HUNT ME

AN IMMORTAL VICES AND VIRTUES NOVEL

HEATHER HILDENBRAND

Hunt Me

Heather Hildenbrand

Edited by Dawn Y. Discreet Edition cover art by Manuela. Necklace design by Alchemy Q Designs. Regular Edition Cover Art by Urban Rex Designs. Model photo by Lindee Robinson Photography. Cover Models: Shannon Lorraine and Sam Parker . Character art: Rachel Doud

GET A BONUS PROLOGUE!

Read Legion's backstory -
Join the Patreon and get access to bonus content,
artwork, and quarterly signed books!
Visit www.patreon.com/heatherhildenbrand

It's a hazy evening in the Crossroads, making my attempt at anonymity that much easier as I head out to meet a new client. The few people I pass on the sidewalk don't speak to me, though several familiar faces nod in recognition and respect. Or maybe it's less respect and more polite caution. Sort of a "Keep your friends close and your friendly neighborhood assassin closer."

Located in what was once the midwestern United States—before humans learned that magical portals had opened throughout the world and supernatural creatures overtook modern civilization—the Crossroads is a tight-knit community that takes care of its own. If that sounds wholesome, it is... at times. But when wholesome and neighborly don't solve the problem, they call me— the poisoner.

Thanks to my nymph mother and dark fae father, my unique magical gifts give me an affinity for coaxing nature along. Basically, that means I'm great at growing things—especially poisonous things. *Thanks, Dad.* Combine that with my halfway decent skill with a blade, and it's safe to say that, if you want someone unalived in this city, you call me.

Not that I just walk around offing people willy-nilly. Supplies aren't cheap in this economy, and I do have morals. Surprisingly strong ones, in fact, considering my line of work. But a girl's gotta eat, and well, we all have our strengths. After a decade of mastering my craft and being very careful about the jobs I take on, my reputation in the Crossroads is more than enough to keep me busy with work.

It doesn't bring me joy or anything. I didn't wake up and choose a profession like this one. No one really does —unless you've got one too many screws loose. It happened slowly and as a matter of survival.

More specifically, Kendall's survival.

Orphaned as a teen, it's not like I had a ton of career options. What I did have was a younger sister to support and no parents left to help. So, I did what I was good at. And I traded any guilt over it for knowing I was protecting my sister from a world that would eat us alive if we let it.

I'll do anything for Kendall—even kill. And those are not empty words. A fact I've proven again and again since our parents died. It's not like I have a choice. Even so, I only target the ones who deserve it.

No innocents, my mother made me promise. She hated the work—a career my father never gave up, not even for her—but she loved him. And she couldn't deny my inherited talents once they showed themselves. My mother was the kindest creature I've ever known, so it's the least I can do to keep this promise to her, considering my decision to follow in Dad's footsteps.

What can I say, the family business pays the bills.

Tonight's assignment is like a hundred others I've done before. A drink at a bar with an entitled douche bag who thinks he's a god's gift to us all, a little hemlock and wolfsbane mixed into his whiskey and Coke when he's not looking, resulting in the asshole taking a little nap from which he won't ever wake.

The client isn't someone I've worked with before. I simply know her as Em, a concerned citizen of the Crossroads. She came recommended to me by one of my regulars, a vampire named Uziah. He owns a club on the outskirts and has facilitated many jobs for me over the years. I trust him—as much as one can trust a guy who organizes professional kill contracts.

At least he honors my requirement for a backstory on my marks.

The brief recon I did on tonight's mark revealed he's just another power-hungry male trying to use our city's newfound infamy to boost his own position. Ever since a portal opened to Tartarus three months ago in the center of downtown, we've had an influx of new faces. Outsiders come to scope out how they might claim this suddenly-valuable city as their own. Almost every other portal that exists in the world is now ruled by a House except for ours. No one has officially threatened us over it, but some people—like Uziah—believe it's better to play offense than defense.

Out-of-towners arrive daily. Some are House emissaries. Some are aspiring politicians. Some just think they have a right to come here and use our lack of House affiliation to set up shop running drugs or weapons. But my fellow Crossroads residents are having none of it.

Word is, neither is Caius, Tartarus' ruler, but the god-king prefers to stay on his side of the portal. There are rumors of a dark dragon who commands Caius' army, a creature powerful enough to wipe out entire legions of men, but so far, he's standing down as well. All of which has apparently sent the message that the Crossroads might be up for the taking.

The fact that one of our own—a Santiago sister no less—has become the queen of hell only makes the story that much more interesting. Reagan Santiago is a former graverobber by trade, and, according to rumors, also the chosen guardian of Caius' soul, which he opened the portal to retrieve. By all accounts, Reagan's survival was not high on his list of priorities in said retrieval—right up until the moment they met and he realized she was his mate.

The rest, as they say, is (recent) history. Hence, the reason for the swell in tourism. It's not just that there's a new portal open in the world. People want to know if there's a power vacuum for the taking.

Spoiler: There's not.

As far as I'm concerned, we don't need gods or death dragons from hell fighting our battles. We've managed to avoid being claimed by a House this long, and our citizens have no intention of letting that change now.

I can't say I'd choose to off tonight's mark for simply

doing political recon, but then I dug deeper and found a list of sexual assault allegations against him.

That's enough for me.

As I walk toward the meeting point, my phone buzzes, and I check the screen, sighing when I see the caller's name. I'm nearly there, which makes talking aloud to someone I care about dangerous, but I take the call anyway.

"Kendall? Is everything okay?" I ask in a low voice.

"Everything's fine," my sister says in a tone that suggests I'm being ridiculous for worrying.

Oh, to be sixteen and blissfully naïve. Not that I ever had that luxury. My parents died when I was sixteen, leaving me to raise Kendall on my own. I've lived with the pressure of that for a decade now, and it only seems to get worse as she gets older. Raising teenagers is harder than offing people, I swear.

"You're supposed to be at work until ten," I point out.

"I got off early."

"What happened?"

"Why do you assume something happened?"

"Experience."

"It was slow. Natalia said I could cut out early." Her tone makes it clear I've insulted her, which would have made me feel bad if I didn't have good reason to assume the worst. Kendall's always trying to sweet-talk me into ... more.

More time out with friends. More shopping. More dates.

It's exhausting. Or maybe that's just life in general. Either way, I'm tired.

"I have a meeting with a client," I say pointedly when she doesn't answer. "Is there something you wanted?"

"Okay, hear me out before you say no—"

"No."

"I said hear me out," she protests.

"Fine. What?"

"A guy from school invited me out—"

"What guy?"

"Chase Lanson. And before you say anything, he's an elf," she says, "nothing I can't handle." I roll my eyes at that. My sister thinks her ability to see the future makes her invincible. But her abilities are hardly accurate, and she has a lot more training to do before they will be. "Anyway, he invited me out for live music, and the place is right next to the bar you'll be at, so I thought maybe I can meet up with him while you're working and—"

"How the hell do you know what bar I'll be at?" I hiss at her, ducking into an alley and glancing around to make sure no one can hear me.

"I pay attention," she says as if it's easy to find out such covert details about a secret assassin's calendar.

Ugh.

My sister is smart as hell, but she has zero life experience, and it shows.

"Kendall, you can't be anywhere near that bar tonight," I say.

"Fine. I can tell him to meet somewhere else."

"No." I pinch the bridge of my nose to ward off a stress headache. "I don't want you out at all."

"Tor, you don't want me to go out any night."

"Exactly. You're sixteen," I tell her.

"Almost seventeen—"

"—and you have school to think about."

"I'm top of my class. And Natalia says I'm making good progress with her lessons."

I shake my head. "Dating will only distract you from your future plans."

"What plans?" she fires back. "I don't even know what I want to do."

"That's my point."

She sighs. "You're impossible."

"I know."

"And overprotective."

"You're welcome."

"And infuriating."

"It's a gift."

She mutters some colorful words, and I brace myself for more of an argument, but in the end, she says, "Fine. I'll see you at home."

My shoulders sag in relief. "Thank you."

"Just be careful," she grumbles.

"Love you, punk," I say, using Dad's nickname for us.

"Love you, too, punk."

I end the call and slide the phone back into my pocket. The fact that she returns the endearment means she's not as mad as she pretends. With a steadying breath, I scan the shadows for any sign of someone lurking or listening. But this part of town is empty of pedestrians, thanks to the rows of abandoned houses and boarded-up businesses.

Satisfied I'm alone, I resume my trek toward the meeting point.

Keeping Kendall caged is becoming increasingly harder, and I know the day is fast approaching when I won't have the power to do it anymore. But I'm determined to protect her as long as possible from any and all danger—including herself. Being sixteen is hard as fuck, but being sixteen in the Crossroads is even harder.

Too many assholes would take advantage of her if they could, and my sister hasn't learned who to trust just yet. Until she does, I'll do it for her.

I turn the corner and see that, up ahead, a lone figure waits, their silhouette faint beneath the cloud-covered moon. My fae senses, already heightened, are razor-sharp in the darkness. In our limited communication thus far, Em doesn't strike me as the type to kill the messenger even before I've delivered the message, but I don't assume anything. I didn't get this far by letting my guard down.

At the end of the block, a willowy figure leans against a battered brick wall, a cloud of cigarette smoke hovering before her like a misty shroud. The expensive coat she wears hides whatever's underneath, including any weapons she might be holding. A scarf is tied over her hair, offering another layer of disguise. Her presence exudes an air of secrecy and intrigue, but it's her eyes that catch my attention—narrowed to slits like a cat and ringed in thick black liner.

I sniff lightly, trying to get a read on her power, but it's not obvious. Shifter of some kind maybe.

I approach her warily, my footsteps barely making a sound on the cracked pavement.

"Em, I assume."

"You must be the poisoner," she says in a raspy voice. "Uziah said you're the best in the Crossroads."

"I'm the most discreet," I tell her.

"Good. I need this to be smooth. No witnesses. Nothing linking you to me. Or him."

I nod, reaffirming my objective. "Discretion is part of the package."

"And no bloodshed."

"That's not my style."

It's true that I'm capable of using a blade or even my fists, thanks to my father's training, but it's not my best talent. It's also not nearly as efficient as poisoning.

Em eyes me like she's trying to decide whether to take me at my word. I don't bother trying to reassure her. She wouldn't have called me here if she hadn't already made up her mind.

"I don't have to tell you the portal has put a target on our backs," she says.

"And yet, you're hiring me anyway."

"This man is a warlock," she says, ignoring my comment. "His ability to sense danger is uncanny. No weaponry can slip past his awareness."

"Good thing I don't use weapons."

"Your... blend—it's natural?"

"Every time."

She hesitates again before saying, "I'm told you don't kill innocents."

"Your mark is hardly that."

"No," she agrees. "He's a monster who uses power to harm the powerless."

"Then we have no problem." When she still looks

skeptical, my eyes narrow in impatience, and I add, "Just because I only target the ones who deserve it doesn't mean I'm soft. Trust me, I'll get results, and I won't lose sleep over it either."

She nods, apparently satisfied.

I do my best not to tap my foot. I might have a rule about harming innocents, but I don't exactly need to stand here and bond with her about it. "And my payment?"

She hands me a small vial, which I snag quickly and tuck into my boot. It makes my hands tingle with its potency, and I scent the contents instantly thanks to my dark fae gifts. Demon tears are hard as fuck to come by, especially around here. But I know better than to ask questions about its origins. And I damn sure don't want to have to explain my intentions for it.

My father spent a lifetime researching the most potent fertilizers for the deadly plants that filled his greenhouse. Turns out few compare to the power of demon tears. Not only do they infuse the poisons with more potency, but they make healing—even for a super-natural—impossible.

A death dealt by one of my poisons is absolute.

It's part of what makes me the best.

"This is only half," I point out.

"The other half will be delivered to you after," she says.

"Good enough."

With a final glance back at her shadowy figure, I disappear into the night, the weight of my mission resting heavily on my shoulders. It's not that I'm worried

I'll fail—I never have, and I don't plan to start tonight—but I can't help wondering if it'll even be enough to succeed. Or if it's only a matter of time before the Crossroads becomes a battle zone in a war for power that no one can stop from swallowing us all.

It's a sobering thought and one I've contemplated many times since that damn portal opened three months ago. The Crossroads has had its share of problems over the years, but it's my home. And more importantly, it's Houseless, which means I don't have to swear my allegiance to some asshole who wants to control me.

Portals have been open in this world for thousands of years, but it wasn't until the one near Portland opened in the middle of a highway nearly seventy years ago that humans realized the supernatural world existed. When that happened, chaos exploded, and the world kind of fell apart.

When the dust settled, the rulers that emerged took control of their own territory, now called Houses, which is just the post-modern world's name for kingdoms and countries. Each House has a king or ruler. And the citizens are subject to their law. The only areas of the world not run by monarchy are No Man's Land—which is, thankfully, exactly what the Crossroads is.

It's every creature for itself out here, which serves me just fine. If that changed, I already know my particular brand of capitalism would be targeted first. Sure, there are peacekeepers and vigilante justice-seekers here, but none of them bother with me, and I suspect it has something to do with the fact that I only ever accept jobs where the mark has it coming.

I know, I know; an assassin with a conscience is weird, but none of that will matter if some hotshot politician takes over our city and tries enacting their own laws. I don't want to think about what would happen to Kendall if I became the hunted instead of the hunter.

All I can do is focus on my part and let that be enough.

While I walk, I reach back and free my hair from the ponytail that's held it up all day. Shaking out my locks, I note the green dye is beginning to fade, letting my brunette roots show through. The sight of it makes me think of my friend Stella and her love of a magical makeover. She left town three months ago after being cheated on one too many times, and while I know she's happy, life has been pretty lonely for me ever since.

I'm not exactly the party girl type. Hell, since my parents died, I haven't even dated, much less made time for friendships. But Stella and Niamh, pronounced Nee-iv, as she's always correcting for the ones who mangle it, managed to draw me out of my shell. I miss Stella. She was apparently our glue because I've barely seen Niamh since our trio became a duo.

As if I've conjured her from thought alone, my phone dings with a text from Niamh.

Hey, stranger. Want to get drinks?

I frown as I type back. **Can't. Working.**

She responds with a sad face that has me shaking my head.

Aren't you? I add.

Uziah made me leave early. Some asshole grabbed my ass, so I choked him out with climbing ivy.

I snort. Niamh is the only other fae I know who has an affinity for plants like me. Except, she doesn't poison people with hers; she just suffocates them outright. Mostly men who get too handsy. Which happens a lot considering she works at a nightclub full of drunk vampires. Not to mention she's drop-dead gorgeous.

Raincheck on the drinks. I need to hear about this. Tomorrow?

She texts back almost immediately: **It's a date.**

The bar is crowded when I arrive, but that's a good thing. Makes my job easier. Believe it or not, the more people present, the less they suspect danger, which makes doing shady shit under their noses even easier. After all, no one assumes you're going to poison a guy in front of dozens of witnesses.

So that's exactly what I'll do.

I scan the rowdy crowd until my eyes land on the slick-looking guy at the end of the bar. Bingo. His rounded face matches the picture Em texted me two days ago. Dull brown hair receding drastically from his large forehead, a pointed nose, and a suit that screams "Look at me; I'm important."

I avert my eyes before I can draw his attention and begin winding my way slowly through the crowded tables. It's happy hour, and apparently, the drinks are strong because the seats are full and floor space is tight as people crowd the aisles.

I slide up to the bar's end opposite from where my mark sits and catch the bartender's eye. She saunters closer, a friendly smile on her narrow fae face.

"What'll it be, gorgeous?" she asks.

"Whiskey and Coke."

She goes to work making the drink, and I glance over at the mark again in time to see him ogling a woman in a short skirt. She's tall and willowy with a dancer's grace. My senses peg her as an elf or nymph. As she walks by him, he reaches out and palms her ass. She rounds on him, glaring, and he grins like her protest only makes it all the more fun.

Wow, he's going to make this easy.

"Here you are." The bartender sets the drink before me.

"Thanks." I toss a sachet of herbs onto the bar in exchange.

"What's this?" she asks.

"Wolfsbane."

Her eyes glint with interest. Wolfsbane is a commodity used mostly for trading for other valuables. What I'm giving her is more than one drink deserves, but hopefully, it'll ensure she never admits to seeing me here if anyone questions her later. She takes the sachet and gives a nod of thanks before walking off to help the next customer.

I take the drink, faltering as a wave of... something washes over me. Dizziness followed by a rush of power that leaves me reeling for a moment. Gripping the bar, I suck in a deep breath and try like hell to remain on my feet as the room tilts.

Then, just as suddenly as it came on, the heady rush recedes. My vision and balance steady again. I'm left with a strange sort of itch on the inside of my skin—a pull toward...something. Or someone.

What the hell?

I blink quickly, scanning the room for some explanation. But no one else seems to have been affected. The bar patrons continue to drink and socialize without missing a beat. At the far end, my mark continues to leer at and grab women he has no permission to touch.

I force myself to refocus.

I have no idea what just happened, but whatever's going on with me tonight, I tell myself it's nothing that can't be fixed by a bottle of wine and a good night's sleep. Stress, that's all this is.

Time to get to work and get the hell out of here.

Moving through the crowd, I use the closeness of bodies as cover to empty a sachet from my pocket into my whiskey. A few swirls of the ice cubes dissolve the powder until the liquid is once again amber-clear. A few more paces and I'm within arms' reach of the mark.

Keeping my back to his, I wait for my moment. Predictably it comes when the short skirt from earlier does another pass. The mark reaches out and brushes her thigh with his hand.

The female rounds on him immediately, cheeks flushing in anger.

I use her disgusted rebuff as a distraction to swap my poisoned drink with his. As soon as I've made the switch, I turn and begin moving toward the exit. Watching him succumb to the drink is easy enough from the window, and it puts distance between me and the crime.

Once I know he's taken care of, I can get home and uncork that bottle of wine I promised myself. Maybe I'll even text Niamh to come on over tonight. We can touch up my hair the old-fashioned way.

Just outside the door, a body blocks my path.

Impatient, I shove past them without bothering to look up. The moment my shoulder makes contact, a jolt slams through me, driving me backward a few steps.

Strong hands land on my hips, helping to steady me. I gasp, reeling at the sudden return of dizzying power rushing through me. When I look up, an attractive male is staring back at me, looking equally stunned.

Not just attractive. He's handsome to the point of devastating. Dark hair falls to the nape of his neck, thick enough that I find myself wondering what it would be like to run my fingers through it. His jaw is covered in a short beard that only adds to the dangerous and roguish aura he puts out. But it's those eyes, nearly black and full of secrets, that hold me still, trapped by their enigmatic depths.

The noise of the bar falls away.

For a suspended moment, nothing else exists in the world but him and me. Something passes between us. Not interest. No, this feels so much more than that. It's heavy and contains a darkness I should be running away from rather than leaning into, hoping for another taste. Whoever this stranger is, he's not safe. So why are my nipples hardening at the sight of him undressing me with his violent eyes?

Slowly, he reaches up and brushes a warm hand over my cheek. I don't move. I barely breathe. The dizziness from earlier washes over me again, the world tilting and then righting itself again—as if the entire axis of my world has just changed.

As the moment stretches, there's a strange settling inside my chest that feels both comforting and alarming. And it's all I can do not to reach for him and run my hands over his body or offer myself to him here and now to be claimed.

The desire to do both of those things terrifies me.

Not because I don't welcome physical pleasure but because I've never felt so overcome with need. It's a threat to my survival, especially in a moment when I can't afford to lose focus.

I take a step back.

At my retreat, his gaze darkens, and fury flashes. For a wild moment, I think he might actually toss me over his shoulder and run off like some kind of caveman. But in the next second, he's gone, slipping out the door and into the night as if he'd never been there at all.

I follow him out, trying to decipher which direction he went.

Inside the bar, someone screams, drawing me back to the task at hand. Dazed, I look through the glass just in time to see the mark toppling off his stool. His skin is grey, and his eyes are frozen. His glass—empty.

I turn to leave just as the bar's door flies open and panicked customers pour out into the street. One of them slams into my shoulder. Another reaches out to steady me before I can lose my balance. I grab her wrist, holding tight for support until I get my bearings.

Magic surges to the spot where I've touched her.

Her eyes widen, her face reddens, and she gasps. I

release her, and she stumbles back. Another fleeing bar patron knocks into her, and she falls—hard.

I rush forward and kneel, panic and confusion leaving me at a loss.

"Hey," I call, "Are you all right?"

She is most clearly not all right.

Her attempts to speak are interrupted by saliva leaking from her mouth. It's soon joined by blood. I can only watch in horror as her skin turns grey and her chest heaves with a failed attempt to draw breath. And then the life disappears from her eyes, and she's gone.

Dead.

I have no idea what just happened, but all her symptoms point to poison. A sniff against the night air confirms it. The scent coming from her flesh, from the blood that's leaked from her mouth, is unmistakable to my dark fae senses.

The unnatural rot of poison.

Panic seizes me.

Scrambling for my pocket, I search for my extra vials of supplies, wondering if one somehow broke in the commotion and jostling. Maybe she touched the sachet of powder, not that a single touch would have been enough. Besides, it's only residue now.

Someone kneels to investigate the dead woman's vitals. I look up and meet the eyes of a man I've never seen before, noting the way he looks between the vial I'm holding and the female dead at my feet.

"What have you done?" he demands.

"Nothing," I say quickly.

"She's dead," he accuses, louder now. "What did you do?"

"Nothing, she grabbed me, and I..."

"Murderer!" the man declares.

People stop and stare, their fear turning to suspicion as they move in closer, encircling me. With nothing left to do for the stranger now dead at my feet, I get up and run away as fast as my legs will carry me.

LEGION

The sexy female fae from the Crossroads haunts me every step of the way back through the portal and into Tartarus. The fact that I witnessed her spike a man's drink and ultimately kill him only makes me more curious about her. Who is she? What wrong did that male commit against her? Every thought and urge I have toward her is unexpected—and honestly, the worst fucking thing that's happened to me in a long time. As is the desire to turn around and hunt her down.

Fighting the temptation to return to her, I end up at Osiris, one of the less popular bars on the outskirts of town, and, therefore, one of my favorite places to frequent. Arriving well before happy hour, I order bottomless shots with a generous infusion of magic in an attempt to drink away the knowledge of the female's existence. My biology makes it nearly impossible to get drunk—partly thanks to the blood of a god that runs through my veins and partly thanks to Tartarus which would have rendered me immortal even if my DNA hadn't—but the magic infusion offers that extra *oomph*. Now, all I have to do is drink faster than my metabolism can burn it.

Two off-duty soldiers come in. Their stares and whispers make me regret my choice. Drinking at home is probably more appropriate, given that I'm the general of Tartarus' army. Seeing the boss get wasted in the middle of the afternoon is gossip that's sure to spread through the ranks. But I've come too far.

"Sir, can I buy you a drink?" one of them asks.

He's green, I can see it in the way he addresses me so casually. Not to mention his uniform marks him as a trainee. Clearly, he hasn't learned rule number one.

I school my features into something more growly, which isn't hard, given my mood.

"What the fuck did you just say, soldier?" I ask.

"I, uh, I could buy you a drink," he says, looking unsure.

"No," I say flatly. "You can't."

"Sorry, I just—"

"What's your name?" I demand.

They exchange a look, and my temper shortens further. "I asked you a question, soldier."

"Lankford, sir. This is Rath."

"Who's your supervisor?"

"Uh, Conway, sir."

"Has he explained the consequences of breaking protocol?"

"Sir?"

"Drinking with your commanding officers is a punishable offense."

The first whiff of fear rolls off them.

Instead of feeling satisfied, my dark mood only makes me feel bad for them.

"Get out of here," I say.

"Sir—"

"I said go!"

They scramble out, and I go back to the task at hand of getting myself good and wasted.

An hour later, I'm barely upright on my stool, which makes this effort a success as far as I'm concerned, when I'm rudely jostled by a new customer sidling up to the bar beside me. Styx gives me a once-over that would make most mortals quake. Despite her small stature, the kelpie is known and avoided by most in Tartarus, though somewhere along the way, her grumpy persona stopped putting me off, and we became something like friends.

Maybe it's our mutual love of the very mortal-like pastime of drinking in a dive bar like this one.

As usual, her dark hair is pinned up into a bun with two metal sticks that look like lightning rods, revealing a guileless face that might tempt one to be fooled into thinking she is harmless.

I know better.

She is one of the most formidable creatures I've ever known.

She is also the most sarcastic.

"Is there a liver-drowning contest I'm not aware of?" she asks, sliding onto the stool next to mine.

Without waiting for my answer, she nods at the bartender, an ogre named Meech who doesn't speak.

"Bourbon. With infusion," she tells him, referencing the same magic additive I used to get wasted. Then she looks over at me, one brow arched in judgment. "Well?"

The alcohol swims in my blood, making me more forthcoming than usual. "I went through the portal."

"The Earth realm was that disappointing, huh?"

"It was ... different than I remember."

She waits, clearly not ready to accept my vague answer. True, I wasn't the same creature back then either. I've always been a dragon shifter with a dark side, but after five thousand years in Tartarus, this world and its magic have made me into its own creation, full of shadows that cling and whisper their violence.

But Styx knows all that. Because she's a shadow creature too. Not to mention, she visited the Earth realm with Caius himself when the portal first opened.

"I witnessed a murder," I add.

"Just one?"

I scowl and reach for my drink. The liquid sloshes as I pick it up. "The assassin was a woman."

"Good for her," Styx declares. "Maybe feminism isn't as dead as I thought."

Another patron cuts her a look. I recognize him as a regular who spikes his own whiskey with wolfsbane because he likes the high. He's an asshole but usually keeps to himself. Tonight, he winks at Styx, and she bares her teeth at him. "Mind your business, asshole."

He looks away.

Styx turns back to the bar just as Meech sets her

drink down in front of her. She drains her glass and hands it back to Meech, saying, "Keep 'em coming, big guy."

Then she turns to me again. "You know, nothing you've said warrants a drinking binge as far as I can tell. I mean, if either of us has a reason to drown our livers after visiting that place, it's me."

I sigh. Styx has zero love for the Earth realm. Or maybe it's what they did to her there. What they did to all of us, casting us here in the first place. And if that weren't bad enough, her recent visit sparked her mate bond, which she's dealing with about as well as I am.

My thoughts drift to the last Februlune—the double moons that incite moon fever in those who've found their mates, forcing the shift and sending them into a frenzy that only ends if they claim their mate. Styx had me lock her up so she couldn't go searching for her mate. If anyone understands my reasons for resisting this, it's her.

"Does this have anything to do with the bitch who tossed you here?" Styx asks, referring to the demon female who sired me.

Once upon a time, I swore vengeance against her. But five thousand years is a long time, and if I'm honest, my time in Tartarus has actually been the best experience of my existence thus far. At least, Caius hasn't ordered me to level entire dynasties for him.

Here, I have a life. A home.

Besides, my mother is gone. And so is the past.

There's nothing left to avenge.

I shake my head. "No. There are many different kinds

of creatures in the Crossroads, but I did not sense any being with power like hers."

"So, she's dead. This is good news."

"Maybe."

Or just gone back to her realm.

Beside me, Styx empties her glass again then hands it off for a refill. She sits, silent and contemplative. Her refusal to fill silences with unnecessary words is one of the reasons we're friends. But I've also noticed how many drinks she's put away since arriving, and I'm starting to think it's more than just support for my dismal mood. Before I can ask, she breaks the silence.

"There's something else, isn't there?"

I reach for my drink, using the move to buy myself time. If I say it aloud, I won't be able to take it back or pretend it away anymore, but in the end, the alcohol pulls the words from my lips. "There was a woman."

"Fuck me," Styx says, throwing up her hands, "there always is."

I cut her a look. Whatever she sees in me has pity flashing like lightning in her eyes. "Damn, what was she, a siren? You look pathetic."

"Worse," I say, misery leaking in around the alcohol making my senses buzz. "My mate."

"No shit?" She looks stunned. I watch as her expression registers the memory of her own mate issues. When she recovers, she says, "I thought you couldn't have a mate."

"So did I."

Her eyes narrow, but they're glassier now, glazed

with the magic infusion. "Wait. How can you have a mate bond *and* a blood oath to Caius?"

"I don't think I can." My voice is hoarse.

She's hit on the real problem I'm trying to drink into oblivion. Her expression softens.

"What are you going to do?"

"I have to choose."

Styx stares at me, sympathy mingling with that dry humor we both know she uses to cope. "Wow, and I thought my life was fucked."

I snort.

She raises her newly refilled glass to me and says, "You lived a good life, soldier. But it's over now."

"Fuck me," I mutter, and then we drink to her dramatic toast.

Out of the corner of my eye, I watch as the drunk eyeing Styx gets off his bar stool and approaches. He sways slightly, but his gaze is firmly set on the female beside me.

I tense, not really worried since Styx can handle herself, but I also don't appreciate the interruption I know is coming. Nor do I think Caius is going to look kindly on us getting into a bar fight. Again.

"Hey, gorgeous," the male leers, and Styx turns to glare at him. "I couldn't help but overhear you saying you wanted to get fucked." He winks. Or tries to. It's more of a slow blink while his jaw hangs slack for concentration. "I think I can help with that."

Fuck. This guy clearly has a death wish.

I brace myself for Styx to gut him right here. Even Meech, the bartender, who is no coward and usually doesn't put up with this kind of shit, makes himself scarce.

Styx merely stares him down, incredibly still on her stool. "The only thing you can help with is my death count," she tells him. "Unless you turn around and stumble away right now."

Mentally, I will him to take her advice.

Under normal circumstances, I'd kill him myself for the way he spoke to her, but my role here in Tartarus is not normal. Nor does it allow me to kill without the permission of Caius himself. In fact, if I witness another citizen committing unsanctioned violence, I'll have no choice but to intervene.

Unfortunately, the dumbass is either too drunk or too stupid to know his mistake.

He doesn't leave.

Instead, he inches closer. To me.

His thumb jerks against my shoulder. "Why don't you drop this asshole and come sit with me," he tells Styx.

"Watch your mouth," I warn, temper heating beneath my skin.

The alcohol fuels my rage, and my blood heats with the urge to turn this asshole to cinders and ash.

"Fuck you," the guy says.

"That's it," Styx snaps, getting to her feet.

The drunk makes a clumsy grab for her, and I snap.

The blood oath prevents me from killing him, but I shove him hard enough to send him flying backward into the empty table and chairs behind us. He crashes against them, sending wood splintering in all directions.

"What the hell," the drunk stutters, but I barely register his words as I focus on his attempts to get up.

Back on his feet, his skin ripples as he shifts into his counterpart: a hellhound from the looks of it.

Good.

I wouldn't want this fight to be easy.

"Legion." Styx's voice is sharp and close.

I ignore her.

She steps in front of me, blocking the asshole from my view.

"You can't," she says.

"Move."

"Caius will have your hide," she argues. "Let me."

"If you harm him without Caius' approval, the blood oath will compel me to intervene against you," I tell her.

She smirks. "You don't think I can take you?"

Before I can answer, the hellhound leaps straight for Styx. I shove her aside and throw myself at him with a roar. The blood bond pulls taut against my desire to kill, but it doesn't prevent me from breaking every bone in his body one by one. Behind me, Styx finishes her drink and watches like the good friend she is while I do just that.

TORI

A half-hour later, blood still pumping with adrenaline and fear, I bypass the house and use the creaky gate to slip into my backyard. An old shed in the back serves as my workshop, and I hurry inside, forgoing the light to keep from alerting Kendall. Using the flashlight on my phone, I search through the cabinets along the far wall, rifling through items until I've kicked up enough dust to send me into a coughing fit.

Finally, I find the book I'm looking for. Grabbing it from the stack, I whirl just in time for the door to bang open and Kendall to fill the opening. She has a kitchen knife gripped in each hand, her expression twisted in fear and determination.

"Stop right there, or I'll cut you in half," she threatens.

"Kendall," I say, shining the flashlight on my own face. "It's me."

She huffs out a breath in strangled relief. "Gods, Tor. What the fuck. You scared me senseless."

"Sorry."

I shuffle over and flip on the light.

Kendall takes one look at me, and her fear returns. "What happened?"

"Nothing. I just didn't want to disturb you, so I—"

"Torissa Emerald Sage, don't bullshit me."

"Your fae senses aren't always right, you know."

"Is that so? And what about my eyesight? Is that also unreliable?"

"What are you talking about?"

"Give me your phone." I hesitate, and she reaches down and snatches it from my hand. With a quick swipe, she sets it on selfie mode and holds it up to my face.

I gasp.

On my chest and throat, my veins are a tangled map of dark gray lines beneath my skin. I pull my shirt up to find the same coloring across my abdomen and down my arms.

"What the hell happened?" Kendall repeats.

My hands go to my pockets then my boot, and I check, again, that my vials are all still intact. They are, right down to the demon tears. Which means none of those are to blame for...whatever this is.

Fear lances through me as I remember the female outside the bar. She didn't accidentally come into contact with a broken vial.

She touched *me.*

And I killed her.

And now... my veins are rotting?

Fuck.

I stare down at the dark veins running beneath my skin, horror and disbelief swirling into a nightmare of dread. I have no idea how it's possible or why it's happening, but the only thing I can think about now is how close Kendall is standing to me. And how lethally dangerous that is.

"How do you feel?" Kendall asks worriedly. "Does it hurt?"

"No," I assure her. "It's fine."

I lower my shirt.

"It is *not* fine. You're—"

"Kendall," I say with forced calmness. "I promise I'll tell you everything, but right now, I need you to back away from me."

She starts to argue, and I snap. "Please!"

"Okay." She backs off, and my shoulders sag.

Before I can offer an explanation, another sound comes from the doorway. We both jump and then exhale as Juniper moves into the light. The older woman's chestnut hair flows freely and wildly down her back—a visible example of her free and wild spirit. At her arrival, the plants surrounding us slowly strain in her direction, and I swear I can hear them whispering to her in the silence.

Juniper is a nymph, like my mother was, and our oldest family friend. She lives across the street but spends the majority of her time with us. She's the closest thing to a parent we have left.

"Tori," she says when she sees me. "Are you—oh." She stops at the sight of my skin.

"Tori was just about to tell us what the hell is going on," Kendall says. "Isn't that right?"

I sigh, knowing there's no chance of keeping this from them. Not when I'm a walking danger to them. Quickly, I recount what happened, leaving out the part about poisoning my mark. Or anything to do with the handsome stranger that I insanely thought might be my mate.

"So, you think this random girl was poisoned because she touched your skin?" Kendall asks dubiously. "That's impossible."

"I don't have another explanation." I look at Juniper, who is quietly contemplative. "Do you?"

She frowns, nodding at the book in my hands. "You checked your father's diary?"

"Not yet. I was about to."

"My kind are not capable of what you're suggesting," she says. "But your fae blood might hold some answers." Her words hold no accusation. She knew my father and never judged him for what he was or what he did as a poisoner. Still, I can't help but feel some judgment of my own toward my dark fae heritage, especially if it's somehow transformed me into a walking, breathing poison.

I exchange a look with Kendall and can tell she understands.

"Tor," she says, stepping forward as if to comfort me.

"Stay back," I say quickly.

She retreats.

Silence falls, and I feel a wall forming between us. It's not just Kendall though. It's everyone. The idea of never touching another living creature is a bleak thought. One I'm not quite ready to process just yet.

"I'm going to read Dad's journal," I say. "And probably sleep out here until I know more."

Kendall nods. "Okay. I'll bring you some blankets."

"Thanks."

She hesitates like she wants me to ask her to stay with me. When I don't, she slips out, leaving me with Juniper.

"She worries for you," Juniper says.

"Likewise," I say wearily.

"It's not easy raising a child. It's even harder when you're still a child yourself."

"I'm not a kid anymore, Juni."

"This world asked too much of you, and you gave it anyway. But you lost yourself. Maybe this"—she nods at my darkened veins—"will help you find the parts you're missing."

My throat tightens as her words hit way too close to the mark. She's right. I gave up everything to provide for Kendall. I was just sixteen when my parents died. A kid. And then I became an adult and a parent in a single moment. It wasn't fair but it was my only option. And now... I don't know if I can put myself back together again. Or how to even begin.

I sigh. "I don't have the luxury of thinking about myself, you know that."

"She is stronger than you think."

"I'm supposed to protect her," I say. "Not be the one to put her in danger."

"Our role isn't to shield them; it's to prepare them."

Her words are a painful reminder of how little preparation I had to become a single parent of a six-year-old.

"What am I supposed to do?" I ask, ignoring her attempts to reassure me. It's a conversation we've had before, but tonight, I'm too exhausted and beaten for it. "If my skin is poison, then what?"

She looks at my cassava plant like it holds the answers. At her attention, the stem moves, angling toward her. Juniper's nymph blood is a siren call to plants, which is why I don't usually allow her to spend much time in my shop. Tonight is an exception. One that will probably leave my plants in withdrawals once she's gone.

"You will figure it out," she says decisively. "And in the meantime, I will look after Kendall."

Juniper leaves me alone, and I spend two hours poring over my father's diary. I've read it before. Hell, I helped him write many of the entries while he was still alive. But I wasn't exactly looking out for any mention of dark fae abilities involving poisonous flesh powers, so it bears another look. Unfortunately, my search yields nothing.

Kendall drops off a blanket at some point, but I end up sleeping in a wooden chair with my head on my desk and wake to the sound of my phone ringing. I reach for it, groaning at the stiffness in my neck and back, and see the caller is Unknown.

"Hello?" I answer.

"Tori, I need to speak with you." Uziah's voice is gruff and strained.

A glance out my shop window offers a sky streaked in

pink and orange as the sun begins to rise over the horizon.

"What's up?" I ask. "You sound like you just went ten rounds at the gym."

"Something like that. Can you come by?"

"Now? The sun's up."

"We should speak in person. Sooner rather than later."

I push to my feet, worry coursing through me. Uziah, the vampire who owns Bite Club and sends a considerable amount of business my way, has never asked to see me during the day. "Okay. I'll be there soon."

He ends the call, and I hurry toward my house. Inside, I listen carefully and catch the sounds of Kendall's even breathing. Creeping silently down the hall, I find her sprawled on the couch, her eyes closed and mouth half-open.

I shake my head.

Her perfectly good bed is just down the hall, but she opted for the couch as if that would somehow help me figure things out.

In my room, I throw on a fresh long-sleeved shirt and pants along with a scarf, hat, and gloves. When I'm satisfied I've covered as much of my skin as possible, I make my way into the kitchen where Juniper is sitting at the table with a mug cupped in her hands.

"Did you find answers?" she asks.

"No." I sigh and rub my stiff neck. "Uziah wants to talk. I'm going to the club."

"Now?"

"Yeah, he sounded weird."

"Be careful."

"Keep an eye on her?"

"Of course."

"Thank you." I close the door behind me and head for my car parked at the curb. I accepted it as payment from a client a couple of years back. Kendall drives it more than I do, mostly to school and work, but the club is on the far edges of the city, and I'm in no mood for public transport. After tossing food wrappers and three different lip glosses into the backseat, I settle in and head for Uziah's.

The club sits just off the road at the edge of town, and while it's not the worst neighborhood, the empty parking lot and eerie quietness that surrounds it make the hair on my neck stand on end.

The large front door is unlocked, though, and I make my way inside cautiously. A guard waves me forward.

"He's in the back booth," he says.

"Thanks," I mutter.

The club lights are all off except for the overhead lighting at the back. Uziah sits in the back booth alone, but I see three more guards hovering near the bar and watching me closely.

"Uziah," I say as I slide into the booth opposite the male vamp.

He looks back at me with crimson eyes that are framed by a full head of salt-and-pepper hair right down to his bushy eyebrows and full mustache. "It's good to see you, kid. You want a drink?"

"No, I'm okay. What's up?"

"Tony, get her a drink," he says, ignoring my refusal.

One of the guards heads around the bar and starts making a drink.

Uziah studies me in a way that has worry creeping in again.

"How'd it go last night?" he asks.

"Last night?"

"The mark."

"I took care of it," I say, heart thudding. "Why?"

"Heard there was a commotion afterward." His expression gives nothing away. And while Uziah and I have always been friendly, I don't like how this feels. Like a summons to an interrogation. Like I'm accountable to him rather than the client.

"These things always result in commotion." Bullshit.

"Hmm," he grunts then takes a drink.

The guard returns, setting a glass in front of me. I don't pick it up.

"Do you need me for another task?" I ask.

"Tell me about the second mark."

My heart drums loudly at that. "There was no second mark."

"You made a second contact," he says.

I hesitate, but he clearly already knows everything.

"Not exactly."

He looks me over, noting the scarf and gloves. "Something you want to tell me?" When I don't answer, he leans in. "I've known you and your family many years, Tori. I hope you know you can tell me anything."

I sigh. "I don't know what happened. A female ran into me. She touched me, and then she fell ill. I... Her exhibited symptoms suggested a lethal poisoning."

"Was she a mark?"

"No," I say quickly. "I didn't know her. I…"

Guilt and fear and worry are a nauseating cocktail in my stomach. I grip the drink, rethinking it. Halfway to my mouth, the smell hits me, and I stop, eyes widening as I look from the liquid to the vampire seated across from me.

"What is this?" I hiss.

"Relax. I had to test you."

"Test me?" My voice rises. "To see if I was stupid enough to drink poison?"

His eyes glitter with something I don't understand. Not malice. Something else. "To see if you're immune."

"Immune to…" I sniff the drink again. "Ricin?" I recoil, knowing how deadly the toxic plant is. "What would give you that idea?"

He doesn't answer other than to continue eyeing me with that weird gleam, which leaves me more uneasy than before. Like he knows something I don't.

"We're done here." I set the glass down and move to the edge of the booth.

"Wait." Uziah's voice is sharp. I glare back at him.

"If you thought I wouldn't scent it, you're mistaken. Poisons are my specialty, remember?"

He shakes his head. "Someone came here. Looking for you. They claimed you acted on a second mark last night."

I slowly turn to face him, thinking through all the possibilities, but there aren't many. "Em."

His brow furrows. "I didn't say that."

"The only other person who knew there was a first

mark was Em, so she's the only one who would call the female a second mark."

Uziah doesn't deny it. "She's unhappy at the outcome of the mission."

"Why? I did the job she hired me for."

"Apparently, she knew the female personally."

My chest squeezes. An innocent. I killed an innocent. And she was someone important to the client. This was so fucked up. "I'll talk to her."

"I don't think you understand. Em is an important player for the organization."

My eyes widen.

He's talking about the Crimson Roses, a small but growing criminal organization intent on taking over the Crossroads. From what I've seen, they're ruthless and unyielding. What they lack in numbers, they make up for in sheer determination. Once you're in their sights, you're dead.

Uziah leads them, though that's not exactly common knowledge in the Crossroads. To keep their members' identities secret, they operate as several smaller units, each with a "leader" of their own. Not even the lower members of each unit know Uziah is at the top. I've been around the gang long enough to know that even Uziah's friendship won't save me from their wrath.

"Fuck."

"Fuck is right. The second mark was a lieutenant sent to report on your effectiveness of the job. She's taking the woman's death personally."

"She thinks I did it on purpose?"

He raises a brow. "Is there another way to poison someone?"

I hesitate.

My silence has Uziah leaning across the table toward me. "Look, kid. We go back a long time, me and you. Your dad once saved my life, and I never did get to repay that debt. Consider this my way of making it even."

Saving a life? Is that what this meeting is?

I glance around, noting the details with fresh understanding. More guards than usual. A meeting after daybreak so others in his organization won't know about it—namely Em or any other Crimson Rose not under his thumb.

Uziah is risking himself to tell me The Crimson Roses are coming for me. And they're not going to stop until I'm dead. Despite the danger I'm in, I can't help but acknowledge my relief. The female was *not* innocent—not if she was a Crimson Rose. My promise to my mother is still intact. At least, I have that for as long as my short life lasts.

I shake off that last thought, refusing to give in to fear. For Kendall's sake, I have to keep fighting.

"What were you really testing?" I ask quietly. "With that drink."

He sits back, studying me. "You tell me."

I look from him to the drink, my thoughts churning —but I can't bring myself to say the words. "Do you know how this happened to me?"

"No."

My eyes narrow. "You have a theory, though."

He nods. "The portal opening brought with it a

magic this realm has never seen. Those who were exposed to that magic...changed."

I've heard the stories. The magic is dark, capable of twisting and changing one's abilities into something else. "You think the portal magic infected me? I've never been near the thing."

"Maybe not the portal but one of its creatures."

My protest dies on my lips as I realize what he's suggesting. The handsome male from the bar... the darkness I felt standing in his presence.

"You think someone from Tartarus did this to me?" I ask, the words strangled as I try to decipher how Uziah could possibly know any of this. Unless Em had others watching. Of course she did. How else would she know what happened to her soldier?

Uziah shrugs. "As you said, it's a theory."

But it's more than that. And now I want to know what he knows—desperately. So I press him.

"You are pretty convinced my skin was the weapon, especially considering you weren't even there."

"I have eyes everywhere, my dear."

I can't help glancing at the guards stationed around the room. Oh yes, they are definitely watching, which means they know about the dangerous stranger. "And what did those eyes tell you?"

"They said you touched her. They said that was all it took."

Uziah produces a vial and sets it on the table before me. The liquid is murky, and I wrinkle my nose at the bitter scent my senses pick up on even through the corked lid.

"The antidote," he says simply.

A reassurance in case he's wrong.

And an encouragement to do a very stupid thing.

I meet his eyes. "Who was the male who touched me?" I ask, needing him to give me something more first.

"They call him the death dragon."

My limbs go limp as the blood drains from my cheeks. "The General of Caius' army? That was him?"

Uziah nods. "He is a shadow dragon capable of destruction beyond this realm's comprehension. And he is more than powerful enough to curse you."

As his words sink in with a cold, brutal awareness, I stare at the drink, trying to talk myself out of such a terrible idea. But I have to know. Not just because of the Crimson Roses. Even if I survive them, what kind of life can I have if I can't touch another creature without killing them instantly?

I need answers. And that starts with understanding what I am now—and what I'm truly capable of. Before I can talk myself out of it, I grab the glass and drain the contents.

LEGION

I'm woken by a small but insistent voice that grows steadily louder at my ear—and a headache that crescendos right along with it. My metabolism might be immune to alcohol and its after-effects, but the magic infusion still lingers in my bloodstream just enough to leave me with a miserable hangover.

"Wake up." Chaya's voice is soft at first. Then, with more force behind it, "Legion!"

I sit up quickly in the darkness, instantly alert at the sight of the fourteen-year-old girl standing in my bedchambers, wearing only her robe.

"What's wrong?" I demand quickly, already straining to hear whatever danger has brought her in here.

Chaya never comes into my bedroom. Hell, it took earning her trust for two years before she'd eat a meal with me, thanks to the horrible life she'd endured before coming to live at Kolgrave Keep. For a creature powerful enough to command the heavens, she's still awfully softspoken.

"Nothing's wrong here," she says quickly, understanding my concern for her and the house. "But Klyn—"

I sit up straighter at the mention of my second-in-command. "What about him?"

"He's at the front gates. He said to get you immediately. I think it's something at the castle."

"Tell him I'm coming." I toss back the covers as Chaya nods and hurries out again. Her small frame makes for nearly silent footsteps as she slips out.

I frown, wondering if she's not yet eating enough. Then I shake away the worry. Chaya was frail and sick when she arrived, but in the two years since, her color and courage have both returned. The fact that she braved waking me just now is proof of that.

Instead, my thoughts drift to Klyn and whatever's brought him to my doorstep before dawn on my day off. Head still thudding with a hangover headache, I hurry to get dressed and curse myself for drowning my sorrows so deeply with Styx last night. A quick glance at my knuckles shows scrapes and bruises from the fight, but any other damage has thankfully healed. Something tells me I'm going to need my strength for whatever's waiting out there.

Klyn's pacing in the entryway when I join him downstairs. When he sees me, his expression only darkens, his bearded face and dark eyes making him look wild and untamed—which isn't wholly inaccurate.

When I get close, he sniffs, and his gaze narrows. Fuck, having a lupin for a friend makes it hard to get away with shit. Before he can ask about the alcoholic magic still clinging to me, I cut to the point of his presence here.

"What happened?" I ask in a low voice.

"An explosion. Took out part of the castle wall."

I pause, stunned. "What?"

"I know. It's crazy."

Crazy is an understatement. I can't remember the last time someone attacked the god-king's residence. A thousand years? Two?

"What part of the wall?" I ask, my thoughts racing ahead toward injuries, targets, and a million other things to be concerned about.

"The southern rim." Klyn pauses as if letting his words sink in. When he speaks again, his voice is heavy with what he hasn't said yet. "That side of the wall gets a lot of traffic."

I tense, knowing he's right. It's the main thoroughfare connecting the towns on either side of the royal house. "How bad?"

"Not sure yet."

"How long since it happened?"

"Twenty minutes ago. I came straight here."

I head for the door, forgoing my usual launch pad in the back of the estate for the open front yard.

Klyn follows me out as I ask, "Suspects?"

"One in custody so far. Caius granted you full authority with the interrogation."

That's my cue.

I stride onto the grass in the darkness that's fast becoming dawn.

"Casualties?"

Klyn doesn't answer, and I turn back to him when I reach the center of the clearing. The morning air is chilled, but it doesn't bother me in this form or the other.

"Six so far," he says, his voice rough. "A couple of guards—and three women and a child. We're digging out more now."

"Fuck." My dragon rises to the surface, begging to be let loose on the fucks who decided to kill innocent women and children.

"I'll see you down there," I tell Klyn, who's already rippling with the change as he takes the form of a massive wolf.

I'm barely done speaking the words before I'm in my dragon form.

Klyn backs off to give me space, and I leap into the air, letting my massive black-scaled wings lift me airborne. Below me, Klyn's wolf is already on the move, sprinting down the mountainside I call home.

Following his lead, I soar toward the castle as fast as I can fly.

It doesn't take long for me to see the smoke. I swoop lower, noting the activity near the castle walls, but my destination doesn't take me quite that far. I head for the ground a half mile south of the wall, landing hard on the small hilltop next to Command, the structure that houses the military's headquarters.

A soldier, Marques, is waiting for me when I touch down. Even from here, I can see he's the only figure standing still while everyone else rushes past. The moment I shift back to my human form, he walks up and holds out a pair of wrinkled uniform pants. One of many

I keep in a storage bin just outside my offices for commutes such as this.

I take the pants and shove them on before heading toward the rear doors of the large building before us. The military's headquarters serves as both a hub for the different companies that serve throughout Tartarus and a prison. And tucked into a lesser-known wing of the basement is my interrogation room.

"Where's the suspect now?" I ask.

"In holding, General. We've got a medic looking at his wounds—"

"No."

He shoots me a look. "He's lost a lot of blood. We need him to live long enough to talk."

I bite back my rage, saving it for the asshole who caused this nightmare. "Who's on-site for the investigation?"

Marques holds the door, and we pass inside, resuming our fast trek. "Caius went with a dozen troops to the portal. Clawford took a task force to look for anyone else involved—"

"Wait, did you say he went to the portal?" I stop and give him my full attention. "Why?"

"That was the target, General."

"Not the wall itself?"

"The wall was their way in," he explains quietly. "They wanted to bypass the castle guards."

Understanding dawns in a haze of fury. The portal is inside an atrium that's connected to the castle. If they went to all that trouble, their goal wasn't as simple as bringing down a wall. "They were trying to break out."

"That's our theory."

Of course. Tartarus started as nothing more than a prison world and even after several thousand years to cool us off, there are still monsters here who deserve to remain locked away.

I think of the innocent lives taken and curl my hands into fists. We come to the conference room, which is full of various commanders waiting on my orders. But I don't stop.

The door opens behind us, and Klyn jogs in, out of breath and wearing a pair of wrinkled slacks he clearly pulled out of the bin.

"Boss," he calls, nodding to the conference room doorway.

I ignore the gesture and start walking in the opposite direction. "Marques, meet me in the interrogation room with the prisoner," I call over my shoulder.

"General," Klyn calls. "Department heads are waiting—"

"They can wait."

Ten minutes later, the door to the interrogation room opens, and a male I've never seen before is shoved through. His hand is loosely bandaged in a mountain of gauze, and his shirt is covered in blood and dust. No, not dust—debris. From the wall he blew to bits earlier.

Fury rises at the sight of him, hellfire burning my throat in an attempt to strike him down where he stands, but I hold it in check.

Behind him, two guards shove him toward me. The sound of his iron chains rattling where they've bound his wrists and ankles is interrupted by the sound of the door being pulled shut with a bang.

The lock offers an ominous click designed to remind the prisoner he won't leave this room alive. From this moment forward, everything I do and say is about getting answers. Even the chair they'll strap him into is made of a magically infused material that is impervious to any of my ... methods, including hellfire.

It's a system I've honed to perfection, and while I don't enjoy it, exactly, there is a dark satisfaction my shadow beast takes from his work. I don't bother feeling guilty about that. This asshole deserves so much worse than what I'm about to do to him.

"Is this him?" I ask.

Marques steps around the prisoner to address me. He managed to make it through my last interrogation without losing his shit, so I promoted him to the position permanently. Pretty sure he thinks it's punishment.

"Yes, General. We found him near the wall right after the explosion."

"And you have confirmation he was involved?"

"The asshole admitted it," he says with disgust.

I give the prisoner a look that conveys everything I am capable of. "In that case, we can skip to the good part."

"He's pretty banged up already," Marques adds.

"Yes, I see that. What's the bandage for?" I ask.

The second soldier finally rounds the prisoner, and I see that it's not a soldier at all. Pol, Caius' closest advisor and one of the most sarcastic males I've ever met, snorts. "Idiot made the detonator too short. Nearly blew off his own hand."

"If he's that stupid, how can you be sure he's the leader?" I ask.

"I'm not sure of shit." Pol gives me a pointed look. "That's your job."

I grunt. "Put him in the chair."

The guy struggles, but Pol shoves him into the chair in the center of the room, and Marques straps him in.

I walk over and lean down until I'm all up in his space. "What's your name?"

"Fuck you."

"Okay then. It's going to be like that." I turn around and walk to the counter along the wall, knowing full well the guy's watching me like a hawk. They always do.

This is the part where they're sizing me up, trying to gauge what sort of methods I intend to use.

I let them think it's the vanilla sort of torture. Five thousand years to hone my craft has taught me that, when it comes to breaking down one's enemy, mind games work better than pain ever could.

Behind me, Marques and Pol stand off to the side, chatting as if the prisoner isn't even here anymore.

"Twenty gold coins says he breaks him in thirty minutes or less," Marques says.

Pol scoffs. "No way. This dude just blew off his own hand. If that wasn't enough to get him talking, it'll take at least an hour."

We've done this routine enough times for me to know half of their banter is foreplay for what I'm about to put this asshole through. The rest is genuine—or it is for these sick fucks.

The soldiers apparently like to bet on my record for breaking a prisoner. I pretend not to notice. That's a mind game too.

"Look," Marques says, drawing attention to the saw I've just added to my pile of toys. "He chose the saw. He only chooses the saw when he's feeling creative."

"Dammit," Pol mutters.

I glance over and see the prisoner watching me. I note a flicker of fear.

Good.

Time to let that build.

I go back to gathering my tools, making sure to draw out the process of holding each one up and then placing it on the wheeled cart. When I'm ready, I roll the cart over to where the prisoner waits, watching.

I grab the hammer and raise it high.

"What's your name?" I demand.

He doesn't answer.

With my free hand, I reach down and peel back the gauze on his hand. The flesh is mangled and coated in bloody tissue. From the looks of it, he's lost all but his thumb, and even that is hanging on by a thread.

He needs a healer.

But he won't get one.

At my touch, he strains against the irons. "Don't—"

"Four fingers gone," I say. "One for each of the women and children you killed today."

He glares up at me, his defiance never wavering. Not

a single shred of regret clouds his expression. It's that lack of repentance that seals his fate.

I smash the hammer against his hand, and he screams. The irons strain as he tries and fails to withdraw his arm. Blood runs from his hand like a wet sponge.

His scream turns to a wail of pain.

"Name," I say again.

"Barbas."

"And why did you bomb the wall, Barbas?"

No answer.

I start to bring the hammer down again.

"Wait! We wanted to go through the portal."

I lean forward, eyes narrowing on his sweaty, dirty face. "Who is *we*?"

"My family and our clan. We're sick of being prisoners. Caius got to leave. So should we."

His voice shakes, but the entitlement remains.

I shake my head. "And you think innocents deserve to die in order for you to take what you want?"

His expression hardens. "Casualties of war."

My patience snaps. I bring the hammer down again, and while he screams, I open my mouth and let the hellfire burning my throat drip onto his arm.

His screams heighten.

The sound of it echoes off the walls, and the monster inside me stirs. *More*, it whispers.

"Whose idea was this attack, Barbas?"

I don't wait for an answer before I let more hellfire drip onto his legs. His pants melt where the molten lava scalds, leaving craters of missing flesh beneath. Through his screams, he wails, "How the hell are you doing that? You're not even shifted."

I smile. "It was a gift from my mother. Now, give me a name, or you'll slow-roast right here in this chair."

An ember slips off the armrest and onto his thigh. The hot coal burns immediately through the fabric of his pants, and he screams again as his flesh burns anew.

"My uncle, okay? It's my uncle. Quincy. He's our clan leader. The one who put this together."

"Where can we find him?"

"The outlands."

"Not good enough."

"Ah! The Western Isles. Fuck. Please don't hurt me anymore."

"That was your choice, remember? Not mine. It didn't have to go this far."

"He's my family. What am I supposed to do? I can't betray family."

"You can if that family is hurting innocent people." I ignore the twinge in my gut as I say the words that hit way too close to home.

Through the pain, he manages to glare at me. "Don't you have family?"

"I did. Once."

"Wouldn't you do anything for them?" he pleads.

"Yes." Darkness presses in around me, old memories that weigh heavily even as I shove them back again. "That's the problem."

He starts to argue, and the idea of whatever he's about to say—to try to convince me of—is too much.

I open my mouth and, using my shadow dragon's powers, breathe the fires of hell over his flesh.

He screams, his form morphing toward some kind of fur-coated shifter before his entire body is reduced to ash.

The sudden silence echoes around me.

"Ugh. I hate when you use the hellfire," Pol mutters. "Smells terrible."

I look at him, my insides churning with a wound that hasn't broken open this wide in a long time. "Put together a hunting party. Tell them to assemble in the courtyard. I'll brief them in an hour."

Pol mutters something and motions for Marques to accompany him out.

They leave quickly. I don't blame them. The smell isn't great, and it's only going to get worse the longer the prisoner's remains sit.

But I don't leave yet.

Instead, I begin carrying the tools back to their respective boxes on the counter. There are plenty of soldiers suited for a job like this one, but I crave the distraction of cleaning up. Even now, the darkness of my past presses in around the edges of my consciousness, whispering reminders of what I am. What I did to earn a prison like Tartarus.

"It smells like shit in here."

I look up at the sound of Styx's voice and note the fact that the door never opened again. Which means she's been standing in the shadows for a while now.

She comes forward slowly. When she gets to the chair, she eyes the prisoner's remains with mild interest then returns her attention to me as she approaches the counter where I stand.

"How long have you been here?" I ask.

She shrugs, but her expression is strained. "I caught the show."

She rubs at her temple, wincing, and I snort.

"You too, huh?"

She scowls. "I blame you for my choices."

"Oh no. I did not tell you to empty the bar of all its bourbon. That was all you."

She glares at me. "Is someone beating on your skull from the inside?"

"Right behind my eyeballs," I say.

"That makes me feel better." She sniffs. "We'll call it even."

I shake my head.

A beat of silence passes, and then she says, "Is that why you went so hard on that asshole just now?"

I go back to straightening and putting away my tools. "It had to be done."

"Right."

"I have the name of the leader," I say even though I know she already heard it earlier. "We're sending out a hunting party to locate him and bring him in."

"I thought Caius said to make it clean next time."

I motion to the unused tools. "I did."

"He gave you the name. We could have called the healer."

I scowl at her. "You're telling me you disagree with my choice."

"Hell no. I would have done the same thing. Besides,

if you'd put him in a cell for holding, the soldiers would have done way worse."

She's not wrong. They're all itching for a fight after what happened with the guardian. Our greatest enemy turned out to be Caius' mate. Good for him. Not great for battle-thirsty soldiers whose war has been snatched away in the name of love.

"Then what is it?" I ask.

"I couldn't help but notice how he mentioned family and betrayal, and, well, it almost seemed personal at the end."

"Fuck off, Styx."

She braces her elbows on the counter, leaning in and pinning me with a look I don't like. "Legion. You're not yourself."

"Is this the part where you say something about how I need the love of a good woman to heal me or something?"

"Actually, I was going to say you should get laid."

I snort, and she straightens, heading for the door. "Caius wants a briefing in twenty. I'll see you in there."

"Yeah, fine," I mutter.

When she's gone, I splay my hands out on the counter, letting my head hang forward, trying—and failing—to clear my mind. The prisoner's last words continue to replay in my mind, conjuring memories that are better left buried. Even after all this time, thinking about it—about her—still feels like a poison inside me.

It's so much worse than any physical pain I've endured. I'd do anything to take it away, but there's nothing strong enough to cut this particular wound out of me.

Family.

The ultimate torture.

The only thing I can do is make sure I never form an attachment like that again. Not with anyone. Especially not a mate.

CHAPTER 5

TORI

I check my phone for what might be the millionth time today and note the lack of notifications. After my visit to his club early this morning, Uziah promised to ask around for some way to stop the Crimson Roses from coming for me, but so far, I've yet to hear back. My worry spikes with each moment that passes without answers.

I need a plan.

Somewhere to take Kendall until all this blows over. If it ever does. But my only real friend in this city is Niamh, and her job at the club makes her too risky of an ally right now. She's already texted me about getting drinks tonight, but I haven't answered her. I don't even know where to start.

All my focus is on making Kendall safe.

Guilt tugs at me a bit for never teaching her the same fighting techniques my father insisted on teaching me. I'd wanted to protect her from the harsher aspects of life, but now I worry I've only made her defenseless.

Juniper still hasn't returned from her sojourn with the tree people. She's always spent more time out there than she does in the city. I think it makes her feel closer to my mother. Usually, I'm a bit jealous of the way she's able to commune with nature, but right now, I'm just glad she's somewhere safe.

Maybe I could talk to Natalia about hiding Kendall for me.

Pulling out my phone, I fire off a text to her.

Hey, can I ask a favor? It's about Kendall.

Her response is prompt as always, leaving me to wonder if the witch saw this coming and has been waiting on me. **Sure, anything.**

Can Kendall stay with you for a few days? I need to sort out a work thing.

I watch as the dots ripple, signaling her typing a response. Finally, she answers. **What does Kendall say about that?**

I frown, confused.

Before I can text back, a knock sounds at my bedroom door.

"Tor, I know you're in there," Kendall calls.

The sound of her voice sends my stress and fear up another notch. Up until that moment with Uziah, I'd almost believed whatever happened to me was a fluke or could be reversed, but drinking that poison proved otherwise. Or, more accurately, the fact that nothing happened to me after drinking it spoke volumes.

Actually, not *nothing*. The black veins spidering across my stomach and arms are gone now. Almost as if drinking that poison healed me.

Whatever's going on, it's clear I'm tainted by some kind of dark magic from the death dragon himself. A creature more powerful and brutal than anything I've ever encountered if rumors are true. Until I know more, I'm not about to risk another accidental touch—especially with Kendall.

"Tor, you have to eat something," she tries again.

"Leave it outside," I call.

"Or you could come sit at the table like a normal person," she says.

Except that I'm not normal.

"I'll stay on the other side of the room," she adds hopefully.

"Too risky."

"You aren't going to hurt me," she argues. "I trust you."

That may be, but I don't trust myself.

"Fine. I'll leave your plate here," she says when I don't respond.

I count to fifty before sliding off my bed and venturing to the door. I stop long enough to pull on gloves that cover my hands and wrists followed by a scarf that covers nearly all of my face and hair. Listening, I make sure there's no sound from the other side before unlocking the door and pulling it open.

Kendall is nowhere in sight, but the plate is set a lot farther out than I expected. I'm forced to take three steps to reach out. The moment I bend down, Kendall pops out from around the corner and slides in behind me, pulling my bedroom door shut.

"What the hell are you doing?" I demand.

"Proving my point," she says, blocking my retreat to isolation.

"Kendall," I warn, taking a step back. I nearly trip over the plate but manage to right myself, sidestepping it and her. "This isn't funny. Or safe. Move out of the way."

"No." She gives me a hard look. "I'm not letting you spend the rest of your life in your room."

"Kendall," I say again, my voice dropping to a whisper. "I'm not safe. I could kill you."

"You won't."

"You can't be sure—"

"I can because I've seen it."

That stops me. "What?"

"I've seen how I go, and it's not by your hand."

I gape at her. "You've seen your own death?"

"Yes." She shrugs like it's no big deal.

Kendall's always had visions of the future, but they've grown more frequent as she's gotten older. And darker. Especially since she began training under Natalia. This is her first vision of death, but I can't help shuddering because I have a feeling it won't be the last.

"How does it happen?" I ask softly, wincing at what I'm saying.

But she folds her arms. "No way. I'm not answering that question."

"If you tell me, maybe I can help stop—"

"You can't." She holds her hand up to cut off my argument. "Relax, Tor. I live to be very old, okay. There's nothing you need to do here."

I exhale, still wary.

What if she's lying just to calm me down?

"Come eat dinner with me," she adds and marches off into the kitchen without waiting for a reply.

Alone, I glance down at the plate that lured me out here in the first place. Curious, I reach down and pull the lid off.

The plate is empty.

I huff and straighten, pausing long enough to make sure all my coverings are still in place. Then, I reluctantly follow her into the kitchen.

Kendall's seated at one end of the table. She looks up and gestures for me to take the seat opposite her. It's already set for me, complete with a huge plate of spaghetti.

My favorite.

"Sit."

Cautiously, I do as Kendall says, sitting and taking a bite. The flavors hit my tongue, and I make a sound of appreciation. When I look up, Kendall's watching me with one lifted brow.

"Sorry," I mumble.

She smirks. "I'll take the compliment."

We eat in silence for a few minutes, and slowly, I relax into the idea that I might co-exist with Kendall this way. If I'm careful. If I don't let my guard down.

But the relief doesn't last. My future stretches out before me, lonely and long. A well of sadness rises to the surface.

"Stop."

Kendall's tone is sharp. When I look up, I find her glaring.

"Stop what?" I ask.

"Feeling sorry for yourself."

"I'm not—"

"It's all you've done since you came home from that stupid bar."

I set my fork down, suddenly not hungry anymore. "I killed a girl last night."

"It was an accident," she reminds me, but I'm not sure that matters.

"One that could easily happen again," I point out.

"But it won't. You'll be careful. We'll figure this out. Together."

I shake my head, thoughts crashing one into another as I try to decide how much to tell her. I've always kept her from the details of what I do—and the life I live as a professional poisoner. But I'm not sure I can do that anymore. And that breaks my heart.

Kendall is quiet, watching me, waiting—because she knows there's more.

"Uziah said the woman was part of the Crimson Roses," I add.

Kendall's eyes widen. "The gang?"

I nod.

"Shit," she says.

Kendall knows only the basics about them, but it's enough for her to understand the gravity of the situation.

"They think I did it on purpose. They're taking it personally."

"Can Uziah talk to them? Smooth things over?"

"I don't know. I haven't heard back from him."

"You have to get out of here," she says, voice rising as worry sets in. "They'll hunt you down, find you here."

"I can't go out there. I'm dangerous."

She sets her fork aside and sits back. "Fine. We'll be ready when they come—"

"No," I cut her off, rigid in my chair. "You will not be here when they come. *If* they come," I amend though we both know it's a futile thing to doubt.

They'll come.

"I am not letting you face this alone," she says.

"Yes you are. It's my job to protect you. I texted Natalia. You can stay with her."

"You got me a babysitter?"

"Just for a couple of days until I figure this out."

"And exactly how will you do that?"

A headache begins to pulse at my temples. "Uziah will find a way out of this."

She scowls. "Bullshit."

"Uziah—"

"Uziah is a vamp out to make a buck. He doesn't care about you. He only cares how he can use you."

"He was Dad's friend."

"He was Dad's *resource*. There's a difference." She softens and ducks her head as she adds, "He came into Spells the other day."

I stare back at her, thrown off by her admission. "What? Why?"

"He asked me to work for him." She lifts her gaze again, and I see guilt flash. "I know, I should have told you right away but—"

"Work for him how?"

"He wants someone who can see the future."

"He wants to replace Stella," I realize. She nods, and a

new kind of fear twists in my gut. "I hope you said no."

"Of course I said no. Do I look stupid?"

Relief courses through me, but it's short-lived. "How did he take it?"

"He promised to be back in a few days so he could change my mind." She hesitates. "I told Natalia I needed the week off."

"Smart. It's best to avoid the situation rather than face him head-on."

"I know."

The fear threatens to drag me down, so I force a smile and tease, "When did you get so street-smart?"

"I haven't changed," she says, brows arching. "Maybe the way you see me has."

I shake my head, unwilling to get into that particular argument right now. "He might be dangerous, but Uziah has connections. If anyone can find a way out of this, it's him."

"Fine, but you have to face this. Stop hiding in your room."

Now, it's my turn to glare. "You're being awfully pushy for a girl who still has a curfew."

She hesitates. "I saw something, Tor." The worry in her tone puts me immediately on edge.

"What is it?"

"A vision. About you. A possible future."

"Tell me."

"In one version, you... don't forgive yourself. You remain locked in this house." Her voice catches as she adds, "You die alone."

Fear and worry clog my senses, but then I remember

her words from earlier. "I thought you said you live until you're old."

"I do." Her concern deepens as she adds, "But I am not with you when—" She breaks off and looks away.

I stare down at my plate, at a loss.

"You have to fight this," she pleads.

"What is there to fight?" I snap, looking up at her again, eyes blazing with fury. "Even if she wasn't an innocent, I killed her for no reason. I am the enemy. How do I fight *myself*?"

She doesn't answer my question. Instead, she scrapes back her chair and gets up, moving to the sink and clattering dishes into the soapy water. Her back is to me, and she's silent so long that I'm certain the conversation is over.

Finally, she says, "There was another future."

My eyes bore holes in her back. "What future?"

"There's a male. Someone ... who helps you."

I pause, my heart racing as I think of the possibilities. But I have a feeling I already know who she means. "Uziah?"

"No."

My mate.

The death dragon himself.

The image of his face is burned behind my eyelids. Amid all the fear, I've thought of him constantly. My body aches for him, which is stupid considering I've never done more than look at him or feel his hand on my cheek. Despite that, I want him as badly as I want to wake up from this nightmare.

"Mom would forgive you, you know."

I blink, snapping out of my thoughts to see Kendall facing me again. Her expression is a knowing one. "She would understand."

I shake my head, my eyes filling with tears. "I know that. But what if the next one…"

"She would want you to have a life."

"What life?" I snort. "It's not like I had one before this."

She crosses her arms, challenging me with the lift of her chin. "So, maybe it's time to make one."

"You mean retire."

She shrugs. "We could go legit. Start a kitchen herb business. One that doesn't include poisons."

I consider that idea, but my mind can't seem to conjure what that future would look like—not without seeing my mate there with me.

Ugh.

"The male you saw," I say slowly, "In that other future… what was he to me?"

"What do you mean?"

"Were we… together?"

"I'm not sure. I think that was part of the choice you need to make—the choice that will save you." She pauses and then cocks her head. "Do you know who I'm talking about?"

"I met someone," I say quietly.

"Who?"

I hesitate, trying to calculate how much to tell her and how much to hold back. "A dragon. From Tartarus."

"No way," she breathes, eyes wide. "What was he like? Tell me everything."

A killer.

A monster.

"Well." I swallow hard. "He's my mate."

"What?" she demands. She returns to the table, keeping her distance, I note. "I cannot believe you sat on this for a whole day. Tell me everything."

My mouth lifts at her enthusiasm. It's the first semblance of normalcy I've had. "He was at the bar when I finished work the other night."

"What did he say?"

"Nothing."

"You didn't speak to him?"

"No, I just felt... It happened so fast, and I think he was as shocked as me."

She shakes her head, amused, but then her expression pinches, and she goes still. "Is he the one who did this to you?"

I hesitate, shaking my head rather than spilling the terrible truth. "I'm not sure, but there was a darkness in him. Something I've never felt before. Strong magic. It made me dizzy. At the time, I thought it was the mate bond, but now I'm not sure."

"You think he cast a curse?" she asks. "A dragon?"

"I don't know." I sigh. "What do you think?"

"I couldn't see the male in my vision, but I think you deserve to know one way or another."

"What do you mean?"

"You need to talk to him," she says as if it's the most reasonable idea in the world.

My heart pounds wildly at the thought of

confronting him. Of seeing him again at all. "And what would I do if it's true?"

She shrugs. "That's a choice only you can make."

Before I can answer, my phone dings with a text.

"It's Uziah," I say, scanning it quickly.

"What does it say?" Kendall asks.

I look up at her, dazed. "He says he told the Crimson Roses the reason I was able to poison that girl is because someone cursed me."

"You told him about your mate?" she asks.

"No, only that a stranger touched me and likely cursed me in the process. I'm guessing he was trying to find a way to take the blame off of me."

"And? Did it work?" she asks.

"Yes," I say, unsure how I feel about this new development. "They said if I can bring them the body of the one responsible for infecting me, they'll rescind their kill order on me."

Kendall stares at me, wide-eyed. "You have to kill your mate?"

"And bring them his body," I add.

Silence hangs between us. I know she's trying to wrap her head around it just like I am.

"Are you going to do it?" she asks quietly.

I look up at her, ready to tell her no, of course not. To kill one's mate would bring an agony unlike any other. But then I see Kendall staring back at me with wide, worried eyes—and I remember my vow. One that promises I'll keep my sister safe, no matter what.

"I don't really have a choice."

LEGION

I shouldn't think of her at all, but I do. I cannot stop. No matter how much I drink. No matter how many enemies I torture or reports I read from my men. Her scent, her eyes, her body—I want it all. And even though I haven't sought her out again since that first meeting, my want is turning to a need so dark and feral I think I might go mad without her.

She must feel it too, our connection.

She must be desiring me as much as I want her. It's twisted, but I comfort myself with the idea that she's as tormented as I am by this invisible force doing its best to push us together. Even if I never plan to take her fully, my dark heart is smug in knowing she wishes I would. She must be dying to touch me. To feel my body against hers. In hers. She must be desperate to seal this bond. To have me claim her.

I refuse to give in to it.

I will not be ruled by yet another bond, especially one that ties my life to another. Being bonded to Caius isn't the worst fate in the world. Not considering the monster who came before him. But a mate is different. It's more than a leash. It's a mortal tether. If she dies, I die.

I refuse to add the weight of that to an already burdened fate.

So, I remain in Tartarus, closed off behind the walls of Kolgrave Keep. My trip to Osiris was a disaster. Styx was mildly amused. Caius, not so much, which means I won't be venturing out again anytime soon. Not until I can find a way to break the mate bond's hold over me. If that's possible.

Whatever happens, I have no intention of claiming her.

As a gloomy afternoon gives way to twilight, Klyn appears in the doorway to the study where I slouch beside the fire. He offers a rap of knuckles to signal his presence though he didn't need to bother. I scented him the moment he entered the estate.

"Come in."

Apparently, I needn't have bothered either as he strides toward me without waiting for an invitation.

I've known Klyn since I arrived in Tartarus five millennia ago and chose the land next to his as my new home site. He is a wolf shifter whose lupin bloodline is descended from the gods, who turned on him and cast him out of Olympus for no other reason than that his strength and cunning threatened their own. Since then, he's roamed the realms as a wild, packless beast.

His penchant for silence has made him an easy companion for someone like me. His ability to find out nearly anything in this realm or the next has made him a valuable resource. He's more than my second-in-command; he's a friend.

"What did you find?" I ask as he comes to stand before me.

"Good to see you too, friend."

I roll my eyes. "Good to see you. What did you find?"

He grins at me then crosses to pour himself a drink. I wait impatiently as he does so and watch as he takes the seat across from mine near the crackling fireplace.

"She's not what I expected." He sips the bourbon he's holding.

I curl my hand into a fist, trying—and failing—to remain patient. "What the hell does that mean?"

The look he gives me tells me he's enjoying this torture. "She's different."

"Klyn, it is only out of friendship that I have not lost my temper. What did you find? Specifics."

"Relax, friend," he says, grinning. "I did the job you asked."

I snarl.

His grin never even wavers. "Fine. How's this for specific? She's half-dark fae, half-nymph, which is an interesting mix to be sure. Both offer an affinity for nature, which makes sense, given her line of work. Anyway, both parents died about ten years back. Car accident. Her only family is a younger sister, Kendall, whom she's raised alone ever since."

I frown. My experience with family has been less than pleasant, but even so, I can't imagine having to raise a sibling alone.

Then Klyn's other words snag my attention.

"What's her line of work?"

"Oh, man. This is the part that cracks me up." He shakes his head, chuckling. "Ready for this? She's an assassin-for-hire."

I frown. "She's a soldier in her realm?"

He nods. "Freelance. Her specialty is natural poisons. That night you saw her in the bar, she was working."

So, she wasn't avenging a wrong that male did to her after all. The disappointment I feel is ridiculous. I don't intend to pursue or claim her, so why do I care if she's a killer like me?

I don't.

As if to prove it, I remain silent.

"You want to know the rest?" Klyn asks.

"No, that's enough."

His brow lifts, but I ignore it. "You sure?"

"What else is there?" I all but snarl.

But Klyn is too used to my foul moods. He doesn't bat an eye as he teases, "Whether or not she's seeing anyone?"

My blood roars in my ears. I lean forward before I can stop myself, teeth bared. "Is she?"

He chuckles again. "Nope. But I had you."

Leaning back, I exhale, my breath shakier than I want to admit. Klyn, of course, notices and continues to smirk as he drains his glass and pushes to his feet. "Her name is Torissa Sage, in case you're wondering."

"I wasn't."

He sets his glass down, angling toward the door before he stops and says, "You want her address?"

"No."

"Suit yourself."

I listen as he lets himself out, my thoughts churning. She's alone. Raising her sister. Vulnerable. Unprotected.

My dragon's need to go to her, to protect her is overwhelming. The feeling goes far beyond any blood vow obligation I've ever experienced.

Before I can think too hard about all the reasons not to, I am up and out the door and heading for the portal. All it takes is a quick exchange with the soldier guarding the portal, and I'm cleared to pass. My position has its advantages and this is one I almost wish I didn't. Without clearance, I'd at least be forced to stay away from her.

The moment I step into the Earth realm, I shift into my dragon and take to the air. The mate bond slams into me, calling me toward her with an urgency that catches me off guard. I could feel her in Tartarus but not like this.

In this realm, the tether that connects us is a screaming siren, beckoning me toward her. I fly faster, harder, if only to burn off the lust that fills me as I imagine her following this strand of connection we share —hunting for me as if she were the predator rather than the prey.

It's pointless to go to her.

And yet, that's what I do.

The mate bond leads me to a small house with peeling paint and a well-tended yard. In the back, a light shines inside a shed. Despite having every reason not to, I land in the trees far enough away that she won't hear it and slowly approach from the woods. I'm nearly at the edge of her yard when I remember I'm still naked from the shift. Doubling back through several yards, I snag a pair of pants from a clothesline and tug them on before making my way toward her home.

Her presence is a screaming neon sign.

Even from outside, I can already scent her, and it takes everything in me not to break down the door and bury myself inside her.

Instead, I watch her from the window.

Her green hair is loose and long, obscuring her face, but the curves of her body hypnotize me as she moves from plant to plant, watering, inspecting, murmuring things to each of them.

A killer.

I snort. *Hardly.*

At the sound, she jerks her face toward the window, and I rear back, melting into the shadows.

I wait, barely breathing.

The shed door opens.

I strain to listen for the sound of footsteps or movement, but there is only silence.

Too much silence.

I press myself against the wall, my body thrumming with lust that clouds my thoughts. My erection bulges painfully against my pants. It takes me a moment to sense anything beyond my need for her.

She's a quiet hunter, I'll give her that. On silent steps only a fae could achieve, she is suddenly standing before me. Her hair is pulled back in a tail now, revealing her face, and I find myself studying her features even while imagining what it would be like to free her hair again. To watch it curtain around her shoulders. To curl my fists around the ends and bow her head back so I can lick from her throat to her breasts.

Her eyes meet mine, and I watch as her breath catches. Her pulse pounds harder, and I nearly drop to the ground at her feet right here and now to give her what she wants.

What we both want.

Her fist swings out, flying quicker than I would have thought her capable. I barely manage to dodge the punch, sidestepping her at the last second.

She glares at me.

I frown. This is not the greeting I expected. "Do you know who I am?"

"That depends on which context you're referring to." Her voice rakes over me, a delicious ripple of pleasure against my senses.

"We met," I say, "in the city."

"Oh, I remember," she says darkly. "It's not something I could forget, unfortunately."

Unfortunately?

"You are my mate."

"Yes, I'm aware." She sighs. "A fact that's equally unfortunate."

Irritation stabs through me. "You would speak to your fated mate that way?"

"I would speak to my enemy that way," she says icily.

"What makes you think I'm your enemy?"

"You're a being from hell, are you not?"

Irritation tightens my expression.

"You are the monster they call the death dragon," she

presses. "An evil creature responsible for wiping out empires and killing innocents."

Anger overtakes confusion. I straighten and close the distance, standing before her. She is smaller than me though she doesn't retreat at my presence. If anything, she looks more determined—for what, I don't know.

"Why did you come out here if not to give yourself to me?"

"Give myself to you?" She stares at me with something like disgust, and my blood boils. "Does that kind of talk really work where you're from?" She shakes her head. "Sorry to disappoint you, but you're the one trespassing on my property. And I didn't come out here to screw you, asshole. I came to kill you."

TORI

The death dragon stares back at me with enough fire in his gaze to burn my skin. The moment I state my real intentions, he's half-ready to kill me, too; that much is easy to read. But he holds back. Rather than analyze the reason why for too long, I get down to what I came here to do. I've spent the last few hours in my shop preparing to hunt him. Only to have him come to me in the end.

It's an opportunity I can't waste.

Unfortunately, firing the arrow I dipped in poison won't work up close, so I improvise. Reaching into my pocket, I pull out a vial. A deadly combination of hemlock and belladonna made more potent by the blood of a dark witch. It's warm to my touch, and I waste no time uncapping it and tossing it at my mate.

He retreats so quickly I almost don't see him move.

The poison lands among the dead leaves where he just stood and the ground it coats immediately turns black as the grass shrivels and dies.

He glances from the poisoned ground to me, his eyes flashing with power and rage unlike anything I've ever seen before. He closes the distance between us as suddenly as he left. Overwhelmed by the magnitude of his presence, I back away, stopping only when my back thuds against the large elm tree behind me.

"You would dare to try to kill me?" he snarls.

His voice is barely more than an enraged breath. The sound of drums beats against my ears. My vision swims with battles and blood and a dragon with scales the color of midnight breathing fire and brimstone at the center of it all.

"There is no try, only do," I say.

His eyes narrow. "I am capable of destroying you with one breath, little fae. You are no match for me."

I know I'm supposed to be terrified at his threat, especially when he's obviously capable of backing it up. But I can't help the anger that surges upon hearing him confirm Uziah's claims. So, instead of cowering like I'm sure he expects me to do, I ask the only question that matters, especially if I'm about to become kindling.

"Why did you curse me?"

He blinks. "What?"

"You cursed me," I say, adding emphasis to each word. "Why? I did nothing to you."

He takes a step back, frowning. "What are you talking about?"

"That night at the bar," I say impatiently. "You touched me."

"I...yes." His expression shifts, and I know he's remembering the way he pressed his palm to my cheek.

Just like I know we're both distracted by the idea of touching one another again. Ugh.

"Ever since that night, my skin is poison," I tell him.

"The portal's magic is unpredictable but it's not my fault—"

"I haven't gone anywhere near that damned portal. Only you."

"I am not responsible for whatever strange affliction—"

"I killed a woman," I snap, temper flaring as I reach my breaking point.

"Yes, I've heard that's your profession." He practically spits the last word at me, and I don't miss the judgment in his sharp gaze.

"How do you know what my profession is?"

"Maybe you're not as good as you think you are."

I bite back another argument, refusing to let him distract me from what he's done. "I killed a bystander that night. A woman who had nothing to do with...my job. I killed her by accidentally touching her. And now her people want to kill me in return."

"What people?" he demands, eyes flashing with renewed determination. "Tell me where to find them."

"Are you even listening? My touch kills people," I say, voice rising. "Don't you understand? I have a sister, and thanks to you, I can never hug her again. In fact, if I accidentally brush her cheek, she'll die. Not to mention the fact that I'll never get laid again. Or hold someone's hand or feel someone's arm around me. I'm so fucked. And it's all your fault."

I watch as he takes in my words. His eyes dart to my

hands, which are bared and hanging at my sides. I consider attempting to touch him now and ending this once and for all, but I stop myself. Maybe it's the defeat I'm feeling, but I can't bring myself to attack him again. Or maybe it's the fact that what I really want is to press myself against him for entirely different reasons. To strip out of my clothes and hand over my body for whatever he'd like to use it for.

He shakes his head. "I am not capable of what you're accusing me of."

Fury rises at his denial. It's enough to snap me out of my lust. I lift my hand, reaching for his throat.

He steps back, but I leap forward.

We do this deadly dance for several more moments, and by the time I'm finished, I'm forced to admit he's faster than me. It stabs my pride and fuels my resolve to kick his ass.

Kill him, Tor.

Call it what it is.

Ugh.

"You are beautiful and deadly, little fae."

I scowl at the way his compliment warms me.

"Deadly is not a thing of beauty," I tell him.

"It is to me."

I huff because, if I'm being honest, he's beautiful and deadly too.

"You will not be able to kill me," he adds, and I glare back at him.

"I've never failed at it before, and I don't plan to start now."

His expression tightens. "Ah, yes, you've killed before."

"Many times."

Something unsettled flashes in his gaze. He looks almost disappointed.

"What? Did you think you were the only one capable of it?" I snap.

He looks resolute. "I have to go."

"Aww. Have I killed the mood?" I ask sweetly.

His hesitation is genuine, though, and I try to figure out how I've gotten to him. "You're not what I expected."

"I'm sorry. Did you want a mate who would fall at your feet and worship you?"

"I don't want a mate at all."

His words sting far more than they should, considering what a monster he is, but I shove that aside and snap, "That makes two of us."

He takes a step toward me, and I throw up my hands. "If you come near me, I'll touch you. And that will be that."

His eyes glitter as he says, "I would destroy you long before you got close enough to harm me."

"I'm not afraid of you."

"You should be."

Before I can answer, he leaps into the air, his dragon form exploding from his flesh and his wings carrying him off into the night.

LEGION

I fly south for an hour before touching down again. After five millennia in eternal darkness, having the open expanse of endless sunlit skies is a newfound freedom for my dark dragon. That freedom becomes more and more like a prison the farther I get from *her*.

My beast craves her. It's more than her beauty though she is the most alluring creature I've ever seen. She is strong. A fighter. A killer.

I will not tie myself to another monster.

I refuse to be controlled.

There's still the matter of her thinking I cursed her. It's a baseless claim though it has me wondering: If not me, then who or what did? Tartarus' dark magic has infected more than one citizen of the Crossroads already, but so far, that magic has been contained to the portal itself. And it hasn't involved curses. Either way, it wasn't my magic that did this.

Still, I can't help but admire her bravery for facing me so fearlessly with her accusations. Then again, maybe it's stupidity. Either way, beneath my obsession for her, and my determination to resist her, I worry.

The very idea of someone intentionally hurting her has a fire curling inside my beast. Before I know what's happening, hellfire unleashes from my throat, raining out over the moonlit sky and falling to the Earth below.

Shocked at the way I just lost control, I stare out at the landscape beneath me, watching as the fire makes landfall. It scorches everything it touches. Farmland, mountains—thankfully, no homes that I can see.

Unfortunately, the fire I unleashed barely scratches the surface of the rage my beast feels, and I feel another burst forming. Half-mad from resisting the fury, I angle higher, determined to keep from razing the town below me.

The madness at not accepting the mate bond is a darkness driving me wild. Even if I wanted to give in, I couldn't, not if she's unable to touch another without killing them. The idea of another creature touching her in the way I want to blinds me with rage. I find myself relieved she cannot. But that also means I can't touch her either.

With a snarl, I turn back and head for the portal back to Tartarus. Someone hurt her. I intend to find out who if only to soothe the beast inside me—to maintain control. But to do that, I need to be free of my restraints.

An hour later, my legs are heavy as I climb the steps to the palace. Pol, Caius' closest advisor, stops me before I've made it to the door. I brace myself for a round of shit.

"Well, look at what the werecat dragged in," Pol says.

I don't give him the satisfaction of a response. Pol likes to push buttons.

"You look like hell," he adds when I don't respond.

"You should see the other guy," I tell him.

"Oh, I heard." Pol chuckles. "Five thousand years of imprisonment, and at the first taste of freedom, you get drunk and lose your shit on one of our own."

I scowl. "That's not how it is."

"Then how is it?"

"That asshole had it coming," I tell him.

"Oh, I don't doubt that. But you must have needed to blow off steam pretty badly if Styx let you have all the fun."

I shake my head, in no mood to rehash it. "Is he in?" I ask, angling my head toward the castle's private living quarters.

Pol waves me onward. "He's expecting you. Hey, next time you want to brawl, call me. We'll make it a fair fight."

I ignore his shit-talking and continue making my way toward the residence.

Pol's wrong. Freedom has nothing to do with it, and I have to believe Caius will let this go. The ruler of Tartarus might have begun as nothing more than my prison warden and bonded master, but somewhere along the way, he became a friend. He'll understand what I did and why.

What he won't like is the favor I'm going to ask.

But I must deal with my mate before I go completely mad from resisting her. And I can't do that if I'm serving another master.

Even now, I can feel my beast stirring for her. To see her, speak with her, touch her—again. It doesn't seem to mind the idea that her touch could kill me. Although, that's a fact yet to be determined.

At the top of the stairs, a young guard perks up at the sight of me. "General," he greets, straightening his shoulders and standing taller.

"Riggs. At ease."

He relaxes but barely. "Heard you went a few rounds at Osiris the other night." He grins.

I stop and stare at him until his grin fades.

"Sorry, sir," he mumbles. "None of my business."

"Damn right it isn't," I tell him before letting myself through the door at his back.

Caius is seated at the end of a long table when I enter. The impressive spread of food is untouched and ignored in favor of the female currently draped over his lap.

"Ahem." I clear my throat, and they reluctantly break apart.

"Legion." Caius eyes me around the curve of his mate's throat which he'd just been licking.

"Your timing is impeccable as usual," Reagan says.

She turns and shoots me a scowl, but the smile that follows is friendly. Since she took her place at Caius' side a few months ago, I've come to know her as warm and open.

She's a welcome addition to Caius' court, though I don't understand the draw to the male before me. He's decent as gods go, but he's still a grump and an asshole. Apparently, there's someone for everyone.

Except for me.

"I can come back," I say, "If this is a bad time."

"No, no, it's fine," Reagan says. "I have a painting to finish."

Caius whispers something to her, and she plants another quick kiss on his mouth before climbing to her feet and leaving us.

When we're alone, he says, "What's on your mind?"

"I would like to speak with you about my service here."

"Your service," he repeats with something like suspicion.

"As you know, I have loyally served under your leadership since I came to Tartarus."

At that, he chuckles. "As I recall, you didn't have a choice since your heritage requires you to be bonded to another being as a matter of survival. I also recall that you made my life hell for it at first."

"How about we focus on the last four thousand years," I shoot back wryly.

He grins. "Took you a while to come around, General."

The joke is short-lived as I focus on what I came to say. "During that time, I've never once asked you for anything."

His grin disappears, and he studies me. "No," he

agrees. "You haven't. But something tells me you'll do so now. Is this about the bar fight?"

"The offender was inappropriate with one of your advisors. I was well within my right as your general—"

"Relax, Styx told me everything. It's fine. Though I wondered what caused you to react so strongly."

I tense. "As I said, he was inappropriate."

"It's not the first time you've dealt with a drunken dumbass," he points out. "Your self-control is usually on a tighter leash."

"You're not wrong." I clear my throat. "That is why I request that you release me from our blood bond."

He nods slowly without an ounce of surprise in his expression. It makes me wonder what he thinks he knows, but I don't ask.

"Releasing you will leave you vulnerable," he says. "Someone else could attempt to bond you to them—"

"They would not live long enough to succeed," I snarl, my temper sending smoke through my nostrils.

Caius holds up a hand, and I check myself, forcing even breaths until my heart rate calms and my beast recedes. "You've served Tartarus dutifully. I hate to lose you, but I understand. Though, I must say your timing for retirement is—"

"Not retirement," I assure him. "I ask only for the blood oath between us to be released. I still intend to do my job."

"In that case, I'm curious as to the reason for your request," he says. "Is there another bond you want to forge?"

My eyes narrow.

He knows. That gleam in his eye is too certain. I have no idea how he knows already, but then, he is a primordial god.

"I have found my mate," I admit.

He smirks. "I know. Styx told me."

My eyes narrow. "She and I are going to have words."

"That might prove difficult. She's gone to hunt for her own mate. Like Oberon should be. Now with you, I'm starting to think there's something in the water here."

I frown. "That's not what I'm doing. And Oberon's hunting his throne."

He smiles smugly. "That's what they all say."

I resist the urge to defend myself and simply say, "I have found her, but I have no intention of claiming her."

His smirk fades into concern, which is almost worse. "I see. Can I ask why not?"

"I will not be bonded to another again."

"What will you do once you've protected her? Will you return to retake the oath with me?"

I hesitate, unused to admitting these words aloud. "I hope to find a way to end the need for it altogether."

"Of course." There is understanding in his expression, as I knew there would be, but there is also pity.

Uncomfortable, I change the subject.

"Does the magic we carry from Tartarus... can it infect another through touch?"

"The portal itself leaked magic when it first happened. But I'm not aware any of our kind has done what you're suggesting. Why do you ask?"

"My—the female is a dark fae with a talent for

poisons. After meeting me, her magic has changed, and now her touch alone is lethal."

"And you think you're responsible?"

"She does," I admit. "I wondered if the magic of Tartarus could affect a curse of that magnitude."

"It's possible," he says, brows furrowing in thought. "I thought I stopped the magic from leaking when I returned here through the portal. But it's possible you carry some of that magic on you. Is she at risk then?"

"I don't know. Not from the poison, I don't think. But there are others who are offended by what she's done with it. She needs protection," I add. "I can do that much."

He nods in understanding. "But you can't take a life I haven't sanctioned."

"Yes."

"What if I sanction it?"

I frown. "Would you?"

He shrugs. "If it keeps you safe from another bond, if you wish it, then yes."

I hesitate. It's tempting. Not because I don't think I can take care of myself but because maintaining the blood oath with Caius means I can't be tempted to mate with her. Then I remember the hellfire I rained down over the Earth realm earlier. The madness that only grows stronger as the two bonds fight for dominance.

In the end, I shake my head. "I think it's best if we end our connection. The mate bond ... it is dangerous feeling both at once."

He nods. "You've been loyal to me, Legion, and in return, I will show you the same respect."

He reaches over and picks up a knife from the table setting then slices his palm open until blood pools in his hand. He walks over and holds the knife out to me.

I take it and make a similar incision in my own palm.

When my own blood has pooled, I take his hand in a firm shake, sealing our blood as one just like we did five millennia ago. The air fills with the scent of brimstone and smoke.

"I hereby release you, Legion Razginath, from the blood oath between us. Your will is now your own."

He releases me, and I watch as the blood coating our hands evaporates, becoming thick, black hellsmoke. I exhale, knowing the demon bloodline that created me acknowledges his decree. My thoughts drift to my mother, but I shove her away. She is no longer a threat to me. And I have finally earned my freedom at last.

My muscles tense then relax as I feel the tether between Caius and me finally snap free.

In the absence of a blood bond with another, a new sense of power courses through my veins. In this moment, Caius is not the only god here. A demon might have birthed me, but a god sired me, and for the first time in five thousand years, I feel the essence of both legacies in my blood.

Inside, my dragon stirs, straining for the freedom of the skies, but I hold it fast in my grip, reveling in the feel of the only will inside me being my own—at last.

"It is done," I say.

"It is done," Caius agrees, still studying me. "Where will you go?"

"Wherever it takes," I say.

"Take as long as you need. I'll speak to Klyn about covering your duties. Your job will be waiting for you when you're ready. You always have a place here, Legion. Bond or no."

I dip my head in acknowledgment and respect. "I am grateful."

I turn to leave. Behind me, Caius calls out, "Be careful, old friend. The heart is a dangerous thing to ignore, and your enemies would exploit any vulnerability."

Rationally, I know he's right, but my beast isn't concerned about enemies. None of those threats feel nearly as dangerous as that unmistakable pull I feel toward a singular fae woman.

For some, the idea of a mate might be desirable. For me, it's another prison sentence. I'm done being captive to any sort of bond—even one that comes with an all-you-can-fuck buffet for life. Now that I'm free, I'll die before I let anyone else trap me ever again.

CHAPTER 9
TORI

I pull my gloves higher on my arms, making sure they overlap with my long sleeves. My scarf smells strongly of the magic Juniper used on it earlier, but at least it remains firmly in place, covering my deadly skin. I wish she'd come with us today, but she promised to ward the house from intruders, and she can't keep up the protections if she isn't there. Trees are very forgetful, apparently.

At least the Crimson Roses have yet to come looking for me. I know it's Uziah's "deal" with them about me bringing the dragon in my place. But I also know the time left on that reprieve will run out soon. And Natalia has been silent ever since I texted her about letting Kendall stay with her, which hasn't left me any options for relocating.

The only real solution I have left is to kill the death dragon. I keep telling myself I would have done it if he hadn't flown off last night, but the truth is a bit murkier than I'm ready to admit.

In the mid-morning sun, Kendall dances around me, her attention captured by the goods displayed in the booths we pass. This farmers market bullshit was her idea and, frankly, I owe her some semblance of freedom. She isn't Rapunzel; I can't keep her locked in the house forever. I did, however, require Juniper's gift of charms to help alter Kendall's appearance so that she wouldn't be recognized. The process had reminded me a lot of my friend Stella and her love of makeovers.

My thoughts drift to Niamh, whom I still owe drinks. I make a mental note to text her later to see if she's heard anything during her shifts about the Crimson Roses and their plans for me.

Meanwhile, Kendall is in her element here. She stops occasionally to ooh and ahh over fabrics and jewels.

Our ultimate goal, though? Donuts.

Alisha makes the best in the city and always sells out before the market closes. It used to be a tradition with our parents to come score the sugary treats on a Saturday morning, so when Kendall suggested the outing, I couldn't say no.

I'm trying hard not to regret that decision.

But I also need to talk to Natalia, preferably without Kendall within earshot.

I trail behind my sister, a silent—grumpy—sentry, exhausted by her enthusiasm, while the pit in my stomach grows heavier and more bitter with every casual contact she makes. I can't blame her, though. I'd gladly suffer twice over if it meant sparing my sister from this kind of darkness.

In the crowded square, someone bumps my shoulder, and the scarf around my face comes loose. I scramble to tuck it in again though Juniper's charm does its work, ensuring the scarf molds right back into place. I'm determined to keep every inch of my skin covered. This is about more than just my skin being a weapon.

Juniper didn't glamour my appearance like she did Kendall's.

I scan the faces of the people around me for anyone who might have recognized me. Or anyone who looks like a Crimson Rose. No one looks my way, though I can't shake a sense of being watched.

I tell myself I'm being paranoid.

Up ahead, Kendall continues shopping, oblivious to the tension I feel. She's talking to a warlock whose jewelry, even from a distance, is nearly as fake as his charm. I get close in time to hear him ask if she wants a reading on her future. I roll my eyes at his obvious pick-up line. Not to mention the fact that my sister doesn't need anyone else to do that for her.

Kendall, however, widens her eyes and leans in. "Can you do that?" she asks.

"Of course." He holds his hand out, and she places hers in it.

I wince.

He pauses dramatically then says, "I see you and your mother having a fight over a handsome male." He winks at her.

Ugh. What a crock.

I clear my throat.

"We should keep moving," I say pointedly. "If we want to catch Alisha."

"I'm not finished," the warlock says.

Kendall flashes him a tight smile. "Maybe another time," she tells him as she withdraws her hand.

"I look forward to it," he says.

I wait until she moves away and then follow her. She slows her pace, forcing me to fall into step beside her.

"You're ridiculous," she says.

"I'm trying to keep you safe."

"He was harmless."

"He was a fraud."

"I know." At my questioning look, she adds, "He had a dagger he claims can kill a dragon. I needed to know if he was trustworthy."

I give her a sideways glance.

"What?" she scoffs. "You think you're the only one good at intel in this family? You know what? Don't answer that. There's Alisha. Come on, I've been craving her lemon meringue."

I leave Kendall with Alisha and slip over to Spells. I'm so distracted by my own thoughts that I don't see the familiar female exiting until it's too late. My shoulder bumps hers, and I reel back, fear pulsing in my throat as I double-check that my skin remains covered.

"Are you all right?" I ask quickly.

Spencer's eyes narrow as she peers back at me. "Who are you?" she asks warily.

"Shit, right, it's Tori." I pull my scarf down to reveal my face.

"Oh."

"How are you?" I ask.

"Just another day in the Crossroads."

I've met Spencer a handful of times—all of them here at Spells. She doesn't talk much and is even more standoffish than I am, but the fact that Natalia seems to trust her led me to extend the olive branch.

"Did Natalia give you my number?" I ask. "I told her it was fine."

"Oh. Yeah. I just haven't needed...you know."

"It's fine. I just wanted to make sure you know you can reach out." I don't even know why I'm saying it. My own life is in chaos, and I might not even survive long enough to answer her texts. But something about her makes me want to be friends. Maybe it's because I see so much of myself in her—in the way she holds herself apart from others.

"I appreciate it." Her gaze darts past me with impatience.

"Well, I better get going," I say. "See you later."

She looks relieved at parting ways. "Bye."

I don't let myself take it personally as I watch her walk off and then hurry into Spells. Natalia is waiting behind the counter. She doesn't look surprised at the way I'm dressed.

"You haven't answered my texts," I say, the words veering toward accusation.

If she's offended by it, she doesn't show it. "Did you speak with Kendall about your request?"

"Kendall understands why I need her to go," I say, confused. "Besides, I want her to keep up her training."

"Your sister's gifts are developing at a rate beyond my own skills to teach her."

"What does that mean?"

"It means I've done all I can for her."

I blink, stunned at the brush-off, especially at a time like this.

"Natalia, I am asking this as a friend. Not as her boss. I need to make sure she's safe while I... take care of some things."

"You should speak with your sister about that." She turns away, busying herself with organizing various jars behind the counter.

"I-I don't understand. We've known each other for years. You... you knew my parents."

She looks up, empathy lining her expression. "I am not turning my back on that friendship, Tori. But I trust Kendall. Talk to her. Trust her like I do."

I stare at the witch, anger churning inside me. Out of the handful of folks I call a friend in this city, Natalia is the last person I would have expected to turn her back on us. The reality leaves me sick. Reeling, I turn and walk out of the shop, all my best plans gone.

Twenty minutes later, I've managed to wrangle Kendall away from Alisha, and we're headed home. The day is chilly, but we opted to walk the three miles anyway since parking would have been a nightmare in this part of town.

"Well?" Kendall prompts when our donuts are eaten.

She carries a small bag for Juniper, but otherwise, we've already destroyed the evidence.

"Well what?" I ask moodily.

"You went out into public and didn't kill anyone," she says brightly. "I told you it was going to be okay."

I snort. "I wouldn't call today's outing 'okay.'"

"What happened?"

"Nothing. Natalia—Forget it."

"Tor, talk to me."

I open my mouth to answer when the hairs on my neck stand up. I whirl, scanning the streets, but I find no one out of place. The mate bond pulses inside me just like it did the night the death dragon showed up at my workshop.

He's close.

I can feel it. But I can't spot him.

"What's wrong?" Kendall asks, following my gaze.

"Nothing," I say, turning back. She looks unconvinced. "I'm just being paranoid," I add.

She doesn't know about his visit the other night. I tell myself it's because I don't want to worry her, but the truth is I'm not ready to explain why I didn't kill him.

"Come on," I tell her. "We need to get Juniper's donuts home, or I might eat them myself."

Kendall snorts. "I'm not risking her wrath, so that's all you."

I glance over at her and do a double-take.

"What is it?" she asks.

"Your glamour," I say quietly. "It wore off."

"Relax." She doesn't look nearly as worried as I feel. "We're almost home."

We're passing the last of the retail shops before our neighborhood when Kendall waves to someone and calls out, yanking me from my thoughts. I look over in time to see a guy her age crossing the street to meet us.

"Who is that?" I ask, instantly tense.

"Chase," she whispers. "The one who asked me out." She cuts me off with a look. "Be nice," she hisses as he reaches us.

"Hey," he says.

"Hey." She beams up at him.

I roll my eyes, which isn't technically *not* being nice since he's not paying attention to me or even knows I exist, considering the consuming look he's giving my sister.

"What are you up to?" he asks.

"Oh, Tori and I were just at the farmers market, stalking the donut vendor I told you about."

"Sounds like fun." Even at the mention of my name, he still doesn't look away from her. And despite my efforts to continue my cynicism, I can't help the stab of jealousy I feel at watching someone look at my sister the way Chase does. Like she's the only thing in the world that matters.

Considering my touch is death, I doubt that kind of devotion is in my future. And it certainly hasn't been in my past. Even my mate looks at me like he wants to eat me alive. There's no worship in his dark gaze, only threats.

"Are you free tonight?" Chase asks, and the question jolts me back to the present moment.

Kendall pauses as if actually considering it.

I'm nearly ready to interject when my senses prickle with awareness again. My gaze shoots toward the shadows, scanning the streets for some sense of danger. But the few pedestrians nearby don't pay us any attention as they come and go. Still, I can't shake the feeling that we're being watched.

Unlike before, the mate bond is quiet.

"Tor," Kendall prompts when I continue scanning behind me.

"Hmm?"

"Chase asked if I'm free tonight."

There.

Out of the corner of my eye, I spot a figure watching us from beneath a heavy cloak. I blink, and they vanish like smoke. Dread curls in my gut, and I fight the urge to toss Kendall over my shoulder and flee. Instead, I turn back to Chase and keep my voice as even as possible.

"She's not," I tell him, earning an immediate glare from Kendall and a sad blink from Chase.

"Oh." He doesn't bother to hide his disappointment, which would've been adorable under other circumstances. Now, it only prolongs our exposure.

The figure is out there, watching us. I can feel it.

"Tor," Kendall begins in a low voice.

"We have to get home." I loop my gloved hand through her arm and use it to drag her away. "Now," I add, letting my urgency leak in.

Kendall looks at me sharply, concern marring her features. She looks back at Chase. "Sorry, I'll call you."

He says something that I don't even hear. Blood pounds in my ears as I hurry us home.

Up ahead, the street is clear, but clouds move over the sun, adding a sense of foreboding.

"Tor, what's wrong?" Kendall asks as we speedwalk toward our little cottage house.

"Nothing."

"It's not nothing. You're scaring me."

"We have a tail," I say as calmly as possible.

"Where?" She cranes her neck, but I yank on her arm.

"Don't look," I whisper.

"Is it a client or a mark?" she asks, surprising me with how focused she is suddenly. How calm.

"I don't know. I didn't get a good enough look."

Lie.

It's him.

My mate.

"Okay, we're almost there," she says, matching my speed easily now.

"I need you to go inside and lock the doors."

She shoots me a look I recognize well. "No way, I'm not leaving you to deal with—"

"I can't concentrate unless I know you're safe," I tell her.

"I can help you. My magic—"

"Kendall, please." We reach the front steps. I stop to face her, letting her see my fear. I hate to make her worry, but I need to convey how serious this is.

In the backyard, a branch snaps.

Kendall jolts.

I tense.

Our eyes meet.

"Go inside," I tell her.

"But—"

"Go."

She finally disappears through the front door. I start for the backyard, drawing a blade from my boot as I go. A moment later, there's an ear-splitting scream from inside the house.

Kendall.

Fear grips me. I race up the steps and shove my way through the door in time to see two vampires dressed in black, cornering Kendall against the wall. One of them has a knife pressed against her throat.

"Get away from her!" My heart squeezes, and I launch myself at the one with the weapon.

The unarmed vampire intercepts me. A crimson rose tattoo peeks out from beneath the collar of his shirt, confirming my fears. I raise my blade, but he knocks it out of my hand in a move so fast I feel the sting in my wrist before I even see him move.

He uses his size to shove us both back—away from Kendall and the other man. My skin is the only weapon I have left, and I don't hesitate to use it. Wrapping my hands around the vamp's throat, I squeeze and wait for my skin to do the rest—only to realize I never took my gloves off.

The vampire snarls at me. My gaze darts up to his face where a pair of angry red eyes stare back at me.

"Uncover her face," the other vamp says.

My attacker uses his size to shove me back, easily breaking my hold on his neck. I stumble, and he lunges, snagging the edge of my scarf. It unravels and falls to the floor, revealing my face.

My attacker's eyes narrow. "It's her."

"Finish it," the other one says. He still has Kendall

pinned. She watches the scene with wide eyes and shallow breaths.

"With pleasure."

My attacker closes the distance between us and plants his fist in my stomach. Pain explodes through me. I fall hard, the hit a shock to my senses. The air is sucked from my lungs, and I wheeze, struggling for air until black dots dance in front of my eyes. When my vision clears, the vamp looms above me, eyes blazing as he waves my own blade in front of my face.

"You don't have to do this," I say, willing to beg if it saves Kendall.

"True. Our orders were to bring you in dead *or* alive." His eyes flash.

"I ... had a deal. I could bring you the one responsible..."

"Now you're dealing with me. You killed my cousin, bitch. I'm going to enjoy this."

"Wait. My sister has nothing to do with this. Let her go, and I won't fight you."

His eyes gleam with twisted malice. "Who said I wanted you to stop fighting?"

A loud crash fills the house as the front door splinters into a hundred pieces. My attacker snarls and pushes to his feet as a dark figure looms in the open doorway.

"Who the fuck are you?" my attacker demands.

There's no answer, and my blurred vision makes it impossible to see his face, but I sense his presence in every fiber of my being.

The death dragon.

"You have touched what doesn't belong to you," my mate snarls. "And now you will pay."

He steps forward, grabbing my attacker's shoulder with one hand and his wrist with the other. The knife clatters to the ground, and the vamp cries out in pain.

Legion releases his grip on the vampire and, for a second, I think he's going to show mercy, but then his fist slams against the vamp's chest. Not against. *Through it*. The sound of bones snapping is quickly overshadowed by the asshole's wretched screams. I watch as Legion yanks the heart free, clutching it in a tight, bloody fist. The vamp's cries cut off, and the life leaves his crimson eyes. Legion steps back just as the vamp's body crumples to the floor in a pool of blood. There's a beat of silence, and then the heart lands on the floor with a juicy thud.

My mate turns to look at the second attacker, who still has his knife pressed to Kendall's throat.

"Back the fuck up or I'll—"

At the far end of the house, the back door opens. "Girls—"

Juniper's voice is pitched high with urgency and fear.

"Run," I scream at her.

The back door slams shut again.

The vamp holding Kendall at knife-point snarls, and I can see in his eyes that he's done waiting. The blade presses into her throat, drawing the first sign of blood.

I scramble to my feet, but my mate is faster. Moving so quickly I can barely track it, he closes the distance and slams the second attacker backward away from Kendall. The moment she's free, she launches herself toward me.

I scramble back. "My scarf," I say, reminding her. "Don't come closer."

She grabs my scarf, tossing it to me. By the time I catch it, the second vamp is dead just like the first one, his heart fully removed from his body.

"Juniper," I tell Kendall, breathless. "Come on."

We head through the back door where my mate has already disappeared.

In the backyard, I count three more Crimson Roses. Two are already dead with their chests exposed and hearts lying in the bloodied grass nearby. The third is about to meet the same fate as Legion stalks him.

On the other side of the yard, a figure bends over something half-buried in a pile of leaves. It looks like a body.

"Stay close to me," I tell Kendall.

For once, she doesn't argue.

The figure stands, its red eyes narrowed on me as we get closer. It raises a knife, aiming it for my chest. I stop, frozen in the line of fire as I realize any attempt I make at getting away will only put Kendall more at risk.

"Down," I hiss at her at the same time I start to duck.

But the Crimson Rose thug is struck by a ball of fire. He screams, and the knife falls as the asshole stumbles away, body burning. I watch as Legion tracks him with murderous calm.

When he's out of the way, I hurry toward the pile of leaves, assuming it's another gang member lying in wait. But when I get close, I stop and cover my mouth with my hand. Behind me, Kendall presses closer.

"What is it?" she asks.

"Nothing." I swallow hard. "Go back inside."

"Is it another one?" she asks, ignoring my order.

Footsteps crunch over leaves, and I whirl, ready to fight again, but it's him. My mate. Behind him, the rest of the gang is dead. Relieved of their hearts. Too late.

"Tori," Kendall breathes, eyeing him.

"He won't hurt you," I tell her, tearing my gaze from his. Despite the way he seems to fill the empty space between us, I know in my heart that much is true. If he were here to hurt me, he would have done it.

Instead, he saved us.

I have no idea why, but none of that matters, considering what I've just lost.

Juniper.

My breath catches.

A sob builds in my throat.

I look down at the body in the leaves and find myself darkly jealous of the dead men. At least, without a heart, I wouldn't feel mine breaking into a thousand pieces.

"Oh gods," Kendall says, stepping around me so that she finally gets a good look at the body in the leaves. "Is that—?"

She covers her mouth, her eyes filling with tears.

I say the words that make it real, mostly so she won't have to. "It's Juniper."

LEGION

Fury and fire burn in my veins. Their deaths were too fast. The beast inside me isn't ready to rest. Not yet. Not when our mate was harmed by their hands. But it's done now, and I find myself drawn to her side if only to reassure myself she is safe. My dragon craves her gratitude. He wants her to need him. But the moment I see the older female dead among the leaves, I realize I don't deserve gratitude at all.

Torissa turns to me, grief and pain swimming in her eyes, and I see her devastation. Whoever this woman was to her, the loss is a blow I can't block for her. I didn't protect her at all. I have only allowed her to be hurt in a different way.

"We have to help her." The younger female crouches over the dead woman.

Torissa looks down at her, sorrow in her eyes. "She's gone, Kendall."

"No. She can't be." The younger one, Kendall, reaches

for the dead woman, but the leaves tremble, and she yanks her hand away.

I tense, sensing for the threat, but Torissa says, "It's all right."

"Tor." Kendall stands and backs away. "What's happening?"

"She is returning to the Earth," Torissa says quietly. "It's part of the process of dying for her kind."

Kendall looks at her, eyes wide and already red-rimmed. "The trees are coming for her, aren't they? Like she always said they would at the...at the end. Like they did for Mom."

Torissa nods, and the branches above our heads begin to tremble, shaking and creaking as they bend. Slowly, the leaves coating the woman's body cover it completely, shifting and spreading until they've formed a blanket. The tree sways, gathering momentum. Around us, all the trees nearby do the same.

The wind whistles around us.

I step closer to my mate, my dragon still on edge from the fight. We're exposed out here. There could be more of them coming. But I don't rush this. I know it won't work to try.

Around the woman's body, the leaves rustle, and the earth beneath gives way. A moment later, the woman's body is gone—swallowed by the ground and ushered into her afterlife by the trees.

In the silence, Kendall sniffles as tears track down her face. My mate, however, is dry-eyed and stone-faced. Her shoulders are rigid, and I can sense the grief she's holding in.

My dragon strains to do something—anything—to help her.

"What was her name?" I ask.

"Juniper." Her expression is slack with shock.

"She was important to you," I say quietly.

"She was like a mother." Her voice is laced with pain.

"I should have been faster," I say.

At my words, the younger one, Kendall, turns to me. "You're him, aren't you? Her mate."

I cast a glance at Torissa, but she yields nothing.

"I am Legion Razginath."

"I'm Tori's sister, Kendall Sage." She gives me a once-over that's more shrewd than I might have expected, considering her fresh grief and her young age.

"Tori," I say, testing out the nickname.

She shudders but refuses to meet my gaze. I tuck the reaction away for later.

"You saved us," Kendall adds.

"Not all of you," I say, glancing at the place where Juniper's body disappeared. "I should have been here faster."

"It's not your fault," Kendall says.

"Are we sure about that?" Tori puts in.

Some of her color has returned—and a look of accusation along with it.

Kendall gives her sister a withering look. "He saved us, Tor. Do you really think he's the enemy?"

"I think we can't know anything for sure right now."

"Who were these men?" I cut in.

"Crimson Roses," Kendall says. "They blame Tori for killing one of their own."

"Is this all of them?" I ask.

Tori snorts. "Not even close."

"We can't stay here," I say, turning to scan the yard. "There will be more of them."

"Where are we supposed to go?" Kendall asks.

Tori closes her eyes. When she opens them again, I can see her struggle to bury the worry away from her sister's awareness. "Maybe Uziah will—"

"No fucking way," Kendall cuts in.

"Who's Uziah?" I demand, jealousy already a hot streak in my veins.

"Not someone we can trust," Kendall says with a pointed look at Tori.

"He's the only resource we have," Tori says.

"Then we have nothing," Kendall snaps.

"Have you seen something?" Tori asks worriedly.

Kendall doesn't answer.

I want to ask what she's talking about, but I know better than to get in the middle of a sibling argument.

"You'll stay with me," I say into the silence.

Tori turns to me, eyes widening. "Absolutely not."

"Don't you live in Tartarus?" Kendall asks.

"Yes."

"Hell, you mean," Tori says to her sister. And then to me, "Not a fucking chance."

"Actually," Kendall says, "It's not a bad idea."

"You can't be serious." Tori looks incredulous. "You do know he's called the death dragon, right? He's killed more people than all of the Crimson Roses put together. And Tartarus is full of monsters just like him."

"Which makes it the perfect place to hide," she says.

"It's dangerous there," Tori argues.

Kendall rolls her eyes. "And it's so safe here."

Tori shoots me a withering look as if to say I should side with her. Instead, I flash her a thin smile. "It's the one place these Crimson Roses can't go."

Tori looks like she wants to strangle me.

Kendall winks at me as if we're co-conspirators.

Despite everything, my lips twitch. The sisters are interesting. No, watching Tori's reactions to Kendall is interesting. Apparently, I'm not the only one she likes to argue with.

"Listen," Kendall says, "if you have a better idea, I'm all ears. If not…" She shrugs.

"I can't trade one killer for another. How do we know he won't kill us the moment we get there?"

Kendall sighs. "Fine. We'll do this officially." She steps forward and holds her hand out for me.

"What is this?" I ask.

"I'd like to read you if that's okay."

"Read me?"

Tori mutters something, which Kendall ignores.

"I have sight," Kendall explains. "Mostly about death. So, if you're planning to kill us, I'll see it."

I hesitate. "And is your gift only focused on the future? Or do you also see the past?"

"Future," she says. "Why?"

"No reason." I glance at Tori, who looks impatient, and then place my hand in Kendall's.

A surge of jealousy slams into me, and I look over to find my mate staring at my hand resting on her sister's. Enjoying her reaction way too much, I wait until she glances up at me again and smirk. Her eyes narrow, and she holds my gaze almost defiantly until Kendall releases me and steps back.

"He's not a threat," Kendall tells her sister.

"You can't know that. It's too broad of a—"

"He *is* responsible for your curse, though," Kendall adds.

"What?" I demand at the same time Torissa says, "I fucking knew it."

"Sorry," Kendall shrugs at me. "But you are. Which means you should really help her break it, you know. It's the right thing to do."

I shake my head.

Releasing myself from Caius in order to protect Tori was supposed to be temporary. A quick good deed—and a chance to get up close with the mate bond to decipher how in the hell this is even possible—and then we'd part ways forever. But now that I've met her, I can't imagine walking away. Something I know she'd gladly do. If helping her break this curse keeps her close, I'll take it.

"I agree," I say, "But in order to do that, I have to take you to Tartarus. It's the only magic that could have done this, which means we'll need—"

"No way," Tori says. "Tartarus is a horrible place. I'm not—"

Behind Tori, a black-clad figure emerges from the woods. He sprints toward us, an axe gripped in his raised hand. He rears back, ready to throw it right at her head. With a snarl, I step in front of her and catch the axe mid-air. Then I hurl it back at him.

It lands, splitting his forehead in two.

Another figure appears behind him, then another, then another.

My beast strains to be let free, to raze this place to the ground with every threat incinerated to ash. But a glance behind me reveals four more vampires charging at us from the opposite direction.

There's no time to isolate the enemy from the ones I want to save.

The need to protect my mate is consuming. It outweighs even my instinct to stay and fight.

"Put your scarf on," I tell my mate.

"What?"

"Do it," I snarl.

Without waiting for an answer, I shift, shredding my clothes and gritting my teeth against the pressure that compresses in on me from the inside out. Black scales replace my flesh, my wings unfurling so quickly that one of the attackers is knocked off his feet, his flesh instantly shredding thanks to the razor-sharp scales that slice through him.

Kendall screams as one of them tries to grab her. Tori races over to put herself between her sister and the threat. I slam my wings downward and lift myself airborne, scorching hellfire building in my throat and begging to be freed.

Wind whipping thanks to my wings, I angle myself toward Tori and Kendall, capturing them in my clawed hands. Then I swoop upward, breathing hellfire as I go. Below me, bright flames cascade to the ground like water, burning everything they touch to ash.

Legion Razginath's dragon is a thing of nightmares. He is bigger than any creature I've ever seen with black, spiky scales that look sharp enough to slice flesh to the bone. Not that he needs those particular weapons, considering the lava-like flames he conjures on a simple exhale. My shock at being snatched into his claws and lifted off my feet is surpassed by the sight of the bodies in our yard burning to ash.

The wind burns my cheeks, my tears turning to ice against my skin as Kendall and I are lifted away from the charred vampires still screaming even as they burn alive—and from the remains of the only life I ever knew.

I assume Legion intends to find a suitable hiding spot outside the city. To my horror, he heads straight for the city center. I realize with agonizing clarity where he's headed just as the arch comes into view.

He dives sharply, ripping a scream from my throat.

Still, he doesn't stop. If anything, he speeds faster.

The fact that he manages to glide along so close to

the ground in order to fly through the portal still in dragon form is kind of impressive—if it wasn't also terrifying. There aren't many things that truly scare me, but watching the pavement race by mere inches below my face leaves me dizzy and trembling. The portal guards are nothing more than a blur as we zoom past them, one of them waving a hand in greeting to the dragon.

The moment we're on the other side, he lurches to a stop and sets Kendall and me on our feet. The whole thing happens so fast, I lose my balance and fall to my knees, bracing my palms on the floor. Kendall does the same.

At the sound of voices, I look up to see a guard approaching. Legion snorts at him which is apparently all the communication necessary because the guard waves us onward. Legion nudges Kendall and me both to our feet.

I manage to stand and, pulling Kendall along with me, we make our way out of a large atrium and through a set of doors that Legion's dragon only barely fits through.

Once we're outside, Legion's wings beat furiously, lifting him off the ground. Just like before, he grabs Kendall and me in his powerful claws and then angles upward.

Our entrance into hell lasts all of thirty seconds before we're once again airborne. As the ground drops away, we soar high into Tartarus' night sky so quickly that I'm positive I've left my stomach behind.

Doing my best not to throw up, I study the landscape below me, fully expecting a hellscape complete with eternal fire and tortured souls. Instead, a city is sprawled around a castle on a hill, their twinkling lights almost peaceful and serene. Beyond the city limits, a thick forest spreads far and wide with a narrow ribbon of a road that cuts through it.

As far as I can see, there's nothing burning and no souls screaming out from eternal torture. In fact, it's peaceful. And so much more beautiful than I imagined it would be.

Soon, the forest below gives way to a mountain—the first of several in a long, unending ridgeline. At the top of the first peak, a gothic castle looms out of the rock, looking as if it were carved into the mountain itself. Halfway down the cliffside, a large waterfall sprays mist into the air where the rushing water freefalls before disappearing into a layer of clouds.

It looks like something right out of a dark fairy tale.

Legion aims straight for a grassy courtyard nestled between the castle entrance and a high stone wall that surrounds the estate. Between the view and the adrenaline, my energy is zapped. By the time he finally sets us down—much more gently this time thankfully—my knees are so weak I can barely stand. Next to me, Kendall is sucking in deep breaths.

"You okay?" I ask Kendall.

"Yeah. You?"

"I might vomit," I admit, and she laughs then winces, clutching her own stomach.

"Ugh. Do not make me laugh right now," she groans.

Drawing in deep breaths, I look around to get my bearings. Behind me, a stone wall encircles the courtyard where we stand, broken up by a wrought-iron gate fashioned in the shape of a dragon with wings spread wide. The large lock holding it closed is both a sign of protection and a prison sentence, so I turn away from it and stare up at the castle before me.

It's at least four stories high with slate gray stone walls and a black roof complete with spires, turrets, and a widows' walk. From this angle, I can't see the sheer drop I glimpsed from above, but I know it's there, making this the only way in or out.

"Wow," Kendall breathes, staring up at it. "This is where he lives?"

I cock my head, assessing. "A bit cliché if you ask me. Like he's overcompensating for something."

She shoots me a look.

I smirk.

When I look back at the castle, my gaze is drawn to the backdrop of the night sky. In the darkness, more stars than I've ever seen on Earth wink back at me. Two moons hang heavy almost directly above us. The sight of them feels like a weird sort of double-vision mind trick that sends another wave of dizziness through me.

Before I can point it out, Kendall gasps.

I turn to see what's drawn her shock and find Legion standing across the courtyard where he's shifted back into his human form. A very naked, very impressive human form. I don't want to stare, but there's literally no other option. A broad chest and rippled abs give way to a perfectly shaped V where his hips point the way to—

"Tori," Kendall hisses, turning away and yanking me with her.

My cheeks heat as the sight of his large cock

becomes permanently stamped in my brain. Even more awkward, my sister has the same image stamped in hers.

Out of the corner of my eye, I see Legion turn and begin walking away.

"Hey," I call as he nears the door of the massive estate. But he ignores me and disappears inside, leaving us alone.

"Where did he go?" Kendall asks.

I don't answer, my senses on high alert as I scan for a way out. We could scale the wall, but I'm not sure if Kendall could keep up. She hasn't trained physically like I have. And besides, it's not like I have a way to get us off this literal mountain before Legion notices we're gone and snatches us into the skies.

"Come on," I say, marching toward the same door Legion used. If we can't run away, I'll have to settle for confronting my captor instead.

The door opens easily when I shove it. Cool, gray stone greets me though the air is warm enough from some heat source I can't see in the large, echoing entryway.

I've only made it a couple of steps inside when a teenage girl emerges from the hall on the left. Her brown hair hangs in a messy braid down her back, and her cheeks are flushed red like she rushed. There's an innocence in her features, but considering the nightmare we're in, I don't trust it.

"Hello," she says.

Tucking Kendall behind me, I pull myself as tall as I can. "Who are you?"

"Chaya." She glances between us. "You must be Tori and Kendall."

"How do you know our names?" I demand.

"Mister Legion informed me."

"He told you he'd be bringing us here?"

"He mentioned your names as he walked by a moment ago," she says uncertainly. "Said you were going to be staying for a while."

A while, huh?

"Can you tell me where I can find *Mister* Legion?" I ask.

"He'll return momentarily. Would you like something to eat or drink while you wait?"

"No."

"Tori." Kendall pokes me and then turns to Chaya. "Some water would be great."

"Of course." She hurries off through a doorway, and I nod at Kendall.

"Good idea. You got rid of her. Now we can—"

"Making yourselves comfortable?" Legion's voice has me whirling, eyes narrowed. He's clothed this time, and I'm not sure whether to be disappointed or grateful. At least, my eyes know where to look.

Then again, they sure knew where to look last time too.

"You can't keep us here," I say, taking a step toward him.

The foyer is massive, and my footsteps echo, but I refuse to be intimidated by his wealth or position. Whoever he is in this world doesn't negate what he did to me in mine.

"You're free to leave anytime," he says, and while his words say one thing, his gaze says another.

"And what about you?" I press.

"What about me?"

"Will you just follow us wherever we go next?"

"Not if you don't want me to. In fact, there are some houses available for rent near the king's residence that you might find—"

"We are not staying in Tartarus," I snap.

He frowns, and I almost lose myself in the small lines that appear between his brows. What would it be like to smooth them with my fingers?

No. He's the enemy, I remind myself.

I fold my arms across my chest to keep from reaching for him.

"It would be unsafe to return to the Earth realm for the time being," he says.

"Right." I snort. "Because Tartarus is such a *safe* place."

"Compared to what waits for you in your realm, I'd say it's your best option."

He's right, of course, which only serves to piss me off. Suddenly, taking my chances with the mountainside sounds preferable.

"I don't have to listen to this." I turn for the door. "Come on, Kendall. We're leaving."

"Um. No?"

I stop short. "What?"

"Tor, Legion is offering protection. We'd be stupid not to take it." Her voice is way too calm, given the circumstances, and I can feel my control slipping. "Besides, he promised to help you break this curse."

"We don't even know him," I hiss.

"He killed those men to save us," she says, brows lifting. "I'd say we know enough."

A headache builds behind my eyelids. "Kendall, you don't understand how the world works. Just because—"

"When are you going to stop treating me like a child!"

Her outburst echoes off the stone walls loud enough to shock me into silence, and I feel the guilt settle right between my shoulders.

"We just lost Juniper," she adds quietly, and I see the grief brimming in her watery eyes. Her unshed tears pierce me like a blade. Guilt pricks sharp between my shoulders, and I relent beneath the weight of it.

"You're right," I say quietly. "Survival is what matters now. We'll stay until we figure this out."

"Thank you," Kendall says softly.

I turn to Legion. "Happy?"

His gaze sweeps over me, leaving me tingly in the wake of his perusal. "Getting there."

I roll my eyes.

"Chaya," he calls.

The young woman who greeted us reappears, holding a glass of water. "Yes?"

"Will you show our guests to their rooms?"

"Of course." She offers the water to Kendall.

"Thank you," Kendall tells her.

Chaya flashes a tight smile then hurries by, leading the way down the hall. "This way."

I follow Kendall out, refusing to look at Legion as I pass. I can't. Not while I'm drowning in my own failure and guilt.

Chaya leads us down the hall, up a flight of stairs, and around a series of turns that make it impossible for me to remember the way back. I'm fairly certain that's her goal, though, when she stops in front of a door in the middle of a random passage.

She pushes open the door and steps back, gesturing to Kendall as she says, "This is your room."

Kendall walks in, and I start to follow, but Chaya stops me. "Yours is at the end."

"I prefer to stay with my sister," I say.

This time, it's Kendall who stops me. She blocks the door and pins me with a serious expression. "Tor, you should go with her."

"Kendall," I start.

"Listen, I'm not mad at you, okay? And I don't want to fight. I just need some time alone." Her eyes, though hard, fill with tears. "Juniper—"

She breaks off.

I nod. "I get it," I say quietly. "I'm sorry."

"It's not your fault. I just... Can we talk later?"

"Yeah, sure."

I step back, and she closes the door with a soft click.

The rejection stings even though I know exactly how she feels.

"This way," Chaya says.

I follow her to the end of the hall, aware that Legion has put me as far away from Kendall as possible.

Asshole.

I push open the door and head inside, thinking of a shower and maybe a stiff drink if I can find it.

"I'll give you some time to rest," Chaya says. "Dinner is at seven."

I turn back, ready to refuse, but she looks so damn friendly, and this isn't her fault. "Do you know how far we are from the portal?" I ask instead.

"The portal? To Earth?"

"Yes. Do you know how long it would take to get there?"

"Three hours if you walk. Obviously way faster if you're flying but..."

Hope sinks in my gut. "Great."

"Do you need anything else?" she asks.

"Do you have any alcohol in this place?"

"There's a bar in your room," she says uncertainly.

"Perfect. See you at seven." I flash her a smile and then shut the door.

More guilt pricks at me for being so short with a girl who has nothing to do with any of this, but I can't bring myself to find politeness in this moment.

As soon as the door shuts, sealing me in, my mind conjures the image of Juniper dead in the leaves in the backyard.

Her body was broken beyond repair.

Her life, lost, for us.

For fucking nothing.

A victim to thugs and monsters.

Because of me.

Tears blur my eyes. Forgetting the alcohol, I pull out my phone, intending to call Niamh, and find the screen cracked and dark. No amount of pressing the power button revives it. Loneliness slams into me then.

With my back against the door, I slide down until I'm sitting on the floor. My grief and pain squeeze my heart, and I pull my knees up, pressing my forehead to them as the tears begin to fall.

Losing my parents was the worst pain I'd ever felt. Until now. My parents' death was a horrible accident, but Juniper's is my fault. If not for me, she'd be here now. And I wouldn't be locked in this damned castle, a world apart from my home.

Sniffling, I lift my head and bang it lightly against the door. Through the blur of tears, I see a bedroom nicer than any I've been in before. The bed is huge with four posts, each with beautifully intricate designs carved into the wood. The mattress is made up with a ridiculous number of pillows and a plush comforter I could sink into.

On the left, glass doors overlook the night sky. On the right is a cozy sitting area set before a fireplace and, beyond that, a doorway that leads into what I glimpse to be a gleaming bathroom.

It's disgusting, being here, draped in luxury and comfort when Juniper is gone.

I have no idea how long I sit like this. Tears fall then dry then fall again.

I grieve for Juniper, for my parents, for Kendall—for me.

I cry until my shoulders and ribs ache from the effort and my insides are hollowed out, empty of everything, including a future that is anything less than bleak and lonely.

Maybe it's no less than I deserve. Not only did I fail to protect Kendall and Juniper from danger, but I've just sealed my fate as a target of the Crimson Roses forever. Even bringing them Legion won't work. After leaving so many of them dead today, the Crimson Roses will never accept someone else's death as a replacement for mine. Killing Legion will not earn me and Kendall our freedom. In fact, I'm not sure there's anything I can do to survive this threat.

Stay here and hide. I can practically hear Legion saying the words, and my muscles tense with frustration. This is what he wanted all along. To get me here to his world—to his home—and never let me go.

He's just won, and he thinks the prize is me. Fuck that. I intend to ruin his victory if it's the last thing I do.

LEGION

Kendall is pleasant company at dinner, but I cannot ignore Tori's absence. If not for her younger sister—and my strained sense of decorum—I would have stormed her room the moment she'd failed to appear. Her insult won't go unpunished. But Kendall's been through a lot today, and I can see the grief she's battling.

Despite her loss, she attempts conversation with me, and I do my best to offer answers. Her manners are, at least, better than her sister's.

"How long have you lived here?" she asks while Chaya serves the soup, quiet as a mouse.

"Four thousand years," I say.

She nearly spits out her drink but manages to keep it down. "Seriously?"

I nearly smile. "Is that shocking?"

"I mean, it's a long time."

"Are you trying to say I'm old?"

"Well, you're not young," she says, and I chuckle.

"Some of the residents of this realm are much older than I am."

"Is it normal for the people of your realm to live so long?"

"Tartarus molds its creatures in many ways," I tell her. "One of them being immortality."

"What about me and Tori? If we stay here long enough, will we become immortal too?"

"It's likely, yes." I hesitate, wondering if I should warn her further. "The magic here will change you, though. You should be aware of the choice you're making by staying."

She looks away, her expression flashing with worry I don't understand. When she looks back at me, I note there's a forced cheer. "Yeah, I'm aware."

"I'm sure word has traveled back in your realm," I say, thinking about the time the portal magic changed a boy into a Corgi.

"No, it's not that." She lowers her gaze to her plate. "I've seen it. Seen myself here in the future. I've seen all of us."

I almost miss her meaning. But then I remember her gift. The Sight.

Interesting.

"What have you seen exactly?"

"Possible outcomes. Probably futures."

"You make it sound like nothing is certain."

"Of course not. Free will changes the outcome constantly. I see possibilities." She glances around the room and adds, "This is one of them."

I get the distinct impression that, for everything she's

telling me, there's a lot more she's leaving unsaid. "Is it a safe future?" I ask. "For you and your sister."

"It's safer than if we'd stayed in the Crossroads."

I don't need sight to tell me that.

"And my part in your sister's curse?"

She shrugs. "I told you everything I know about it, sorry."

I'm not quite sure that's true, but I decide to save my questions.

We eat in silence.

My thoughts drift immediately to my mate again. I can feel her one level above us—hurting. She's been hurting all afternoon. I can do nothing to stop it. I remind myself I don't want to stop it, but it's a useless effort. Not mating her is one thing. But feeling her in pain is like a knife slowly twisting inside me.

At least, when she was on the other side of the portal, there was a distance to this awareness. Now, she's here, and I can't turn it off. My mood darkens as I try to imagine enduring this for the foreseeable future.

"You're friendlier when my sister isn't around."

Kendall's words startle me out of my brooding thoughts. "Is that a compliment or a challenge?"

She shrugs. "An observation."

Her openness prompts an observation of my own. "She doesn't trust me."

"She doesn't trust anyone."

"She trusts you."

She snorts. "Yeah, right."

Her expression clouds, so I clamp my mouth shut, unsure what I've said wrong. Finally, I can't take it anymore. Setting my fork aside, I push my chair back and stand.

Kendall looks up. "Are you leaving?"

She looks stricken, and I glance around for some consolation.

"I need to check on ... something. Chaya will stay until you're finished."

I don't wait for her answer before heading upstairs.

Outside of Tori's room, I force myself to pause and knock.

"Who is it?" I hear from inside.

Rather than give her the chance to refuse me, I push the door open and step inside.

Tori freezes mid-stride, her eyes widening. "What the hell are you doing in here?" she demands.

She's wearing a satin robe that ends at mid-thigh, revealing more of her body than I've ever seen.

"What the fuck are you wearing?" I demand.

"A robe," she says like I'm the one being ridiculous.

I stare at the hemline. At the skin it reveals. The soft, touchable, delicious-looking flesh I desperately want to touch—

"Hello?"

Her harsh voice snaps me out of my fantasies. I meet her gaze evenly despite every fiber of my being wanting to strip her out of the thing and bury myself inside her.

"If you didn't want me to wear it, you shouldn't have put it in here," she snaps.

"I didn't."

Chaya stocks the rooms. I've never asked to see the

pieces she chooses. I've never visited guests in this…state.

"Hey, asshole." She snaps her fingers, and I blink, realizing I'm staring again. "This is my room," she snarls. "You have no right to barge in like this."

"I think the words you are looking for are 'thank you.'"

"Excuse me?" Her eyes flash with temper. And though she's infuriating me, I can't help the thought of taking her like this. Furious, arguing. Watching her come beneath me with fire burning in her gaze.

"For saving you. And your sister," I add. If she wants a fight, I'll give it to her. "You're welcome."

"Actually," she says sweetly, "you're close, but I think the words I'm looking for are fuck you."

I take a step toward her, vibrating with barely controlled need and temper. "Your mouth is going to get you in trouble."

"What are you going to do, kick me out? Please do."

I stride toward her, but she backs away, leaning against the balcony doors with wide eyes.

"You can't touch me," she blurts. "I'll hurt you."

Very carefully, I reach around her and click the latch open so that the doors spill outward. She stumbles back a step before catching her balance. Straightening, she glares at me.

My lips curve in a smile that, judging from her flaring nostrils, only makes her angrier. I don't move, happy to take all her ire. She wants games, fine. But I will have her in the end.

My dragon takes what it wants. She will be no different.

"I've survived many dangerous creatures in my life, little flower. I have no doubt I can handle you."

"Fine." She stops moving away from me and holds out her hands in challenge. "Give it a try then. Let's see if you're right."

I remain where I am.

She smirks. "What's wrong? Worried about a little poison?"

I frown, realizing my desire to touch her is quickly becoming an obsession. And I'm not the only one if her scent is any indication. What would she do if she didn't have her lethal touch as an excuse to keep me away?

Maybe then I could fuck her and be done with it. Get her out of my system. I wouldn't have to claim her to enjoy her.

It's a problem I'd like to eliminate.

"I know a witch who deals in curses," I tell her roughly. "We'll meet with her tomorrow."

"Why would I do that?"

"To find a cure for this... ailment."

She studies me for a long moment and then turns away, crossing her arms. "No."

"No?" My brows lift at that. "You don't want to hug your sister again—?"

"Don't." She looks back at me, her expression vicious. "You do not get to use Kendall like that. Besides, if being cursed keeps me from being touched by you, then maybe I'm better off."

I smirk. "I thought you wanted me to go ahead and

give it a try. Didn't you invite me to try it the other night when I came to see you outside your workshop? Which is it, little assassin? Do you want your hands on me or not?"

"I wanted to touch you to kill you, you idiot."

"Yes, I remember your thirst for revenge. It was an amusing attempt."

"Don't flatter yourself. For revenge, I'd have to have feelings about you. This was a contract kill, nothing more."

My eyes narrow, and the lust winks out. "Excuse me?"

Danger coats my tone. She must sense the change in me because she tries to back away. Except, she's already pressed against the railing, fully at my mercy unless she wants to take her chances with gravity.

When she realizes she's trapped, she glares up at me defiantly. "The Crimson Roses offered me a deal. Your life for mine."

"And you accepted," I say in a low voice.

"Abso-fucking-lutely."

Her defiance is beautiful, though that's twice now she's tried to kill me.

If she were any other creature, I would strike her down here and now. Slash her throat with a claw. Drip hellfire onto her flesh. Shove her off the balcony and be done with it. End her before she can end me.

But I do none of those things.

Instead, I feel the fury in me become a pulsing want. No, a need. To consume her. Devour her. To make her beg for me. In a way that has nothing to do with saving her life.

I lean in, dangerously close to her lethal mouth, and watch as her pupils dilate with the same need thrumming in me. "Tomorrow, we'll see a witch about curing you, little assassin," I whisper. "And this time, don't bother trying to hide in your room."

TORI

The hallway is dark and empty when I slip out of my bedroom hours later. Around me, the castle is so quiet and still that I can hear my own breath. It's unsettling. I keep waiting for Legion to jump out at me and do something completely insane like kiss me.

I haven't stopped thinking about his promise to find me a witch. Or how badly I want him to—and not for any other reason than wanting *him*—which is stupid. He's the one who did this to me. Ugh. My desire for a cure is making me desperate.

I can't trust him, I remind myself. He might have brought us here for protection, but remaining here forever only makes it a prison.

No, the only person I can count on here is myself—and Kendall.

I knock on her door as lightly as I can, hoping Legion's not actually hovering nearby, watching me like some kind of stalker. Thankfully, Kendall's door opens before I have to knock again.

"Hey," she says, hair rumpled. "Can't sleep?"

"Not a wink. You?"

In answer, she simply pulls the door open and retreats.

I slip inside, clicking the door shut behind me.

Kendall's room is set up like my own, plush and cozy and stocked with clothes and essentials from the looks of her pajamas.

"Where'd you get the PJs?" I ask, thinking of the robe Legion had looked so scandalized over earlier. Clearly, he hadn't picked out the items in these rooms. But why bother stocking them at all?

How often did he bring females home?

Ugh.

Why did I care?

"Chaya provided them," Kendall says, climbing into bed and pulling the covers up around her.

Chaya. Right. The girl who'd greeted us downstairs when we arrived.

"I don't get it," I say, perching on the far edge of the mattress. "Is she related to him or something?"

"No. Legion found her living on the streets a few years ago. He brought her here to live with him. I don't think she has anyone else."

"Why would he do that?" I ask.

"I don't know. Maybe he's a decent person."

I snort. "Or maybe he's forcing her to be his slave."

"You always believe the worst in people."

"It's called survival." I stop myself before I can lecture

her on all the reasons I have to worry in a world like ours. Instead, I change the subject. "This place isn't what I expected."

"Me neither," she admits.

"It's kind of beautiful," I add reluctantly.

"Chaya says the village down the hill is really fun, especially on the weekends when they do a farmers market. We should go sometime."

"I doubt we'll be here long enough for all that."

Kendall doesn't answer.

For a long moment, we sit in silence in the dark room. My thoughts drift to Juniper. To the memory of her body being reclaimed by the Earth. The images of the trees being scorched right along with the Crimson Roses Legion rained fire upon. And my chest aches with grief.

"How are you?" I ask quietly.

"Better, I guess," Kendall says with a heavy sigh. "Not great. But better. You?"

I blow out a breath. "Same."

She nods, staring down at her hands.

Tears burn my eyes. I blink them back.

"Listen, I'm sorry," I begin, and her head comes up.

She studies me warily. "For what?"

"For bulldozing your ideas and not trusting you."

"You were scared," she says, sadness etched into her words. "So am I."

I nod. Tears threaten again, but I blink them back. "Did you... Have you seen anything new since we've been here?"

"Why?" Her sadness shifts into suspicion. "What did Legion say?"

"Legion? Nothing. Why?"

"No reason."

"Kendall."

She sighs. "This place is good for us," she says. "Good for you."

"That's cryptic."

She smirks. "Natalia says being cryptic is all part of the customer experience."

I snort.

Finally, this feels like familiar ground. "You want to elaborate, oh wise one?"

"You'll soon meet your destiny," she says, pitching her voice dramatically low and sinister.

"Wow." I roll my eyes. "That's incredible. Do you need to see my palm to read my lifeline?"

She sobers quickly. "Not anymore."

"Is this about what you told me the other day? About dying alone?"

"It's the opposite," she says. "That's what I'm trying to tell you."

"So, that future is gone?" I ask hopefully.

"As long as you're here, it is."

"Here," I repeat. "With Legion."

"He seems like a pretty decent guy, Tor."

I glare at her. "Are you actually seeing visions, or are you just trying to hook me up with the dragon stalker?"

She grins. "Why can't it be both?"

"You're ridiculous. You know what they say about him, right? He's a killer."

"Wow, that's the pot calling the kettle black, don't you think?"

I scowl. "I am not the same as him."

"You're not that different, either."

"He's an army general," I point out.

"He fights for his cause; you fight for yours."

I start to argue with her and then catch myself. "Okay, before this devolves into another fight, I came here to ask you for advice."

"Really? Wow, this place is changing you."

"Ignoring that," I grumble.

She laughs. "Okay, what advice?"

"Legion wants me to meet with a witch tomorrow."

"For?"

"To ask about what's happened to my skin. To see about a cure."

"That's great." Her eyes light up, but then my expression has her frowning again. "Or it's not great?" she tries, confused. "I thought you wanted answers."

"I do. I just... can we trust the people in this realm?"

"Tor, you're his fated mate. Do you really think he'd let you get hurt?"

"I mean, I was going to kill him, so... yeah."

"Right, but he doesn't know that." I wince, and her eyes widen. "You told him?"

"It slipped out," I say.

"Tor."

"He presses my buttons, and then I don't think."

"Okay, first of all, no one is killing anyone. And second, he's not going to let anything happen to you. He wants to help you."

"That's what I'm worried about."

The way she lifts her brows knowingly has me

wondering how I ever doubted her street smarts or wisdom. "You like him. And you're terrified of that, aren't you?"

"Stop being so fucking insightful," I mutter.

"Okay, how about this? I'll come with you to meet the witch. And if I get any visions that it's a setup, you can shake everyone's hand, and we'll call it a day. Deal?"

I sigh, knowing this is probably the best compromise I'll get now that Kendall's on Team Legion. "Deal."

A knock at my bedroom door pulls me from sleep. Groggy, thanks to hours of lying awake, listening to every creak the wind brings, I groan and roll over. The knock comes again, louder.

"Ten minutes," I call, cracking an eyelid to see the same nighttime sky as before.

It's not even morning.

Ugh.

I grab my pillow and cover my head, drowning out the world as I attempt to drift back to sleep.

I'm nearly there when the door flies open, startling me enough to yank me upright. Legion strides in, looking particularly delicious in dark cargo slacks and long sleeves shoved up to reveal inked forearms.

"Good morning, mate."

Mate.

It's the first time he's really called me that. Hearing it does weird things to my insides. Before I can interpret the sensation, he stands over me, his gaze eating up the length of my body covered only by a thin sheet. I'm very aware of the thin layer of separation and the way it does nothing to hide my hardening nipples.

"You sleep naked?" he asks, his voice rougher than usual.

"You seemed offended that I made use of the robe," I toss back at him. The truth is I often sleep naked, but I refuse to give him personal details. He has me physically; he doesn't get to have any other parts.

He doesn't reply, but his expression darkens, and the air between us crackles with tension. I refocus on all the reasons he should not be looking at me like that.

"What did I say about barging into my room?" I ask sharply.

His gaze flicks back to mine. "I don't remember."

Liar. "Don't do it," I say through clenched teeth.

"We have an appointment with a witch."

"I made no appointment." I lie back and pull the blanket over me to make a point about sleep—and to hide my body's response to him in my room.

Burying my face in the pillow, I wait, wondering how long it'll take him to give up and leave me alone. A second later, the blankets are ripped from my body.

I gasp, staring up at where he's moved to the foot of the bed, my covers gripped in his fists. He doesn't let his eyes roam my exposed body, but I know he sees. Somehow that makes it worse.

"Chaya is on her way up with a few extra clothing items," he says.

"You can't be serious. It's the middle of the night."

"It's always the middle of the night here," he reminds

me, and I groan. "You have ten minutes to shower and another ten before I'll come looking for you again."

Finally, he breaks eye contact and lets himself look at me. My breasts, my stomach, my thighs—which are squeezed shut to hide the fact that I'm already wet.

It's the most erotic thing I've ever felt, and he hasn't even touched me. Then again, if he touched me now, it would take about three seconds for me to come.

And three more seconds for him to die.

"And if I don't?" I ask.

His gaze snaps to mine. Even though my breathless voice gives me away, I make sure to put fire in my glare so he knows it won't be that easy.

"If you don't," he says slowly, "I'll be forced to punish you."

"You can't touch me," I say.

"Not with my hands," he agrees. "But there are many other things you'd enjoy me using to bring you the plea-sure of my punishment."

I don't dare ask what he means by that. The glint in his eye makes it clear I've reached the edge of this conversation. One more word and he'll show me exactly what he intends to do. And I'm absolutely sure, in this moment, I wouldn't stop him.

CHAPTER 14

LEGION

My control slips with every step I take away from her. Darkness creeps in at the edges of my awareness, eclipsing reason until my fists tremble with my shadow beast's power. Seeing her naked was a stupid mistake. All that bared, flawless skin just begging to be explored. But it's the double full moons I spotted through her balcony doors that are the real threat. Februlune—the moon fever. If I still had any doubt the mating call between us wasn't real, I'm now convinced it is.

The only creatures affected by the double moons are fated mates being pulled toward one another. To resist brings out the shadow beast like nothing else. I've seen the destruction—the madness—firsthand. I never thought it would be my turn.

My shadow beast snarls for me to turn around and give in to its desire. To bend her over and take my fill of her. If I weren't trained in torture, I'd undoubtedly give in. Resisting only invites more madness, but I do it. I won't take her against her wishes. She's clearly unaffected by the moon fever, or I would have seen it. Felt it.

So, I walk away from her, my blood singing for hers.

It doesn't matter that she agreed to trade my life for hers. I would have taken the same deal if I'd been in her shoes. But it's not just a warrior's understanding. It's more. Not even this need to possess her—thanks to the moon fever—is to blame. For some reason I can't make sense of, I've already forgiven her for an act I have killed countless men for in the past. Maybe it's the mate bond, but I'm beginning to care for this woman.

When I reach my bedroom, I slam the door and then loose the roar that's building in my throat. It shakes the stone walls—probably hard enough that the rest of the castle feels it, including her. At least, there was no hellfire this time.

I need to find a release before that happens again.

The fact that I'm even fighting off claiming a mate is still hard to believe. My bloodline shouldn't even be able to have a fated mate. My mother saw to that. I'm nothing more than a predator on a leash. A beast to be captured.

And no matter how badly I want that female in the bed down the hall, I refuse to let her imprison me.

Unfortunately, reminding myself of that fact does nothing to solve the painful erection I'm sporting. Nor does it alleviate the darkening desires that are slowly taking hold in my mind.

I spend the next twenty minutes in the shower, my hand wrapped around my hard length, imagining her mouth locked around me instead. She wants it—not like I do, thanks to these double fucking moons, but still. I can scent her desire for me, but she's not letting herself give in to it. And the longer she resists, the harder it's becoming for me to keep my hands off her.

She thinks her touch will kill me.

I believe her.

But I'm beginning to think not touching her will have the same effect.

The madness whispers to me that I'm not wrong.

My body shudders with the force of my orgasm, and I hope it's enough to help me survive her today.

Dressed and more or less composed, I don't bother looking for her downstairs. She's made it clear she won't be ordered anywhere. Instead, I turn toward her bedroom. And I'm so excited at the idea of punishing her for disobeying me, I almost miss the covered figure darting down the corridor that crosses this one.

I catch up with her just as she reaches the door to the terrace gardens.

"Going somewhere?"

She whirls, and I note she's at least wearing the clothes I asked Chaya to deliver, including the gloves and scarf. My gaze lingers on her breasts, and I remember how she looked in that bed earlier. The shock on her face when I ripped that blanket off was priceless, but the sight of her bared body eclipsed everything else. I'm already hard again just thinking about it despite my shower session.

The frenzy stirs in my blood, and I shove it down, using every bit of torture technique I possess to remain in control.

"How did you get these?" she demands.

"What are you referring to?"

"My clothes," she says impatiently. "They're mine. How did you get them here?"

"I went and got them last night."

Her eyes widen. "You were in my house?"

"It was easier than trying to shop when I didn't know your size," I say. "Although, now that I have it, I'm sending Chaya to get you a few more items today."

She glares. "You had no right to go through my things."

"Would you prefer I let you keep wearing the same blood-stained clothes day after day? Or the ill-fitting borrowed garments of my past guests?"

I think of the robe. Actually, I thought of the robe throughout the night. I even checked her dresser at home for anything similar because I want nothing more than to strip her of any other clothing so she's forced to wear only thin satin garments with short hemlines. But it's not exactly practical for transport.

She doesn't answer.

I keep my smile to myself, feeling like I've won a round.

"We should get going," I say. "The witch doesn't take kindly to tardiness."

But she doesn't move. "If it's always dark here, how can you possibly know that it's morning?"

"We do keep time here," I say, my brow rising.

Her eyes narrow, and she changes the subject. "Why are you following me?"

"We have plans."

"*You* have a plan. I didn't agree to it."

"You are that afraid of touching me?"

"I'm not afraid of you at all."

"Prove it then. Come with me to see the witch."

She glares at me, and I know my challenge won't go unanswered. "Fine. But the moment my curse is gone, I'm leaving Tartarus. Without you."

"You can leave when the Crimson Roses are no longer after you."

Her brows lift. "Even if my curse isn't gone?"

"Of course. I only want you to be safe."

It's a lie. I want so much more than that, but now's not the time to negotiate those terms.

She bites her lip, and I find myself completely fucking mesmerized by the sight of her mouth. "How do I know you're not trying to lure me away to kill me?"

My brow lifts. "I thought you were the one with that agenda."

She scowls.

"Besides, I should think your poisoned skin is enough of a defense against anything I might try."

The list of what I might try is much more extensive than she knows.

"You breathe fire," she points out. "My skin won't stop that."

"I guess that means you'll have to trust me."

"Well, I don't. Speaking of which, where's Kendall? She promised to come with me and—"

"She won't be joining us."

"Excuse me?"

"This witch does nothing without payment. I've arranged for you and only you. If you bring Kendall into this, I can't guarantee the witch won't demand something of her in return."

Not to mention how fucking dangerous Tartarus is today. The moon fever isn't the first impression I want to give her of this place, either. If I'd known it would affect me, I would have never bargained with the witch for today's appointment.

Tori bites her lip.

I track the movement, completely distracted by it until she sighs and says, "Deal."

I gesture to the door at her back, pretending I'm not fighting the urge to press her against the stone wall and fuck her until she comes or I'm dead or both. "After you."

She pushes through the door into the moonlit morning. I follow her out then fall into step beside her, heading straight for the back terrace where a large open courtyard of pavers doubles as my launch pad.

She casts me a sideways glance. "Don't smile like that."

I start to deny it before realizing I am, in fact, smiling—sort of. It's more of a smirk as my thoughts remain on the sight of her mouth and how I'd imagined it in the shower locked around my hard cock.

I clear my throat, interested in where her thoughts have gone—or in anything that might distract me from my tenuous control. "Why not?"

"You have an untrustworthy smile."

I throw my head back and laugh. "You are so much more interesting than I expected."

She frowns. "What did you expect?"

"A ruthless killer."

"I *am* a killer."

"No," I say quietly, my thoughts taking a turn into darker territory. "You're not. Not like I am."

"But I *have* killed people."

We reach the courtyard where the wind whips more sharply. I turn to face her, noting the stubborn set of her expression. It's already become familiar to me, and I find myself wanting to reach out and trace my thumb over the way her mouth has pinched tight in determination.

"Did your parents love each other?" I ask.

"Excuse me?"

"Your parents. Did they love each other and use that love to create life?"

"I guess. What does that have to do with—"

"I was birthed by a demon female who disguised herself as the lover of another creature and stole his seed. Hellfire and darkness are in my veins. My soul is tied to the underworld and my heart..." I hesitate, unwilling to give away my secret no matter how pure her intentions seem.

She softens, and there's a flash of pity in her blue eyes that has me clenching my fists. Pity is for the weak.

"Your heart?" she asks softly.

"It is dark and empty," I snap. "I have wiped out entire armies, ended entire civilizations, with one breath of hellfire, and lost no sleep over it. Can you say the same?"

She frowns, her expression hardening again. "No. That's horrendous."

I don't miss the judgment in her tone, and it hits me square in the chest, painfully sharp. Regret churns in my gut for having shared any of my past with someone like her.

"You have nothing to fear from me touching you," I tell her, angry though I can't name why. Tempers are always shorter on the dual moons. "When the curse is lifted, I will return you to your world, and we will resume our separate lives."

She nods. "Fine."

I glance out at the open sky that rises to meet the edge of the courtyard. My thoughts and emotions churn, building toward a storm I can't seem to calm. Not while I'm standing beside her.

Whatever control I'd had earlier is strained to a thread now. The need to shift is overwhelming. Stupid fucking moons.

"I've changed my mind," I say, not bothering to look over. "I'll get the witch and bring her here."

"What? Why? I thought—"

I don't bother to explain. Even if I did, it wouldn't make sense. She's gotten to me in a way I don't understand. "Stay here. I'll return at the end of the day."

"The end of the day? Are you serious?"

I stride toward the stone wall where the cliff's edge offers a fast getaway. Behind me, Tori calls out, but I keep going, needing an escape before I completely lose my mind and do something stupid. Like touch her.

When I reach the wall, I shrug out of my clothes and step up onto the ledge, calling my dragon forth. It is quick to respond, berating me for leaving her this way but no less willing to help me fly off into the darkness alone.

Legion's mood swings leave me confused and pissed off. Not to mention his little comment about his *past guests*. How many other women has he brought home anyway? Ugh. Why does it even matter? Alone on the ledge, I stare out over the skies where I'd watched him shift into his massive dragon and soar out of sight. The wind is cold as shit up here, but it's also beautiful the way the clouds seem to wrap themselves around the distant mountain peaks, their snowy caps reflecting in the moonlight.

Both moons are completely full, their glow nearly as bright as a coming dawn. For a moment, I wonder what it would be like to live in a world of perpetual darkness. I'd always imagined Tartarus as some dark hell filled with evil and ugliness. But now, seeing the beauty of this place under a blanket of serene moonlight and twinkling stars, I have to admit I might have been wrong about this world.

Turning away from the ledge, I wander the gardens,

appreciating the vitality of the plants. Deep blue ferns and ivy the color of amethyst twinkle beneath the moonlight. It's kind of amazing how a world plunged into permanent darkness has found a way to grow things. Their life force sings to my fae blood, though what echoes back at them from inside me is much darker than it's ever been before. Here, I feel powerful.

I feel safe.

Finally, when my hands and nose are numb from the cold, I make my way back through the garden and into the Keep. The hall is still empty, the house still quiet. When I get to Kendall's room, her door is open, and she's not inside.

Doubling back, it takes me several wrong turns to find my way downstairs and into the dining hall. Kendall is seated at the table in front of a plate piled high with pancakes.

"Morning," I say.

"You're up early," Kendall offers.

"Unfortunately, my wake-up call was not optional."

Her brow lifts, but before she can ask, I add, "Any chance I can get what you're having?"

"I'll split it," she says, grabbing an extra plate. I start to protest, but she says, "Chaya is nowhere to be found, and the cook was impatient to leave too."

"Cook?" I repeat. "How many people live here?"

And why haven't I put more effort into doing recon before now? I'm clearly losing my edge.

"Three or four maybe? I don't know. The others have kept to themselves."

"Do they all, like, work for him?"

"No idea. The cook wasn't exactly talkative this morning."

"Where's the kitchen? I'll make it myself."

"If you'd met the cook, you'd know that is not a good idea. Here."

She passes me a plate with half her pancakes, which I take gratefully. "Well, I guess it's just you and me then."

"Where's Legion?"

"He left," I say flatly.

At her questioning look, I scowl down at my pancakes—which are delicious. Tartarus is really growing on me.

"What do you mean he left?" Kendall asks.

"First, he said we were going to see the witch but, then he changed his mind—and his mood, apparently— and left without me."

"When is he coming back?"

"Tonight, I guess." I take another bite of pancakes, knowing she's about to launch an interrogation about what happened to make Legion leave. Questions I have no interest in answering. "How are you feeling today?"

My question successfully derails her, but it also sends the mood spiraling.

Kendall sets her fork down and picks up her juice but doesn't drink it. My chest squeezes as the silence stretches.

"Juniper would have loved this place," she says at last.

When she looks up at me, her eyes are shining with tears, but she's smiling.

I smile back. "She would," I agree. "All the stone and natural elements are exactly her style."

"Last night, I could have sworn I felt her with me," she admits.

My smile fades, my mouth tightening with grief. "I'm sure you did. Her body might be gone, but her spirit isn't."

She nods then takes a sip of juice. "What do you think Mom and Dad would say if they could see us now? In Tartarus of all places."

She's changing the subject, but I let her. Besides, her question isn't rhetorical. Kendall was so young when they died. I know it's harder for her to remember them, so she relies on my stories.

Putting aside the heaviness from before, I smirk. "Mom would have Legion eating out of her hand."

Kendall grins. "And Dad?"

"Dad..." I shake my head.

"What?"

I meet her curious gaze, a new plan forming as I imagine exactly what my father, a dark fae poisoner, would do. "Dad would be getting prepared."

"Prepared for what?"

"To go back and finish this."

"Tor," Kendall starts.

"Look, they're not going to stop unless I stop them. And I refuse to hide forever. I will not live the rest of my life in exile."

Kendall grimaces, but she doesn't argue. "What kind of preparation do you have in mind?"

"I need supplies. My kind of supplies."

"You want poisons."

I nod. "You said there's a village nearby. We could go see if they're having the farmers market."

"Poisonous plants aren't exactly your typical farmers market offering."

"Not in plain sight," I say with a shrug. "You just have to know who to ask."

"And you know who to ask," she says wryly.

"Not yet. That's why I'm bringing a fortune teller."

She snickers. "Well played."

"C'mon," I say, "Maybe they have donuts."

Ten minutes later, Kendall and I are both at least a pound of pancakes heavier and headed out through the terrace gardens. My hands and face are covered, protecting Kendall and anyone else from my skin. Overhead, the double moons offer more than enough light to navigate, casting the flowering hedges in a happy glow.

"Are you sure this is the best way out?" Kendall asks.

Up ahead, the terraces begin to rise toward the edge of the cliff where Legion took off earlier. I glance around, suddenly feeling as if we're not alone out here, but there's no one else in sight.

Kendall seems unaffected, so I force my paranoia to the side.

"The front gate is locked," I tell her. "But I saw a path back here earlier."

"And you don't think Legion will care that we went out?"

I catch myself before firing off a rant about autonomy and not giving in to the resident dragon like he's some kind of prison warden. Instead, I say lightly, "We'll bring him back a donut just in case."

Kendall grins.

"Wow, this is beautiful," she says, admiring the gardens as we walk.

"Yeah, no poisons though," I say wistfully. "This way." Just before we reach the last terrace, I turn left. The path veers downward with small stone steps cut into the ground. It's a sharply descending cutout, only wide enough for one of us at a time.

At the bottom, there's an iron gate where we pass through a narrow breach in the castle wall. On the other side, the stone pavers end, and the trail widens into a dirt path.

Kendall falls into step beside me as we walk.

I cast furtive glances toward the sky. Legion's departure was tense and abrupt enough that I felt sure he'd stay gone a long while. But now that we're out here, without leaving so much as a note in our absence, I'm suddenly hoping we'll be back before Legion returns with his witch. He won't be happy to find we've skipped out on him, and I don't want to be close by when he realizes we're gone.

"This place is not what I expected at all," Kendall says, and I turn my attention from the skies to the terrain.

The mountainside is dotted with craggy rock formations interspersed with thick pines that press in on both sides of the dirt road. The scent of cold pine needles is refreshing, and the moonlight reflecting down at us offers a cozy blanket of peace. Or it would be peaceful if I wasn't going to come home to a grumpy, obsessive dragon, risking his wrath in the process.

"Look, a road," Kendall says excitedly.

I hurry to keep pace as she runs to the intersection ahead. Thanks to the trees, I can't see around either corner. As I get near it, the hairs on the back of my neck stand on end.

"Kendall, wait!"

On our left, a brown bear rounds the edge of the trees. Its fur coat is mangy and missing in places like it's been in a fight recently. Its yellow eyes glow in the low light, wild even for a shifter, and I watch as it scans the clearing with teeth already bared. Like it just wants to attack something.

The moment it spots Kendall and me, it goes utterly still.

I stand frozen as the moment stretches like time suspended. I want to call out that we're not a threat, but something holds me back from making noise. Something about the animal is off.

From somewhere farther away, a howl sounds.

The bear flinches as if the howl woke it then opens its mouth and lets out a guttural roar. When it finishes, it starts running straight for my sister.

"Kendall!" I race toward her and shove her aside at the last second. The bear's claw catches my hip, and I'm sent to the ground as pain slashes through my side.

When I look up, the bear is gnashing its teeth at me, its glowing eyes focused like a predator about to strike. I see a madness in its eyes—a lack of control that tells me there's no stopping this thing, not short of killing it, anyway.

"Tor," Kendall says, her voice trembling with fear.

"Don't come any closer," I tell her, scrambling to my feet. I wince at the pain that shoots through my left side when I walk but force myself to keep moving.

The bear growls, facing us down with the confidence of a predator who knows it has cornered its prey. I try not to think about it. Instead, I focus on Kendall.

"I'm going to draw it away from you," I tell her. "When I do, run into the trees, and find one to climb."

"What are you going to do?"

"Don't worry about me. Climb, and don't come down until I tell you."

"Tori, you can't fight that thing." Kendall's voice shakes again, and my throat clogs with emotion I can't afford to let myself feel right now.

"I don't need to fight it," I tell her, forcing a confidence I don't feel. "I only need to touch it, remember?" She doesn't answer.

The bear blows an exhale through its large nostrils. I bend my knees, preparing to sprint.

"Get ready."

"I am," she whispers.

"Go!" I let out a roar, waving my hands and running toward the thing for about three paces.

It snarls angrily and charges.

With a scream that's half-battle cry and half-terror, I take off down the road. The bear follows, and I know immediately that I am not nearly fast enough to give Kendall the time she needs to get to safety.

The only thing I can do is take this asshole down.

While I run, I shed my gloves and jacket, dropping them as I go.

Behind me, the bear closes in, its massive claws scratching the dirt as it eats up the distance. I can feel its breath on my heels. Feel its madness in my bones.

Now or never.

Veering off the road, I grab hold of the first tree I come to and use my momentum to swing myself around to meet the creature head-on. It snarls and snaps its teeth as it whizzes past. I manage to brush my hand against its hind leg then stumble as I nearly face plant.

The beast careens to a stop and rounds on me, already coming again.

I straighten, eyes widening as raw fear pours through me. There's nowhere left to go. My touch should have—

From above, an enormous scaled wing crashes through the treetops. It slams into the bear, sending it flying sideways where it hits the ground, sliding to a stop.

The roar above me is deafening as the black dragon lands in the center of the road. Its glowing yellow eyes are narrowed in rage as it stalks closer to the bear.

For a moment, fear squeezes my chest, and I want to warn Legion to be careful. But the scent of rot hits me, and I take a step toward the bear, needing to see, to know that I wasn't wrong. Two steps are all I need to watch as the poison spreads and the bear succumbs.

It falls onto its side, breaths shallow, as the rot spreads from its leg to its hindquarters.

I glance into the trees, gaze sweeping for Kendall. She's not in sight, which means she must be hiding. But I need to know she's safe. I'm just about to skirt past Legion to look for her when a ball of fire shoots from his mouth, consuming the bear.

The heat burns my cheeks, and I retreat as lava and ash rain down over the whole area. When I look back at where the bear lay before, there's only bone and embers now.

My stomach lurches at the smell.

I turn and hurry into the trees, ignoring Legion, which isn't easy when he's the size of a house. I can feel his anger pricking at me right between the shoulder blades. But I focus on finding Kendall, making sure she's okay.

"Kendall," I call out.

A second later, she emerges, unharmed. Her eyes widen at the sight behind me, but I'm still doing my best to ignore the showdown I know is inevitable.

"Are you—?" Before I can ask if she's okay, a hand closes over my shoulder, and I whirl, jumping away from the touch out of reflex. My arms and face are completely exposed, but Legion, back in human form, glares at me without a care that he came so close to being poisoned.

"What the hell are you doing?" he snarls.

I force my gaze to remain on his face despite the fact that he's gloriously naked—and clearly unaffected by the cold weather. A fact I notice out of the corner of my eye and only serves to make it harder to focus on his words.

"Kendall and I were walking to the village," I say.

"Are you insane? Do you have any idea the danger you put yourselves in?"

I cross my arms, refusing to let him make me feel bad. "I had it handled."

"That bear is the least dangerous thing out here. You should consider yourself lucky that's the only thing that found you before I got here."

"Before you got here?" My eyes narrow. "You mean when I took care of the thing myself?"

"That bear would have taken you down long before it succumbed to your poison."

"I guess we'll never know," I snap, irritated that he might be right.

"You and I agree on that at least. Let's go."

"No, thanks," I tell him. "Kendall and I are going to finish our outing."

"Um, actually," Kendall says. "Just curious but what else is out there, exactly? And how is it worse than the bear?"

I turn to see her standing several yards back, her hand held up at an awkward angle in front of her. It takes me a moment to realize she's blocking Legion's body from her view. It might have been funny if I wasn't so furious.

"Demons, hellhounds, vampires," Legion tells her. "And those are just my closest neighbors."

"Are you saying everything in this world is going to try to kill us?"

"Today? Yes."

"I don't believe you."

But one look at Kendall and I can see she does. "He lives here, Tor. He would know what the dangers are."

"He's just trying to scare us so we won't leave that prison he calls a castle. I refuse to be intimidated by his fear tactics. We can—"

Pain slices through me, radiating out from the center of my chest. I suck in a sharp breath, doubling over. Legion is there instantly.

"What's wrong?"

"I don't know," I manage through clenched teeth.

Kendall hurries over, but I wave her back. "Don't. I need my gloves."

"Where?" Kendall asks.

"Near the road."

"I'm on it." She hurries off.

Legion hasn't moved away. I take a step back, needing distance, but he only follows.

"Back up before I accidentally kill you," I hiss through another bout of stabbing pain.

"Tell me what's happening to you," he says in a strained voice.

I glance up at him, but the expression he wears is unreadable. If I didn't know better, I'd think I pissed him off. But I've seen him angry, and this isn't it.

"I don't know. I..." Another wave of pain comes, and my knees buckle under the weight of it.

Legion leans in and sniffs. "You smell like blood."

I glance at my left side where the bear's claws got me. "It's not that deep. I'll heal."

He growls.

"That's not what hurts," I add.

Kendall returns, breathless. She holds out my gloves, and I manage to yank them on. The scarf and jacket are harder because every move causes more pain. Eventually, I manage to get my face wrapped up as much as possible.

The moment I'm covered, Legion stalks forward and scoops me into his arms. I gasp then struggle, panicked I'm going to accidentally brush him with my skin.

"What are you doing?" I demand.

"Taking you home."

"Put me down," I insist. "You'll get yourself killed."

"Only if you keep wiggling," he says, tightening his grip against my struggles.

He starts up the road the same way Kendall and I came down. She falls into step beside him, clearly fine with the way he's manhandling me. When I realize I'm trapped, I give up struggling. Partly because I don't want to accidentally murder him and partly because everything hurts and fighting only makes it worse.

"I'm going to pay you back for this," I say quietly.

"I expect nothing less," he returns, a dark smile flashing down at me.

Resigned, I let myself be carried back to my fancy prison by the warden himself.

LEGION

Tori is limp in my arms as I hurry toward the castle. I can't tell if she's sleeping or succumbing to the pain. Urgency drives me, leaving me to wonder if shifting and flying wouldn't be faster, but I don't want to cause her more pain by wrapping my claws around her for a flight.

All I can think about is the moment when I landed and saw her being attacked by that bear. The only reason I made it in time was the mate bond screaming her fear so intensely that I felt it all the way up into the clouds as I flew. In that moment, the moon fever was nothing compared to the fear I felt at losing her. Even now, possessing her is far less important than saving her. But the pain she's in now is a threat I can't see or kill.

I am helpless.

The castle is quiet and empty when we push through the doors. The entire staff takes Februlune off at my request. It's always been a precaution, but today, it's an inconvenience that has me gritting my teeth all the way through the halls.

"Kendall, there's a first aid kit in that closet," I say as we pass it. "Can you grab it and bring it along?"

"Sure." She falls back while I hurry onward.

When we reach her bedroom, I settle Tori in the bed then reach for her blood-soaked shirt so I can inspect her wound. She yanks away from me, her expression tight. "You can't touch me," she reminds me just as Kendall appears in the doorway with a box of medical supplies.

"Kendall, check the medical kit for gloves," I say.

Kendall opens it and comes away with a pair that are clearly too small for me. When she realizes it, she slips the gloves on herself. I move aside to give her access, snagging a robe and wrapping it around my still-naked body.

Tori tries to pull away from her sister, but Kendall's expression hardens.

"Stop moving," Kendall says firmly.

Tori goes still, and Kendall peels back the bloodied shirt. It's already sticking a bit where the blood has begun to dry, and Tori winces as the fabric pulls at her wound. The blood that coats it makes it hard to see the depth of the gashes, but from what I can tell, the cuts have already begun to close.

It's her blackened veins that steal my attention and leave my insides hollowed from fear.

"Shit, Tor, it's happening again," Kendall says.

Tori looks down and then grimaces before falling back again. Her expression is pinched like she's in pain, and a thin sheen of sweat lines her brow.

"What is that?" I ask.

Tori doesn't answer.

"We don't know," Kendall tells me, "But it happened last time she touched someone."

"How do we heal it?" I ask.

"I'm not sure," Kendall says.

Tori doesn't offer anything else. The mate bond is full of her pain—driving me mad with helplessness.

In the silence, a bleakness settles inside me that I can't allow.

"Gods, I was so scared that bear was immune," Kendall says to no one in particular.

"Not immune," Tori says, too pale between the darkened veins now creeping up her face. "His size and insulation slowed the poison."

Kendall doesn't answer. Her concern for her sister is evident as she gently cleans the bloodied wound.

"I'm going to get the witch," I say roughly.

"She's not here?" Kendall asks.

"She insisted on transporting herself." I frown, thinking of how Tori's scent had hit me the moment I landed earlier. How her trail led me straight down the back stairs and out of the safety of the Keep. I leash my temper and say, "I'll be right back."

"I'll start patching this up," Kendall says, pulling up a chair.

I slip out, wondering if the witch will be enough to help or if I should go for a healer instead. That will take time, but I don't know what else to do. Every step I take away from her increases my worry, but I shove it aside. She'll be fine. She has to be.

Stopping off at my room, I trade the robe for fresh clothes. My boots take long enough to lace that I spew curses until I'm finished. But I needn't have bothered with shoes, apparently.

A figure is already waiting in the foyer downstairs when I arrive. Half-woman, half-goat, the glaistig stands with hunched shoulders, leaning heavily on her wooden walking stick. From beneath thick, silver hair, she peers at me with bright green eyes as I approach.

"Broca," I greet. "You made it."

"I told you I would transport myself," she says in a gnarled voice.

"Yes, I didn't think..." I have no idea how she got through the locked gate much less the front doors, but I stopped questioning the creature and her methods years ago. The image of her as an old crone is one of several I've seen her take—none of which, I suspect, are her true form.

"Well, are you going to stand around all night or take me to the girl?"

"There was an incident on the road earlier that left her injured. She needs a healer."

She perks up at my words, her eyes alight with morbid curiosity and no trace of true concern. "What kind of incident?"

"A bear attack on the road."

She puts up a gnarled hand. "I'm not a healer, dragon."

"I know what you are," I say, all too familiar with Broca's cryptic prophecies. She talks in riddles, but she's not been wrong—or at least, not that anyone can decipher. And she's older than Tartarus itself. I need her kind of knowledge.

"She has another ailment that I'd like you to examine. Something with dark magic. Something I've never seen before."

"If magic has tainted her, a healer will be useless anyway. Your payment has been received. Take me to her."

I hesitate, considering the wisdom of this. But Broca is right. If magic has done this, only magic can undo it. And I won't risk Tori's life to protect my secret. "This way."

Broca is silent as I lead her through the house and into Tori's bedroom. She doesn't comment on the fact that this is her first invitation to my home or remind me that few of Tartarus' royal inner circle have ever been invited to the Keep, including her. Knowing Broca, I'm sure every creature this side of the portal will hear about her visit here soon enough. We both know the general of Caius' army, the dragon of death, allowing visitors in his home will be the gossip of the century. And Broca's not the most discreet.

I can only hope she doesn't sense that I've severed the blood vow to Caius. That's one piece of gossip I can't allow to get out.

At Tori's bedroom door, Broca stops and takes in the sisters, the younger one perched in her chair worriedly chewing her nails and the older one looking far too small and helpless in the large bed. The dark veins have spread to her face now, their spiderweb lines a tangled map beneath her skin.

At the sight of us, Tori sits up, eyeing the glaistig warily. "Who are you?"

"I'm Broca, the ancient one."

I roll my eyes at the old hag's dramatics. She likes hyping herself up, which isn't going to win her any points here.

"I don't like witches," Tori says.

"Good thing I'm not a witch then," Broca tosses back, which only makes Tori look more nervous. She glances at me, but I don't bother trying to explain Broca. No one can.

"Besides," Broca goes on, studying the map of veins across Tori's face and throat, "I don't like anyone with darker magic than me, so I guess that makes us even."

"You can sense dark magic on me?" Tori asks.

"*In* you," Broca corrects. "I sensed it from a mile out. In here, it's practically choking me." She moves toward the bed, and Kendall stands, blocking Broca's access.

"Get out of my way, halfling," Broca says.

"Not until I know you're here to help," Kendall says.

"If I wanted to kill you, you'd be dead already," Broca tells her, a sharp edge lacing her words. The air around her crackles with power, but Kendall doesn't back down.

"Give me your hand."

Broca rolls her eyes. "You can't be serious."

"Give me your hand, or leave."

Broca casts me a glance, but I remain silent. The girl has a right to protect her own.

To my surprise, Broca merely scowls and places her hand in Kendall's. Almost immediately, the crone's face morphs into that of a woodland spirit followed quickly by a young woman with cascading red hair and smooth, youthful skin.

Kendall's eyes narrow.

Tori gasps.

Broca rips her hand away, but her latest form remains. A young woman with unmarred skin and bright green eyes glares at Kendall accusingly. "What are you?" Broca demands.

"A halfling," Kendall says with a smirk. "You said it yourself."

"You have the sight. A powerful—"

"She's not going to hurt you," Kendall tells Tori.

"You're sure," Tori says.

Kendall shrugs and steps back. "There's a one in fifty chance but..." Kendall's gaze flicks to me. "She won't get far."

I consider her meaning as Kendall steps back and Broca approaches Tori. The glaistig perches on the edge of the bed and reaches for Tori's gloved arm.

Tori recoils. "You can't."

I expect the glaistig to ask why, but she only says, "Will your gloves protect me?"

"Yes, but..."

Broca takes Tori's gloved hand in her own. "Hmm. What happens when you touch someone?"

"They die," Tori says.

Broca pulls away, frowning. "How?"

"Their veins blacken beneath their skin, the infection spreading over them until their heart stops."

"And your veins?"

Tori sighs. "I don't know why, but both times I've touched someone, this is how I end up."

"How long did it last the first time?"

Tori doesn't answer.

"About twenty-four hours," Kendall chimes in. "I noticed it was gone after that."

Broca starts to respond, but Tori interrupts. "That's not true."

Broca's eyes flash. "What is true?"

"I... drank something. Poison."

"Tor, what the fuck," Kendall says.

"You what?" I echo.

Tori averts her gaze from us and looks only at Broca. "I drank a lethal dose of Ricin. It fixed my skin immediately."

Kendall mutters something about stupidity, but I can only stare at my mate, who has apparently decided to play with her own life.

Broca looks unconcerned by all this. She reaches into the folds of her clothing and produces a vial of dark liquid. "Here."

"What is that?" Kendall asks anxiously.

Tori takes it with her gloved hand and sniffs lightly. Her gaze never leaves Broca's. "Poison hemlock."

Kendall's eyes widen. "What are you—"

But I already know what she's about to do. "No," I roar.

Tori uncaps it and swallows the contents before I can reach her.

Kendall yells. Broca merely watches with a look of

calm anticipation. I drop to my knees beside Tori's bed, heart thudding.

But Tori only sits quietly. She looks over at me, some emotion swimming in her eyes. I can't read it, and I'm too afraid to ask her what she's thinking—or feeling. The mate bond doesn't offer any clues, either. If she's in more pain, I can't sense it.

Finally, she exhales, and her eyes clear, the glassy look she's worn since the bear attack gone at last.

"Tor?" Kendall whispers, full of hope.

"It's helping," Tori assures her.

I'm very aware I'm still on my knees on the floor. Like a desperate man begging. But I can't remove myself. Not until I know she's all right.

Color returns to her cheeks, and then, before my eyes, the darkness in her veins fades until it's completely gone.

Tori looks up at Broca again. "Thanks."

Broca waves off the gratitude as I knew she would. "You are dark fae," the glaistig says, her green eyes bright with curiosity.

Tori nods. "My father."

"And your mother?"

"She was a nymph."

Broca's eyes brighten with a gleam I can't decipher. She glances over at Kendall before continuing. "You are good with nature? Manipulating life?"

Tori's expression hardens. "Plants. Not humans."

"Tell me about the pain."

"It was sharp. Like being stabbed."

Her words distract me as I climb to my feet. How does she know what it's like to be stabbed?

Before I can ask, Tori's eyes narrow at the glaistig. "I thought you were here to answer my questions, not the other way around."

"Do you have enemies?" Broca asks, completely ignoring Tori's comment.

Tori snorts.

Broca's brows lift at that. "I see."

"Is it a curse?" Tori asks.

Broca doesn't answer. Her green irises morph to cloudy white as she calls forth her power. In the distance, thunder rumbles. Broca begins muttering quietly. The air in the room warms, and my skin prickles. I take a step forward, not sure whether to intervene or not. But then Broca stops, and the pressure subsides.

"Well?" I demand.

"She's cursed."

The glaistig stands, and Tori leans forward, suddenly earnest. "That's it?"

"What else is there?" Broca faces me, a shadow darkening her gaze.

There's more, but she won't say it here.

"How about telling me how to fix it," Tori demands.

Broca glances over her shoulder then back at me. "Stop touching people," she says and then walks out.

"Is she serious?" Tori demands.

"I'll be right back," I say and follow Broca out into the hall.

She's fast, and I don't catch her until we're at the end of the hall near the stairs. Instead of taking them, she keeps moving, somehow seeming to know her way around despite the winding turns of this place.

"Tell me the rest of it," I say.

She casts me a sideways glance that does nothing to ease the worry tightening my chest. "Walk with me."

I walk with her to the back doors that lead to the gardens, waiting for her to say more, but she continues silently onward, all the way back to the courtyard where the narrow stairs lead down to the road. The wind is stronger here, whipping her red hair against her collar. I bite my tongue, knowing if I push her, it'll only make her more difficult.

"Who is the young one?"

Her question is not one I expect. "What?"

"The girl. The seer. What do you know about her?"

"Kendall? She is dark fae and nymph like her sister. I don't know much else."

"Has she had training?"

"I have no idea."

"Hmm." Broca frowns, clearly caught up in her own thoughts.

My patience slips another notch. "Tell me about Tori, and I'll consider finding out more about Kendall."

She huffs but doesn't argue my offer. "She is your enemy then."

"What?"

"Tori. She is your enemy. That is why you cursed her?"

"I didn't curse her."

Broca's eyes flash. "What is this, some kind of test? Do you doubt my ability?"

"Of course not. I wouldn't have asked you to come if I didn't trust your ability."

"Then stop lying to me," she snaps.

My temper threatens to unleash at that. "Watch your tone, old woman."

To her credit, she doesn't flinch. "Your bloodline has cursed that woman. If you don't want to share your reasons, that's fine by me. But don't call me here to fix something you broke."

She turns away, and I grit my teeth in an attempt to keep from yanking her back. "Wait."

She turns back, scowling.

"I didn't do this on purpose. Tell me what's wrong with her."

She studies me for a long moment, and I reconsider the idea of using physical means to draw answers from her. Finally, she says, "My ancestors called it poison-kissed. An ancient curse meant to torture and punish. A fate worse than death, they said. It's a complicated spell requiring power even I don't possess."

I shake my head. "I'm no glaistig. How could I have done this?"

"Could be your family."

I shake my head. "I have no family."

"I don't have an answer for that, but the curse is sealed with your blood."

"How do you know it's my blood?"

She grunts in disgust. "I can smell your demon blood from here."

I ignore the insult. "How can I ease her pain?"

Her eyes glitter, clearly unconcerned about Tori's pain. "Find out if Kendall has had training."

I bite back the urge to drown her in hellfire. "Only if you tell me how to ease Tori's pain."

"Her pain will grow worse every time she touches another. Refilling the poison well seems to replenish what was lost. I'd start there."

"You want me to keep giving her poison?"

"Do you have a better idea?"

I don't answer, and she turns to go, walking slowly toward the far edge of the courtyard where a steep staircase offers the only way off the grounds.

"Wait," I call again. "How do I break it?"

"You can't."

She starts to walk off, but I rush after her. "Wait. There must be a way."

She sighs. "The curse can only be broken through an offering made from the one who cast it."

"And if I can't find the one who cast it? If they're dead?" I ask.

She shrugs. "It's broken when she's fully drained of the curse's poison."

"Drain the poison. Fine. And then she'll be cured?" I ask hopefully.

"Then she'll be dead."

TORI

"Well, that was complete and utter bullshit."

I stare at the door where Legion just left with his joke of a witch—or whatever the hell she is. The sight of his broad shoulders as he leaves has my stomach flipping. His reaction when I drank that poison is now an image burned into my brain. The concern—no, fear—he wore as he knelt beside me touched some part of me I'd long since locked away. Rather than admit how much it freaks me out, I scowl and refocus my irritation on the goat woman who told me zero things I didn't already know.

"We can get another opinion," Kendall says, but her attention is also on the door where the old woman—young woman?—just left.

"When you checked the future, did you see how pointless she would be?" I joke.

Her gaze swings back to me, her lips curving wryly. "I was too busy checking to make sure you weren't going to kill her."

"If she hadn't left so quickly, I would have. It would have made the pain worth it."

Kendall softens. "How are you feeling?"

"Good. Better than good. In fact..." I shove the covers off me and swing my legs over. Some part of me braces for pain at the movement, but I feel none. Drinking that poison solved everything—which is honestly a disturbing fact that I don't allow myself to think too hard about. But at least the pain and my dark spider veins are gone. And so is the wound on my hip.

"Whoa. What the hell do you think you're doing?" Kendall demands.

"Getting out of this room."

"Tor." Kendall's voice is a warning.

"What?" I snap.

Hurt flashes in her eyes, and I feel instantly terrible.

"I'm sorry," I say quietly. "I just wish... I could use a hug," I admit.

Her smile is sad. "Me too."

My eyes sting with tears, and I look away, blinking them back before they can fall. This curse has never sucked more than this moment.

"Do you think Juniper's spirit is at rest?"

The question throws me off. "Of course. Why wouldn't it be?"

"I just thought... Legion charred the place pretty good before we escaped. Do you think it hurt her spirit? The fire?"

"No."

"How do you know?"

"Juniper's in a place where she can't be hurt," I tell her.

She nods, but I can see the grief so close to the surface.

"We should have a service for her," I say, and in this moment, I feel horrible for not thinking of it before now.

Kendall's expression is a mixture of hope and uncertainty. "Here?"

"Sure. Why not? We can honor her memory from here just as easily as anywhere."

"You're right." She brightens. "That's a great idea. When should we do it?"

"How about now?"

"You mean in here?"

"Of course not, Juniper needs to be remembered outside." I walk to the wardrobe and snag a fresh shirt, discarding my blood-soaked one. Then I grab my scarf, rewrapping my face as I move toward the door. "Come on. I know a place."

I half-expect Legion to be camped outside my door, ready to lock me inside. But the hallway is empty as I lead Kendall toward the back doors. Not even Chaya has made an appearance, which is weird, considering how attentive she's been until now.

It's a strange sort of quiet. Not like the other times I've come this way. But I tell myself it's just me and the weird day I've had.

Outside, rather than following the wide path that I know leads to the stone courtyard Legion likes to use as a dramatic exit, I turn left at the first crosspath, heading deeper into the thick gardens. Here, the path is narrow, the tall hedges and climbing ivy pressing in around us. It's comforting and peaceful, like being wrapped in a cocoon.

"Oh, this is perfect," Kendall says from behind me.

At the end of the path, a thicket of trees sprawls to our left, the woods extending down a heavily-graded hillside. On the right, the cliff's edge that seems to wrap around the entire backside of the property rushes up to meet us.

Wandering into the trees, I find an acorn on the ground and pick it up. Kendall waits while I choose a spot and then bury it beneath a few inches of dirt. When I'm done, I stand back and look over at my sister. "Do you want to say anything?"

"Sure." She looks down at the freshly turned dirt, softening. "Juniper, you were a second mother for me. You were always there for us and made sure I felt loved and cared for. You taught me how to cook. How to take care of the earth and how to tap into my own power. I love you and miss you so much."

She sniffles and then nods at me, eyes watery.

I look down at the loose dirt, my heart aching. "Juniper, we are so grateful for your sacrifice. You protected us when—" Emotion clogs my throat. I swallow hard against it. "I will never forget what you did for us. Tell Mom and Dad we love them."

With tears streaming, I call on my gifts and send a burst of power into the acorn. A moment later, the dirt loosens, and a seedling sprouts from the ground. It winds its way upward, thickening as it goes until a young tree stands before us. The trunk is thin but strong, and the leaves that sprout from the narrow branches are a healthy green.

"It's perfect," Kendall says, sniffling.

The leaves shimmer in the moonlight then begin to split. I stare, confused and a little horrified, as the leaves multiply into groups of three, taking on a very specific teardrop shape.

Kendall reaches for the tree.

"Stop!"

She jerks back. "What?"

"Don't touch it," I say.

"Why not?"

Fear curls in my gut. "It's poison."

"What kind of... Oh, wait, is that poison oak?"

"Yes."

Kendall turns to me, eyes wide. "How? You planted an acorn. This should be an oak tree. I don't get it."

"I don't know how," I say, staring at the leaves like I can will them to return to what they're supposed to be. But they remain unchanged.

"Maybe your gifts are changing," Kendall says quietly. "Now that we're in Tartarus."

"Maybe," I agree, though the truth twists its way into my thoughts.

This curse is dangerous.

It's spreading even when I don't touch something. Even when I don't want to grow and spread poison, that's what I've just done. I take a few more steps away from Kendall, putting more distance between us as she talks about Juniper's memory.

When our little memorial concludes, I fake exhaustion and escape to my room before she can read my fear. The moment I'm safely away from her and back inside, I pull my scarf off and shake out my hair. My need to always be covered head to toe is starting to wear thin. It's not like I have another option, but my annoyance is there nonetheless. An annoyance that quickly turns toward brooding.

Over Juniper. Over Legion and the way he knelt beside me in obvious fear when I drank that poison. And over this curse that only seems to feel lighter when I'm brimming with poison. But ultimately, I'm brooding over a future that's looking more and more bleak with every day that passes.

I'm so lost in my own thoughts that I almost don't see the dark figure blocking my bedroom door.

"I see you're feeling better."

Legion's voice startles me, and I brace myself against the wall, catching my breath. "You scared the hell out of me."

"I have that affect."

His mouth quirks up. It's a smug look that should ruin the fact that he's devastatingly handsome. But it only makes it harder to breathe.

My heart thuds wildly, and I become very aware of the effect he has on me. "What do you want?" I ask, a little breathless.

"I came to check on you, and you were gone."

"Kendall and I had a memorial service for Juniper."

"I am sorry for your loss."

"I grew a tree," I say, not even sure why I'm telling him. "In the woods beyond the gardens."

"Were there not enough trees already for your liking?"

I roll my eyes. "It was meant to be a memorial for Juniper."

"Ah."

"Anyway, don't touch the tree, okay?"

"If this tree is so personal to you, why put it out in the open?"

I huff impatiently. "It's not personal, it's poison oak."

He studies me for a long moment. "Was poison oak special to Juniper?"

"No, I... It was an accident."

He frowns, concern etching lines around his mouth that I want to trace with my finger. "I don't understand."

"I don't either."

A beat of silence passes between us where it's clear he's waiting for me to elaborate. When I don't, he changes direction, his gaze skimming my face and throat now exposed thanks to the scarf dangling from my gloved hands.

"How are you feeling?"

"Better. Or I was before I grew that damned tree."

"I thought poisonous plants were your thing."

"It started as an acorn," I explain. "The damn thing should've been a harmless oak tree. Being able to change a seed from its origin is new."

"What do you think it means?"

I sigh. "It means I'm not the only poisonous thing on your property anymore. Tread carefully."

"Are you worried about me?"

"Of course not," I snap, hating the way he flashes

that smug smile again. And the way my body responds to it. "Just... don't touch it."

"Only if you promise to stay inside for the rest of the day."

"What? Why?"

His expression darkens, and I can practically scent the lecture on his tongue. But then he seems to change his mind and says evenly, "Today is something called Februlune. It's a dangerous time for anyone to be out in Tartarus. Especially those who are not familiar with this place."

"What the hell is a Februlune?"

"It's what we call the moon fever, and it only occurs when both of our moons are full at the same time. I believe your world has something similar."

"The full moon on Earth calls to shifters," I say. "I can't recall it being dangerous."

"That's because the shifters of Tartarus are shadow creatures, which makes our response to the double moons more intense. Tempers are shorter. There is a decline in humanistic characteristics as the animal within drives them."

"And this happens every month?"

"Every three months."

"I see. So, double full moons make your people feral?" I ask, thinking about the bear. It had definitely lacked any sense of humanity.

"Not feral exactly. It's more about mating. If you've identified or met your mate but have not yet claimed them, the moon fever will drive you mad with the urge to get to them. You'll attack anything else in your path along the way."

I study him, wary now as his words sink in. Not just the danger out there but also in here.

"You've identified your mate," I point out quietly.

"Yes."

"Do you have... moon fever?"

"Yes."

He looks entirely calm as he says the word, and I'm not sure whether that makes him scarier than I previously thought or simply immune to me. Maybe I'm just not that desirable.

Ugh.

"Do you?" he asks.

I frown. "I don't think so."

His expression is unreadable, and I wonder if he's questioning our connection too. Maybe our mate bond is weak. Or not real. Or part of this weird curse. Maybe it's fake.

Maybe I'm nothing to him; a girl he accidentally cursed at a bar. A mess to clean up.

"Am I..." I can't bring myself to voice those fears. Then, I'd have to admit that's exactly what they are: fears. Because, if I'm being honest, even though I don't want to claim him, I want him to want me.

I want to feel desired once before I die, which might just be sooner rather than later.

"Shifters experience it more intensely," he says, and I whip my gaze back to his, wondering if he can read my doubts.

"So, the bear was experiencing this moon fever," I

say, heading back to more solid ground. "And that's what drove it to attack?"

He nods, his gaze darting to my hip where the bear slashed at me. "It'll be over by tomorrow."

"Is that why no one else is here today? Because of Februlune?"

His mouth twists. "It wasn't safe for them here."

"Because of the bear?"

"Because of me."

"Oh."

I wait, but he doesn't say more and it only leaves me with more questions. And more doubts. But I'm not sure how to voice any of them.

"Why did you want to go to the farmers market?" he asks.

I hesitate, unsure what to tell him. I can't decide where we stand or how much to trust him. In this moment, we feel less like enemies and more like awkward roomies, but I have no idea how long that will last.

"Were you running away?" he asks.

"No," I say, shaking my head.

"Then what?"

"I wanted to get supplies," I admit.

He frowns. "Is there something else you need? More clothing—"

"No. It's... I wanted to get some poisons," I admit. "More than just the stuff my body's producing," I add when he looks confused. "If I'm going to fight the Crimson Roses, I need to be ready."

His expression darkens instantly. The awkward

roomie vibe vanishes, and suddenly we're back on opposite sides again. "*You* are not fighting anyone."

"Of course I am. It's *my* problem."

"You're safe here."

"Safe. Right. Like with the bear?"

He growls, but I refuse to back down.

"It's not just about me. Kendall will never be safe either as long as I have this target on my back. I have to deal with it eventually. And to do that, I need supplies."

"And where does killing me fall on your list of things to do?"

I glare at him.

"Don't tell me you've changed your mind about bringing them the death dragon in your place?" he taunts. "My life for yours, remember?"

"I'm still considering it," I say.

His lips twitch knowingly. "Fae aren't supposed to lie, you know."

"No, but nymphs can. I have my mother to thank for that gift."

"And what would your mother say about me—the death dragon who saved your life?"

His words land like a blow.

I look away, fighting the emotion clawing its way through me. My mother... she'd have so much to say about the state of my life. About the mess I've made. And yet, I can't help thinking she'd like Legion. She'd thank him. And tend to his garden. Commune with the magic of this realm. She'd love it here. She'd love him. Someone who could handle my temper and irrational need to argue things to death.

Seeing him through her eyes hurts.

Legion says he has this supposed moon fever, but where's his urgency? His madness? Am I that undesirable that he can just stand here before me looking bored or angry or anything but the way I feel about him?

Suddenly, it's all too much. And I refuse to let him see that.

Without offering him another word, I step around him and into my room. I can feel his gaze following me, but he doesn't try to stop me as I shove the door closed, shutting him out as far as I'm able.

TORI

Cleaning off the blood and dirt is easier than healing my aching heart. So, that's what I do. After an hour's soak in my giant bathtub, I am starting to come around to the luxury of this place. Not that I will ever admit that to a soul, especially Legion.

He pissed me off earlier, but our conversation also served as a reminder of one very important fact: He's my enemy. And I don't care what he says about this curse, I know he's the one who cast it. I can't let myself forget that again.

Toweling off, I wander back into the bedroom and pull open the wardrobe against the wall. For the first time since arriving, I don't grab the first thing I see and instead take the time to dig through what's here. It's stocked with clothing—some I recognize from my own closet at home and some unfamiliar though perfectly sized. There are even extra gloves and scarves to choose from.

I also find a hairbrush and various creams in the bathroom drawer, which I try to hate but just can't. Even if these things were put here for his "other guests," and even if they were chosen by a fourteen-year-old girl, I'm grateful for the fact that they're here at all. For the first time in a decade, I'm not the one who has to think of everything.

I decide right here and now to enjoy the safety this room offers me as long as I can. And to find some way to repay Chaya for letting me have this reprieve. Kendall's safety and my survival are still mine to figure out, but for now, just this once, I don't think about any of it.

I spend the entire afternoon in my room, mostly because it's the only place I can risk not being covered in layers of fabric. It's only been days since this curse took over my life, forcing me to cover every inch of my skin or risk hurting the ones I love, but it feels like years. I find myself enjoying the simple sensation of sitting around, exposing my skin to the air.

Soon enough, I run out of distractions, leaving my thoughts to wander all sorts of dark places. Eventually, I'm forced to leave if only to find more supplies to keep me busy. And food wouldn't hurt either, as evidenced by my growling stomach.

After rewrapping my face and donning fresh gloves, I slip out of my room, stopping at Kendall's door, but after a swift knock and a look inside, I find the room empty. At the bottom of the stairs, Kendall's voice reaches me from the dining room. Chaya responds, and I start heading that way, hoping to use the meal time to find out more about Chaya and thank her for the clothing and toiletries.

But before I make it that far, two male voices drift toward me from the opposite direction. Curious, I follow the sound until I reach a set of heavy wooden doors cracked open wide enough to scent cigars and wood smoke wafting out.

Moving silently, I inch closer, peering through the opening to see Legion sprawled in a large chair. He holds a glass in one hand while the other rests casually on the armrest. His hair is a bit more tousled than I've seen, and his expression is relaxed—almost friendly.

Whoever sits opposite of him says something, and Legion throws his head back and laughs. I stare at him, completely mesmerized. He's nearly unrecognizable to me, like he's allowed himself to let his guard down. Something he doesn't do with me, apparently.

The stranger across from him says, "Do you believe her?"

"About my bloodline?" Legion asks, his smile fading as the familiar shadows darken his gaze. "I don't know."

"Does she have a reason to lie?" the man asks.

"Everyone in Tartarus has a reason to lie," Legion says.

The stranger chuckles. "Good point."

Legion sips his drink and stares into the fire. I study his profile, admiring the angle of his jaw and the curve of his cheekbone.

"So, you're just going to keep her locked up here forever. Pining for her but never touching her?"

The stranger's words snap me out of my daydreaming.

"Go to hell," Legion grumbles.

Ditto.

"And her sister?" the man says. "Two for one?"

Fury lashing, I shove the doors open, pushing my way into the room so I can face the stranger. His brown hair is thick and messy, hanging over his ears with a bushy beard covering the lower half of his face. There's a wild streak in his eyes but it doesn't strike me as dangerous. Then again, my temper considers me the most dangerous thing in the room by far.

"My sister is none of your business," I snap at him.

"Tori," Legion begins.

"And you." I round on him, and he freezes halfway out of his chair. "You don't own me," I say. "I will not be locked away here or anywhere. Not by you or anyone. The moment you are not useful to me, I will go."

His expression tightens, a dangerous shadow crossing his features. He pushes to his feet slowly, towering over me, though I refuse to step back.

"You will go when I allow it," he says, his voice deadly calm.

Behind me, the stranger gets to his feet. "I'm just going to let you two..."

I spin to face him, backing away so they're both within my sights. Removing my scarf is more of a power move than anything—a reminder that I'm lethal and not to be fucked with.

"Who are you?" I demand of the stranger.

He looks from me to Legion. I don't take my eyes off

him to see what Legion says, but the man relaxes. "I'm Klyn. I work with Legion."

He holds out his hand to shake.

"Tori." I smirk and start to take my glove off.

His eyes flick to the movement. He smirks and withdraws his hand. "Right. Well, I'm going to let you two work this out. None of my business."

"If you touch my sister, I'll kill you," I tell him.

"Relax, little fae. I'm not going to hurt you."

"Or my sister," I press.

"Or your sister," he repeats.

He shoots Legion a look of amusement that has me itching to press a finger to his throat. "Good luck," he adds and then walks out, chuckling.

When he's gone, I turn back to Legion. "Tell me about your bloodline."

"No."

"Why were you two talking about it and then me and Kendall? What does it have to do with—"

He stalks closer. Out of instinct, I back away until my shoulders hit the wall, sending a picture cockeyed though neither of us pays it attention. He looms over me, his temper barely leashed beneath the surface. I watch as the storm gathers in his dark eyes.

It should be scary. On some level, I know that anyone else would find him completely terrifying right now. But instead of fear, I fight the urge to kiss him. To offer him everything I have. To let him take me—in whatever way he wants.

My breath catches, and I can't think. Not when he looks at me like this.

Not when he's so close.

His mouth hovering within reach, teasing me.

Taunting death.

"You are here because it's not safe for you anywhere else." His voice is low, the roughness raking over every inch of my poisoned skin. "You are not free to go. Not until I say it. You are mine until I let you go."

"You don't want me," I say. "Even if you could touch me, you said you wouldn't want to. Why are you doing this?"

His gaze drops to my mouth, and for a harrowing second, I think he's going to kiss me. His words from the other night ring out in my head. That dying from touching me would be worth it.

"You are mine to protect," he says. "Mine to touch or not. No one else's."

His words send a burst of heat straight to my core. I hate that his possessiveness turns me on. I hate that the mate bond has reduced me to this. To him. More than anything, I refuse to let him see how much I want that touch. From him and no one else.

"Tell me about your bloodline," I whisper.

His eyes flash with something I can't read. He steps back. His chest rises and falls with heavy breaths, and I know he's just as affected as I am. Just as frustrated. Just as turned on.

"No."

I glare. "You're keeping something from me. I want to know what it is."

"Whatever I've kept from you is none of your business."

"Then I'm none of yours either," I hiss.

His eyes narrow. "Everything about you is my business."

"You don't get to say I belong to you and then refuse to tell me anything about you."

"That's exactly what I get to do."

"Ugh. You're infuriating."

"Right back at you, darling."

I stare at him, wildly violent thoughts running through my mind. The idea of choking him to death is particularly appealing right now.

"I love when you look at me like that," he says.

"Like what?"

"Like you want me."

"The only thing I want to do is kill you."

He steps closer, his breath warm and delicious against my face. "To attempt that, you'd have to touch me. Does the thought bring you pleasure?"

"You have no idea."

"Oh, believe me, I do. I've already taken three showers today just to relieve myself of the madness of the moon. I want you so bad I can't think straight."

I blink, stunned.

"You didn't seem bothered earlier. You were so calm."

"This morning, finding you naked in your bed, I almost took you right there. The moon fever is like nothing I've felt. *Wanting you* is like nothing I've felt. But seeing what that bear would have done... the idea of losing you outweighed all else, even the moon fever itself. I can bear anything except losing you."

His words untangle me.

"I want you too," I blurt before I can take it back. "And it pisses me off."

He grins like he's just won something.

I scowl. "Don't look so smug about it."

But his smile darkens into desire, and I find myself unable to look away. "Show me."

"What?"

"Show me that you want me."

"What do you—"

"Sit."

He gestures to the chair I found him in earlier. Before I can refuse, he crosses to the door and shuts and locks it. I don't move. Part of me wants to scream and fight my way out. But that part is no longer in charge.

Before I can stop it, my feet are moving. Walking to the chair. Sitting down. Looking up at him.

"Take off your shirt."

I don't move, and he strides over, kneeling in front of me. Dangerously close to my bared face.

"Take off your shirt," he repeats, his voice low and husky.

I shiver, feeling the words rake over me.

"Why?" I ask.

"I want to look at you."

Knowing he can only look and not touch is a heady feeling. A power that makes me feel safe enough to bare myself this way. A challenge that I know he can't meet.

Slowly, I peel my shirt over my head.

But then he pushes to his feet and peels off his own shirt. Dropping it onto the floor, he steps back and takes a seat in the chair across from me. His dragon tattoo gleams, almost as if it's moving on its own with each new lift of his arm. Firelight dances over his muscled torso, casting shadows along the planes and ridges of his abs.

I wonder what it would feel like to trace those ridges with my fingers.

"Now, your pants."

His words snap me out of it. I jerk my gaze to his. The same challenge I felt a moment ago is reflected in his dark gaze now.

Maybe that's what has me standing and stepping out of my pants.

My heart thuds wildly in my chest.

This is crazy.

I don't even like him.

He's my enemy.

And yet... I want him to see what he'll never have.

I want him to want me.

"Your turn," I say, daring him.

He stands and pulls off his pants then sits again, powerful muscles contracting along his thighs and biceps with the movement. My gaze is drawn to the impressive bulge in his boxers.

My mouth goes dry.

"Now, the rest," he says.

I hesitate.

He leans forward, his eyes hungry and demanding. "I want to see you, little poisoner. Let me look at what I can't have."

His words echo my thoughts. Before I can stop

myself, I reach around and unclasp my bra, letting it fall to reveal my bare breasts.

Legion snarls and leans forward. He moves so quickly that I jerk back, my eyes widening.

He looks up at me and smirks then sits back again. He lifts up just enough to peel his boxers off. I watch as he palms his cock, pumping it lightly. My nipples harden, and my desire heats me from the inside out.

Maybe I'm not immune to this moon fever after all.

"Do you like what you see, little poisoner?"

I glance up and find him watching me with an intensity that makes my skin tingle. "Do you?"

His smirk is sexy as hell. "I think the answer to that is fairly obvious."

I bite my lip, eyeing his hand around his cock, imagining what it would feel like inside me. The sight of him so turned on by me is empowering.

Feeling brave, I reach down and slide my fingers over the fabric of my panties. Legion tenses. His gaze is locked onto my hand.

It's incredibly arousing watching him watch me.

I keep my eyes on his hand and explore my body with my fingers.

"I want to see." His voice is strained.

I look up to see him studying me, and instead of answering, I stand up and slide my panties off. Then I sit again and part my legs. Nerves creep in then. I've never bared myself like this before. It's more vulnerable than I know how to be.

But Legion clicks his tongue. I meet his gaze and find acceptance. Arousal. Need.

"Let me see," he says again, his voice raw.

I did that to him.

Reduced him to … this.

It's the encouragement I need to keep going.

Circling my fingers around my clit, I focus on my pleasure. Legion makes a sound of approval. I glance up from where he's pumping his cock, and he nods at me.

"Don't stop, little poisoner. Show me how you like it."

I push one finger into my pussy. Then two. My breath catches at the delicious sensations of it. Not just touching myself but having him watch me do it. Legion adjusts himself in his chair, and I know he's fighting the urge to reach over and offer his own fingers for assistance.

"You are so fucking gorgeous," he says.

I increase my pace, rubbing my thumb over my clit. My breathing sharpens, and Legion pumps himself faster. It's incredibly erotic watching him watch me. I can feel my orgasm already building.

His eyes are intensely focused on me, but he's no longer watching my pussy. He's staring right at me. Into my eyes. Seeing parts of me I've never shown a single soul.

It's the way he slips past all my defenses that has me gasping as I come. Pleasure washes over me in waves, more powerful than any orgasm I've ever experienced alone.

Across from me, Legion leans back, pumping himself faster, until his own release has him groaning.

I feel his relief almost as sharply as my own when his

orgasm hits. It's the first glimpse of emotion I've felt from him. The first moment I sensed anything through the mate bond.

It startles me.

I wonder if he felt it too.

When I meet his gaze, the hunger is still there, still poised on the edge of a knife. But I notice a smug possession that hadn't been there before. I don't know what to do with that—especially while I'm still naked and more vulnerable than any lack of clothing could cause.

"That was so fucking sexy," he says.

The way he watches me robs me of my voice. "I..."

"I may not have cursed you on purpose, but your curse is mine to break," he adds, his voice rough.

I look up at him, hope and fear and need and what feels a lot like trust all blooming inside me.

"I'm going to find a way to touch you."

His words ignite a hope inside me that is scarier than any threat to my life.

"You don't believe me," he says.

I look away, emotion swirling, threatening to pull me under. "It's easier to hate you," I whisper.

"Then hate me, my little assassin. Even while you come for me, while you scream my name and beg for more, loathe me. It won't stop me from claiming you in the end. From killing for you. From draining you of every drop of cursed poison in your veins. You're mine, little poisoner. There's nothing you can do to change that."

LEGION

Late into the evening, I pace my study where traces of her scent still linger. The heat from the crackling fire is nothing compared to my own raging emotions. Not being able to touch her is fucking with my head. Even with Februlune behind me, the darkness threatens to take hold. The longer I resist her, the closer to the edge I veer.

Knowing I'm the reason for her curse only makes my torture worse. Telling her the truth about it would paint me as the monster. Then again, I've never pretended to be anything else.

A light scraping sounds at the window. I look up to see a hawk staring in at me. Its gaze is sharp and pointed as it watches me stalk over to the ledge where it waits. I push the glass open and pull the string tied to its ankle. A piece of parchment comes loose. The moment the message is in my hands, the hawk flies off.

Unrolling the paper, I read the note.

The Western Isles are secure. Suspect in custody. -Caius

I frown, walking to the fire and dropping the parchment into the flames. The news is good. It means the threat at the wall is behind us. But I can't help but feel as if something much bigger is on the horizon. A threat I've yet to identify. One that will attempt to take from me the one thing I never thought I'd want in the first place.

Tori's presence through the mate bond makes it impossible to think of anything else. Not while both moons are still full.

I need to see her. To feel her. To know that she's safe. My dragon will not rest until he's reassured.

Storming from the room, I follow the scent of her straight to the library. Shoving the doors open, I find her bent over the table, studying a thick volume. She jumps at my sudden arrival, but I bury my guilt at startling her. Besides, the shadow beast inside me is all about hunting its prey. Seeing her off balance only feeds his enjoyment.

"What do you want?" she asks warily, candlelight dancing over her cheeks.

I don't answer her.

Instead, I keep going, crowding her until she scrambles back and runs right into the wall of shelving. Her eyes are wide, and her lips part as she brings her gaze to mine, her head tilting to accommodate our height difference.

Her scarf and gloves are gone.

Getting this close is dangerous. But so is staying away.

"You look so fucking sexy," I growl.

Her expression flickers with surprise. "Don't..."

"Don't what?"

"Don't talk to me like that."

"You don't want to hear flattery?"

"Not from you," she says.

Her thudding heart contradicts her words. As does her scent.

My lips curve. "Liar."

Her eyes narrow, and I watch, enjoying the way her temper creeps up on her slowly. It's fucking amazing to watch her get worked up like this. My cock hardens, painfully erect against my pants.

"Why aren't you wearing your scarf?" I demand.

"Because I was alone," she says pointedly. "I thought I was safe."

"You're never safe from me, little assassin."

Her chin comes up in defiance. "I told you before, you don't scare me."

"Noted. I'll try harder."

Before she can argue, I reach down and stroke her clit through her pants. She gasps, jolting a little at the unexpected contact, but she doesn't attempt to pull herself away. The fabric of her pants is just thin enough that I can feel the shape of her. Just like I can feel the way she tenses at my touch, arching into my hand ever so slightly.

"What are you doing?" she whispers.

Her eyes are locked on mine now, her breath shallow as she watches me intently.

"I'm reminding you what you have to be afraid of."

"You aren't going to hurt me," she says, a flicker of uncertainty in her eyes.

"I never said I would. But you're just as scared of pleasure, aren't you?"

She bites her lip, and I increase the pressure of my hand, rubbing her harder. She presses into my touch ever so slightly, and my cock throbs.

"Even if I could…" she trails off, unwilling to say the words, which only makes me increase the pace. The need to see her come apart, in any way I can, drives me onward.

"Even if you could," I prompt.

Her eyes darken, and the scent of her lust grows stronger. I inhale, my gaze dropping to her mouth. To where her tongue darts out to wet her lips. Fuck. I want her so bad.

"If I could touch you," she whispers, "I wouldn't let you claim me."

"You sure about that, assassin?"

She doesn't answer me, and I watch as she tips her head back against the shelving, her eyes closing lazily. "No," I growl, flicking her clit hard enough to make her jump. Her eyes fly open. "Don't you dare look away."

I stroke her clit, flicking it and teasing it as she arches toward my hand.

"Eyes on me, do you understand?"

She nods.

With my free hand, I cup her breast through her thin shirt. My blood heats as I realize she's not wearing a bra. Through the fabric, my thumb and finger find her nipple, flicking it and pulling it as I rub her clit harder.

"Legion," she whispers, her gaze pleading with me now.

"That's it, little assassin," I whisper, leaning in close to her exposed mouth. So fucking close. "Hate me. Even as you come for me."

"Please," she pants, breathless.

"Now," I demand and am rewarded with a soft moan as she finally falls apart in my hands.

The orgasm shatters me. It's almost embarrassing how easily I come considering we didn't actually have sex or even remove our clothes. But his gaze is unwavering even after I've quieted. And he still hasn't removed his hand from where it rests against my clit.

It's like he refuses to give me the space I need to collect myself. In fact, I get the distinct impression he might not be finished with me yet.

"That was…"

I don't know how to finish. Mostly because I can't bring myself to compliment him even now. Because, in this moment, I want to do more than compliment him. I want to open for him, let him protect me, take care of me. Maybe it's not a matter of wanting. Maybe I just don't know how.

As predicted, he smirks in triumph. "Yes?"

"A surprise."

His smile widens. Still, he doesn't take his eyes off

me. It's unnerving the way his gaze leaves me nowhere to hide. Heat pulses between my legs, wanting round two. Wanting nothing between us when I come again.

"Why are you looking at me like that?"

"I want to kiss you," he says quietly. "Very, very badly."

"Oh." My breath hitches, and I find myself studying his mouth.

The full lips. Thick stubble. I reach over and slowly slide my glove back on. He watches, silent, as I lift my hand and run my gloved fingers over his cheek.

His eyes darken with a lust I can feel building all over again inside me. His fingers move against my clit. I run my hand along his jaw and over his mouth. He makes a sound like a growl and nips at my fingertips then presses his lips to my gloved palm.

It's erotic but also incredibly sweet, and I find myself fighting the urge to peel my clothes off for him. My poisoned skin has been my armor, but suddenly, it's a barrier too.

As if he's trying to torture me, he steps back and peels off his shirt. Then he returns to where he stood before, leaning closer than is safe. His fingertips brush my clit again, and I nearly purr in pleasure.

With his other hand, he grabs my gloved wrist and presses my palm to his now-bared skin. Slowly, I run my hand over his broad chest and rippled abs, tracing the dragon tattoo that covers half his chest and biceps. He shudders beneath my touch, and, for the first time since we met, I realize I hold just as much power over him as he does over me.

It's thrilling.

In this moment, I can't remember my reasons for not wanting him. Or for hating him at all. The death dragon is mine to command. Mine to pleasure.

Slowly, almost lazily, his hand starts to move against me again. Despite my orgasm from a moment ago, I grit my teeth against the frustration of wanting another one. No, not just another orgasm. His body touching mine. His fingers inside me. His cock—

"What are we doing?" I whisper.

I expect him to answer snarkily about testing one another. Instead, he surprises me by speaking earnestly. "I want to help you break this curse. And then I want to make you come with my bare hands over and over and over again."

He watches me, his expression tense with a concentration that makes it hard for me to think or even breathe.

"Will you let me help you?" he asks.

"I..." My thoughts are jumbled. I try to think past the distraction of his body. Gods, he's beautiful, though. And the delicious torment of his touch, even through the fabric of my clothing, is enough to make me agree to almost anything.

His eyes flash, the dragon slits peering back at me for a blink before they become once again human irises. "What was that?" I ask.

"My beast is very close to the surface," he admits.

"Because of the moons?"

"Because he wants to protect you."

"You...you call yourself a shadow beast," I say. "What exactly does that mean?"

More importantly, what am I getting myself into if I agree to let him help me?

"This world contains a dark magic that permeates everything and everyone in it. Whatever power or gifts we brought with us, the realm took those gifts and infused them with its own nature."

"What nature is that?"

"One filled with shadows. In those shadows, we are brought closer to the spaces between life and death. We are made stronger by these shadow spaces. Or we are ruled by them."

"What happens if you're ruled by the shadows?"

"Madness."

I swallow hard, fairly sure I should be frightened by that answer. "How do you keep from letting that happen?"

"There are several factors," he says, watching me closely. "The most powerful of all is the primal hunt ceremony."

"What's that?"

"A celebration where a mated couple is officially announced in front of everyone."

"Chaya told me about that. It's like a wedding, right?"

"Sort of."

I try to decipher his expression with a growing sense of unease. "Why do I sense that it's actually nothing like a wedding?"

"As part of the ceremony, one mate hunts the other. When they're caught, the mating is consummated."

My mouth falls open. "In front of everyone?"

"The hunt usually takes place in the woods, but yes."

My mind reels back, searching for a safer topic, but there really isn't one. Not in this line of questioning. "And if you don't claim your mate or complete the primal hunt or whatever... you go mad?"

"I am stronger than the shadows, little assassin. Immortal and unkillable. It will take much more than a dark nature to bring me down."

I shudder, despite his reassurances, caught up in the twisted picture he's painting. It feels like a lot of pressure, suddenly, to help keep him sane. Not to mention the whole public sex thing.

"Okay," I whisper. "I'll let you help me."

"In that case..." He leans closer, and for a wild moment, I think he's going to kiss me. But then he pulls back, easing away from me.

I feel cold at the sudden loss of his presence and wrap my arms around myself to keep from shivering.

"Get some sleep, assassin. Tomorrow will be a busy day."

CHAPTER 21

LEGION

A knock at my bedroom door has me hurrying to answer it. The hour is late, but I'm already bracing for another crisis. Chaya stands on the other side. The moment she sees me, her sharp gaze sweeps me, assessing. I don't bother to answer the only question she came here to ask. If I'd claimed Tori, she'd scent it. And I certainly wouldn't be in bed alone if I had.

"Is everything all right?" I ask.

She lifts a brow. "Why do you always assume something's wrong?"

"Habit." I hesitate and then add, "But is it?"

"Everything's fine. I just wanted you to know everyone's safe and accounted for." She studies me. "How did everything go here?"

I swipe a hand down my face, unsure where to even begin.

Chaya smirks. "That good, huh?"

"The sisters decided to walk to town this morning."

Her eyes widen. "What? Why would you let them do that?"

"I was out," I say, feeling defensive at the reminder of the danger I allowed.

"Are they okay?"

"They're fine."

"Uh-huh. And you?"

The moon fever. She insisted I should have left today and let her stay to guard the sisters, but my obsession wouldn't allow it. I don't bother to tell her that, if the circumstances haven't changed before the next double moons, I'm going to do more than leave. A few months ago, I locked Styx up to keep her from hunting her mate; she'll do the same for me if I ask. The problem is I'm not sure the madness won't be permanent by then. Not to mention I have no idea how to keep a beast like mine chained.

"I handled it."

I can see she has questions, but she doesn't press it. "As long as everyone's in one piece." She turns to go, adding over her shoulder, "Klyn sent word to meet him in half an hour."

"He's back already?" I ask, frowning.

She shrugs as she pads silently down the hall. "'Night."

Klyn is already waiting for me at the edge of the garden when I make my way out just after midnight. His hooded silhouette is nearly invisible against the back-drop of thick trees, but my senses are keen. Impatience has me quickening my pace to meet him. Half my thoughts are still on Tori and the way she responded to my touch earlier. A touch that only left me craving her even more. The other half are on her words. She agreed to let me help her. To stop fighting me. It's the closest thing to a truce we've achieved, and I don't intend to waste it.

At my approach, Klyn looks up from where he's studying one of the rosebushes. His recon mission didn't last nearly as long as I expected, and I can't tell if that's good or bad.

"What did you find?" I ask.

"Hello to you too," Klyn says wryly.

"Hello," I grumble. "What did you find?"

"Did you see this?" he asks, pointing to the bush.

"I've seen it a thousand times," I say, impatience making my tone curt. "They're roses—"

"Not the roses. These dark vines covering them."

He moves aside. In the darkness, I note thick, charcoal-colored vines weaving through the branches and wrapping tightly around the rosebuds trying to unfurl. I scowl, ready to blast him for wasting my time on harmless ivy, but my eyes track the vines where they continue creeping beyond the rosebushes. Since the last time I stood here—mere days ago—the vines have wound all the way to the atrium of the garden, choking out several of the lower-lying plants already.

"This wasn't here a week ago," Klyn says.

My gaze snaps back to his. "It's Tori," I say quietly. "This curse is affecting her gift for plants. Turning them to poison."

He snatches his hand away. "You're telling me this vine is poisonous?"

"I don't know for sure, but I advise not touching it."

He stares at me for a beat. "Good plan."

"What did you find?" I ask.

He sighs. "Not the information I wanted."

I tense, not sure how to feel about that answer. I sent him to the Earth realm in an attempt to uncover anything more about this curse or how to end it. And Klyn's never returned from a mission empty-handed. "What does that mean?"

"It's as you said. There's no trace of your bloodline anywhere."

By bloodline, he means my mother. Neither of us wants to say the word, but she's the only possible culprit here.

"Last known whereabouts?"

"The trail is over a thousand years old, so I can't say for sure. I hired a tracker to follow it, and we'll know more in a few days."

I bite back the frustration of hitting a dead end even temporarily. Not that I want my mother to be alive, but this curse came from my blood—and I can't rest until it's broken. "I need confirmation," I say.

"You'll have it. We won't stop looking until we find the answers," Klyn says.

"And the Crimson Roses?" I ask. "Did you look into them?"

"From what I can tell, the Crimson Roses make up the city's organized crime. The gang, which is mostly vamps, is divided into several smaller cells, each with its own hierarchy of leadership. They do it this way to keep the lower members from knowing too much about those at the top. Makes it kind of difficult to uncover the identities of the key players."

My brows lift at that. "Are you saying you couldn't get a name?"

"Hell no. I'm saying you should appreciate my resourcefulness. The people who are after Tori are the same ones who hired her for her last job."

"Klyn, give me a name."

"She goes by Em."

"Vampire?"

"Not sure. The members I spoke to all gave differing answers."

"What exactly does that mean?"

He shrugs. "That's all I know."

"I thought I was supposed to appreciate your resourcefulness."

"I'm just keeping some of the mystery alive for you. So you feel like you did some of the work yourself."

I shake my head. "Where do I find her?"

"There's a club on the outskirts of the Crossroads. Apparently, it's a hub for the gang. Owned by some vamp named Uziah. She's been seen there a few times."

I frown.

"What?" Klyn asks.

"Uziah. Tori mentioned that name back at her house. From the sound of it, she has a history with him." Jealousy has me tightening my hands into fists.

Klyn notes my reaction. "You want me to ask around at the club? See if I can set up a meeting?"

"No, I need you here. Caius sent word that the suspect from the bombing is in custody, but there's still the debrief, and I'm sure there are a million reports to write."

"You're making me do your reports? Again?"

"What can I say? You're the best."

He snorts. "I'll try to suck at it from now on."

"Too late. Your secret's out. Besides, this is my problem to handle."

"You do realize her connections would make it easy to set that meeting, right?"

"Yes."

"You're going to take her out there?"

I look over at the dark vines. "I have to do something. We can't go on like this."

Klyn snorts. "That's for damn sure."

"What the hell is that supposed to mean?" I glare at him, but that only makes him grin wider.

"Your blue balls are making us all grumpy. Go get laid, boss. The world will still be waiting for you to burn it down when you get back."

I lie awake well past midnight, the memory of Legion's touch still lingering on my aching body. Instead of sleeping nude like usual, I dress in a thin layer—just in case. Part of me hopes Legion will show up for an encore and touch me like he did in the library. But the other part knows that would be way too dangerous. Alone, I retrace his movements with my own hand. The thin fabric of my panties offers the same delicious friction from earlier, and I send myself over the edge into orgasm quicker than I expect. But it's not the same. And it's not nearly enough.

Legion's promise from earlier replays in my mind. I can't deny I want what he's offering: to break this curse and let him make me come with his bare hands.

I know I should hate him for what he did to me, and maybe I do. Maybe I'm just tainted by my own poisoned heart, but I want Legion despite knowing he did this to me. And despite knowing what he's done in his past. Maybe that makes me a monster too.

When I finally drift off to sleep, my dreams are filled with him. I'm at the primal hunt, being watched by a crowd, though I want him so badly, I don't care. He chases me down—hunts me—and I let him catch me, my entire body yearning for what comes next. He kisses me, touches me, his hands and his tongue tracing the dark veins on my skin—right up until the moment he succumbs to a slow death. The last thing he whispers in my nightmare is "You win."

In the morning, I shove aside the guilt that pricks at me. It's stupid to feel bad for killing a guy when it was only a dream. But the idea of hurting Legion even if it means saving myself leaves me strangely off-balance today.

Kendall's already gone when I check her room. I find her in the kitchen, her hands covered in flour as Chaya and the cook instruct her on forming the dough for bread.

"Hey," I say, relieved to see her settling into this place so easily. "Have you seen Legion?"

"Not since breakfast," Kendall says.

"Oh, I didn't realize I missed it."

"By about an hour," the cook says with pointed disapproval.

"Sorry. I guess I overslept."

The awkward silence leaves me feeling like a fourth wheel, so I excuse myself and snag some fruit for a quick breakfast on my way out.

Legion isn't in his study, nor do I run into him in the library. My gaze lingers on the spot where I stood while he touched me last night. My body heats at the memory, and I pull myself away reluctantly before continuing to wander from room to room.

While I explore, I find myself imagining a life here. In Tartarus. In this house. Wearing gloves and scarves for the rest of my life. Unable to touch another. And while I want nothing more than to be free of this stupid curse, for a fleeting moment, I almost convince myself I could be content like this. I could live out a quiet life, no more need to kill anyone. Or maybe I could go back to growing poisons. I'm certainly better at it than ever. I'd contract myself to the king rather than the outlaws this time. No more looking over my shoulder. Kendall and Chaya could be together. The idea of it feels almost peaceful. Almost enough.

Until that future vision is shattered by a familiar deep voice that somehow reaches all the way inside me and yanks away the lie that I could ever be happy not touching him.

"Looking for me?"

I whirl where I stand inside an empty guest room and find Legion standing in the doorway. The fact that I didn't hear him arrive is evidence of how distracted I am. But the way my entire body reacts to the sight of him is proof that what happened between us isn't something I can ignore.

Whatever we're doing here, it's changed.

"I... this room is beautiful," I say, trying to find my bearings.

He doesn't look away from me as he says, "Chaya chose the furnishings. I'll tell her you said so."

My stomach tightens as jealousy spears through me.

Ridiculous. She's fourteen? Fifteen? There's nothing between them. Still... she takes care of him. Of this place. I don't like how it feels to imagine it. A life without me in it.

"Why?" I can't help but ask. "Why do you furnish the rooms so beautifully? Why do you stock them with clothing and toiletries?"

"I found Chaya four years ago. Her parents died when she was six, and her uncle sold her to pay his bar tab when she was eight."

My eyes widen as the horror of that punches me in the gut. "That's horrible."

"She's been through a lot," he agrees. "When I found her, I brought her here and gave her a room. Clothes. Food. It took her two years to talk to me." He smiles wistfully, remembering.

I can only stare at him, struck by this compassionate, caring side. Who knew the death dragon moonlighted as a philanthropist? Embarrassment flushes my cheeks as I realize I'd assumed he forced her to serve him here, and all along she'd been here willingly.

"So, you keep the rooms stocked for others like her?" I ask.

He shrugs. "We help anyone we can. None of the others have stayed. Well, besides Brigita. The cook," he adds at my confusion.

"She was a rescue?"

His mouth quirks. "Sure, if we're calling it that. And I wouldn't use that term to her face. Anyway, it's something I can do for those who need it, so I do."

The way he says it is so simple, so matter-of-fact. And my heart melts.

It's not something I saw coming, and I'm not prepared for the way my walls crumble.

"How long have you lived at the Keep?" I ask, suddenly interested in filling in more of the backstory for the man I'd assumed was a monster.

"Four thousand years," he says.

I blink, a little overwhelmed at trying to imagine being stuck here for that long. Or anywhere, for that matter.

"That's a long time to be imprisoned," I say.

"Prison is made in the mind," he says, frowning. "And I was in prison long before I was cast into Tartarus."

"I see."

I don't, really, but he doesn't elaborate.

"And the first thousand years," I say. "What was that like? Where did you live then?"

"I didn't live anywhere. Putting down roots would have meant accepting my fate, and I didn't want to do that for a long time."

"What changed your mind?"

"Friendship."

Whatever I'm expecting him to say, it's not that. The death dragon being won over by friendship—in a prison world, no less—shatters another layer of judgment and stereotype I've been carrying.

"You're not what I expected," I say finally.

"Neither are you."

The way he looks at me reminds me of the way he

watched me touch myself. The moon fever clearly wasn't the only reason for that night. I lick my lips, remembering what it felt like to know how much power I held over him.

To know how much he wanted me.

The silence between us stretches, but it's charged now. Full of a tension that's less hostile than the other times before.

Whatever shift happened last night, an even larger one has just happened today. In this moment. I don't know what to do with that. Or if he senses it too. But I need to find my way back to solid ground. Fast.

I'm not here to fall for him. I'm here to survive. Except that, the more time I spend with him, the more intertwined those two things become.

"Can we talk?" I ask, nerves dancing in my belly. "Somewhere more private?"

"Of course. He steps aside, motioning for me to go first. When I step into the hall, he points and says, "Last door on the left."

I follow his directions, almost positive he's staring at my ass while he follows me. At the end of the hall, I push through the closed door only to stop at the delicious scent of him filling the space so entirely. It's not just scent either. There's a presence of him here unlike anywhere else in the house.

My gaze sweeps the room. A large bed with mahogany posts sits on my right, framed by two windows overlooking the back garden and, beyond that, a gorgeous view of the open sky. The bedspread is a deep crimson color that reminds me of the hellfire he breathed that day in my yard. Velvet curtains done in crimson and black hang on either side.

Opposite that, a desk and chair sit near a charcoal-colored loveseat that is draped in a soft throw blanket and matching pillows. A stack of books sits on the floor, crooked and ready to topple over.

I whirl at the sound of him behind me.

"This is your bedroom," I say, noting how cozy he's managed to make the space. It reminds me of Chaya's words. A safe space.

"Do you like it?"

I glance at the bed. "It's…cozier than I expected," I admit.

He smirks. "Bed's even more comfortable than it looks."

Before I can answer, he pushes the door shut with a click, sealing us in together. My heart thuds. My body pulses, and the thrum beneath my skin is full of anticipation. The memory of last night washes over me. The knowledge that he can make me come without being skin-to-skin is a thrill, but it also makes me feel desperate for a world where barriers aren't needed. Because, somehow, even standing several steps away from him feels incredibly intimate.

"What would you like to discuss?"

"Legion," I say, not even sure how or where to start.

He waits, giving me time.

"Last night," I say finally, and his gaze darkens. The mate bond pulls taut between us, both of us straining toward it.

"Did you like it, my little poisoned flower?" he asks, his voice low.

I swallow hard against the urge to tell him I liked it so much that I played an encore alone. "Did you mean what you said?" I ask instead.

He blinks, but there's no hesitation when he says, "Yes."

He doesn't even ask what I'm talking about. For some reason, that makes me believe him even more.

"You said today would be busy. What did you mean?"

I almost expect him to refuse to answer me. Or to make up some bullshit alphahole story about what he's going to do while I sit and twiddle my thumbs. Either one would have ruined what we've built so far.

So, I'm shocked when he says, "Tell me about Uziah."

"What?"

"He owns a club where the Crimson Roses do business, right?"

"Yes, but how do you know about him? Or the club?"

"I had Klyn look into the people who are after you. He said the client who hired you for your last mission is the one who's after you now. He couldn't dig up much else on her, so we need another angle for information."

I sigh. "I only know her as Em. But Uziah won't help us. He's already done all he can."

"And what exactly is that?"

"He's the one who made the deal for me. To trade your life for mine."

His eyes narrow. "And the one who sold you out to them."

"He was a friend of my father's, but that doesn't make him one of the good guys," I say.

"Yes, that's clear."

"Look, this is how things work in the Crossroads. It's not like Tartarus."

"And how does Tartarus work?"

"I guess I wouldn't know. I haven't seen it."

"Would you like to?"

The question throws me off. "I don't know. What do you mean?"

"Come into town with me. Let me show you around."

I stare back at him, not sure where this is coming from. "What happened to a busy day of curse-breaking?"

"I asked Klyn to help me track down someone who might be able to give us answers, but he hasn't found them yet."

My brow goes up at that. "Another goat woman?"

"No. Someone in the Earth realm."

"Okay." I draw out the word, hoping he'll elaborate.

"We'll know more in a few days."

"And in the meantime, you want to play tourist in your own realm?"

"I want to show you this world has more to offer than being a prison."

"Isn't that what it's been for you?"

"At first," he admits. "But then it became an escape. And from there, a home. A chance to stop running."

"What could you possibly have to run from?"

His expression darkens, a shadow haunting his eyes so deeply that I know he's holding something back from me. "So, your father's former friend specifically offered a deal for the death dragon, huh? What else did Uziah say about me?"

"That you're capable of destruction beyond this realm's comprehension. But everyone in the Crossroads knows that."

Legion doesn't answer.

The silence leaves me more convinced of a secret hanging between us.

"What's this really about?" I ask.

"My... reputation offers a challenge that is irresistible to the greedy and foolish."

His voice is hard now, his expression unyielding, as if I've somehow offended him. It makes no sense.

"What are you talking about? Your reputation is that of a killer. They call you the death dragon. Who would be stupid enough to mess with someone like that?"

He gives me a pointed look that has me rolling my eyes. My temper is a streak of impatience that has me snapping, "Don't change the subject. Tell me what this is about."

He sighs. "My bloodline is a commodity I can't afford to expose."

"Excuse me?"

"My bloodline. You asked why Klyn and I were talking about it the other night. This is it."

I study him warily. "Why can't you expose it?"

"Because it would make me even more of a target."

"A target?" I think of how valuable and rare dragon parts are in the Crossroads. Scales, tears, blood, even toenails. I know several treasure hunters in the Crossroads who would kill for a score like that. Uziah's guys, especially.

Still... this is Legion.

I can't see a single one of them getting the upper hand against him.

"I don't understand," I say. "Everyone in Tartarus knows you're a dragon, and they haven't targeted you for it. Hell, you're the general of an entire army. I'm pretty sure no one's coming for someone in your position."

"It's not about being a dragon."

"What is it about?"

"My blood, specifically."

"I don't—"

"I was sired by a god and birthed by a demon."

"You..." It takes me a second to recover from that one. "Your father was a god?"

"A good one, from what I'm told." He lifts a brow. "Is it so shocking that I might have some good in me?"

I feel my cheeks flush, and I glance away. "I only meant it is an unlikely pairing, a demon and a god," I explain.

"Yes, apparently, my father was under the mistaken impression my mother was a fire fae. He didn't discover her true nature—or intentions—until after she conceived."

"You mean she tricked him into getting her pregnant?"

"That's her favorite part of the story."

"Why?"

"My mother cares about nothing and no one apart from power. For centuries before I was born, she razed civilizations, cut down her opposition, and took entire peoples as slaves to serve her. But it wasn't enough. Humans were too easy to conquer. She wanted supernatural kingdoms. When she realized she could go no farther in her domination without help, she began to seek a tool of destruction to accomplish her goals. Since a weapon like me didn't exist to her satisfaction, she decided to breed one herself."

"Wow, she sounds lovely."

He grins crookedly. "Where do you think I get my charm?"

I snort, but my amusement dies quickly. "Are you saying your demon mother made sure you're more like her than your father?"

"I'm saying that was her intention, yes." His tone is sharp, twisting with a self-deprecation matched in his gaze. "Dark magic was involved in making me. Helping to shape my qualities and my gifts to her liking. She only needed his seed. And his DNA. She bent everything else to her own will. She made me what I am."

"And what is that, exactly?"

"The death dragon, of course." Bitterness coats his words. "The monster of nightmares, apparently."

My anger softens as the darkness in his eyes is finally recognizable: self-loathing. "Do you think you're a monster?" I ask.

His gaze snaps to mine. "Do you?"

"Do I think you're a monster?"

I'm tempted to offer a quick and definitive yes. That would be the obvious answer given all the stories about him—and the things he's just essentially admitted to doing. But for some reason, it doesn't feel quite so obvious anymore. Or true.

"I don't know how to answer," I hear myself say. "The rumors about you…"

He steps closer, crowding me, challenging me. "What about the rumors?"

His voice is silky now, but I know better than to take it at face value. I've pissed him off. "They say you have wiped out entire armies single-handedly. Destroyed empires. Ended dynasties."

His gaze darkens. "Is that a question?"

"It's a lot of innocent lives."

Fury flashes in his dark eyes—nothing more than a tiny flame in the center of his irises. "Yes, my mother would be very proud."

I ignore his sarcasm and the rage brewing beneath it. "Where is she now?"

"Gone."

"Gone as in she ran to the store or gone as in…?"

"Gone as in she's the one whose war crimes put me here in the first place. When they came for me, she ran. Left me to take the fall for her. Every clue I've found since then suggests she is no longer living."

"I'm sorry."

"I'm not." He watches as I process his words. I wonder if he knows I'm thinking about my own parents now. And how much I miss them. "She wasn't a very good mother," he adds as if that makes the loss matter less.

"Well, then, I'm sorry for that too," I say softly.

Something flashes in his gaze. His expression intensifies, but it's not grief or truth between us anymore. This is desire. The way his eyelids lower and his gaze flicks to my mouth.

He leans forward, and I hold my breath, hating that I have to stop him.

"Legion," I say, my voice cracking because, in this moment, I actually want to let him touch me. To let him kiss me and claim me and never let go.

At the sound of his name, he jolts, and I can see the moment he remembers himself—and remembers all the reasons he can't do this. Disappointment turns to a fury that I don't fully understand.

Before I can figure out what caused the change, he backs away. "I have a meeting."

"A meeting?" Didn't he just ask me to go out sight-seeing with him today? "Where?"

"What?"

"Where is your meeting?"

When he finally answers, his tone is curt, his expression completely closed off. "At the king's residence."

"Oh."

He doesn't say anything else before he turns and walks out.

His dark eyes flash with something that is so unexpected I almost miss it. Hurt. The death dragon is hurt. Not angry. The surprise of it leaves me at a loss. The idea that I could possibly have the power to hurt him, that he cares what I think so much, is not something I know what to do with.

I don't go after him.

Maybe I should, but I have no idea how to heal whatever wound I've just opened in him. I'm still standing at the window in his room when I see him stalk through the gardens and onto the launch pad. He shifts, shredding his clothes, before diving off the side of the ledge and vanishing into the sky.

CHAPTER 23

TORI

An hour later, I'm sitting in the garden, surrounded by rosebushes now blooming black and gray, when I see Legion return. He doesn't notice me, and after what happened earlier, I decide to keep it that way, ducking out of sight as he stalks through the gardens and into the house. Part of me wants to go after him. To pick a fight. Not because he deserves it but because it's the only way we've connected until now. It's familiar. Knowing I've hurt him is far more uncomfortable than knowing I've pissed him off. But I don't get up.

Soon, the doors open again, and I glance through a gap in the rosebushes to see Legion re-emerging. He's dressed in pants and a black tee that stretches across his broad chest, showing off his muscled arms. He strides toward the far side of the Keep before disappearing around the side of the estate. I frown, confused. The only thing over there is a steep hillside of thick trees, so I wait, unsure what he could possibly be doing.

A moment later, I hear voices including a child whooping and yelling in excitement. Curious, I stand to investigate. But by the time I round the corner, they're gone.

Frustrated and confused, I return to the house, nearly running into Kendall as she strides toward me.

"Hey," I say, "I was just coming to find you. Want to hang out in the garden with me? Watch me try to grow some poisons?"

"Oh." She blinks and looks away uncertainly. "Um."

I zero in on the jacket she wears. "Are you going out?"

"Yeah, that's what I came to tell you. Chaya has to get some things for the house, and she asked if I want to go into town with her."

"Kendall, it's not safe. Legion—"

"Legion already cleared it."

"Seriously? He's sending you off alone?"

"Actually, he's coming with us." She eyes me with a smug sort of knowing. "He sent me up to ask if you'd like to join us."

Instead of convincing me directly, like he'd tried doing earlier, he's resorted to using Kendall. Sneaky asshole.

"Fine," I say. "Let's do it."

"Really?" Her eyes widen like she didn't expect me to agree. "I thought you were going to be way more difficult."

I glare at her. "I am not difficult."

"Please." She rolls her eyes, laughing, as we descend the stairs. "I had money on the whole 'Kendall, you have to be street smart about this. People are assholes and the world is dangerous, blah blah blah.'"

Her voice lilts dramatically with her impression, and I laugh.

"Spot on impression," I tease. But my smile fades quickly. "Actually, I'm starting to think I'm not the best person to be giving you life advice. So far, your choices are a hell of a lot better than mine."

"I'm glad you're finally starting to see who the real adult is here."

I stick out my tongue at her. "Punk."

"I rest my case," she says then sticks out her tongue in return. "Punk."

I laugh, feeling lighter than I have in days.

Downstairs, Chaya is already waiting in the large foyer.

"Hey," I say to her, hoping to make up for my complete rudeness thus far. "Thanks for inviting me along."

"Of course. I'm happy to show you a less violent side of Tartarus," she says, eyes sparkling with humor.

"That sounds great," I say with a smile. "And thanks for all the clothes and supplies."

"Of course. I know what it's like to come here with nothing." Her expression flashes with shadows, but she blinks, and everything brightens. "Maybe you can help me stock up for the next guests. Pay it forward."

"I would love that," I tell her.

Legion appears. His gaze is immediately drawn to me. He seems completely recovered from earlier. In fact, his dark eyes gleam with charm at the way he's maneuvered me into his plan.

"Glad to see you're joining us," he says.

I smirk. "I couldn't turn it down."

His grin widens. He glances past me, saying, "We're just waiting on—"

"I'm here!"

A boy of about five or six runs into the foyer with enough momentum that he slides to a stop. His eyes are bright, and his grin is wide as he looks from Legion to Chaya. "Can we go?" he asks eagerly.

I study him in surprise. Something about seeing an innocent child in a realm I'd always thought of as hell has broken a stigma for me. I hurriedly wrap my scarf more tightly around my face. This kid's energy is unpredictable. I don't want an accidental brush to end his life.

"Where's your father?" Legion asks, tousling the boy's hair.

"Here." Klyn appears, looking a little disheveled. "Damn kid is way too fast," he adds, and I'm even more stunned.

Klyn? The grizzly, bearded guy is a dad?

Legion grins at him. "What's it like to get old?"

"Fuck off," Klyn says, and the boy's eyes widen.

"Dad, you said—"

"I know what I said. Can we get moving?" Klyn asks.

Legion chuckles. Chaya takes the boy's hand, but he twists around, staring up at Kendall and me like he's just now noticed us standing here.

"Hi," he says shyly to Kendall.

"Hello." She smiles back at him, and he lowers his eyes then turns to me.

"Are you Mr. Legion's girlfriend?"

"Um." I can feel every single pair of eyes fastened on me now.

Klyn snorts. I glare at him but am distracted when I note that Legion's grinning widely, clearly enjoying this.

"Why is your face covered with that?" he asks when I don't answer.

"I'm Kendall." My sister holds her hand out. "That's Tori, my sister."

"I'm Bron," he says, shaking her hand, completely distracted from his questions. "I'm a wolf shifter. What are you?"

"Bron, it's rude to ask people that," Chaya says.

"Why?"

"Come on, kid. You can ride up top." Legion opens the massive front door and snags Bron's hand on his way out. In the next second, he swings Bron up and onto his shoulders as if the kid weighs nothing at all. Watching the two of them together makes it strangely hard to breathe. I look away, making sure to stand back to give everyone else plenty of room. When I look up again, Legion's watching me. I startle at his attention, but he shocks me even more by tossing me a wink and then turning away again.

I blink, a little stunned by this new flirty side of my mate. Broody and angry I can handle. Fun and flirty? I have zero experience with any of that.

I wait until everyone has filed out before bringing up the rear.

Outside, the waning double moons offer plenty of light to navigate by as our little parade makes its way out of the front gates—which are now unlocked and wide open, I note. From there, the path heads down a gently sloping grade that is all too familiar until we reach the same intersection from yesterday.

There's no trace of the bear. Not even the scent of a dead animal. Images of those claws and snapping teeth fill my head, but I shove them away. Legion wouldn't bring us out here if that were a risk today. Especially not a child.

It's not until we all fall into step on the wide dirt road that I realize we're going to walk the entire way. Not that I'm complaining since it beats being dangled by a dragon thousands of feet in the air. But it makes me wonder if they have any other modes of transport here. From what I've seen, Tartarus isn't modern like Earth. Not a single car or cell phone spotted so far. And if I'm being honest, the slower pace of life is a relief for me. There's a peace here I've never felt on Earth.

At the front, Legion walks along with Bron on his shoulders. The kid doesn't come up for air as he chatters on, asking fifty million questions. Klyn walks beside them, joking and laughing easily. My chest tightens at how natural they are together. How easy and established their friendship seems.

It makes me think of Stella. And Niamh. And how, even with them, I held myself apart. Always focused on my responsibility and keeping Kendall safe. Spencer, the girl I met at Spells, was the same way. Standoffish but not rude. Just... apart.

It makes me wonder what happened to her to cause it. And whether there's anyone out there making her feel safe enough to let her walls down. I never saw it coming, but Legion's doing that for me.

Just ahead of me, Chaya and Kendall walk close beside one another, talking quietly. I watch them for several minutes, grateful Kendall has found a friend here. Life back home was isolating even with her job and Natalia's training.

At least, Uziah can't get to her here.

For the remainder of our walk, I'm lost in my own thoughts, cataloging worries.

Nothing attacks us, but that doesn't stop my anxiety from inventing scenarios to worry about. Feral bears are hardly the only threat. A town full of people is, in many ways, far more dangerous, and by the time we reach the outskirts, I'm certain I've made a mistake in coming at all.

At the first sign of people, I draw my shoulders in tighter and make sure my scarf is secured. No one else seems concerned, but I continue scanning the crowded market area, making sure no one is coming too close as they wander the vendors set up in the square.

Several people call out to Legion and Klyn. They're casual with the dragon general. Friendly, even. Legion addresses them all by name, asking about their families and whether business is good. It's not what I expected, but then, neither is he. And if I'm being honest, neither are the people in the market. There's no trace of the danger from the other day left here. People are chatting, kids are playing soccer in a tight circle, and mothers push babies in strollers.

It's so normal. And charming.

"I thought the farmers market only happened on the weekends," I say to Chaya.

"This is a Februlune celebration," she explains. "Every three months, they extend the market days for celebrating newly mated couples. Tonight, they'll host parties and joining ceremonies for anyone who has just mated."

"Oh." My gaze flicks to where Legion is browsing a booth farther back. "So, like a wedding? That sounds like fun."

She gives me a strange look. "I take it Legion hasn't explained our customs to you yet?"

"I guess not. Is it something I should worry about?"

She shakes her head. "I'll let him tell you about it sometime."

I watch as Chaya and Kendall disappear into the thick of the crowd. Out of pure habit, I bite my lip, debating trying to go after them, when a voice sounds beside me.

"She's safe."

I look over to find Legion standing beside me and realize he's right. I blow out a breath, glancing around. Bron and Klyn are nowhere in sight.

"Where's everyone?"

"Bron wanted a pastry from Mel's. Klyn knows better than to tell the kid no, especially about pastries."

I can't help but smile at that. "I know the feeling. Kendall's favorite place to go at home is the donut shop."

"And what is your favorite place?"

I hesitate, caught off guard by the question. "I don't know," I admit. "I mean, donuts are great. I love them. But... I guess I've never thought about it before. Kendall always came first."

"Well, maybe you should."

"Should what?"

"Think about it."

I'm not sure how to respond to that. Or even how to do it. Before I can tell him so, a young male soldier rushes up to us, his uniform pristine, his buttons shining in the moonlight.

"General," he says, offering Legion a salute.

"Riggs." Legion returns the salute, frowning. "I thought you were assigned the royal residence. What the hell are you doing way out here?"

"The king sent me, sir." His eyes dart to me, and he adds, "May I have a word?"

"Sure." Legion brushes a hand over my elbow, as if touching me even through my jacket isn't the most dangerous risk to everyone in this realm. "I'll be right back," he murmurs.

I watch as he follows the soldier far enough away that I can't hear them. While they converse, Klyn returns with Bron, who is eating a pastry like it's a popsicle. Most of the icing has already transferred to the kid's face, but he looks thrilled nonetheless.

"What's going on?" Klyn asks me, nodding at Legion.

"Don't know," I say.

He watches but makes no move to join them.

Finally, he turns back to me. "You're good for him, you know."

"Are you trying to say I make him a better person?" I joke.

"Nah. He's a grumpy asshole lately," Klyn says, and I can't help but laugh. "But he's starting to wish for more for himself. And that's a first." He is somber as he says, "Thank you."

His gratitude rattles me, but I manage to nod before he glances back to where Legion and the soldier are talking. I look over just as Legion breaks off from the soldier. The young male heads back the way he came as Legion rejoins us. He looks troubled, and my stress instantly skyrockets.

"What is it?" I ask, trying to prepare for something as equally horrific as feral bears.

He looks at Klyn as he answers. "Caius thinks the incident at the wall warrants a bigger solution."

Klyn glances at me like he's not sure whether to speak freely. "I see," he says. "And does he have a suggestion for that solution?"

Legion scowls. "Paintball."

"Excuse me?" Klyn asks.

"He's ordered a mandatory week of war games. Thinks it'll help the men blow off steam. We're starting with paintball."

Klyn shakes his head. "Does he remember what happened last time we did this?"

Legion grins. "He says Styx is banned from playing, so we're fine."

Klyn cackles. "In that case, put me in, coach."

"Who's Styx?" I ask.

Legion's gaze swings to mine. "A friend. One I'd like you to meet, actually."

"Boss, you're supposed to be on leave," Klyn points out. "You can sit this one out."

"And let you win?" Legion snorts. "Not a fucking chance."

Klyn laughs.

"Are we going to play games, Dad?" Bron asks hopefully. Blue icing is smeared across both cheeks and his nose. It's adorable.

"Dad has to go to work, son, sorry," Klyn says. And it's clear from his expression that he really is sorry to have to leave Bron.

Legion motions to someone over my shoulder, and I turn to see Chaya and Kendall returning, both with a bag in each hand. Kendall gives me a look that says, "See, I'm safe." My gaze zeroes in immediately on her shoes, which are mysteriously soaked despite the clear blue skies.

"Ferth is getting stingy with his apples," Chaya complains to no one in particular. "He keeps this up and I might have to send a few more rainstorms his way."

"What happened to your shoes?" I ask.

"What?" Kendall looks down. "Oh."

"Whoops," Chaya says, wincing. "Sorry."

"It's fine," Kendall says, laughing, and then to me, "Chaya showed me her gift of negotiating."

At my expression, Chaya says, "I have a way with the weather." As if to illustrate, there's a rumble of thunder overhead, though no clouds mark the sky. A second later, a bolt of lightning cracks against a rock nearby. It splits in two, leaving only a puff of black smoke in its wake where the electricity burned the stone.

"Wow," I say, my gaze swinging back to Chaya. "That's incredible aim."

And a deadly gift if necessary.

"Thanks." She ducks her head but not before I see her cheeks go pink at my compliment.

"Chaya, Klyn and I have to go in to work," Legion tells her, clearly used to her threats. "Can you take Bron home with you?"

"Sure." Chaya perks up at the subject change. "He looks like he could use an apple to balance out the dessert." She winks at Bron.

"Oh man, I never get to do anything fun," Bron whines.

"Hey, I'm fun," Kendall protests.

"I mean playing games and stuff," Bron says, obviously unconvinced.

"How about hide and seek?" Kendall says, eyes gleaming.

Bron looks her up and down then scoffs. "I'm a wolf. I'll find you so fast."

"Oh, we'll see about that. Fae are very stealthy hunters."

"You're on," Bron says, grinning.

"Thanks, Chaya, I owe you one," Klyn tells her. He chases Bron down and plants a kiss on his son's forehead despite the boy trying to wriggle away. "Be good," Klyn warns him.

Bron waves, grinning mischievously and agreeing to no such thing. "Bye, Dad."

"I guess I'll see you guys later," I say, moving to follow Chaya and the others.

"Come with us," Legion says, stopping me.

After being so secretive and hell-bent on locking me in his house, his invitation surprises me. "What?"

Klyn looks between us uncertainly. "Uh, I hate to state the obvious, but I don't think she's a viable option for war games, boss. Poisoned hands and all."

"She can watch from the box," Legion says, still looking at me. "Come."

"Why?" I can't help but ask.

"I want you there," Legion says, "And..."

"And," I prompt.

"Reagan asked to meet you."

My eyes widen. "Reagan as in the queen of Tartarus?"

"Yes."

I look at Klyn, trying to gauge how worried I should be about this summons. But he merely shrugs. Legion's expression gives nothing away either.

Still, I hesitate, unsure about letting Kendall go off alone on that road, but Chaya speaks up before I can say anything.

"I'll protect her," she tells me firmly, and any doubt I had is squashed at the hardness that flashes in her gaze. Underneath the shy, self-conscious exterior is a warrior willing to fight and defend. I think of what Legion said about her past and know my assessment is right. This girl is a fighter. That, at least, I can trust.

"Thank you," I tell her.

She nods.

Kendall grins and waves at me from where Bron has already fallen into step beside her.

Even knowing Kendall is in good hands, no one's more surprised than me when I turn to Legion and say, "Okay. Let's go play some paintball."

TORI

It turns out the walk from town to their military base is fairly short. When we get close, I see the crowd converging on what looks like a large stadium and instantly tense up at the idea of moving through so many bodies. But Legion takes my gloved hand and guides me to a side entrance. Klyn follows us inside but then peels off in another direction with some comment about making sure he and Legion are team captains.

Legion leads me through a series of halls, up a flight of stairs, and out another door where I find myself standing on a balcony overlooking the large arena. It's crowded on the turf below, but where we stand, its nice and open. And we're alone.

"Thank you," I say, pulling off my scarf to enjoy the fresh, open air.

"For what?"

"Bringing me up here."

"Oh, this isn't for you. It's the best view of the arena,

and I want a witness for when I mercilessly destroy Klyn and his team."

I lift a brow. "I didn't realize you were so competitive."

"Didn't you?"

I shake my head, but the door opens behind us before I can answer. An attractive female steps out. Her gorgeous brunette hair is piled high in a bun, and her pretty eyes are fixed on Legion.

"There you are." She smirks. "Klyn said you were hiding like a little bitch because you didn't want him to beat you again."

"Liar," Legion tosses back easily. "You're just pouting because Caius said you can't play."

"Caius knows I'm too much for these assholes anyway," she says before swinging her gaze to me. "Hello. You must be the one driving Legion to drink."

"Excuse me?"

"Really?" Legion says.

She ignores him and extends her hand. "I'm Styx. Legion's most badass friend."

"Most annoying," he mutters, but she only smiles wider at me.

"Hi." I take her hand with my gloved one and find myself caught in a firm grip. "Tori."

"Well, Tori, it's apparently you and me in the peanut gallery." She arches a brow at Legion. "Unless you're punking out after all."

Legion looks at me uncertainly.

"Don't use me as an excuse to punk out," I tell him.

"I'll be back to get you when it's over," he tells me, still warily eyeing Styx.

"Don't worry, friend. I'll take good care of her."

"Yeah, that's what I'm afraid of," he grumbles as he leaves.

When we're alone, Styx turns to me and says, "What did they bench you for?"

"Excuse me?"

"They won't let me play because I electrocuted a full platoon last time. It was an accident, well, mostly, but everyone's so sensitive in the workplace these days."

I stare at her, trying to decide whether she's serious. The metal sticks holding her hair in place make me think she probably is. Especially when I put that with Klyn's earlier reaction about her being banned today.

"My touch kills people," I say.

"Nice one," she says.

"So, you and Legion," I begin. "Are you guys close? I mean have you...?"

She immediately holds up a hand. "Whoa, let me just stop you right there, Twenty Questions. Me and Legion are friends. That's it."

"Right, sorry."

"Seriously. I've known that dude for five fucking millennia. In all that time, we've gotten into many a drunken brawl, not to mention the brawls where we were sober. My point is, if we haven't boned before now, I think it's safe to say you have nothing to worry about."

"Point taken," I say, feeling awkward for even broaching the topic and wondering when it might be polite to bolt.

But she continues like we weren't just talking about hers—or Legion's—sex life, nodding down at the field. "Legion and Klyn are assholes about war games by the way. Don't be fooled by the name of the game being paintball. This is going to get ugly, especially if Klyn wins."

"Nothing about that surprises me. Legion's terrible about not getting his way. Why should a game be any different."

Styx snorts. "I think I like you."

I smile, and we both spend the next few minutes watching the two teams assemble on the field. Legion and Klyn are, apparently, team captains, and make a huge show about who they pick for their sides. Styx points out some of the men, naming them, but mostly so she can tell me who she almost paralyzed last time they did this.

She's kind of scary—and fun.

The door opens, and another female joins us. Her dark brown hair hangs loose around her shoulders, and hazel eyes are quick to assess me. I've never met her in person before, but her family is known well enough in the Crossroads that I recognize her anyway. Reagan Santiago. Queen of Tartarus. Looking strangely normal in her jeans and tank top.

"Mind if I join you?" she asks.

"Nope. You're right on time," Styx tells her. "They're just about to start."

"Perfect." She closes the door behind her and walks right up to me. "I'm Reagan. You must be Tori. It's nice to meet you."

"Hi." I start to shake her hand, but nerves have me yanking it away again despite the gloves protecting us both.

Reagan doesn't seem to mind though. In fact, she says, "Sorry, I totally forgot about your situation. Handshakes are probably not a great idea, huh."

"No need to apologize. I'm still getting the hang of being this close to people."

I glance at Styx whose hand I shook without a thought earlier. She shoots me a wink as Reagan answers, "I'm sure. And then you're forced into Tartarus on top of it." She doesn't wait for me to respond before adding, "I know what it's like, believe me."

"Thanks."

"I heard about your Februlune adventure," she says. "How are you? Sounded like a close call."

I tense, but there's no trace of teasing or lecturing in her tone. Only concern.

"Wait, what was a close call?" Styx asks.

"My sister and I decided to go for a walk and ran into a bear with moon fever," I say. "Apparently, he decided we were in his way and dealt with us accordingly."

"Shit, why didn't Legion warn you?" Styx demands.

"Good question," I say.

"Well, at least he was there to intervene on your behalf," Reagan says.

I hesitate. Clearly, she didn't realize I'd been the one to stop the bear. I'm just about to clarify that fact when Styx speaks up.

"Good thing he was the one to make the kill."

I tense. "Why is that?"

"Tartarus has strict laws about outsiders killing our own," Styx says. "And I doubt Legion would have enjoyed having your head on his chopping block."

At that, I go still, struck silent by the reality of what she's saying. Legion knew what I'd risked by poisoning that bear. That's why he'd finished it himself. So he'd be the killer, not me.

He'd saved me. Again.

No wonder he'd been furious.

It hadn't just been about the bear nearly killing me. If anyone found out what I'd done, he'd have to kill me too.

The realization sends shockwaves through me, but I do my best to shove it aside. When I look up again, Reagan and Styx are both watching me carefully.

"I'm really sorry," I say. "I had no idea."

"It's fine," Reagan assures me, reading some of my panic. "Legion explained everything. It's all behind you now. I think Caius read him the riot act for not telling you about the moon fever sooner. If anything, it's his fault."

"Oh, I bet adding that guilt to the pile has made him such a peach to deal with," Styx says with a snort.

At my expression, she adds, "Though nothing will top his first millennia in Tartarus. Gods, he was a bastard to deal with."

"Were you two friends then?" I ask.

She barks out a laugh. "Uh, no. We made it a hobby to try to kill each other. But we sort of bonded over it and became friends. When he finally got over his pouting, anyway."

Down on the field, a whistle sounds.

Reagan walks to the railing, glancing at the assembling teams. "Who are the captains?"

"Legion and Klyn," Styx tells her.

"I figured you'd be down there with them," Reagan says.

"Caius banned me," she says haughtily.

Reagan laughs. "For good reason from what I've heard."

Styx looks offended. "Whose side are you on, my queen?"

"Yours," Reagan says, grinning, "Always."

"Good choice."

We all go back to watching the game, which is a much more organized and intense battle than I first imagined. Even from up here, I can tell Legion is brutal. And Klyn is no less competitive. It might be just a game, but none of the soldiers seem to be holding back as they tackle and pummel one another in between shots.

"What's the occasion, anyway?" I ask the two females beside me. "For the war games? Legion said Caius decided to do a week of them. Is this an annual thing?"

Styx shoots Reagan a questioning glance.

"There was an attack on the castle wall recently," Reagan tells me.

"Oh. I didn't know. Was anyone hurt?"

"Yes," she says quietly. "Several people were killed."

"That's awful, did they catch who did it?"

"Oh yeah, Legion made sure to get a name from the asshole who set it off," Styx says.

"Legion got the name?"

"He's in charge of interrogation," Reagan explains.

"He's almost as good as I am at it too," Styx adds.

Reagan smirks. "Anyway, they just brought in the guy who set it all up," she finishes.

"That's great. But... how does a game of paintball help?"

This time, Styx is the one who answers. "It's not just the attack on the wall. Sorry, Reagan."

"No, please." Reagan waves at her to keep going.

"The Tartarus army has spent the last several thousand years preparing for battle," Styx explains. "The guardian who held the king's soul was the ultimate target." Reagan smiles ruefully at that. "But we were always preparing for a full assault. Whatever it took to get his soul back. That kind of prep builds tension. The thirst for battle and blood. But, turns out the situation has resolved another way."

Reagan snorts, and I realize she's much cooler about finding herself mated to a god than I feel about being mated to a death dragon. But the sharpness in her gaze tells me she wasn't always this chill.

Styx grins at her before adding, "The peaceful turn of events left our army with a lot of pent-up fight in them and nowhere to put it."

"And they need to blow off steam," I finish.

"Bingo. Oh." She leans forward, her gaze completely caught up on one of the men down below.

I watch as someone fires a shot at him, but by the time it hits the male's skin, the paint slides right off what looks like a stone bicep. The soldier who fired complains, but the male yells out, "The shot is only good if it sticks!"

The male glances up at our balcony, his gaze aimed right at Styx.

"Is that...?" Reagan starts, following the direction of Styx's stare.

"That's Corvin," Styx says without taking her eyes off the male.

"Is he your mate?" I ask.

She grimaces. "It's complicated."

"Welcome to the club," I say, instantly wishing I could take back the words. These are Legion's friends, after all. Not mine.

But Reagan and Styx both shoot me a small, knowing grin, and before I know it, I find myself grinning right back.

Legion is bruised and bloody when he returns to get me after the game. But his smile is brilliant. Reagan has already gone, but Styx waited with me. She snorts at the sight of his smug face then shakes her head and says to me, "He's going to be unbearable now. Good luck."

"Thanks," I tell her, but she's already slipping out, her attention focused on the male she called Corvin where he waits for her just through the balcony door.

"Hey," Legion calls out. "Nice work today," Legion tells the male. He looks at Styx. "Next time we do drinks, bring your boyfriend. He's cool."

Styx frowns. "He's not my—"

"I'll be there," Corvin says with a crooked smile.

Styx scowls and walks off. Corvin follows, still smiling.

When we're alone, Legion's grin becomes more relaxed.

"Well, what did you think?" he asks.

"You pummeled them," I say, and he laughs.

His smile is rare, the sight so unexpectedly beautiful that my breath catches. But the smugness in the curve of his mouth has me shaking my head.

"Gods, Styx is right. Are you always like this when you compete?"

"Only when I win." He winks and adds, "And I never lose."

I shake my head then tighten my scarf to cover my smile.

Klyn refuses to walk home with us, which Legion finds hilarious. He and I end up walking alone in the moonlight, his good mood a contrast to my thoughtful one, given everything Reagan and Styx told me today.

"How did it go today?" he asks, "with Reagan and Styx?"

I cast him a sideways glance. "Nervous about me meeting your friends?"

"I'm always nervous about Styx."

I smile at that. "Yes, I can see why. She's great. Scary, but great. Especially after she—"

I stop short, my cheeks flushing with what I've almost confessed.

"After she what?" Legion asks, his suspicion bordering on fury.

"Nothing," I assure him. "She didn't do anything wrong."

"Knowing Styx, I find that very hard to believe." His expression darkens as he adds, "I'll speak to her about it. Don't worry, she won't bother you again."

"No, please," I say quickly. "Do not speak to her

about it. It was my fault. I thought you two had...you know."

He stares at me, confusion slowly turning to understanding. "You were jealous."

"No," I scoff. "Not jealous. Just...curious."

He grins. "Right. Curious."

"Shut up," I grumble.

His grin widens, but he lets it go. "And Reagan?"

"She was really nice." I hesitate then add, "And forthcoming."

His smile vanishes and he has the good sense to look nervous. "About?"

My brow arches as I say, "The laws about an outsider killing a citizen of this realm—including a bear with moon fever."

His expression clouds. "She shouldn't have mentioned it."

"Why not? Was it a secret?"

He doesn't answer.

"Your secrets are going to get you into trouble," I warn.

He looks over at me, his expression darkening. "I know."

Those two words speak volumes for all the things he's not saying.

"What was today?" I ask.

"What do you mean?"

"Why did you bring me with you?"

"I told you, I want you to see this place as more than a prison."

I might have believed him this morning, but now,

after what Reagan told me about the bear, I'm not so sure. "You're stalling."

"Stalling for what?"

"I know you. You might not be the evil monster everyone thinks you are, but you are ruthless when it comes to protecting the people you care about. So, why haven't you gone back to my world and destroyed every one of the Crimson Roses?"

"I'm glad you recognize that I care about you."

"Don't change the subject."

His lips twitch, but the smile never comes. He stares out into the distance, and I know I've struck on the truth.

"I don't believe it's a coincidence that this Uziah made you a deal to hunt me," he says at last.

"What do you mean?"

His mouth flattens into a hard line. "When my mother fashioned her weapon, she made sure I was to be wielded by a master always."

"I don't understand."

"My immortal life requires a blood oath to another."

"Is that what you meant about others wanting your blood?"

He nods. "My very existence is contingent upon being blood-bonded to another. A master with the power to command me. To bend me to their will."

"Wait. Your mother did that to you?"

"I think she knew the god's essence in me would make me powerful enough to resist her evil intentions, so she created an insurance policy against any hint of rebellion in me."

"Your mother bound you to her so you'd have to carry out her orders even if you didn't want to?"

"Yes."

I try to imagine a parent doing that to their child, but I can't. It's too horrible. "How old were you when she first bound you?"

"Six."

My stomach roils with what he's telling me. "She deserved to be locked in a prison world more than you did."

"Maybe. But being sent here was the best thing that could have happened. Caius learned of the blood bond and demanded I bind myself to him. At first, I fought it. Fought him. But he wasn't like her. I wasn't forced to kill or destroy against my will. He earned my loyalty and respect—and my willingness." He casts me a glance as he says, "I unbound myself to Caius when I met you."

"I'm glad," I say, shuddering. "No one should ever be trapped like that." My relief is short-lived as I note the heaviness in his gaze. "Wait, what do you mean your immortal life? What happens if you stay unbonded?"

"I'm not sure," he admits. "My shadow beast couldn't be happier, but I'm not sure that's a good thing."

"Well, at least you're free."

"I wasn't meant to be free," he says quietly. I hear a twinge of bitterness in his words that leaves me desperate to help him.

"Is there anything I can do?"

He hesitates and says, "Accepting the mate bond would give you that same power over me."

Suddenly, his resistance makes complete sense. "I would never do that."

I glimpse a vulnerable trust in his eyes as he says, "I'm starting to believe that."

I flash him a small smile since that's all the reassurance or comfort I can give—and tuck my gloved hands into my pockets to keep from trying to offer anything more.

Maybe that's why my next words tumble out before I can stop them. "My mother would have liked you."

"What?"

"You asked me what my mother would say about you. She would have loved you. She had this way of reading a person's character. Of getting past whatever they'd done or mistakes they'd made. She saw through it to someone's heart." I glance up at him. "I promised her something before she died."

"What's that?"

"I promised I wouldn't kill innocents." He studies me with an intensity that has me looking away. "So, I would never order you to do the things your mom did," I add quietly.

When he doesn't answer, I force myself to look over at him again. When I do, I note the wry smile curving his lips.

"What?" I ask.

"You're never what I expect," he says, shaking his head. "An assassin with a code. Who would have guessed?"

"When you say it like that, you make it sound so...cute."

"It is cute."

I scowl. "I'm badass. Not cute."

"Of course, my mistake." The smile vanishes, but the amusement in his eye remains.

Off balance, I refocus on the conversation at hand. "So, you believe Uziah knows about your need to be bound to someone?" I can't quite bring myself to say the word 'master.' Nor do I let myself think about anyone commanding Legion against his will. "But how would they know?"

"That's what I'd like to find out. Very few know my secret even here, and I trust them all implicitly with that truth."

"The Crimson Roses wanted me to kill you," I point out. "That would have made a blood vow impossible."

His smirk from earlier returns with the same level of smugness. "It's cute that you still think you could have done so."

I glare at him. "It's cute that you still think I won't."

He laughs, and the mood lightens, but I'm not finished putting all these pieces together. Nor can I ignore the trust required for him to finally tell me all of this. The more of his trust he gives me, the more I want to give him in return.

"So that's why you haven't gone to the Earth realm to face them? You're afraid they'll try to bind you?"

"Not afraid," he says, eyes flashing. "Not for myself. But I won't risk you."

"Honestly, I half-expected you to sneak off in the middle of the night and go without me already."

"I've considered it," he admits, earning another glare.

"Why haven't you?"

"I had wanted to go in with more information, namely how in the hell they found out my secret, but so far, Klyn's hired tracker hasn't brought us any useful intel."

"When you do go, I'm going with you."

He doesn't answer.

"Legion," I warn. "I'm serious."

"I know," he says finally. "Okay."

"Promise me."

He scowls. "I promise to take you with me."

"Good," I say, but my worry is a dark cloud that follows me all the way home. Without a blood vow, what will become of Legion? And what happens to us when my long yet mortal life comes to an end?

Kendall is waiting for me when I step inside my room. Her expression is tight, and I immediately tense.

"What's wrong?" I ask.

"I had a vision," she says quietly.

"What was it about?"

"You. And Legion. There's something dangerous about his blood, Tori. Something people will kill for."

I sigh. "He told me about it earlier. His mom—who sounds like a real asshole by the way—used dark magic to invoke the need for him to be bound to a master if he wants to remain immortal."

"What kind of binding?"

"One that makes him subservient to whoever rules

him. Forcing him to obey their commands even against his will."

She stares at me for a beat, not quite surprised but not reassured either. "The kind of commands that lead to wiping out entire armies?" she asks quietly.

I sigh. "Yeah, pretty much."

"Gods. His own mother did that to him?"

"I know. Trust me, if I ever meet her, I'm going to show her exactly what I think of her parenting choices."

Kendall snorts. "What did Mom always say? Kill her with kindness?"

I grin. "Exactly."

Her amusement fades quickly, replaced by that same worry from before. "Well, whatever this binding is, it puts him at risk. You're not the only one being hunted, Tor."

"What did you see?" I ask. "Is it Uziah?"

"Yes, but he's not alone."

"Who else?"

"I don't know them, but... he faces them alone, Tor. And he loses."

"He's immortal," I argue. "Unkillable. He can't lose."

Her gaze is haunted as she shakes her head. "There are worse things than death for someone like him."

I shudder, thinking back to Legion's promise to take me with him. Clinging to it. Especially now. "He's not going alone," I assure her.

But she doesn't look relieved.

"Is there something else you're not telling me?" I ask.

"I think I need to go with him too."

"Absolutely not. It's way too dangerous."

"Uziah wants me," she says. "You can use that. Distract him—"

"No way. I am not using my little sister as bait."

"Listen, I know it sounds crazy, but there's something I'm supposed to do."

"Like what exactly?"

"I don't know." Her expression clouds. "The vision isn't clear."

"Of course not." I throw up my hands.

"Look, I'm trying, okay?"

I sigh. "Kendall, I'm not trying to diminish your gift. I just... I can't let you put yourself in danger. Not for this."

"What if you fail without me there?"

"Then I'll die knowing you still live here where it's safe."

She glares at me, and I brace myself for more of an argument. But she only shakes her head, no less angry but apparently not in the mood to argue as she strides for the open door.

"Something's coming," she tells me ominously. "And it's going to take all of us to beat it."

Chaya, Kendall, and Bron are a captive audience at dinner as Legion regales everyone with a very embellished version of the game right down to the moment of his victory. Klyn, who arrived just before the meal, scowls from his seat, which only adds to the others' amusement. It's the most social I've ever seen Legion, but it only makes me more concerned about the secret he shared with me earlier.

He didn't come out and say he ended the blood bond with Caius for me, but he said he did it after he met me, which tells me enough. The fact that he's waited to face the Crimson Roses—a gang he's capable of destroying with one breath of his hellfire—tells me even more.

He's vulnerable.

Kendall's vision proves it, though I don't let myself dwell on her predictions. I can't. Somewhere along the way, I began to care for the death dragon. The thought of losing him now cuts me deeper than I ever thought possible.

After dinner, Legion and Klyn close themselves in the study. For once, I don't eavesdrop. Instead, I spend the evening playing board games with Chaya, Kendall, and Bron. The kid's exhausting, endless wells of energy combined with a chatter that doesn't stop. Chaya takes it all in stride, even conjuring a small cyclone of wind that knocks Bron off his feet again and again as he tries to push through the force of it. He ends up wearing himself out from laughter more than anything else. By the time Klyn comes to collect him, I'm yawning and thinking only of sleep.

Legion walks me to my room, quiet enough that I wonder what he and Klyn spoke about. But he doesn't say.

"You were great with Bron," he tells me.

"That kid is exhausting," I say.

He chuckles. "It's a team effort to keep up with him."

"Where's his mother?" I ask.

He frowns, his gaze distant as if caught in a memory. "Leah had childbirth complications. She passed away when Bron was a few days old."

"I'm so sorry. That must be hard for Klyn. Were they mates?"

"Not fated, no. But they were clearly meant for each other. She softened his edges. Now, Bron does that. And we all do what we can to help."

"You're his family," I say, and he nods.

It's another way Tartarus has broken through all my stereotypes. The idea that the people here care this much about one another—it touches parts of me that really needed to know the world still had this kind of goodness in it. It also makes me realize I'm not the only one who will be affected if something happens to Legion.

When we get to my door, I turn to him, a sudden worry chasing off my tiredness.

"You're not going tonight."

"Going?"

"To the Earth realm," I say. "To the Crimson Roses. Promise me you're not going tonight."

"Why would you think—?"

"You and Klyn are not subtle, you know. Locking yourselves up in that room all night to plot and plan."

His mouth quirks. "Is that so? And what exactly do you think we plotted?"

Another day, his attempts to draw me into a back-and-forth like this would work. Tonight, I'm too far gone with concern. "I'm tired, Legion. Promise me you won't go tonight."

His smile vanishes. Worry lines his dark gaze. "I promise."

"Thank you." I push my door open and step inside before I can ask for more than that. "Good night."

Despite my exhaustion, sleep is not easy. Not even the relief of removing the layers of fabric covering my lethal skin is enough to relax me. After a lifetime of having only Kendall to protect, I've now apparently added Legion, Chaya, Klyn, and Bron to the list of lives I refuse to endanger. It's a weighty responsibility with no easy solutions.

I could try to make another deal maybe. Some kind of negotiation with Uziah. Though I have nothing he wants except for the things I refuse to give. Em isn't a better option. I don't even know her much less understand what sort of motivation would change her mind from taking her revenge.

Kendall's warning only makes it worse. More and more, her visions revolve around death, making it hard to see what sort of plan or choice allows us to avoid that fate. All I have is Legion's promise to cling to. He won't go without me. At least, not tonight.

Eventually, I sleep fitfully, my dreams full of poisoned deaths with no one left to protect by the time I've finished killing.

The following morning, I'm up and dressed and about to seek out breakfast when someone knocks at my door. Pulling it open, I'm surprised to see Legion.

"Hi."

"What's wrong?" he asks.

"Nothing. I just didn't expect you to knock."

He smirks, his gaze flitting lower as we both remember the eye-full he got last time he barged in on me first thing in the morning. "I like to keep you guessing."

My thoughts drift to the moment we shared in the library. A moment he hasn't tried to repeat since. Granted, it was risky as hell to do in the first place, but I can't help wanting more.

Legion clears his throat, and I realize belatedly what he must be sensing through the mate bond.

"Are you free right now?" he asks.

"Depends on why you're asking."

"Don't look so worried." He grins. "I have a surprise for you."

"Now, I'm definitely worried."

"Come on. I think you'll enjoy it."

I follow him out and through the halls until we arrive at the back doors. He holds the door for me to follow him out then pauses at the bottom of the steps.

"Close your eyes."

"Absolutely not."

"You don't trust me?"

"Not as far as I can throw you."

"That hurts. Didn't I promise to keep you safe and I have?"

"So far," I allow.

"And Kendall?"

"Maybe. But I'm not sure I can handle any more surprises for a while."

His teasing vanishes, and he says, "I would never let anything happen to you."

I don't answer. It's too much of a reminder of what kept me awake last night. I have no doubt Legion will protect me—but I'm not ready for what that might cost him.

"Close your eyes, little assassin."

This time, I do as he asks.

"Good girl. Now, give me your hand." My eyes fly open. His lips twitch. "Your gloved hand," he adds pointedly.

I shake my head but offer him my hand anyway.

"Eyes," he reminds me.

I shut them and am immediately enveloped in darkness. All I know is the sensation of his hand wrapped tightly around mine, and my entire body warms to it. He's right, he would never let anything happen to me. So, one foot in front of the other, I let him lead me ... wherever it is he's taking me.

"Now, walk this way," he says, using our joined hands to lead me into the gardens. After what feels like forever, he says, "Stop here."

I do as he asks and wait, listening to a series of creaks and rustles that suggest something other than rosebushes and ferns.

"Are you leading me into some torture chamber?" I joke.

"I guess some might call it a torture chamber," he says.

At that, nerves dance in my belly, but he never once lets go of my hand. I hear a click then another creak.

Finally, he says, "Open your eyes."

With a steadying breath, I do.

The first thing I see is a doorway pushed open as if beckoning me inside whatever structure stands before me. I look around, noting we're in the very back of the gardens just before the forest encroaches. Dark, poisoned vines crawl over the plant life, but right here where I stand, they've been cut back, and in the clearing stands a wooden structure I've never seen before.

"What is this?" I ask.

"Go inside and see for yourself."

I take a tentative step through the door he's pushed open, and my eyes widen at the number of plants that have been packed into the space. Not just any plants either. Recognition hits me as my eyes land on a familiar pot of wolfsbane. Juniper gave it to me for my birthday two years ago. Beside it is potted hemlock my father and I planted as seeds, and beyond that, several pots of brightly colored oleander that my mother got for me the last time we went shopping together.

I take another step then another until I reach the back of the greenhouse and spot the stack of notebooks and journals set out on the small desk in the corner. My eyes well with tears at the unexpected gesture that speaks volumes in so many ways.

I whirl and find Legion standing in the doorway.

"These are my father's journals," I say.

"Yes."

"And my plants."

"Yes."

"How?"

"I brought them here."

"You left? But you promised—"

"I didn't seek out a single Crimson Rose. I kept my promise."

"You could have been captured," I say.

"But I wasn't."

I want to argue, to unleash the mountain of fear at the idea of him being in the Earth realm alone. In my backyard, no less. But the magnitude of the gesture makes it hard to hold onto my anger.

"I know it's not the same as being at home in your workshop, but hopefully it helps."

I stare at him, not even sure he's the same person as

the smug as hell, self-centered dragon who first came to my backyard and demanded I tell him how desperate I was for him.

"Is it okay?" he asks when I don't say anything.

I swallow hard against the lump in my throat. "Yes," I somehow manage to say without crying. "It's very much okay."

He exhales, suddenly looking far less tense than before.

I offer him a small smile, my heart pounding even though he's standing well out of reach. "This is the nicest thing anyone's ever done for me."

His mouth quirks. "I see. Saving your life is insignificant compared to gifting you with a greenhouse full of potted poisons."

"Funny. But yes. I guess that's how I rank kindness."

His dark gaze glitters. "And how do you reward such kindness?"

He hasn't made a single move toward me, yet I feel him intensely as if he were standing in my personal space. The reality that this is as close as we can ever be is like a bucket of cold water.

I blink, hope draining away like the tide. "I guess we'll never know."

LEGION

In the small hours of the morning, I stalk through my quiet house like an angry shadow. Sleepless hours passed with me lying in bed, but when my erection became too painful with no satisfying release in sight, I got up and wandered. Thoughts of Tori have me on edge. The memory of her expression, when I showed her the greenhouse yesterday, is an image that will forever be etched into my mind.

Her emotional reaction drove my beast to near-madness. I left her alone under the guise of letting her work and spent the day hiding in my study. I'm caught between needing to flee her presence and refusing to leave her alone.

It's nearly dawn now, and there is not a room in this house where I don't feel her presence. Somewhere along the way, I stopped hating the bond. I stopped hating her.

What I feel... Even if I could put it into words, I don't know how to tell her. Not without admitting this last secret I've kept. The one that would ruin her toward me forever. Giving her that greenhouse full of poisons was the only way I could think of to show her how much she means to me. But even that ended on a sour note.

I've never wanted a thing I couldn't have before.

And I've never wanted anything more than I want her.

But having her is impossible.

Even if we found a way to break the curse, it would undoubtedly involve telling her where the thing came from in the first place. And I know Tori well enough by now to know that kind of betrayal would break us... irreparably.

Keeping her here with me—and keeping her cursed —is the most selfish thing I've ever done. But the guilt has never been so heavy as when she looked at me in that greenhouse and wanted me. In that moment, without the curse, she would have been mine.

Instead, I'm here, in my study, drinking whiskey at five in the morning, and daydreaming about killing things just to cheer myself up. But maybe it doesn't have to remain a daydream. The Crimson Roses are still out there, which means they are still a threat to my mate.

Klyn's tracker has yet to return with useful intel, but I'm done waiting. My shadow beast needs an outlet. Maybe when Tori is safe, the madness will be bearable. Or maybe it's the madness that drives me to decide.

I down the last of the whiskey I'd poured and set the glass aside, heading for the launch pad. My thoughts drift to Klyn. He'll want to know I've left, but now that I'm on the move, I can't bring myself to delay long enough to tell him.

My shadow beast drives me onward, and I let him.

Outside, the morning air bites my cheeks, but the chill is refreshing to my senses. It'll feel even better against my scales.

I'm nearly through the gardens when I see the familiar silhouette. Still, even though I recognize Tori immediately, I falter in confusion at seeing her out here so early. She's wrapped in a thick cloak that clings to her curves despite its bulk. My heart lurches at the sight of her, my feelings even stronger than my physical desire. I shove them all aside as I approach.

"I didn't realize you were awake."

She crosses her arms, looking defiant. "You thought you could sneak out before I woke up?"

"I'm not sneaking anywhere," I say. "This is my house."

"In that case, you don't mind me tagging along."

I frown. "You don't even know where I'm going."

"Then why don't you tell me?" she asks.

Her expression makes it clear she's already guessed. It takes me a moment to figure out how she knows.

The mate bond.

Fuck.

"You're staying here," I tell her firmly.

Her eyes flash with fury though it doesn't surprise me. "You promised me you'd let me come."

"I also promised to keep you safe. That promise is more important."

"No. You don't get to justify this. And you don't get to break your vow to me."

Any other day, her temper would turn me on. Today, it only feeds my determination. "It's too dangerous."

"But not for you?" I start to reply, but she cuts me off. "Kendall had a vision about you." She pauses and then adds, "She saw you go alone, and it ends in you losing."

"Those visions are subjective of a thousand different choices along the way."

"Fuck, Legion." She throws up her hands. "If you aren't going to care about living through this, at least care what your death would do to me. We might not be claimed mates yet, but if you died, I probably would too."

If she'd yelled it, the words would have cut less than they do as she delivers them quietly.

I hate the pain in her eyes that goes with them.

Seeing it weakens my resolve. She's right. I wouldn't survive losing her either. I'm barely surviving resisting her, and I'm only doing that because touching her would kill me. Otherwise, I would have claimed her as mine long before this moment.

"I don't plan to die for you," I tell her. "Not unless there's no other choice left for me. Believe me, little assassin, I want very much to live for you instead. To find a way to touch you. And claim you. And make you mine like I'm already yours. That is why I'm going to end this today."

She exhales, her expression softening at my words. "I want a mate who lets me fight beside him." Her mouth curves in a devious smile. "I also want to fight you but only because I love when we make up."

I flash a small smile at that but shake my head. "Using your gift causes you pain, remember?"

"Then I won't use it."

My brows lift at that.

She rolls her eyes. "Fine. I might. But I'll try not to. Look." She holds up her hands to show the gloves covering every inch of skin.

"Your face," I say.

She pulls something out of her pocket. When she pulls it over her head, I see that it's not a scarf but a sheer mask shaped perfectly to her face.

"Where did you get that?" I ask.

"Chaya got it for me. Apparently, she understands I should be part of this."

I ignore her attempt to bait me. Instead, I focus on the mask that will only make her more vulnerable. The damned thing covers every inch of her face, including her eyes.

"You're willing to fight blind?" I ask.

She shoves her gloved hand out, driving a punch straight into my gut.

I grunt, my muscles tensing too late. It doesn't hurt exactly, but she makes her point anyway. "Not blind, apparently."

"Not blind," she confirms, stepping back.

I can hear the smugness in her tone.

She crosses her arms again, feet planted as if she's bracing for a fight.

"If you say no, I'll find my own way," she adds.

"Yes, I have no doubt about that." I shake my head. Short of tying her up, I can't make her stay put. And letting her face the Crimson Roses alone is not something I'm willing to do.

"All right, little assassin. But I won't carry you like prey this time."

She eyes me warily. "What does that mean?"

"It means, this time, you'll ride on my back." I can't help the darkly delicious thoughts that follow my statement. Or the wink I give her when I add, "Until such time you can ride my front, that is. Now, come on. Daybreak is here, and I intend to hunt a Crimson Rose for breakfast."

She shudders at my words, though I don't know if it's my promise to let her ride my cock someday or my vow to kill her enemies that's caused her blood to stir. Either way, I strip, dropping my clothes to the ground at my feet and calling my beast to the surface before I can distract us both with any more empty words.

Being airborne is not an experience I want to repeat, but I'm done sitting around. So, I spent all night making my peace with the necessary evil of being carried through the skies like a sack of potatoes, only to be faced with the idea of riding on his back instead. Even the sight of Legion shifting and becoming a giant black-scaled dragon isn't enough to distract me from the mental image of me riding him... in every way imaginable.

By the time he looks down at me with those glowing orange eyes, I know my face is flushed, and my core aches with a need that's been unfulfilled for way too long. His nostrils flare, and I realize he's scented my desire.

Ugh.

I am instantly grateful for the mask I'm forced to wear. That's a first.

"Let's hurry up and get this over with," I say.

The dragon snorts, and hot air washes over me. His

size and sense of power are intimidating, but I know with absolute certainty Legion would never hurt me. When he responds by lowering himself to his belly so I can climb on, the gesture alone earns a new level of trust. He's willing to make himself vulnerable. That means something.

His scales are smooth beneath my hands, but I'm careful to avoid the row of spikes as I climb up to his back and settle there. With gloved hands, I grab onto the raised row of scales behind his head and call out, "Ready."

Only then does he slowly push to his feet.

I look down at the ground, already feeling a little unsteady at how far up I am. But then his large wings spread, beating downward to create a powerful draft of air. Then he walks over to the cliff's edge—and steps off it.

For a harrowing moment, my stomach lurches into my throat, and a silent scream sticks in my open mouth as we freefall. Slowly, I realize we're not falling exactly as Legion angles us so that we're coasting slowly downward.

Semantics.

The effect on my stomach is the same either way.

My hands grip tightly to the raised scales as I try very hard not to throw up. My body tilts as his scales suddenly become slick with the moisture in the air. Panic slams into me as I imagine myself sliding right off his back and plummeting to the ground.

In the midst of my panic, he levels out his body, pointing his nose straight ahead. On either side, his wings beat powerfully once, twice, and then we're soaring. As the minutes tick by, thrill replaces fear, though I'm not sure I'm ready to admit, even to myself, that I might actually like flying.

And I certainly don't plan to admit it to him.

Sooner than I expect, he banks gently as we near the ground again. Up ahead, is an open hillside that slopes up toward a castle that's even larger than Legion's estate. A wall wraps around it, but the gate in the front stands open, and even from here, I can see a small amount of foot traffic passing in and out of the gate.

On the left, a small portion of the wall has been demolished. I realize this must be Caius' castle. The explosion Reagan mentioned left its mark.

Legion lands on the hillside with surprising grace. I do my best to match that grace as I climb down, but in the end, I'm just lucky not to fall on my ass. My knees are a bit weak from the adrenaline, so I'm glad for the moment to collect myself as Legion wanders off to shift again.

When I look up, he's pulling on a pair of pants I didn't even know he had. My gaze snags on the perfect V of his hips just before he pulls the waist up and buttons them. I look up and find him watching me. Again, thank the gods for this stupid mask. And the wind for carrying off my scent, hopefully.

"You okay?" he asks, infuriatingly smug.

"Where did you get the clothes?" I can't help but ask.

"I carried them in my teeth. You were probably too distracted by me taking them off in the first place to notice."

I do my best not to react to how right he is. "Let's go."

I stalk off down the hill, but Legion's large hand wraps around my arm, and he pulls me to the left, chuckling.

"This way."

"The portal is over there," I say. "I remember coming through it when we arrived."

"Yes, but we're going to make a stop first."

"What kind of stop?"

"You'll see."

I have no choice but to keep up with his brisk pace. By the time we reach the bottom of the hill, the people nearby begin to notice us. Soldiers mostly. Some in uniform, some not—but they all pause to salute Legion.

I get several weird looks thanks to my face covering, but I don't dare take it off with so many others around. The closer we get to the large building looming ahead, the more nervous I become at the idea of a crowded space.

When Legion holds open the door for me to enter, I hesitate.

"What's wrong?" he asks.

"Everyone will stare," I whisper.

He pins me with a look that's both fierce and comforting as he says, "Let them."

I step through the door, and Legion follows, grabbing my gloved hand as he takes the lead down the hallway. On both sides, we pass doors, some of them open but most closed. The ones that are open offer a glimpse into an office, each of them empty, which makes sense considering how early it is.

Near the far end, an open doorway leads to a large conference room, but Legion doesn't stop until we come to the main doors. There, a large reception area features a high counter, and behind it, a male in uniform springs to his feet at the sight of us.

"General." He salutes Legion, casting me a wary look.

"At ease, Whitman," Legion says. "Where's Klyn?"

"Not here yet, sir."

"Thanks. As you were."

Legion tugs my hand, and we continue past the confused guard through a side door that Legion unlocks with his hand print.

"Sir, is she—"

The guard's voice is lost as the door closes behind us, sealing us inside a low-lit hallway. The doors are all equipped with scanners for entry, but Legion bypasses the first few.

"Where are we?" I ask as he stops in front of a door halfway down and presses his palm to the scanner.

The lock disengages, and Legion motions for me to enter.

I have no idea what I was expecting, but a large room containing wall-to-wall weapons is not it. I stare open-mouthed at the rows of daggers, short-swords, and various other uniquely deadly items.

"Is this the entire army's weapons cache?" I ask.

"This?" Legion turns back from where he's crossed to a small keypad. He frowns at me. "No. This is just for the officers."

"Damn." I whistle. "I guess joining organized crime has its perks."

His mouth quirks. "Crime, huh? I thought the army was for defending its leaders."

I lift a brow. "Isn't Tartarus a prison world?"

He goes back to punching in some code. A second later, a click sounds, and another display wall is revealed. This one isn't full of weapons though, and I immediately take a step back.

"No fucking way."

Legion grabs an armored breastplate off the wall. When he swings his gaze back to mine, there's a full fire blazing in his eyes. "No fucking way you're going without it."

He takes a step toward me.

I take a step back.

"I'm not wearing that."

"You're wearing this and this," he says, pausing again to snatch a thigh plate off the wall as he comes for me. "Or you're not going."

My back hits the closed door, and I glare up at him. "You planned this," I accuse. "Bringing me here and forcing me to wear this crap. It's why you agreed to let me come so easily."

"The fact that you thought I'd let you just walk right into what I have planned for those monsters, without so much as a steel plate of protection strapped to your body, is remarkably naïve, little assassin."

"Exactly," I say. "*Assassin*. I'm scary. And dangerous. I don't need all this showy shit. It'll only slow me down."

"Hold this," he growls.

He shoves the breastplate at me. When I don't take it, he bares his teeth and says, "Just fucking hold it."

I snatch the breastplate, letting it dangle in my hands. He grasps the edges and lifts it so that the breastplate is held flat against my torso. Then he backs away five paces and snatches a bow off the wall.

Before I realize what he intends, he's taken an arrow out of the quiver, notched it, and let it fly. It slams into the breastplate hard enough to vibrate my wrists painfully before the steel-tipped arrow clatters to the ground at my feet.

In the silence, I stare at Legion, not sure whether to scream or fight or just walk out. "You just shot me."

"It's not for show," he says simply.

"You just shot me," I repeat through clenched teeth. My temper is like molten lava poured through my veins. How did I ever think this asshole was nice?

"You wear the armor, or you stay here."

"Or go alone," I say, dropping the breastplate and turning for the door.

His hand closes over my arm, pulling me back to face him. I yank away from his grip and look up at him. His eyes are blazing almost as brightly as they do when he's in his dragon form.

"I wasn't asking," he says in a deadly quiet voice.

"I don't take orders from you, *General*."

Whatever power I think my temper holds is nothing compared to the way he stares at me now. "I'm not ordering as your general. You are not a mere soldier to me, little assassin. You are so much more than that. You are the breath in my lungs. The beat of my heart. If you are injured or—"

He stops, his breathing ragged, his eyes blazing with an intensity I feel in my core.

"Just wear the armor, love."

Love.

I am not proud of the way my knees weaken and my heart skips a beat at the silly nickname. Nor am I proud of the way my ovaries practically hum inside me. I should be better than this, and yet...

"Fine."

His lips twitch almost imperceptibly. I tell myself it's a sign that I've pleased him—not that I want to—and not him just being smug as fuck about winning the argument.

The armor is surprisingly light and easy to move in, thanks to whatever magic has been woven into the material. I don't dare admit that to Legion, who stands surveying his work once everything is strapped into place. Finally, he grunts, which apparently is alphahole code for "looks good."

"Happy?" I ask.

His eyes snap up from my thigh coverings to meet my stare. The gleam from earlier returns. "If I say no, what will you do about it?"

My stomach flips at all the ideas that spring to mind. Ideas that are all impossible or lethal at the moment. "Take it all off," I say, knowing full well that would only make him suffer.

. . .

"I look forward to the day I can call in that dare," he says, and my heart tugs wistfully as I let myself imagine it.

He reaches above my head, pulling down a sword and its belt that are mounted to the wall. I watch as he straps it to his waist then starts for the door.

"Whoa, where do you think you're going?" I demand.

"We need to get moving if we're—"

"Are you going in this form then?"

"I want to be able to stick close to you."

"What about your armor?"

Impatience flashes in his gaze. "I hardly need—"

"If I have to wear this crap, so do you."

"Tori."

"Why did you insist I wear this?"

"Because I need you to be safe."

"Exactly. I deserve the same thing."

"You do know I'm immortal, right?"

"You do know my sister's visions are reliable, right?"

He looks ready to argue, but after a heavy sigh, he turns around and grabs a chest plate from the wall. I watch as he straps it on, followed by a few more pieces.

When he's done, he's not nearly as covered as I am, but it's enough.

"Satisfied?" he asks.

The gleam in his eye is either a sexual innuendo—again—or a way of baiting me into another argument. I don't trust myself in either scenario.

"Let's just get going," I mutter, turning for the door.

His chuckle is quiet at my back.

I ignore it and march out the way we came in. When we emerge into the lobby again, a few people are entering through the main doors. They salute Legion and glance uncertainly at me.

Legion leads me past them and out the doors. Outside, he sets a brisk pace down a walkway that leads straight toward the castle gates. We pass more soldiers as we go, each of them with a salute for Legion and a curious stare aimed at me.

"Am I going to get into trouble for wearing this?" I ask as we walk.

"Are you worried about being punished?" he asks with no small amount of enjoyment written on his features.

I scowl. "I'm already in hell. Not sure what more you guys could do to me."

"Oh, I have lots of ideas."

I don't have an answer for that one, so we walk in silence, passing through the gate with barely a word exchanged between Legion and the guards. As we get closer to the castle, we encounter more guards and more salutes.

"Sir," several murmur with respect and admiration reflected in their expression.

I get more stares.

Likely wondering who the masked warrior is beside their beloved General.

But no one stops us, and soon enough, we're through the portal and out the other side into the Crossroads. It's deserted here other than the Tartarus guards posted at the portal entrance.

One of them is a woman Legion addresses as Clara. After a quick conversation that involves several dubious glances from her, he breaks off and returns to my side.

"What is it?" Legion asks as we leave the fountain and head for my house. The area is a lot more deserted than I expected. Dead trees and a lack of grass surround the entire portal area. Coating it all is a layer of blackened char marking a clear perimeter where the portal magic has infected our realm. Even the fountain is now stained black.

Tartarus guards keep a watchful eye on it all, making sure no Crossroads citizens come into contact with the dark magic residue.

"I'm surprised," I say, "I thought the portal would have drawn more folks by now."

"Tartarus is being very selective about those they allow to pass through. Clara has guards keeping people outside the perimeter of the portal's magic. We don't want anyone else infected or hurt."

I glance up at him and find a hard expression. "Did something happen?"

He glances at me then back to the road, his watchful gaze scrutinizing everyone we pass.

"Legion?"

He cuts me a look as if I've interrupted some distracting thought. "No."

"Reagan told me about the explosion," I say.

He looks at me, surprised, but then nods. "We hunted down those responsible."

"Yes, I heard you're second best at interrogation."

"Who— Styx."

"Yeah." I smirk at his scowl, but my smile fades

quickly. "She said you got the name of the guy who set it all up."

"I did what had to be done."

A shadow passes over his expression. It's a glimpse behind the mask of the death dragon. One of so many he's shown me so far. He doesn't enjoy hurting others. But he also won't hesitate if it means protecting the ones he cares about.

He doesn't want to kill innocents either, I realize.

"Good," I say, drawing a look of surprise from him. "I'm glad you're keeping people safe."

He doesn't answer, but I can feel him relax at my acceptance.

We walk a bit in silence.

My armor earns me stares from the people we pass. I do my best to ignore them, but it feels strange to be back here. Like a lifetime has passed in my absence. Maybe that's because, even in such a short amount of time, I've changed, but this world hasn't.

"Are you sure about stopping at my house first?" I ask. "You said you were here the other night and you didn't run into anyone. Maybe they aren't watching the place after all."

"They're watching."

He doesn't meet my gaze.

"Legion," I say, my tone a warning.

His expression tightens, and he continues to look straight ahead as he says, "I may have been inaccurate with the details of my visit."

"Inaccurate," I repeat, glaring daggers at his cheek.

He glances at me then away again. "There may have

been a couple of other visitors during my time collecting your plants. And I may have neutralized them."

"Do you think this vague military-speak is going to trick me into not being pissed at you?" I ask.

He looks over at me, an evil grin playing at the corners of his mouth. "I had hoped."

"How many?"

He sighs. "Three."

"And what did you do with the bodies?"

He shrugs. "I left them. They deserve to bury their own dead. I can't do it all."

I don't know what to say to that.

My temper cools as I realize, even more important than his omission—lie, technically—is the fact that he's right. It's daylight, which means the club will be empty. Vamps don't love the sun, but it won't stop them either. Letting them come to us is the smartest play. Going home will be like sending up a bat signal to let the Crimson Roses know where we are.

"We're going to talk about this later," I grumble.

Legion has the audacity to wink. "I look forward to it."

When my house comes into view, emotion slams into me. Grief weighs heavily as my gaze darts toward the backyard—the last place I saw Juniper.

I make my way toward the front door, glad to bypass the backyard and all its memories. Beside me, Legion tenses. There's no visible change in our surroundings, but I somehow just know he's poised and ready for anything. It reassures me.

When we reach the front porch, Legion grabs my arm.

"I'm going in first," he says, daring me to argue.

But since I already know how that will go, I simply wave him through. He gives me a smug smirk before proceeding. His large frame fills the entire doorway, making it impossible to see whether a threat stands on the other side. But when he doesn't yell or launch himself into an attack, I exhale, assuming the way is clear.

He stalks slowly through the house, but I linger in the foyer, inhaling the scent of home and staring around at a house full of things that bring back so many memories. Tears burn my eyes. Juniper may not have lived here, but I see reminders of her everywhere I look.

A photo of her and Kendall grinning at the camera from last Christmas. A throw blanket she brought over when I had a cold the year after my mother died. Her artwork hanging above the couch. A lump forms in my throat, and I blink back the tears that threaten to overtake the senses I know should remain on alert for threats.

I end up in my bedroom, my gaze sweeping the space for anything important I might need. A tiny vial sits on my dresser, and I swipe it, tucking it into my pocket just as Legion returns from his sweep of the house.

"All clear," he says.

I'm glad again for the mask that hides my emotions, but somehow he knows because he closes the distance, his hand coming up to cup my cheek in a surprisingly affectionate gesture.

"It's all right to be sad," he says quietly.

"How do you know I'm sad?"

"Because I feel it. Through the bond."

"I miss Juniper."

"She fought bravely."

"She was a warrior," I agree. "In her way. Like my mother. They were against violence and death, but they were fierce."

"That must be where you get it from."

My chin comes up in defiance, which is stupid considering everything. "Don't forget that I actually have killed though."

"You may have taken life, but you are not a killer. There's a difference."

Unlike before, this time when he says it, there's no judgment. In fact, it's admiration I see reflected in his dark gaze.

A noise comes from the backyard, and I tense.

Legion whirls toward the back door, already moving. I follow, chasing him through the kitchen and out the door into the yard. I catch a flurry of movement near the trees—a figure disappearing at the edge of the charred yard—and Legion races after them.

I start to follow but stop when the scent of blood hits me. It comes from the direction of my workshop, and I look over to find the door hanging open. Even from here, I can see it's empty of plants. The plants Legion carried from here all the way to his home in Tartarus—for me.

But the scent of blood is strong, so I follow it, stepping into the shadowed interior. In the back of the space, on the floor, is a body lying prone in a pool of blood that's slowly saturating the wooden plank flooring.

Whatever happened is still fresh. My heart squeezes as I approach.

I crouch, peering below the worktable, and gasp at the sight of Chase Lanson, the elf Kendall had a crush on. Rounding the table quickly, I lean down beside him, hoping to find a pulse. But his throat is nearly gone, ripped messily open by narrow slashes that look a hell of a lot like teeth marks.

Fangs, actually.

Vampires did this.

My eyes catch on something on the floor nearby. I pull off the fabric covering on my face and stare at it, my stomach tightening into knots.

A crimson rose.

Legion appears in the doorway, his eyes burning with intensity.

"Did you catch them?" I ask, pushing to my feet.

"I let one go to deliver our message," he says in a deadly promise. "What is it?"

"Chase Lanson." I swallow hard. "Kendall's friend. He must have come looking for her when she didn't show up to school. Gods, he's only a teenager. And now he's dead." I hold up the flower. "With a crimson rose left behind."

Legion's dark eyes blaze with contempt. "They will pay for his life. Come on."

I follow him out, glad for the fresh air, inhaling gulps to clear the chaos buzzing inside me. But I don't keep going like I know he wants. When he sees I'm not following, he turns back, impatience flashing.

"He died because of me," I say, still trying to process all of it.

The dead elf.

The calling card I know only belongs to one person.

And it's not Em.

"No," Legion says roughly. "He died because of evil creatures who think they can destroy without consequence."

"This rose... it's Uziah's thing. He told me once it was the mark of the leader. He went on and on about it too, spouting some elitist bullshit." Legion doesn't answer, letting me process it. "Do you think they mistook him for me? He was in the workshop..."

"I think Uziah wanted to get your attention. To make you come looking for him."

He's right. I can feel it. That's why the crimson rose was left behind. So I would know. So I would come for him.

I square my shoulders. "Then that's what we'll do."

The dead male in Tori's workshop is a message. It's also exactly why I didn't want to bring Tori along. But she's the only one of us who knows where this club is. And even though I can see the need for vengeance in her green eyes, I have no intention of letting her get close enough to carry it out. Uziah and his gang of monsters will burn today.

We take Tori's car, which is uncomfortably small, forcing me to bend and bunch my knees toward my chest just to fit into the seat. It earns a snort from Tori, which I decide is worth it—right up until the moment she enters the flow of traffic on a busy road. The terror of allowing her full control behind the wheel of this contraption is unmatched in my long life.

She glances over at me, but my eyes remain glued to the path before us as if my watching it unfold can somehow prevent certain death.

"You good?" she asks, and I can hear the laughter in her voice.

"That depends," I say as she guns it and dodges past another vehicle that is apparently going too slow for her liking. I grip the armrest. "How many times have you crashed?"

"None," she says as if offended. "How many times have you?"

I drag my gaze from the road and glare at her. "None."

She smirks despite the gravity of what we're about to do. "Are you scared?"

"No." I look back at the road.

She snorts. "Imagine how I felt when you carried me into the air that first time."

Finally, we leave the busy streets behind. Fewer cars and even less foot traffic line the roadway here. I tell myself that means we're less likely to accordion this hunk of metal against another.

Eventually, we pull into an empty gravel lot and park. I study the large building with blackened windows. The sign above the door says Bite Club.

I climb out of the car, glad to be done with it, and survey the surroundings. It's quiet but not peaceful. There's a forgotten or sinister energy to the rows of houses that line the street across from us. Several windows are boarded over. All of the lights are out.

A cloud-coated sky blots out the sun of this realm, casting a gloom over everything. Despite that, Bite Club looks to be in decent shape with newer repairs.

There's money here.

And power.

The unspoken kind.

The kind that does what it wants, caring for no one outside its own walls.

The kind that has betrayed and threatened my mate.

I look over and find her staring up at the club, the mask dangling in her hand. Her shoulders are set, but her expression sends a dagger straight through my heart. She has had almost no one to turn to in this world for far too long. And the vampire she once considered an ally has made her circle one less.

I will kill him for it.

"Put your mask on," I tell her as gently as I can, given the bloodlust pouring through me now.

My dragon is a shadow beast out for vengeance. The lack of a mate bond or a blood oath only makes him more chaotic. But at least, my will is my own. I cannot be stopped and I cannot kill anyone or anything I don't choose to.

Today, I will destroy everything that has hurt her, and I'll do it with zero regret. Still, it's a strain to keep from giving into the bloodlust and completely losing myself to the fight. Doing so would mean risking Tori's safety even further, so I leash the beast as best I can.

Thankfully, she does as I ask. The armor is still in place, but I reach over and double-check the fastenings for good measure. Then I unsheathe her dagger and shove it into her gloved hands.

"Promise me you won't touch them," I say, thinking of Broca's warning about what will happen if she drains herself.

"I'll try, but if they—"

"Promise me."

She stares back at me. Even through the mask, I can feel her irritation. But she doesn't argue. "I promise."

I exhale and then take the biggest risk of all. I lean over and kiss her through the fabric mask.

She jerks back, gasping and wrenching herself several steps out of my reach.

A moment passes, and I know we're both waiting to see if I went too far.

But I feel fine.

A second later, I close the distance and kiss her again, this time grabbing her tightly enough that she can't escape.

She doesn't try to.

Instead, she leans in, pressing her covered body against mine. Her lips are yielding and demanding. The kiss is warm, stirring my blood and my cock, but it's not the access I need. Not with the layer of fabric between us.

I want more of her.

I want all of her.

Forever.

I step back, holding her gaze. Up close, I can just barely make out her eyes on mine. There's an emotion in them I can't read. And we don't have time. Not yet.

After...

"Come," I say, turning for the club entrance. "When we get inside, stay behind me."

She lets me lead, and my dragon is all too pleased with himself at her display of trust.

The front door is locked. I half-expect some kind of charm spell to strengthen against intruders, but a hard shove snaps the lock free, and the door swings open.

I hesitate, unsure whether they're the stupidest vamps ever or smarter than I'm giving credit with some kind of latent alarm system I'm not expecting.

A slow, deliberate step inside proves it's both.

A screech splits the air, and a blur of something solid though small careens toward me. Stringy hair hangs in the face of alabaster skin.

I draw my sword, slicing through flesh and bone as if it were paper. The banshee goes silent, dead and in pieces at my feet.

"What the hell is that?" Tori takes a solid step away from the remains that are currently leaking viscous fluid onto the floor. The air fills with the scent of rot and brimstone.

"It's a nightmare," I say quietly, my stomach swirling with sick recognition. Suddenly, the idea of simply burning this place to ash is not enough.

I need answers before I can do that.

"What's a nightmare?"

"It's a kind of spell or charm made by a demon. This one was fashioned as a banshee, but they can come in any form, shape, or size, depending on the power the creator wields. They're used as deterrents or alarm systems as they're not very powerful, but they distract well enough."

I take another look around with fresh eyes.

"I've never even heard of them."

"That's because they aren't from this realm."

"How the hell did it get here?"

"That's a great question," I say. And not one I'm going to like the answer to. "Stay close."

I make my way slowly through the empty club, careful to stay ahead of Tori. The silence after the screaming is unsettling. Or maybe that's my own trepidation at finding a demon-made creature here in this place.

A creature I've seen a million times before.

My heart hammers at the idea that, after all this time, all the searching—

In the darkness, a figure moves through a narrow opening at the back wall and steps into the room. Broad shoulders draped in a suit. A swath of dark hair combed into submission. Sharp, crimson eyes.

He is middle-aged in appearance, but my senses tell me he's much older than that. His pale skin is deceivingly fragile-looking. I know better.

"Hello, Legion. We've been waiting for you, son."

CHAPTER 30

TORI

The sight of Uziah sends rage coursing through me. Juniper's face flashes in my mind followed by Chase's body lying dead on my workshop floor. The people Uziah hurt deserve justice. I grip my knife tighter, on the verge of shoving past Legion and burying the blade in his chest until his heart is free of his body. But his words to Legion stop me in my tracks.

Son?

"Who are you?" Legion asks in a low voice.

He is absolutely still, a snake coiled and ready to strike.

"I am Uziah Jafarov, your father."

My jaw drops, thankfully covered by the mask I'm wearing.

Legion's eyes narrow in disbelief. "My father was a god, and you are hardly that."

"There are many names for an ancient like me. God, Original, First One," he says. "It is all the same."

Legion's body trembles, and I realize he's holding back rage, though barely. "You're lying."

"I have lied to others in my life, but not to you."

"Bullshit," I say, stepping forward so that I'm shoulder-to-shoulder with Legion. He doesn't stop me; a sign of his shock. I glare at Uziah and tell him, "Legion doesn't drink blood. He has no vampire qualities. He can't possibly have come from you."

"The vampires you have come to know in your modern world are not like me," Uziah says, though his attention remains on Legion. "I am much older than this realm. Created by the primordial magic of the first portal to connect the realms. I sustain myself on life force. In this world, in this age, I do that with blood. But I am not the same as these other creatures. I am Timeless. I am a First One. Raw power runs in my blood. And yours, boy."

Legion is silent beside me.

I have no idea if he believes this nonsense, but I refuse to pretend he's telling the truth. "This is crazy. You have zero proof to back up anything you're saying. You're the leader of a gang, for hell's sake."

Rather than contradict my words, he looks me up and down, noting my covered skin. "Hiding your best gifts, I see. Nothing has changed then."

"Your men killed my friend," I say, anger spearing through me. "And an innocent kid. Don't deny it was you. I saw the rose."

"I'm not denying anything."

"After assuring me you had nothing to do with the Roses who put the bounty on me," I say with disgust. "You pretended to help me, offered me that deal to hunt down the one who did this in exchange for my survival. The whole thing was a setup. You betrayed me. Betrayed my father's trust in you."

His eyes flash with the first hint of anger. "Your father understood business comes first. Something you do not. Though, I must say I appreciate your willingness to mix business with pleasure." He glances at Legion. "You've gone and brought my true quarry right to my doorstep."

Confusion clouds my anger. "How could you possibly know I'd meet Legion? Much less bring him to you?"

"From the moment you came to me with poisoned skin, I recognized the signs," Uziah says.

"The signs?" I echo, still trying to understand how he made the connection.

"Tell me how to break the curse," Legion says.

"You know I can't do that." Uziah looks at Legion with a hunger that lacks any trace of humanity. Like Legion is nothing more than an object to obtain.

"I don't understand," I say, "How does Uziah know —" but Legion interrupts.

"You wanted me; I'm here," he snarls. "Now let her go and call off the bounty." He turns to me and adds, "Drive to the portal. The guards will get Klyn and he'll—"

"Legion, no," I start, but Uziah interrupts.

"One condition," the vampire says.

"Name it," Legion snaps.

"Give me your blood oath."

"What?" I say at the same time Legion snarls, "No."

Something passes between the two men that I don't understand, but there's no time to ask.

"It's time to leave." Legion grabs me, yanking me toward the door at our backs.

Confused, I let him pull me along, glancing back at Uziah. He stands alone in the dark club, watching us go, though I highly doubt there aren't hordes of Crimson Roses waiting in the wings. Still, we can't just leave without finishing this.

At the door, I plant my feet and wrench my arm out of Legion's grasp. "What are you doing? We can't walk away," I hiss. "He'll just keep coming after us—and killing innocents."

"We'll find another way," Legion says, his voice strained.

"Your mother sends her best, you know."

Uziah's voice rings out, and I watch as Legion stiffens. He looks back at Uziah, a flicker of concern flashing in his blazing eyes. My shock leaves me speechless, but not Legion. In fact, he doesn't look surprised at all.

"Where is she?" Legion asks warily.

"She ran an errand," Uziah says, his smile smug. "She'll be so pleased to see you. We've spent eons waiting for that portal to open."

"We?" Legion echoes dubiously.

"Your mother contacted me after you were imprisoned. She asked for my help bringing you back to her side, and I agreed. It's time for you to take your place in this family."

"I will never do her bidding again," Legion snarls.

He shoves me toward the door, but Uziah calls out

again. "You can't have her, you know. The curse forbids it."

This time, I'm the one stiffening and rounding on the vampire. "What do you know about my curse?"

Uziah looks quickly between us, and the smugness that settles around him is impossible to miss. He looks at Legion like I'm not the one addressing him and says, "You haven't told her?"

"Told me what?" I demand.

Legion doesn't answer.

I look back at Uziah, who appears all too eager to fill me in.

"Legion's mother laced his blood with a curse. If he should ever meet his fated mate, Maricha's magic would leave them unable to touch. Unable to complete their bond." Uziah's gaze hardens as he says to Legion, "The only blood bond you will have is with me or your mother. The sooner you accept it, the safer she will be."

I look between them, horrified. "Your mother cast this curse on me?"

Legion doesn't answer, but the guilt that flashes in his depthless eyes is all the confirmation I need.

"And you knew?" I accuse.

"Yes." His voice his hoarse, his eyes refusing to meet mine.

"This is what you meant that night with Klyn. About your bloodline. You've known and kept it from me. Trying to make me doubt what I've suspected all along." Rage, betrayal, fear—my stomach swirls with all of it. "I'm going to be sick," I whisper.

Legion watches me warily, but I don't give him the

satisfaction of my attention. I drag my gaze back to Uziah, and the triumphant look he wears reconfirms that his claims are true.

"You asked me to deliver him," I say flatly. "I have. Our dealings are done. If I see a single member of the Crimson Roses, I will kill them. We are done, do you understand me?"

Uziah waves me off. "Whatever you say, little assassin."

"Don't call me that," I growl, and then I walk out.

Legion follows me, but I refuse to look at him as I walk to my car. When I get there, I stop and turn to him, hating that he has the nerve to look sorry for his lies.

"Tor—"

"Don't," I snap. "You don't get to say anything, and you definitely don't get to apologize. You knew your mother did this to me, and you lied about it. We're done."

"I didn't know," he says quickly. "When we met, I didn't know about the curse."

"When?" I demand. "When did you know?"

He hesitates. "The day the glaistig came to the Keep," he says quietly. "She told me the curse came from my bloodline. I figured it had to be my mother. Her way of keeping me trapped and bonded to only her."

"And you didn't think I needed to know? It made me a target."

"I wanted you to..."

"What? To fall for you? To trust you?" I snort. "Look at how that turned out."

He starts to respond, but I block him out, wrenching

open my car door and climbing inside. The moment I do, I hit the locks.

He frowns in at me. "You can't go out there alone. It's not safe."

"Watch me," I say through the window, hating that he's probably right.

I'm not naïve enough to take Uziah at his word in there. He'll keep coming for me if only to get to Legion—whom he apparently wanted all along. This was never about me. I was a means to an end. A tool.

I certainly feel like one now.

Regardless of how safe I'll be alone, I'm not about to be in an enclosed space with Legion. Not while I'm angry enough to strangle him—with my bare hands. The irony isn't lost on me that I've come full circle, right back to entertaining the idea of actually killing my fated mate.

Instead, I start the car and hit the gas, spinning gravel as I drive off, and leave Legion Razginath in the rearview—forever.

LEGION

I let her go despite every cell in my body screaming at me to stop her. The way she looked at me—the devastation and accusation in her gaze burned a hole straight through a soul I didn't know I possessed. The only thing I want to do is chase her down and make her forgive me, whatever it takes. Unfortunately, the scores of Crimson Roses soldiers closing in on my position make that a very bad idea. I refuse to let them hurt her, which means dealing with them first and earning forgiveness later. At least, this way, she'll live long enough to eventually, hopefully, stop hating me.

I watch the car drive off until it finally disappears, but all my focus is on the approaching gang at my back. They've been lurking in the woods since the moment we arrived. At first, I'd been confused over why they didn't attack. But then Uziah made his offer. And his reveal.

My father wants my blood oath.

Now that I've refused to offer it voluntarily, he'll try to take it by force.

Footsteps behind me tell me the enemy is done hiding.

I turn to meet them, sword drawn as I channel my guilt and loss into the rage my dragon is straining to unleash. Scales form along my arms and back, a half-shift that leaves me with a much stronger armor than the stuff I wore for Tori's sake today.

Across the lot, Uziah stands amid a dozen vampires. They all watch me with a deadly stillness, waiting for his order.

"Last chance to come willingly, son."

"I am not your son. And you will not have my blood oath. I would die first."

His eyes glitter with the gauntlet I've thrown down. "That's my least favorite option, but it's your choice." He nods to his men, and they attack at once, vampire speed blurring their bodies so that every counter-move I make is on instinct alone.

The power of gods and demons swims in my blood. The fury of my shadow beast is an unyielding madness as I give in to the hunger for blood—a hunger that apparently came from the male who sired me. A vampire god.

With rage fueling me, my sword cuts through the inexperienced vampire soldiers like paper. Their screams ring out, cut short by their swift death. One by one, they fall, and with each one I bring down, the shadow beast inside me rages hotter and brighter.

Bloodlust overtakes me until all I see is their blood to be spilled.

I lose myself to the battle, my mind nothing more

than an algorithm for battle plans, constantly re-adjusting itself to the flesh I've yet to carve. When I'm finished, silence rings out, a clang of victory that leaves me empty and alone in the parking lot now littered with dead vamps. Their hearts lie beside their broken bodies.

I look down to find my sword clutched in a hand that's half-man, half-dragon. Claws extend sharply from my scaly fingers, each one coated in blood. Black scales cover my arms, turning to flesh where my shoulder meets my chest.

The adrenaline lacing my blood finally wanes as thoughts of my mate eclipse everything else. She's vulnerable. Not safe. I can't let her leave, no matter how much she wishes I would.

I wipe my sword on my pants and sheath it then head for the road.

"If I can't have you, I'll take her."

Uziah.

He vanished during the fight. I whirl, looking for him, but he's hidden himself well among the trees behind the club.

"If you touch her, I'll make you beg for death before I give it."

"You'll come to me eventually, boy. One way or another. It's your choice how hard you make this decision."

"Why don't I come to you now?" I taunt. "Face me yourself. End this."

He doesn't answer.

Coward.

I start toward the trees, determined to find him and

end this once and for all, but then he speaks again. "My men will have caught her by now. Pledge yourself to me now, or it'll be too late for her."

I stop.

Panic replaces the cooling adrenaline in my veins, spurring me back toward the road. I shift as I run, clutching my sword in my teeth. The moment my wings appear, I take to the skies, racing after my mate. She can hate me all she wants as long as she's alive to do it.

TORI

My eyes blur with tears so badly that I lose sight of the road. This cannot be happening. I'd just begun to let myself trust Legion, to think he was someone I might have a future with, and now all that trust is shattered. It hurts so much more than I want to admit, but there's no turning it off. Hot tears continue to fall until I'm blinded by them. With a jerk of the wheel, I brake hard and pull off to the side of the road until I can regain control.

Kendall is my priority now.

I have to find us a safe place to go. Because I damn sure won't be staying at the Keep. But there's also nowhere else safe for us in either realm. Another wave of tears threatens as I realize how truly alone I am in all this. Without Legion...

It's only me against the entire force of the Crimson Roses.

My bravado toward Uziah was just that. We both know he won't stop coming for me. This was never about the female I accidentally killed outside that bar. It was about using me to get what he wanted. It's almost refreshing to see that he's dropped his act of pretending to care about me or look out for me. At least, all his cards are on the table now. Unfortunately, that card just so happens to be death.

My spiraling thoughts are interrupted as something heavy bangs against the roof of the car. I shriek, flinching and trying to see what hit me. The car's frame creaks as whatever it is moves off the car onto the pavement beside me.

Through the window, I see a very large, very angry-looking vampire. A rose tattoo peeks out from beneath his shirt, wrapping around his thick neck. He stares me down for a long moment as my heart races and adrenaline pumps.

With my hands in my lap, I pull my gloves off and prepare to do whatever I can to touch him without getting myself killed in the process.

Slowly, heart pounding, I climb out of the car, knowing I have a better chance if I go on the offensive. If I drive off, he'll just peel the car apart like a fucking onion. The vamp's eyes gleam like his job just got a whole lot easier.

"My touch is lethal," I tell him, hoping the knowledge will at least slow him down.

He snorts. "Mine is worse, bitch."

I force my expression to remain unmoved. "You sure you want to test it?"

A blur of movement approaches, and a second later, three more vamps have joined the first.

Fuck.

My odds just went from bad to impossible.

I reach for the door handle, prepared to get back in and make a run for it. If I can make it to the portal, maybe the guards will grant me asylum into Tartarus—

A loud wind rushes in, scattering leaves and whipping branches. Above, something dark blots out the light. A screech splits the air, and I know exactly what sort of monster is descending.

Legion is a demon-eyed dragon wrapped in fury.

He lands with chunks of lava leaking from his mouth, dripping onto the pavement where it melts the asphalt instantly.

The vamps' eyes widen.

The larger one who arrived first hardens his expression and plants his feet. "Rip his throat out," the vamp orders to the others. "We'll see how easily he spits fire then."

The vamps attack quickly, each of them trying and failing to pierce Legion's scales. The dragon's tail swings out, knocking the men off their feet.

The larger one turns away from them and stalks toward me.

I reach for the car door, but he's too fast, slamming it closed again and breathing against my ear. "You smell delicious, little fae. Let's see how you taste."

With my bare palm, I reach for him, but he's yanked away before I can touch his skin. Legion snatches the man with his teeth, ripping into him before tossing him aside. The injured vamp lands on the other side of the road. I note the other vampires are already strewn across the bubbling pavement, each one bloodied and unmoving.

Legion stalks to my attacker and pins the man to the ground with a large, bloodied claw. Smoke curls from the dragon's nostrils, and a moment later, a lick of flames leaks from his mouth, engulfing the vampire until his screams are cut short.

Finally, the dragon turns to face me.

I stare at his glowing eyes, a thousand feelings racing through me. The urge to go to him is strong. I find myself scanning his large form, checking for injuries.

I shouldn't care.

But I do.

And that's exactly why I turn away and fumble with the driver's handle. Warmth hits my hand, and I stop, turning to see Legion's dragon inching closer. His large snout nudges my hip, and I sidestep mostly out of instinct so I don't brush him with my exposed skin.

He stares at me with a sadness that pricks at my heart.

"I can't," I say simply.

He huffs, and a small whiff of smoke escapes his nostrils. His frustration reignites my own temper, and I turn away, wrenching open the car door and sliding inside before he can stop me.

I avoid his glowing gaze as I rev the engine and hit the gas, swerving back onto the road—as if I can somehow outrun him. But he doesn't move even when I speed off, and I watch in my rearview until his mournful eyes disappear.

My heart aches with a sense of loss, but I shove the

pain down, reminding myself he's the enemy. And you can't lose what you never had.

I'm nearly back to the city when the car is accosted a second time. I gasp, swallowing a panicked shriek as I imagine Uziah's men regrouping and doubling their efforts. This time without a watchful dragon to rescue me.

Instead of stopping, I hit the gas, speeding up and heading for the portal.

The sound of metal being scraped is followed by the roof being punctured. I glance up to see a long, blood-stained claw poking through the car's roof. Then another. Then another.

Suddenly, the road beneath my tires drops away, and my entire car is being lifted into the air. Wind roars outside, and I glance out the window to see large black wings beating wildly against the air—gaining altitude fast.

Treetops fall away, and my stomach drops to my knees as the dragon above me banks sharply right and I'm carried off across the skies.

TORI

Realizing my power windows still work at a thousand feet elevation is possibly the weirdest part about my current situation. I lean my head out the open window and scream at the dragon currently stealing my car with me in it. Not to mention, he's flying in the opposite direction of the portal that will take us home.

"Put me down, asshole!"

Legion ignores me and keeps flying.

I hastily roll the window back up to avoid a flock of incoming birds.

After that, Legion simply flies toward the horizon. The ground beneath us changes as we fly away from the Crossroads and any other sign of life inside it. After a few minutes, hills and valleys and farmland slope toward mountains and rivers and lakes.

I grip the steering wheel like some kind of life line when he suddenly dips toward the ground again. My knuckles whiten, and my breathing stops as the rocky mountaintop comes up to meet me far too fast. At the last minute, everything slows, and my tires once again touch the ground.

I jostle as if I've hit a pothole, and then everything goes still.

The dragon retreats, and I watch in the rearview as the beast shifts into the man I know; the man I have every reason to hate.

I watch him approach in the side mirror, my temper swirling at the sight of the naked, handsome, infuriating man who's just saved me then abducted me—again. Climbing out of the car, I glare at him, mask and gloves off in a silent dare.

"Tor," he says, relief lacing my name like a prayer. The sound of my name in that voice sends shivers through me, but I refuse to let him see how affected I am.

"Don't," I say coldly.

He stops, scanning the length of me. "Are you hurt?"

I hesitate, but there's no point in worrying him. "No." I frown at the blood and dirt coating his body. "Are you?"

He softens. "No."

"Liar." I gesture at the shallow cut on his ribs.

He brushes me off. "It's nothing."

I want to argue. To tell him the very idea of him being harmed terrifies me. But I don't want that to be true anymore.

"Why did you bring me here?" I ask.

"Uziah threatened you," he says. "He told me he won't stop until..."

He doesn't finish, but we both know what he means.

"He can't get to me in Tartarus," I say, still not sure why he brought us all the way out here.

He shakes his head. "The portal wasn't safe. He would have laid a trap."

"How do you know?"

"Because that's what I would have done."

I study him, remembering what Uziah claimed. About being his father. "Do you believe him? About being your... you know."

His eyes flash with a pain I've seen before. The pain of his past. "It's possible. He knew things no one else could have."

"About the blood oath?"

He nods. The pain in his gaze becomes a plea. But I haven't forgotten how we ended up here.

"That's something you'll have to deal with alone," I say. "I need to get Kendall and find somewhere safe for us—"

"I *am* safe for you," he insists, eyes flashing.

"You don't get it," I snap. "You're the one I need safety from."

He stares at me like I've just slapped him. Then he blinks, and the anguish I see stabs at me, tempting to crumble the walls I've built around my heart in the last hour.

"I will never let anything happen to you."

"Why?" I shoot back.

"What?"

"Why bother offering me a vow like that? You don't want to mate me. And I don't want to mate you."

Lie.

But I'll make it true.

I have to.

"Why bother continuing this charade? Let me go, Legion. It's over."

"I can't do that."

"Because of this stupid mate bond." I roll my eyes. "It's not like we claimed each other. We can still say no."

He stares back at me with what feels like more secrets. Hurt stabs at me at the reminder of what he kept from me. And if there's more—I can't take it.

"Let's just be done with this," I say, lifting my chin with a challenge in my hard gaze. "You could reject me."

"No," he growls with enough force that I cross my arms against the urge to step back.

This time, I let a threat edge into my voice as I say, "I could reject you."

His dark gaze flashes with a flicker of flames in their center. "You won't."

The certainty in his words pricks my pride. Instead of remembering all the reasons why I shouldn't do it—all the reasons I don't actually want to—the words fly from my lips if only to prove him wrong and wipe that smug-ass look off his face.

"Legion Razginath, I rej—"

He roars, closing the distance between us and shoving me back against the car. My breath is stolen but not from the impact. It's the look in his stormy, pain-filled eyes that has my lungs squeezing and my heart pounding. His breath on my face—the taste of it in my mouth—and his full lips hovering so close I can practically feel them on mine already. The chaos in his eyes reflects the raging emotions I feel for what we are to each other.

"Don't," he pleads.

In that word, I hear what he won't say. He wants me. And he wants me to want him.

I can't deny that I do.

I want him more than I've ever wanted anything or anyone.

That's precisely what I hate about him.

No, it's the betrayal I hate. The way I opened myself up to him—a first for me—and he cut me.

"You don't want this any more than I do," I argue, desperate now to be rid of this force that continues to draw me back to him even when it hurts. "You told me that yourself. Why are you making this so difficult?"

A shadow crosses his handsome features, further darkening his expression. For a moment, there's a vulnerability in him. A glimpse into the raw, real truth that lies buried so deep. "Even without accepting the bond, we are connected," he says quietly.

"If you're talking about this curse, you can go fuck—"

"I'm talking about my feelings for you. And your feelings for me."

"Those feelings aren't real. They're the mate bond luring us in."

"You know it's more than that."

"No, I don't," I say stubbornly.

"I never wanted you as a mate," he says, hurting me even though he's said it before. "So, it's not the mate bond. Because even with it drawing me to you, I was going to resist. To walk away. But then I got to know you.

And something changed. I became willing to help you. And every day we spent together became better than the last. You're not what I thought you'd be. You're kind. Compassionate. Smart. You make my life better, Torissa Sage. In every way."

My resolve softens with every word he utters. I blink back hot, angry tears as I say, "What does it all change, though? Nothing. I'm still cursed. And your crazy parents are still after you."

"Exactly. Rejecting me won't change anything either. They will still come for you to get to me."

"And I will still be cursed," I say bleakly.

Pain flashes in his dark gaze. "But the bond between us offers one edge that will help."

"What?"

"The madness that comes from resisting it. Resisting you." His voice is raw, his eyes haunted. "My shadow beast grows stronger every day that passes without claiming you."

"Why does that sound like it's not a good thing?"

His smile is crooked and darkly rueful. "Because I might actually go mad over it. But the bloodlust is a power all its own. A power we'll need against what's coming."

"And by that you mean your batshit parents."

"Yes."

My eyes narrow. "You refuse to reject me because our connection makes you more able to kill and destroy?"

"Hmm. Now that you mention it, I think we've both enjoyed a few other perks as well, little assassin."

"Screw you," I mutter, but there's no fury left in the words.

His eyes flash with pure lust, and in response, I feel the same desperate need tightening in my own core. "Unfortunately, that's not on the table," he says. "Though, as you know, there are other options."

I nearly rock my hips toward him, remembering that night in the library, the way he brought me to orgasm with the friction of his hand through my clothes. But then I remember my poisonous skin. And whose bloodline caused it. And the secret he kept about it all this time.

He made my life better too. That's what made his lie hurt so much.

"You wouldn't live long enough to enjoy any of them," I tell him darkly.

One touch. That's all it would take to end this. Something tells me it wouldn't be difficult to slip past his defenses either. To convince him to forget why we shouldn't. To press my exposed flesh to his.

"You underestimate me, sweetheart. I'm tougher than you think."

"Your ego is going to get you killed."

"I have no ego when it comes to you, little assassin. But you underestimate my determination to have you."

For some reason, his words pierce me—a final blow.

Something inside me snaps. Ten years' worth of loss and loneliness and holding my shit together by a thread. Since the moment my parents died, I remained closed off —until Legion. He was the first and only one I ever let see the real me, including all my worries and fears and vulnerable places.

And he hurt me.

The pain he caused me becomes rage and a determination to hurt him too.

"You're the one who underestimates," I say, my bared hands twitching at my sides.

His smirk spikes my temper all over again. "We'll see."

Ugh, it's time to wipe that disgustingly sexy smile from his face once and for all. Stepping away from him, I hold his gaze and slowly peel my armor off then my jacket. Finally, I'm standing before him wearing only a t-shirt and my jeans. Legion's gaze is hungry as it roams my body. I don't move, letting him look, letting the exposure of flesh distract him just enough to lower his guard.

I strike fast, using the element of surprise to my advantage as I rush at him, hands bared and reaching for his throat.

He doesn't see it coming. I know it because I see clearly the eye-widening shock as I close the distance. His recovery is just enough for him to sidestep me, and my fingers meet only thin air.

Frustrated, I whirl and rush him again.

He dances out of my reach easily, that stupid smug smile still flashing at me. With a battle cry, I try a third time, anticipating his feint and lowering my head, tackling him with a shoulder in the gut. I feel the moment my skin touches his and my heart lurches but there's no time to react. In the next second, he loses his footing, and we both go flying off the edge of the rocky cliff.

I scream, watching the hard ground below rising fast to meet us, too fast for anything but death. Before we have a chance to hit the bottom, Legion shifts, scales replacing flesh as large, leathery wings appear. There's no time for a recovery, not even with wings, but he's not trying to escape the fall.

Instead, his enormous wings curl forward, cocooning me inside them. A second later, Legion slams into the ground, and the impact jars me. The wings pull tighter, suffocating me while saving me from a fatal impact.

An impact I barely feel because Legion takes it for me.

He makes no sound as he hits the ground. His wings unfurl, and I'm dumped onto the ground in a heap of dust and pebbles. Scrambling up, I lean over Legion's dragon form, searching for a heartbeat.

Thud... thud... thud.

There.

My shoulders sag in relief.

"Legion."

He doesn't answer. I resist the urge to shake him awake.

"Legion," I call, louder now.

Fear twists inside me.

I felt my head connect with his shoulder earlier. And then his wings touched my skin when he used them to save me, which means the fact that he's unconscious might be from the fall—or it might be from the poison in my skin entering his bloodstream.

The idea that I might have just killed him leaves me sick and panicked.

"Legion!"

My scream is guttural, echoing around us and bouncing off the hills we've landed between.

A rumbling follows, and for a fleeting, hopeful second, I think Legion is waking. But then the ground beneath me trembles, and the rocks on the hill above us begin sliding. Horror dawns slowly then with terrifying clarity as the landslide worsens. Giant boulders are uprooted and careen toward the bottom of the cliffside where Legion and I wait like sitting ducks.

"Legion, wake up," I call urgently.

Above me, enormous boulders bounce and roll at startling speeds. The rumbling grows louder. Closer. The ground beneath me cracks and fissures just as a boulder the size of an RV flies right toward my head.

Without thinking, I throw myself over Legion's dragon form, hoping to shield him from the inevitable. Just before the boulder would have reached us, the ground beneath gives way. Suddenly, I'm weightless, both of us swallowed by the earth, falling, falling...

LEGION

Flying is my specialty. Falling is not. Throbbing pain across every inch of my body wakes me with a groan. Trying to get my bearings, I blink, my eyes taking longer than usual to focus. Still in dragon form, I'm on my back in a pile of rubble. My right wing is pinned beneath a large rock, and my ribs are screaming.

Rock walls surround me on every side. Above me, a small opening in the Earth suggests how I got here. It's nearly completely sealed by large boulders, making the light in this cavern almost nonexistent.

Sifting through foggy thoughts, I try to connect how I got here. Last I remember, Tori came at me on the mountain. She touched me. Fuck, the poison. So far, there's nothing in me to suggest I'm dying. Well, other than the pain of falling hard on my ass in this cavern.

Then I remember how we got here. We fell. I shifted to shield her from the fall and then—

Fuck. Tori!

I see her several yards away, half-buried beneath a

pile of rock and dirt. She doesn't move. Determined to get to her, I force myself to sit up, groaning at the piercing pain in my wing as it's stretched taut from my movements. Doubling back to the boulder pinning me, I shove it aside with a clawed hand and then hurry to Tori. The dirt and rock are easy enough to scrape away with my dragon's claws.

Fear is an acid on my tongue, and I grit my teeth against my dragon's resistance to shifting back to my human form. It'll make the healing process twice as long and three times as painful, but I have to get to her. To feel her pulse against my hands.

When I get close, I see that her breaths are shallow and barely audible to my sensitive ears. The moment my scales are swapped for flesh, I begin carefully picking away at the rubble half-burying her.

"Tori," I call.

She doesn't move, and fear grips me harder.

"Tori." I raise my voice, letting urgency creep in. Her pulse is there, but her eyes remain closed. I pull the rocks off her, scanning her for injuries. Beyond a few shallow cuts and scrapes, I don't spot anything. Then, I notice her veins darkening beneath her skin. They go from blue to gray to black, and fear beyond anything I've known grips me, squeezing my heart until it threatens to break apart. In this moment, I know with absolute conviction that this woman is the only reason I'll ever have to live. Without her, I am nothing.

"Tori." My voice is hoarse, but even so, it echoes in the silence of the cavern.

There's no heartbeat.

I realize with horror that her breathing has stopped.

Pain and rage build inside me until I'm trembling with what feels like an earthquake in my bones. I will not outlive this grief.

No longer caring whether her skin remains lethal, I pull her lifeless body into my arms and hold her against me. The feel of her bared skin against mine is a pleasure I can't remember feeling in all my thousands of years. It is also the most exquisite pain—experiencing it without her eyes open. Without her alive to share it.

Reverently, I lean down and brush a kiss over each of her closed lids.

When I sit up again, I feel it. A tingling in my lips. It spreads fast, sending a numbness across my mouth and down my throat. My hands tremble.

Fear grips me.

Not for myself.

But if I die here like this, who will save her?

I need Tori to live, dammit.

Urgency driving me, I run my hands over her body, frantic for something—anything—that could help her before I succumb to the poison.

When I reach her hip, I feel something solid in her pocket. Pulling out a small vial, I remember how Broca gave it to Tori to help her heal.

I have nothing left to lose and no time left. My left side has already become paralyzed. Knowing it's my only shot, I use my right hand to uncap the vial and pour the drops of liquid down Tori's throat.

The moment I do, the scent of the vial's contents

slams into me—a scent I know all too well and have spent five thousand years trying to forget.

Demon tears.

The shock of it here, now, has me reeling. I realize too late these are not just any demon tears.

These tears belong to my mother.

Did Tori know that?

Where the hell did she get them?

And what effect will they have on my mate's survival? My mother always claimed the tears of a demon were lethal. A poison that packed potency unlike any other.

I can do nothing but wait.

A full minute.

Then two.

My right side becomes paralyzed. I slump to the side, leaning heavily on a large chunk of rock. My breathing slows. Hope is a light that grows dimmer by the second.

Another minute passes.

Tori doesn't wake, and my hope bleeds away.

The grief closes over me, and I'm sucked beneath its anguished depths as I try to accept that I've truly lost her. I'm so immersed in the pain that it takes me a moment to realize the numbness is gone. I lift my hands then my arms and notice they're back to normal.

The poison is gone.

I'm not going to die after all and the reality of that knowledge crushes me. How can I possibly live without *her*?

My grief sends me spiraling. I reach for her then, pulling her close and whispering her name.

The sudden warmth of Tori's skin jolts me back to the moment.

I stare down at her as her cheeks begin to flush and her closed eyelids twitch. The scent of magic hits me then. A rotting, burning smell that reminds me of the creature who set all this in motion.

It pours out of Tori's mouth, a dark green cloud that clogs my nostrils and sticks inside my mouth.

When the last of the smoke has dispelled from her mouth, she gasps, drawing in a sudden breath as her eyes fly open and find mine. Relief floods me.

Something even more powerful than the mate call slams into me. Love. Unconditional, irrevocable love. I vow to never let this woman go again.

"Legion." Her brow furrows, and she glances up at the cavern's ceiling.

"Hello, gorgeous." I smooth her hair back, grateful for the sight of her flushed cheeks and the rise and fall of her chest as she breathes.

"Are you hurt?" I ask.

She shifts in my arms, frowning. "Sore." She glances down at her bared arms and notes the bloodied scratches. "I feel strange. The mate bond. Gods, it's strong. Did you do something?" Her eyes widen as she finally realizes I'm touching her. "Legion, stop. You can't—"

She pulls away, and I release her, mostly so she'll calm down. She scrambles back, staring at me with growing fear. "You're going to die," she chokes out.

"I'm not. The curse is broken."

"What? How?"

"Where did you get the demon tears you had in your pocket?"

Her hand goes to her pocket.

I hold up the empty vial, and she stares at it.

"You drank it?" she asks.

"No. You did."

"I don't understand. I touched you. Even before we fell. You should be poisoned."

"I was."

"Then how...?" She trails off like she can't bring myself to voice the words.

"You weren't breathing." My heart squeezes all over again as I relive nearly losing her. "You were dying. Maybe already dead. I think your... I think it neutralized the poison's affects in me."

"How am I alive now?" she asks quietly.

I clear my throat, shoving aside the grief and fear I'd felt a few minutes ago. "I remembered how poison helped heal you before, so I gave you the vial of tears from your pocket. The scent... these were my mother's tears. Where did you get them?"

"Em," she says. "I took this as payment for that last job. She was supposed to give me more after, but we never got that far."

My gut tightens as I begin to understand. "What did Em look like?"

"I didn't see much except for her dark eyes. She was wearing a long coat and a scarf." She stares at me. "You think Em is your mother?"

"I don't know. I searched for her when I first visited

this realm. When I couldn't sense her, I assumed... If it is her, she's cloaked herself somehow."

She shakes her head, watching me warily.

"What is it?" I ask.

"The mate bond. It's so much stronger than it was." Her face flushes as she adds, "I can feel you. Like a magnet being pulled."

I smirk. "Are you saying you want me?"

"I'm saying..." She blinks, her gaze sharpening. "Do you think the curse dimmed the mate bond? Is that why I wasn't half-crazy on Februlune?"

"The way I remember it, you were pretty crazy for me." I smirk, and it feels so damn good to joke with her in this moment.

"I'm serious. I was so scared there was something wrong with our connection." She takes a deep breath. "But now... it's all I can feel. How did demon tears break the curse, exactly?"

"Broca said the curse could only be broken by an offering from the one who cast it. I think my mother's tears were the offering."

The hope in her eyes has me forgetting everything else. Thoughts of my mother are shoved aside, and I reach for her, pulling her back into my arms where she belongs.

My shoulder throbs with the effort thanks to my still-healing wound, but it's nothing like it was when we landed here.

"Hey—" Tori struggles against me, but I hold tight until she gives in. Still, when I look down at her, there's fear in her gaze as she studies my face and chest anxiously. "What if you're wrong?"

"Darling, I've been holding you and touching you since we landed down here. If the curse was going to kill me, it would've happened already."

She sighs. "You're right. I just don't want to risk losing you," she admits.

"Do you mean that you'd be upset if I died, little assassin?"

She flinches, but the vulnerability in her gorgeous eyes grows. "Yes," she whispers. "Very upset, actually." Her gaze dips to my mouth, and desire stirs in my still-healing body.

"Strange, considering you recently tried to kill me," I say.

"I'm sorry," she says, her voice breaking as tears fill her eyes. "You lied. I was angry."

I tuck her hair behind her ear, enjoying the softness of her skin beneath my fingers. "We should work on our conflict resolution."

"We should," she agrees, her eyes unwavering on mine.

The air between us thickens with the scent of desire. Not mine. Hers.

I don't bother asking permission. Not for this. I've waited too damn long already. If she doesn't like it, she's welcome to try to kill me again.

With a growl, I crush my mouth to hers. She gasps and tenses then melts. Her hands come up to thread in my hair and pull me closer. I lose myself in the taste of her on my tongue, the feel of her body against my hands, the sounds she makes as I claim her mouth. My kiss is a silent promise to do the same to her body and her soul.

My hands trace over her hip, hooking into the waist of her pants. Without breaking our kiss, my fingers loosen the buttons, and I yank the fabric aside, sliding my fingers through her wet heat. She gasps and rocks into me, and I slide a finger inside her, then two.

"I've owed you this since that night in the library," I tell her.

My voice is ragged, but I don't care. The feel of her body against mine is a drug, and I'm already hooked. Since the moment we met, I've wanted nothing more than this. Now that I have her, the reality is so much more potent than anything I imagined.

"Legion," she whispers as I slide my fingers in and out of her.

"You feel so good," I tell her.

She grips my neck, tightening her hold as her tight walls contract around my fingers. I don't stop, pushing into her and watching, rapt, as she comes apart for me. When she whimpers my name, I steal the sound with another kiss.

Overwhelmed by the feel of him, I melt into Legion's touch, riding the wave of pleasure until I'm lost to my senses. His fingers drive me up and over the edge faster than I ever thought possible. All the while, his eyes never leave mine, the glint of desire mixing with a devotion I didn't expect and am not sure what to do with. I feel his hardness against the back of my thigh, and almost immediately, I can feel another orgasm building at the idea of having him inside me.

"Legion," I whisper, sitting up so I can straddle his lap. "I need you."

He doesn't stop touching me, his fingers massaging my clit, as he holds my gaze. "I've wanted to touch you like this since the moment we met."

He slides a finger inside me, drawing a sharp breath from me as he watches my expression closely. Like he's drinking in my pleasure. Drawing it out. Like we have forever for this.

I'd like to think we do.

His eyes are hooded now and almost dangerous with the desire sparking in them. "I want to watch while you come for me, little assassin."

His words send a shiver through me. His other hand comes up to cup my breast, his thumb brushing over my nipple.

"Do you like it when I touch you like this?"

An hour ago, I would have said no. But it would have been a lie.

Still, I can't help but think how close we are to talking about sex—an act that would seal the mate bond. Now more than ever, I understand Legion's resistance to being bound again. And I refuse to ask him to do that even for me. This will have to be enough. I care for him too much to ask for more.

I press kisses to his jaw, his cheek, his mouth. "Yes."

His answering growl is punctuated by a sound from above.

Both of us go still, listening to the sound of voices from the opening in the cavern ceiling. I look up, trying to make out the words of the strangers. Trying to figure out if they're friend or foe.

Legion holds a finger to his lips, signaling to be silent. I button my pants, heart pounding both for his touch and for the possible danger. Naked and covered in bruises and scratches, Legion stares up at the opening high above our heads.

There's a small wound on his shoulder blade that's nearly closed. I realize I never asked if he was injured from the fall. I still can't believe my curse is broken. Or that the demon tears I've been carrying belong to

Legion's mother. Or that Em might actually be Maricha.

The voices drift down, and I catch bits and pieces.

"…landslide. Probably a cave-in or sinkhole."

"Help me move this rock so we can see if they're inside."

I glance around, looking for a place to hide, but there's nowhere we won't be seen, not from an aerial view. Legion takes my hand, pulling me close against his body. I hate that I can't enjoy the feel of him, but my panic blots out any sense of pleasure.

Above us, rocks are cleared out, and the opening grows wider, letting in more light. A second later, two sets of crimson eyes peer down at us.

"Well-well, what do we have here?" one of them calls.

"Right where Maricha said they'd be," says another.

I tense.

Legion pulls me close and whispers in my ear, "I'm going to shift and take us out of here."

"Can you fly?" I ask, noting the injuries along his back and shoulders.

"Don't have a choice," he says grimly. "Ready?"

I nod at him, wide-eyed as one of the voices above says, "It's like fish in a barrel."

The other vamp laughs.

Legion motions for me to stand back, and I scramble up onto a pile of rubble against the cavern wall. He grimaces as he transforms, and I watch with concern, wondering if the shift is causing him pain that he's not telling me about. But a second later, an enormous black-scaled dragon stands before me, wings unfurling and twitching a bit as he shakes himself out.

His gleaming eyes turn to me.

I scramble over the rubble and onto Legion's back.

Overhead, the vamps are rolling the rocks back into place, trying to seal us inside.

"Let's go," I say.

Legion crouches low and then shoves off the ground, his wings beating furiously. Dirt kicks up as the edges of his wings brush the cavern's walls, but he doesn't stop until we're catapulted upward.

His head smashes through the opening the vampires are trying to re-seal. Boulders and debris go flying, and the vamps scramble back. The wall of stones is enough to slow our momentum, and Legion's dragon perches precariously on the edge of the opening. He scrambles to climb up and out of the cavern, and I cling to the raised spikes on his back, trying not to think about the sheer drop waiting if we fall back into the cavern.

On my left, I see one of the vampires holding a box of some kind. His eyes widen at the sight of Legion attempting to break through the last of the boulders blocking our way out.

"There," I say, alerting Legion to the threat.

He roars, spraying flames that incinerate the grass and plants in its path. The vamps scatter left and right to get out of the way. The one with the box pulls his arm back and throws it in our direction.

The box hits an outcropping of rocks at Legion's feet and explodes.

I'm thrown off Legion's back at the force.

There's an ear-splitting roar as Legion's dragon slams against the rocky ground. I land not far from him, the pain of the impact against my hip dragging a cry from my lips. Legion's dragon pulls itself to its feet with a concerning amount of effort. From here, I can see a fresh wound gaping open along his scaled leg. Legion sways, clearly shaken. When the dragon turns to our attackers, the rage in those glowing eyes is terrifying.

Another wave of flames unleashes on the vamp who tossed the bomb. The man is engulfed, his mouth frozen in a scream that never reaches my ears. Out of the corner of my eye, I spot the second vamp running away.

Legion's fire doesn't let him get far before he's turned to ash.

I exhale, allowing relief to overtake my fear, but it doesn't last. Movement along the ridge draws my eye. It takes me two long heartbeats to register what I'm seeing, but when I do, horror eclipses my sense of victory.

Crimson Roses move swiftly, their ranks pulled tight as they approach with vampire speed. I count at least two dozen before Legion is there, his dragon's snout nudging my shoulder in a silent plea to move.

I try, but the pain in my hip has me falling back again.

"Just go," I whisper. "Don't let them take you."

He snarls, flashing his teeth in a clear refusal.

Something slams into the ground nearby, loosing dirt and rock as it lands with a clang against stone. We both look over. A blade lies on the ground, it's handle intricately carved with symbols I've never seen before.

Legion rumbles from somewhere deep in his chest.

It's a sound of fury but also fear. That, more than the dozens of Crimson Roses coming for us, scares me.

"What is it?" I ask, but I don't get my answer.

Another blade flies, this one finding its mark in my thigh.

Agony, unlike anything I've known, rips through my skin.

A scream rips from my throat.

Beside me, Legion roars his rage.

I stare down at the knife, too paralyzed by the pain to touch it. The handle is carved with the same symbols that, despite being foreign to me, send a ripple of dread down my spine.

Fire erupts in my veins.

Dizziness washes over me, and the scent of something burning fills my nostrils. Dark green smoke leaks from the wound.

I look up at Legion with wide, fear-filled eyes. "It's poison," I croak, biting down on the scream building inside me. "And I'm not immune anymore."

LEGION

I stare down at the blade in Tori's leg with suffocating dread. The symbols, that hilt—the sight of it sends waves of memories through me, none of them good. My mother's preferred weapons aren't simply forged steel. They are sentient spirits; essentially demons in their own right. I'd forgotten what they were capable of. If they're here on this mountain, it can only mean she is too.

Scanning the horizon, I'm drawn to the far ridge.

She's different than before. Cloaked as a shifter. But it's her. The way my blood responds to the ancient darkness that clings to her is unmistakable.

My reaction costs me.

Before I can find a way to counteract the dark and ancient magic, the Crimson Roses reach us. I burn them all, destroying and incinerating and giving myself over to my shadow beast nature.

I use my dragon's body to shield Tori, but we're

running out of time, and the damned enemy keeps coming. Farther up, on the ridge, two figures watch the fight—such as it is.

No, they watch me.

And they know they have me.

I can feel her gaze on me—her quiet certainty that I will submit—and it makes me sick.

I fight harder.

When the last of the Crimson Roses has been burned from this earth, I look up at them. My stomach churns, and my beast recoils at the sight of her.

My mother.

She walks beside Uziah, her steps slow and measured. She could have unfurled her dark wings and flown here, but that would have meant making haste toward the woman she's just poisoned.

At the sight of her venom-laced stare, my dragon trembles with rage and desperation. I hate her more than I want to live. But I love Tori more than either of those things, so for her, I stand my ground. And bide my time. All that matters is saving Tori. I'll do anything to ensure her survival, and they know it.

As they approach, my mother's mouth quirks upward in a smug smile. Uziah is not nearly as subtle. His flash of teeth is unapologetic as they stop before me.

"Hello, son," he calls.

I shift back to my human form, uncaring that I'm coated in dirt and blood. "Don't call me that," I snarl.

"Don't be rude, Legion."

I glare at my mother. Her skin is flawless, her beauty

untouched by time. But I'm not fooled. Her ugliness is buried deep beneath the surface.

"You don't get to order me around anymore," I tell her.

"I'm still your mother."

"Actually, you lost that right a long time ago. You're nothing to me."

She cocks her head. "Is that why you spent your first night back in this realm searching for me?"

My hands ball into fists. "A shame I didn't find you sooner. Your death could have saved us all this trouble."

"Ah, the cloaking spell. Powerful, isn't it?"

"Not powerful enough," I say. "It's gone now. Your rancid scent is all over this mountain."

Her eyes flash at my insult but she maintains her cool. "You assume the cloaking spell was for you." Her gaze flicks to Tori. "Besides, if you'd found me, you might not have run into her. And then you would have never cursed, oops, I mean *met* your mate."

Her taunting snaps my control.

With a roar, I give in to the fury building inside me and consume them both with hellfire. When the flames clear, they are both unaffected and glaring at me.

"Have you forgotten I am immune to your tricks?" my mother calls.

"You've lied before," I say with a pointed look at Uziah. "Figured it was worth testing."

"I never lied," she says.

"You told me my father was a god."

"When he was made, no other word existed for what he was," she says with a shrug.

"You told me he was a good male. That you tricked him by appearing to him as someone else."

"Good is a bit subjective. But that last part is true," Uziah says, his crimson eyes flashing with the first hint of animosity toward my mother. "She did take the form of another when she came to me that night. And I won't lie and say I didn't feel betrayed. But I came around eventually. As will you."

I bare my teeth, allowing the heat and smoke to pour from my mouth as I snarl at the vampire asshole who sired me.

"Are you done being dramatic?" my mother snaps. "We have work to do."

"Legion?" Tori gasps.

I glance down to see that she's pale with a sheen of sweat coating her skin. Her eyes are glassy, and my fear threatens to paralyze me as I watch her succumbing to a slow death. I never thought I'd wish for her poisoned skin, but I wish it now. At least then she'd have a chance against the infection.

The fire inside me winks out.

I cannot carry her away from here. Not when she'll die and the only person in the world with the power to save her is watching me, waiting for me to realize the decision has already been made.

I shove my beast down, ignoring its desperate pleas to stay and fight. Or even to flee.

"Let her go," I say, voice raspy from the hellfire still burning my throat. "It is the only way I will come with you."

Something grips my throat. An invisible hand squeezing until my breath catches. My mother's magic is an unseen thing, but that only makes it more dangerous.

"It's hardly the only way," my mother says, and despite the purr in her voice, my muscles tense and coil at the invisible grip her magic has on me already. It's nothing I can't fight off—for now—but I don't. All that matters is saving Tori.

"We both know the blood oath must be taken willingly," I snarl, my words choked. The invisible cord my mother's wrapped around my throat squeezes tighter. When she doesn't release me, I spit the words, "Now who's being dramatic."

Uziah turns to her. "Darling."

The invisible vise releases me. I remain where I am, my body shielding Tori. She is wheezing now, the poison working its way into her organs.

"Heal her," I snap. "Or I will unleash what I have and all that I am against both of you."

My mother lifts her hand, and the first knife, the one that missed, is suddenly airborne as she calls it into her palm. She comes forward, and I watch her warily.

"You look strong," she says, eyeing me like one would any weapon.

"Strong enough to find a way to destroy you," I say.

She kneels beside Tori, unaffected by my threats. "This is the one Fate chose for you."

Her tone makes it clear she means the words as an insult. My hands curl into fists, but it's Tori who speaks.

"You're Em, his asshole mother."

"And you're the bitch who brought him back to me."

"He's not yours." Tori's eyes flash with a conviction and strength that make my heart swell. But underneath that strength, she is fading.

"Well, he'll certainly never be yours, will he?" my mother says with malicious enjoyment.

"You really thought cursing my skin would keep him from falling for me?" Tori fires back. "Honestly, I think it brought us closer, so thanks for that."

My mother's eyes narrow.

"Heal her now," I demand, but my mother's already wrapping her hand around the blade's hilt.

"No. Don't save me if it means–" Tori tries to move away, but Maricha pulls the knife free.

Tori makes a guttural sound and clutches her leg. Maricha utters a string of words—ancient magic, dark and strong enough to shudder through me as I stand beside them.

Tori gasps, and the wound changes from black to red. A dark green smoke, viscous and toxic, escapes the wound. Tori coughs as the poisoned curse is withdrawn, leaving behind a jagged wound that looks painful but survivable.

I exhale.

Maricha stands, gripping a blade in each hand. She whispers a few more words to them, and the bloodstains vanish. When she looks up at me, impatience lines her hard expression. I know I only have moments left before she demands I hold up my end.

I kneel beside Tori, schooling my expression to hide the storm raging inside me. My back is to Maricha, my body shielding her from witnessing my exchange with my mate.

She still hasn't realized her curse has broken, and I don't plan on giving her proof of it now. That would only endanger Tori all over again.

Tori meets my eyes, tears slipping down her cheeks. "You shouldn't have done it," she whispers. "I wasn't worth the price."

"You are worth everything to me." My voice is hoarse, my hand trembling as I stroke her cheek quickly before either of them can see it. "Never forget that. Never doubt my love for you."

"Legion." Another tear escapes.

"Enough of this," Maricha snaps. "It's time."

I push to my feet, turning away from Tori before I can change my mind and do something pointless like fight. Facing one of them might have been possible, but both Uziah and my mother together are too risky, especially with Tori still injured.

"Fulfill your end, or I'll bury a poisoned blade in her heart," my mother says.

I stalk to where she stands beside Uziah and snatch the dark blade from her hand. With only the slightest moment of hesitation, I draw the tip across my palm until blood soaks my skin.

My mother takes the blade from my hand and does the same to her own.

I open my mouth to begin reciting the old words that will bind us, but Uziah stops me when he grabs the knife and draws blood across his own hand.

"What are you doing?" Maricha demands.

"Joining all three of us," Uziah says.

My mother's eyes narrow. "That's not what we talked about."

"No, but it's what we'll do." He looks at me. "I bind you to me, Legion Razginath, son of darkness and damnation."

My mother looks murderous, and for a weighted moment, I think she might attack him. But then she speaks up, reciting the same words he's just uttered.

"I bind you to me, Legion Razginath, son of darkness and damnation. Son of my womb." The words she adds at the end make her eyes gleam with a smugness she aims at Uziah.

It's all I can do not to roll my eyes at their pettiness.

"Your turn," my mother prompts.

It takes everything in me not to look back at Tori. "I bind myself to you, Maricha Razginath and Uziah—"

"No!" Tori screams.

Uziah's eyes widen at something over my shoulder just as Tori throws herself at him. He manages to dodge her attempt to upend him, stumbling against Maricha who screeches at him and shoves him away.

Tori glares at them, her hands trembling as she lifts them at her sides. Beneath our feet, the ground trembles and cracks open. Maricha and Uziah take a step back to avoid being swallowed up. I watch, stunned and proud, as thick, dark vines climb out of the fissures, crawling across the ground toward my mother and the vamp who sired me. The curse may be broken, but this part of Tori's power has remained.

Maricha screams and calls out an ancient command to her magic. "Lissnim Roraouth Azrepkeer!"

Thick green smoke licks over the ground, consuming the vines and turning them to ash as it hurries toward Tori. I roar, my dragon surging to the surface. I rush toward her, the blood from my palm dripping over the vines and flames as I run toward my mate.

Something wraps around my ankles, burning like acid, and I'm yanked to the ground.

"You are mine, blood of my blood." My mother's declaration sends a boom through the skies.

Uziah's hands on me are rough as he hauls me up.

The dark green cords remain wrapped around my ankles, burning lengths of rope made of hell-magic that burns as it eats through my flesh. I twist and pull against them, but they don't break or bend.

Tori screams my name as a bolt of that same dark magic hits her shoulder. It singes her clothing, and she cries out, hunching over as the scent of her burned flesh fills the air.

"Stop!" I don't wait to see if they've listened before I raise my bloodied hand and rush to say the words that complete the binding. "I bind myself to you, Maricha and Uziah. I am blood bound at your command and yours to wield as you desire. My will is yours. It is done."

I lean over and grab Uziah's hand, pressing his bloodied palm to mine. The sky cracks with a response. My mother appears, clearly worried about being left out of the binding. She grabs my bloodied hand and presses it to her own.

The sky cracks again.

Across the divide of broken earth, Tori screams.

I turn away from her as I feel the old familiar leash wrap itself around my heart and mind. The binding is done. And I am once again ruled by monsters; a mateless prisoner, eternally trapped.

I watch, helpless and devastated, as Legion binds himself to the two monsters before me. Uziah's betrayal is a cut I will never forgive, but it's Maricha who makes my blood run cold. The evil that lives in her depthless feline eyes is something I've never encountered. Then there's her twin blades. The way they respond to her suggests a sentience in them. I've never faced anything like it. Not even from Legion.

Seeing Maricha now, I realize I was so wrong about the things I said to him before. Or the things I thought of him when we met. Legion was never evil. But she is, and I have no idea how to stop her.

"It is done," she declares, dropping Legion's hand and stepping back like touching him makes her uncomfortable.

The green smoke binding Legion's ankles vanishes right along with the thunder as if the magic knows the show is over.

Legion doesn't meet my eyes, but I refuse to let this be the end.

"Legion," I start, but Maricha's eyes flash, and she cuts me off.

"We're done here. It's time to take your place," she says to Legion. "Come."

"You will never have my obedience outside the blood oath," Legion growls.

"Have it your way," Maricha says.

She utters words too low for me to hear, but Legion is clearly affected by them. I watch as he turns and follows her, head down, shoulders curled.

Uziah starts to follow when Maricha barks out one last command. "Bring her. She'll be a useful motivator."

Legion whips around, eyes blazing, as Uziah comes for me. I lift my hands, preparing to call on the dark vines again. I'm not sure how it's possible that I can still wield them without the poison curse, but I'm not in a position to question it either.

Uziah must sense my intention because he stops and watches me warily across the narrow divide still open between us.

Maricha glances back and gives an exasperated sigh. "For hell's sake." She lets her blade fly faster than I can see it coming. I don't get the chance to move before it's buried in my ribs.

I gasp, stumbling.

Legion roars at Maricha. "You vowed to keep her alive."

"No," Maricha says. "I vowed to heal her wound, and I did."

"Breaking your vow will end the bond," he warns.

"I have broken nothing," Maricha snaps.

She looks back at me and whispers some words I can't make out. The blade twists as if moved by an invisible hand, and a force like I've never known slides over me, claiming me with its iron grip. I'm sucked into its depths of unconsciousness, my scream never making a sound.

I wake propped up on the floor of a stone cell. My tongue feels thick, and my head pounds with a searing headache. That's nothing compared to the pain of trying to get up. My ribs burn with agony that only intensifies with each movement. Careful to keep my torso as still as possible, I pull my blood-soaked shirt up and inspect the damage. It's not the stab wound I expected—especially considering the last thing I remember is being impaled by that bitch Maricha and her poisoned knife. But instead of a single wound, my skin is an intricate map of shallow cuts. They mar my skin in thin red lines that look like pure chaos until I notice a strange pattern they've cut on my flesh.

Some kind of symbol.

Beneath the burn of pain, dark magic pulses through it.

I try to move again, gritting my teeth against the resistance that meets my efforts. The thin red lines inking the strange symbol blacken as the agony worsens.

It reminds me of the curse and the dark veins it caused when it activated.

Fear grips me as I wonder if she somehow learned the curse was broken and cast it all over again.

I'd rather anything else than to be kept from Legion's touch again. The thought of him alone has me thinking of strategy. I need to conserve my energy if I'm going to have any hope of escaping this hellhole.

I go still, letting my shirt fall and my hands rest on the cool stone floor. With my head tipped up against the stone wall behind me, I survey the space. Thick stone surrounds me on three sides. The fourth is nothing but iron bars that have rusted and begun flaking from age. The air is stale and musty. Wherever I am, it's old and likely forgotten by the rest of the world.

Through the cell door, I see more stone extending down a wide hall until the space opens into what looks like a larger cavern. Dim light emanates from fixtures mounted on the stone walls.

If I squint, I can make out an iron door on the far cavern wall. Symbols have been carved into its surface, not unlike the one currently carved into me. A window with iron bars offers a glimpse of a stairwell that leads up.

I don't see even a shred of daylight anywhere. The damp, musty smell suggests a windowless space all around.

Underground then.

The question is in which realm?

No, the question is where is Legion?

I refuse to leave without him even if escape becomes an option.

Settling in to wait, I remember Kendall's prediction that Legion would go alone and it would end in his death. She gave no indication she'd seen our failure as a team, and I cling to that now.

It's not over.

It can't be.

I don't have to wait long before the distant door opens and a figure steps through. Not Legion, judging by the slimmer stature, but not Maricha from the height.

Footsteps sound, echoing off the stone walls as the figure approaches my cell. Finally, the visitor's face appears from the shadows as he steps up to my cell.

"Hello, Torissa," Uziah says smoothly.

"Where is he?" I snarl, the sight of him sparking instant rage.

"My son is no longer your concern," Uziah says. "Are you comfortable? Can I get you anything?"

"Comfortable? Are you fucking serious? I'm laced with some kind of poison and locked inside a dirty dungeon who knows where. What do you think?"

"Maricha's mark was a necessary precaution," he says. "We had to make sure you wouldn't resist transport. As for your accommodations, you're right, I'll get you a blanket.

"A necessary precaution. Of course. Well then, I forgive you since you explained your reasoning."

His crimson eyes flash with impatience. "If it's any consolation, the original plan was to kill you outright. But it seems you are a strong motivator for the death dragon, thus your value to him has kept you alive a little longer."

"Gee, I'm so grateful."

His eyes narrow a fraction. "Sarcasm won't get you that blanket."

"I want to see Legion."

"You're not exactly in a position to make demands."

Fury heats me from the inside. I call up my magic, whispering to the vines that have proved faithful so far. Nothing happens.

I look back at Uziah, who watches me knowingly. "Your magic won't work here." His gaze flicks to my ribs.

I frown, realizing the symbol Maricha carved into me must have something to do with my fae magic being blocked. I take comfort in knowing the power is only being cloaked and not gone forever. I'm going to need all the help I can get to defeat these two assholes.

"You will regret this," I tell him.

His smile doesn't reach his eyes, but it holds the full weight of his certainty as he says, "If I do, you will not live to see it."

He turns to go before I can figure out what the hell he means.

"Wait," I call.

He turns a bit impatiently.

"Where are we?" I ask. "What realm?"

"The Earth realm." His expression lightens with a hint of smugness as he adds, "Don't you recognize it? My club has proven to be the perfect stronghold for what Maricha and I are building together."

"We're beneath the Bite Club?" I ask, shocked.

He winks. "Impressive, isn't it?"

"Actually, it's quite the opposite. I don't get it. What does a god need with a street gang who uses a nightclub as their headquarters?"

"The club merely provides a modern-day façade for the prison I carved millennia ago. As for the Crimson Roses, they have always been a means to a greater end. One of many tools and empires I have built for myself over my life. But none of them are greater than the power of my own son. I raised a small army to help me get him back." He pauses and then says, "Yet, in the end, you did it all on your own."

I don't answer, and he retreats as quickly as he came.

A moment later, the door creaks and then bangs shut behind him.

In the silence, I think through his words, turning them over and over until I can find the clues they offer. If we're underneath the Bite Club, that means we're in a position to be found. Legion is important to Caius and the people of Tartarus. I have to believe Klyn will come looking when he doesn't return.

But how long before they figure out there's a dungeon below the club?

In the meantime, whatever Maricha and Uziah are ordering Legion to do, it can't be good. In fact, it must be pretty terrible if they're using me as leverage, especially when their order alone is more than enough to compel him.

Before Legion was cast into Tartarus, he destroyed entire empires and civilizations for his mother. I have no doubt that's what she plans to order him to do again.

Guilt pangs through me as I think about what's happening to the people of the Crossroads. No number of innocent deaths is worth my life. Especially not an entire city of people. But as long as I'm stuck in this cell, I have no way of stopping Maricha and Uziah. No way of breaking their hold over Legion with their blood oath. As long as I'm here, bound by dark magic, my mate is doomed to be a pawn. A very dangerous, very effective one at that.

CHAPTER 38

LEGION

My dragon writhes against the cage of the blood oath. Five thousand years in Tartarus has changed me. Where my dragon nature strained against being bound with such a leash before, the shadow beast I've become opposes my restraints with endless fury. Even so, my own capture pales in comparison to Tori's. Watching Maricha carve into her was the worst torment I've ever felt—far beyond the suffering of my own fate. And Maricha knows it too. Maybe letting her discover my weakness for my mate is a good thing. Tori is still alive. Locked in the dungeon of this wretched place but alive. There is still hope.

I stand before Maricha and Uziah now, my shoulders stiff and muscles tensed with the fury churning inside me. They sit like a ruling king and queen in their high back chairs that one of the soldiers set up on the stage of the vamp club. While the rest of us stand below them, taking our orders.

Around me, Bite Club is dimly lit and full of Crimson Roses.

I hate that I didn't see this coming when I was here before. Then again, who would have guessed a ten-thousand-year-old demon with aspirations for world power ruled from a dance club on the outskirts of an otherwise free city?

Then there's Uziah. He's ambitious and cunning, but he leads with his ego. Already, I've seen the way my mother looks at him. She's putting up with him. There's no love here. She's not capable.

"Legion, are you listening?" My mother's sharp voice slashes through my thoughts.

"I'm trying my best not to," I say.

Her eyes narrow. "You will listen and obey, or you know what will happen to your little vine witch."

Hellfire sears my throat at her words, but I shove it back. "What happened to the civilizations I conquered for you, Mother? You ruled from a real throne last I saw you. And now, you're sitting in a nightclub, surrounded by subpar security guards. Where are your armies? Your warriors? Your kingdoms?"

Her eyes narrow. "I will not explain myself to you—a servant."

"Fine. What about him? Your partner? My father? Does he know how much power you had and lost?"

"I understand the burden of immortality and all its consequences," Uziah snaps, rushing to my mother's defense. "Time is the thief of power. But we will rebuild and reclaim at last."

I shake my head.

My mother nods her agreement, her wrath cooling to disdain as she begins her instructions. "You will start with the portal site. We have our soldiers planting explosives at key locations near the square. When they go off, the surrounding buildings will be leveled. You will pile the rubble around the portal to seal off any intervention from Tartarus. When the area is secured, you will return to the air and burn anything that moves to ash and dust."

"You want to burn the entire city?" I scoff in disgust at their twisted plan. "If you kill everyone, who will bow to you?"

"I don't give a shit about this gods-forsaken city," Maricha scoffs. "I want to show the Houses what we can do. And when they come for us, we'll conquer them all. By the time we are finished in this realm, they will all cower beneath us."

"You don't think the Houses will put up a fight?"

"They can try." Maricha's eyes gleam with the familiar light of greed. It has always blinded her, but it's worse than I remember, even for her. Five thousand years of biding her time has made her reckless. It will be her downfall, though whether I live to see it is another matter.

"And Caius? He is a god and a formidable enemy. More powerful than even you."

"He is busy ruling an entire realm," she says with a huff of dismissal.

"By the time he realizes what's happened, it will be too late to stop us," Uziah agrees.

"And what of the other creatures like me?" I press.

"Shadow beasts?" Uziah asks. "Anything in Tartarus will be trapped when we detonate the portal area."

"Dragons. I am not the only dragon shifter in this realm, you know."

Maricha waves my claim away. "No other dragon can do what you do."

"Are you sure about that?" I ask.

She levels her calculating gaze on me then turns to look at Uziah. "You told me he was the only one."

"He is," Uziah says, wide-eyed. "As far as I know."

I hesitate, debating on whether to divulge this particular information. I don't want to put another at risk, but Maricha needs a wake-up call. "There is another in this realm," I say, "I can sense him. And another still in Tartarus."

"Where is the one you sense in this realm?" Maricha snaps.

"I can't be sure of that. Only that it exists."

She eyes me shrewdly, assessing for my lie. But it's the truth; I can't sense anything beyond what I've told her. Nor do I know whether it'll come for me if I attack this place. I almost hope it does. These people don't deserve what she plans to do.

"Maricha," Uziah begins.

"Recon was *your* fucking job," she hisses at him.

"He clearly senses what others can't," Uziah says, but that only seems to piss her off more.

"There are witches for that. Dark magic. Apparently, I must think of everything." She huffs.

"None of the witches saw an unfavorable outcome.

The female fae's sister is a Seer. I had planned to use her—"

"You had *planned*?" Maricha echoes.

Uziah's eye twitches at her shrieking tone. He looks at the soldier closest to his chair and gives a subtle shake of his head. Their division might be something I can exploit—

"Regardless, you go tonight," Maricha announces, drawing wary looks from the Crimson Roses. "We've prepared long enough."

The soldiers look to Uziah, who nods, and they all murmur their agreement. This time, Maricha doesn't miss the acknowledgment of their leadership. Her fury flashes in her eyes.

"Legion, you are hereby ordered to choose my commands over Uziah's should one contradict the other."

Uziah rounds on her, his glare lethally sharp. "You are overstepping our agreement."

Maricha meets his gaze unflinchingly. "I am only cutting the edges as you have done."

"What are you talking about?"

"Your men pretend to listen to me but continue to look to you for the final word. I am only evening the playing field."

"Maricha."

"Legion," she says, ignoring him. "You have your orders. You are dismissed for now."

I'm halfway to the door before I realize the blood vow's magic has yet to seal her orders. Unsure, I turn back to where Maricha and Uziah are locked in a heated conversation on their makeshift thrones. Clearly, there's no love between them. Not even trust.

And I realize it's now or never.

Too cautious to hope, I will myself to turn around. My body complies with the movements, and soon, I'm standing before them once again. The shock in me is mirrored in Maricha's expression when she notices I've returned.

"What the hell are you doing?" she demands.

Uziah's expression is crinkled in confusion, like he hasn't fully understood the gravity of the moment.

"No," I say simply, bracing myself for the magic of our blood vow to ignite against my words.

Before she can respond, a weak connection springs to life. One both familiar and welcomed in its existence. The mate bond. Through it, Tori's life force sings back at me, and I cling to it. A light in the darkness. A loophole in the dark magic forcing my will to bow to my mother's.

I have no idea how it's possible or why it's only happening now, but I cling to it like a lifeline. Her presence is a beacon in the darkness.

"The vow has been taken." Maricha pushes to her feet and makes her way down the steps toward me. Uziah follows, his confusion turning to concern. "There is no refusing me now," she adds.

I plant my feet, determined to stand as long as my free will lasts. "I have just done so, and there is no pain, no leash. No dark magic putting me in my place."

I watch her outrage build, her eyes widening as she stops before me. "Impossible," she breathes. "There is nothing more powerful than the blood oath."

Uziah glances from her to me, thoughtful. "There may be one thing," he says quietly.

They exchange a look, and I see the moment the truth dawns on Maricha.

"I will end her," my mother screeches, whirling and heading for the door that leads to the dungeon where they've put Tori.

Fear grips me.

"You kill her and you will never have my cooperation," I call out.

Maricha looks back at me. "And if I allow her to live?"

There's no offer of mercy in her words. Only manipulation. And I'm not naïve enough to think she won't still attempt to kill Tori in the end, no matter what we agree to in this moment.

"You will take me to her now. Give me one night with her. In the morning, I will carry out all your plans willingly. That is my offer and, frankly, your only choice if you want to use me for this destruction."

Maricha is silent as she thinks it over.

Uziah looks at her, and when she glances at him, he shrugs. "Works for me. It's not like he can touch her anyway."

Maricha looks back at me, clearly unconvinced. "You expect me to rely on nothing but your honor?"

I shake my head at her. "You can't comprehend it because you have no honor of your own. But if that's not enough, I will let you carve one of your symbols into my skin. Use it to command me whatever you wish from now until dawn."

Maricha's eyes gleam. Her runes are powerful, but

they are temporary thanks to supernatural healing. If they lasted, she might have preferred them over the blood vow as they are much more twisted in their compulsions. Offering her this is something she won't refuse.

"Whatever I wish?" Her lips curve, and I know she's going to agree. "All right. One single night together with my mark." She takes out her knife, its curved tip catching the light so it gleams with dark promises. "Come. Let us begin."

CHAPTER 39

TORI

I hover between sleep and awake for what feels like hours though it could have been minutes or days. Time has no meaning in this place, not with my thoughts darkening toward defeat. I strain to hear some sign of life outside my cell, but the walls mute everything. Either that, or they've abandoned me, and I'm dying a slow, lonely death.

The clang of the outer door opening jerks me fully awake. With shallow breaths, I stir, straining to make out the figures entering the cavern. The pain of Maricha's marking has begun to ease some, so I sit straighter, leaning forward with a grunt.

I see guards first. Crimson Roses if I had to guess, and sure enough, when they step closer to the iron bars, I see the tattoos marking them as such. Maricha comes next, the hatred burning in her gaze making my stomach clench. Unbidden, my eyes dart to her hands and then her clothes, searching for those twisted knives she likes so much.

Maybe she's back to carve into me some more. The thought has me tensing and bracing for a fight. But then Maricha moves aside, and I see a face so familiar and welcome that I ache at the sight of him.

"Legion," I say, disbelief mingling with relief.

He watches me with a tight expression, a storm roiling in his eyes as he takes me in. My heart lurches, everything in me reaching for him.

"Open the door," Maricha orders, holding out a key she produces from her own pocket. One of the guards steps forward to unlock my cell.

I have no idea what's happening, but Legion's calmness steadies me. Still, I manage to climb to my feet, gritting my teeth against the discomfort of my stiff limbs being forced to move again. The symbol carved into my middle protests, but I ignore it, eyes locked on my mate.

As soon as the door swings open, he steps into my cell.

My eyes widen as Maricha nods at the guard and he swings the door shut, locking it and handing the key back to Legion's mother.

"What's going on?" I ask.

"We're roommates," Legion says as if we're not both being locked in a dungeon. As if we're sharing an apartment rather than a prison cell.

"Remember your vow," Maricha warns him.

"Remember yours," he growls at her.

"What vow?" I ask.

"We're spending the night together," Legion tells me.

"And tomorrow, you will conquer the realm in my name," Maricha reminds him.

"Our name," Uziah adds.

"Conquer which realm?" I ask warily. And why was she giving Legion a gift like this?

"Yours," Legion says after a beat.

I stare at him, realizing he's serious. The entire Earth realm? Is that possible?

"In the meantime, enjoy your evening," Maricha says, clearly not interested in catching me up on her plans. Her eyes gleam with a sick enjoyment. "If you can."

"What does that mean?"

Maricha utters words I don't understand. My body tenses, and I wait for the symbol carved into my body to reignite. But the pain never comes.

Legion grunts, gritting his teeth, and I realize he's the one being affected by her words.

"What did you do to him?" I demand, taking a step toward him.

That's when I notice his shirt is plastered to his chest with a wetness that sticks to his skin and stains the fabric from the inside out. Dark, almost black wetness.

Blood.

She's carved into him too.

"Only what he agreed to," Maricha says with obvious glee. She waits until Legion raises his tortured gaze to hers. Then she says, "Here is my command, death dragon. Kill her."

I gasp, but the sound is drowned out by Legion's snarl. He takes a step toward the bars, and Maricha flinches before catching herself.

"We had an agreement," he roars.

"I agreed to let you spend the night with her,"

Maricha says. "I never agreed that she'd be alive while you do it." She flashes a smug smile. "You are so sure you're able to defy my orders, prove it."

"Legion," I say as his gaze swings to me with a jerky motion. His gaze is darkening by the second, his eyes swirling with the storm that always comes before he attacks something.

"I am part of you," I tell him softly. "Remember who I am to you. Your mate. Your heart." I nearly choke on the last word, hoping like hell that it's true. "You can't kill your own heart."

"Stop wasting time." Maricha's words are cold and cruel, but it's the blank, obedient look in Legion's eyes that sucks the air from my lungs. He comes toward me, and I back away, shrinking into the shadows of my cell. For all the good it will do.

If Legion carries out her vicious order, there's nothing I can do to stop him.

"You kill her and you lose your leverage tomorrow." Uziah's voice comes from behind the wall that is Legion. I can't see him or Maricha around the broad shoulders and large body of my mate, but Maricha makes a sound of frustration, followed by a long pause where all I hear is my own erratic heartbeat as Legion closes the distance with death in his eyes.

"On second thought," Maricha says thoughtfully. "Don't kill her yet." Her command stops Legion in his tracks, and I exhale so heavily that my head swims.

I step aside, no longer cornered by him.

Maricha comes into view again in time for her to say,

"Treat her as your enemy from now until dawn." The smile she aims my way is full of victory.

Legion glares at me with hands clenched into fists. Every muscle in him remains coiled and ready to fight me, but he doesn't move closer. Maricha's words are a blow to my heart. She has preserved my life but only so she can dangle Legion in front of me without ever letting me have him.

"And rest," Maricha adds, the word ringing out as a clear command. "Tomorrow, you fulfill your birthright."

Satisfied, Maricha nods at the guards, and they retreat along with Uziah, who trails behind them. I listen as their footsteps disappear down the hall and the cavern doors clank closed. Then there is only silence. And Legion, assessing me as if I'm the snake coiled to strike.

"Legion," I say quietly.

"Stop." He pauses, ears trained and listening.

A beat passes then two.

The silence stretches between us.

Finally, he lets out a breath and says, "Come here, little assassin. I need to hold you."

I'm too stunned to comply, but he closes the distance and pulls me into his arms. His warm breath is on my neck, my cheek—then his mouth finds mine, and I let out a sound of relief. Of need.

His tongue crashes against mine. His grip on my body tightens. There's nothing gentle or reassuring about the way he touches me, but I don't need either one.

I need Legion, exactly as he is. Exactly as he's always been.

Fierce, deliberate, mine.

I kiss him back like I'm drowning, and for a long moment, that's how I feel, sucked under by a current pulling us both along toward some end I can't see coming.

When he finally eases back enough to let me breathe, I gasp, clinging to him, staring at him as if I could memorize this moment. "How?" I whisper. "She said—"

"She said to treat you like my enemy." His grin is deliciously deviant. "And this is how I've treated you as my enemy since the moment we met."

I laugh, my relief turning to joy and escaping my body into the cold, dampness surrounding us. "Hells, you're right. She has no idea what she just said."

"None." His grin dims, and his gaze cools. "If her first order had stood, I might have killed you."

"No, you wouldn't," I assure him.

But we both know he's probably right.

"How are you doing with all this? With her? And...him?"

"I am better now," he says quietly. "I needed to see that you're safe."

"I'm okay," I assure him. "But this symbol blocks my magic. Otherwise, I would have used whatever roots lie outside these stone walls to tear this place to the ground."

"Hmm, maybe dial that back until we're both out of here."

I grin. "I'll do my best." My smile fades quickly as I say, "I'm sorry your parents are assholes."

He grunts, amusement flashing across his face before

being replaced by somber shadows. "I should have killed her on that mountain." He looks at me, his palm cupping my cheek. "I'll fix that problem soon if it's the last thing I do."

"Don't talk like that," I tell him.

"I resisted her order for me to fight for her tonight," he says. "The blood vow didn't work. It's why she made the bargain to let me see you."

My eyes widen. "Does that mean the vow is broken?"

"Not broken. But... the call toward you was strong enough to let me resist."

"That's great news. Right?"

He sighs. "It wouldn't have lasted. I could feel the blood calling to me. My resolve would have crumbled eventually. I managed to get down here before that happened, but... it's not exactly a long-term solution. Besides, it ended with her carving into me, and I wouldn't have resisted that order."

I bite my lip, knowing he's right. We have the stolen moments she's given us, and that's all. For a fleeting moment, I wonder if she knows about the loophole in her words or that the curse is broken between us. I wonder if she did this on purpose, knowing one night in Legion's arms is going to make watching him go that much more painful.

"Do you think she knows I can touch you?" I ask.

"No." He sounds certain. "She would kill you if she knew."

"Why?"

"Because it would mean we would be free to do this."

He strokes my cheek again, and the answer slams

into me. My chest expands with my sharp inhale of breath. I study Legion, my heart pounding, as I consider it. As I consider whether he'd ever agree to giving himself over yet again.

"What is it?" he asks, studying me intently.

"Claim me."

"What?"

"Claim me as your mate. Bind yourself to me. It's the only way to break their hold over you."

"Tori."

The sting of rejection burns my eyes and squeezes my heart. "If you want me to, I'll release you," I whisper. "When it's over, I'll reject you. You can be free."

"Tori," he says again, his voice rough. "If I claim you, that will no longer make you my enemy."

I frown, realizing what he means, what he's afraid of. "You think her first order will return. That you'll try to kill me."

He snorts, a wry smile quirking his mouth. "Not just try."

I smirk back, enjoying the banter even if it only lightens the mood for a moment. "You underestimate me, death dragon. As usual."

He grins, but it fades quickly. "I don't want to risk you."

"Tomorrow, you will be forced to carry out her orders. And there will be no stopping them. You will never be free. We have to risk it."

His expression tightens, and I can see a refusal in his eyes. Instead of letting him utter it, I grab him and kiss him, pouring everything into it. Every drop of emotion and feeling I've held back. Every ounce of my want and my need. All of my trust, finally freely given.

"Legion," I whisper against his mouth. "I love you."

His answering growl sends a shiver of pleasure through me. His hands grip my hips as he lifts me against him. I wrap my legs around his waist as he crashes his mouth to mine, walking us back until I hit the wall. His hard length presses against my core. I grind myself against it, already breathless and desperate for him.

The symbol etched into my skin burns with each movement, but I don't care. The mate bond has never felt this strong before, nor has my desire for the dragon standing before me.

When we met, this kind of vulnerability would have terrified me. But for once, I don't try to hide how badly I need him.

I let him see—and feel—it all.

In answer, Legion's desire is an awareness that blots out everything else. Suddenly, his hands are everywhere at once. Cupping my cheek, tangling in my hair, gripping my throat as he tips my head back and trails kisses down to my collarbone. I let my eyes flutter closed in pleasure, but he grabs my face, pulling my gaze down until we're eye to eye.

"Keep your eyes open, little assassin. I don't want to miss a single moment of your pleasure."

I obey, holding his gaze as his hand drops to the hem of my shirt. He peels it off me then does the same with my bra. He reaches for me, cupping one of my breasts with his rough hand and sucking the other into his mouth.

A wave of pleasure rises, and I grip his shirt, needing to feel his skin against mine. He winces, and I suddenly remember the bloody carving on his chest.

"Sorry," I breathe.

He grunts, and I release his shirt, resolving to be gentler. Before I can tell him to leave it on, he leans away and peels the fabric over his head, tossing it aside.

"Don't apologize for touching me," he says.

Then, he reclaims me with his mouth, sucking one of my nipples between his lips until I gasp. His hands are at my hips then wrapping around to palm my ass.

I am lost to the sensations of him touching me. Whatever I imagined, the reality is so, so much better. My nerves are sensitive, my body aching and craving more even while he sends me higher.

"Legion," I whisper.

"Feeling impatient, little assassin?"

"Yes." The word is a plea, and he answers by slipping his hand into the waist of my pants and sliding his fingers into my already wet panties.

I rock my hips to meet him, and he leans in, chuckling darkly against my ear. "I'm here to please you, but that doesn't mean I plan to give in to your demands. You're my enemy, remember?"

His words are a challenge that makes me want to fight with him almost as much as I want to come for him. Clearly, he wants to do both—and for some reason, it only turns me on more.

I open my mouth to blast him with a snarky response when he slides a finger deep inside me. My words are stolen as he pushes his finger slowly in and out of me.

Then two fingers. His thumb brushes over my clit, drawing a sound of approval from my lips.

I wrap my arms around his neck, holding tight as he sets an excruciating pace of delicious pleasure.

"Yes, just like that, little assassin. Don't let go of me." He presses his forehead to mine, increasing the rhythm ever so slightly as I rock my hips to meet him.

My pleasure builds, and his mouth finds mine as I come apart.

When my shuddering cries quiet, he pulls away from me, and I hate how much of a loss it is. But then he's lowering me to the floor and pulling my pants off. Then he reaches for my panties. There's a ripping sound as he loses patience and tears them free.

I look up at him looming over me in the dimness, his broad shoulders and muscled torso blotting out everything else in this cold cell. My eyes catch on the bloodied symbol Maricha carved into his skin.

I reach for it with tender, careful hands, tracing lightly near the slash marks. Legion hisses, and I stop.

"Does it hurt?"

"Nothing about this moment hurts, love."

He stands, shucking off his pants, and I drink in the sight of him naked and erect. Even wounded, he's breathtakingly beautiful. His dark eyes glitter as he lowers himself over me.

My heart pounds, but it's not from fear. Only anticipation and impatience. And so much fucking love.

"I have imagined this so many fucking times," he says.

His cock is hard against my thigh, and he reaches down, positioning himself at my entrance.

"I dreamt of it," I admit. "I dreamt of the primal hunt. Of letting you catch me. Claim me. But no amount of dreaming even comes close to the real thing," I whisper back.

His mouth curves in a sexy smile as he pushes inside me.

I gasp, my eyes widening at the way he fills me, stretching me and sending waves of pleasure through me at the way he fits so perfectly. Then he begins to move, and I shudder, wrapping my legs around him until he seats himself fully inside me.

For a moment, he pauses there, drinking me in with his dark gaze.

"I want to hunt you," he says darkly. "To fuck you. While the world watches. So they know you belong to me."

I gasp as his words send a dark thrill shooting through me. "I want that too," I tell him.

"When all this is over," he promises. "I'll take you home, and we'll do that."

Slowly, he eases back and rocks against me again. And again. And again. His pace is steady, but it's not enough. Need claws through me, driving my body until my hips are rocking and bucking, urging him faster.

Legion's eyes darken as he watches me, silently daring me to look away from him. But I don't. I can't.

"Don't stop," I tell him, panting, aching, pleasure building.

"We're past that point, little assassin." His voice is

rough, his breath ragged as he slams into me over and over again.

My own release is so close that I can feel myself hurtling toward it. Legion tenses, his pace faster as he rocks against me. I reach up, grabbing his face and pulling it down to mine in a hot, frenzied kiss.

He growls against my lips and pulls back to flash teeth that have suddenly elongated to that of his dragon. He pauses, a question in his eye.

"Do it," I urge him. "Claim me."

He lowers his mouth to my throat, and his lips land on the hollow space there. A flash of pain is followed by waves of pleasure as his sharpened teeth break the skin in a bite that is followed by a rush of power.

Legion gasps.

Before he can recover, I sit up and bite his shoulder until I taste his blood on my tongue. Legion groans, and I know I'm not the only one rewarded with a renewed sense of euphoria.

The mate bond crashes over us both, the emotion and power of it overwhelming to my senses.

Legion drives into me harder, his arms holding me, his eyes raking over me as he sends us both hurtling up and over the edge of our release.

His name is a cry that echoes off the stone walls as I come apart in every sense of the word. Every single part of me seems to shatter and then remake itself in that moment.

Legion shudders and then bows his head as he finds his own release alongside mine.

I wrap my arms around him, reveling in the feel of his

skin against mine. His body against mine. His soul part of mine now.

When we're both able to catch our breath, I look up to find him watching me. At the look he wears, emotion ignites inside me. A sudden sense of fate surrounds us in this cold, damp dungeon. A bond I never could have imagined feeling with another creature.

Mine, a voice inside me declares.

My enemy, the death dragon, Legion Razginath, belongs to me. And I belong to him.

LEGION

The sight of Tori splayed out before me, bared and full of my cock, stirs something inside me. It's more than the mate bond. It's a depthless emotion I've never let myself imagine was possible. Love.

She is, in this moment, no longer my enemy. She is my one true love. Bracing myself for some forced urge to harm her, I wait and watch her chest fall with the last heavy breaths as she recovers from our mating.

"What is it?" she asks.

"Just enjoying the view."

She gives me a look that says she's not fooled. But since no such murderous urge has taken me yet, I bend and kiss her to prove my point. She opens for me so easily, and I shove my tongue into her mouth greedily. I'm determined not to let this night together be our last.

She breaks our kiss to rasp, "If you don't stop this, you're going to have to finish it. Again."

I grin at her, my cock already stirring at the thought. "Is that an order, little assassin?"

She goes still, and I realize too late what I just said. Her expression falters, but I stroke her cheek, holding her gaze on mine.

"Look at me," I say. When she brings her eyes to mine, I tell her, "You are not like them. And I am not afraid of this. Do you understand me?"

"I won't ever trap you, Legion. I swear it."

"Belonging to you is not a trap at all, little assassin. You have made me free."

Her eyes widen at the implication of my words. "Are you sure? Did it... is your vow to her broken?"

I hesitate, and her sharp gaze doesn't miss it. "Something is different. The presence of the leash I felt before is gone. But I won't know for sure until..."

"Until she comes for you."

I hate the fear that springs to her eyes, and there's only one thing I can think of to wipe it away now. "Come here." I pull her up and rearrange us so that I'm sitting on the floor with her straddled over my lap.

Her arms come around my neck, and I wrap mine around her waist, smoothing her hair as I press kisses to her chest and throat.

"Tomorrow will come soon enough," I tell her. "Tonight, it's you who comes."

She laughs. "That was terrible."

I grin, knowing it successfully distracted her. "But is it wrong?"

I push my hardening cock against her hot core and she tightens her grip on me. Even though I've just finished with her, desire slams into me all over again, and I adjust her, reaching for my cock, but she beats me to it. Her hand wraps around my length, and she strokes me slowly.

I bite my lip, holding back a groan. This woman is much more dangerous than I ever knew if one touch can rule me this way. The look in her eyes says she knows it too.

"Assassin," I growl.

"Dragon," she returns, way too smug.

I lift her up as she uses her hand to guide my cock to her entrance. Then I pull her hand away and drive into her so hard that she gasps. She clenches around me, a velvet iron grip that makes me twitch.

"Fuck, you feel good," I say.

She rolls her hips forward, and all I can do is wrap my arms around her and meet her thrusts with my own until we're both lost in one another all over again.

Through the mate bond, I feel her enjoyment, which only heightens my own. My hands tighten at her hips as I lift her up then pull her down again. She pants my name, sweat slicking our bodies as she bites and nips at my ears and throat.

My dragon surges beneath my skin, the monster inside me fully leashed by the woman riding my cock and ruling my heart in the same breath. When she lets herself go, my control snaps. My release shudders through me, wave after wave of pleasure, until we're both panting and gripping the other like a lifeline.

If this is what it's like to give my heart and soul to another creature, I'm more than willing to have my will joined with hers at last.

CHAPTER 41

TORI

Footsteps against the stone floor wake me. My discarded clothing covers my back like makeshift blankets, and my cheek is pressed to Legion's shoulder. Reality crashes in around me, and I bolt upright, noting how Legion still sleeps sprawled on his back with me draped over him like a blanket. At the sound of the approaching footsteps, I scramble off him, fear gripping me.

"Legion," I hiss, shaking him awake as I scramble backward to put distance between us. "Legion."

He opens his eyes and sits up nearly as fast as I did, his frown deepening as he becomes aware of our current state. My eyes drop to his bloodied chest. The symbol hasn't healed yet, which likely means he's still vulnerable to Maricha's magic. But that's not what worries me now.

"You're naked," I whisper, scrambling into my pants. "She'll know—"

"What in the hells is going on here?" Maricha's voice is sharp and cutting.

I meet her gaze through the bars and nearly flinch at the fury she aims at me. Before I can answer, she turns her ire on Legion. Shock and fury line her expression.

"Your order was to treat her like your enemy," Maricha says.

I can practically see the gears turning in her mind as she witnesses evidence of what she believed to be impossible.

"And I have done that." He stands, clearly unconcerned with his nudity, and hands me my shirt with a wink. "Darling. I believe this is yours."

"Legion," I warn.

He cuts me off with a searing kiss.

When he pulls away, his eyes dance with a smugness that stills my fear. He turns back to Maricha. "This is how I've treated her since the moment we met."

Maricha's eyes blaze with fury. "Impossible. Her skin is poison."

"Ah, the curse," Legion says. "That's broken. Thanks to you, Mom."

"You're lying."

Legion runs his hand along my shoulder and down my arm as he says, "Am I?" Maricha looks ready to explode at the casual way he touches me. "We really are grateful you provided such an effective antidote to Tori the night you met her. Your own tears? We couldn't have done it without you."

Maricha's face flushes as she realizes what he means. "Step away from her," she snaps. "That is an order."

I stiffen, waiting to see if her orders will have any effect on him now that we're mated. The bond between us fills with a serene reassurance. Legion sending me his love. But beneath it is pain. The symbol isn't making it easy for him to resist.

Still, he doesn't move. "No."

Relief mixes with new fear. I scramble to dress, knowing Maricha won't hesitate to react once she realizes Legion doesn't answer to her anymore. I barely get my shirt and pants on before Maricha screeches her wrath.

"You will die for this, you little bitch!"

A blade flies straight for me, but Legion pulls me out of the way so the blade clangs against the stone where I just stood. Maricha fumes and draws another knife.

This one she lifts to her lips and infuses it with whispered words that make the small hairs on my arms stand on end.

"Move," Legion roars, shoving me toward the other side of the cell just as Maricha throws the second blade.

End over end, it veers toward us as if set on me like a missile to a beacon. It sings past my ear before clanging into the stone beside my head.

Legion snarls and grabs my hand, pulling me behind him as we both turn to face Maricha. But she doesn't attack again. Instead, she utters some kind of incantation. The blades rattle then lift into the air and fly back into her hands.

"You will both regret crossing me." She looks at Legion. "You have reached the end of your usefulness. What a fucking disappointment."

She whirls, screaming for Uziah as she hurries back down the hall.

When she's gone, we both get dressed again. I hurry to the cell doors and rattle them against the lock. "We need to get out of here," I say. "She's going to come back with something much worse than a knife."

Legion steps up beside me. "Tell me to kill her," he says.

"What?"

"Command me. It'll ensure I find the strength to open this cage. We can escape."

"No."

His eyes flash with impatience. "I'm not afraid of being commanded. Not by you."

"I don't care. I won't do that to you."

"It's the only way to beat them."

"Then we find another way."

He glares at me. "There is no other way."

"There has to be."

I step back, pacing in frustration as I try to think of another option.

"If she returns, she'll bring more men than I can fight," he says quietly.

I don't respond, but he doesn't let up.

"They'll kill you first. Slowly. They'll make me watch. It'll break our bond by severing our souls. And when you're gone, she'll use her dark magic to save me from following behind you in death. I'll be bound to her again, with no way to break free. Forever."

By the time he's done talking, his voice is rough. I hate that he's right. That this is the only way.

"What if you hate me?" I ask.

"I could never hate you, little assassin. You are in my bones. Etched into every space of my heart. And there's not a damn thing you can do about it."

I bite my lip, touched at his words but torn in my choice. I don't want to hurt him. How can I love him if I impose the one cage he's always feared?

Across the cavern, the dungeon door bangs open.

Multiple pairs of footsteps march toward our cell.

"I order you to kill Maricha Razginath."

My words are no more than a whisper. Pained. Awful—because of how badly I want him to carry them out.

Legion steps back, his eyes narrowing as they take on a special, horrible gleam. I watch, terrified I've somehow transformed him into a monster. But then he swoops in and plants a sweet kiss on my cheek. "Your wish is my command, gorgeous."

His words are cheesy, his grin even worse. And I know nothing has changed. Except for the fact that he's now a soldier under my command; a death dragon with one single target in his sights. And he won't stop until she's dead.

I can't say I'm sorry about it either.

Maricha leads the charge as she marches down the hall toward our cell. Her hair whips out behind her, wide eyes full of intended pain and destruction. Legion ushers me back, and I press myself against the wall, waiting for him to make his move.

He simply stands and watches them approach.

Maricha stops several yards away and motions for

the men with her to come forward. "Subdue him. Get me the girl," she snaps.

Legion was right.

She's so predictable.

The vampires hesitate, all of them eyeing Legion warily.

"For fuck's sake," Maricha snarls.

She mutters something and sends a blade flying so quickly that I don't see it coming. Neither does Legion. He grunts as it lands in his shoulder then grunts again as whatever magic it's laced with takes hold.

He falls to one knee, gripping the bars for support.

"Legion," I say.

"I'm fine," he rasps.

Sweat lines his brow. I can feel him fighting off whatever it is. Or trying to.

"Done," Maricha says. "Now, bring me the girl."

A vampire comes forward, rattling keys in his hand. The rest of them watch me and Legion with wary, crimson eyes. My mate stares steadily back at them, exuding a stillness that I can tell sets them on edge.

The door of our cage creaks open and swings inward.

The guards crowd in, fangs elongated and various weapons drawn, all ready to obey Maricha's commands.

The vampire with the keys takes a single step inside before Legion shoves to his feet, yanking the knife out and brandishing it at the other soldiers. His roar is deafening, and his body shifts as he moves. In one step, his hand is clawed and his arm covered in scales. Another step; he's pierced the throat of the closest vampire before hurtling him through the door at the others. Half a dozen of them are tossed onto their asses.

"Run," he roars at me.

Another step and his legs are coated in impenetrable scales. More claws. His back is coated in scales and spikes. His tail swipes from behind while his claws clear a path at the front.

This cavern isn't tall enough or wide enough for his dragon form, but he doesn't stop trying to shift. Through the bond, I can feel his struggle to fight against whatever magic Maricha laced her blade with. Before Legion's dragon can fill the space and cut off my exit, I duck beneath him and race out of the cell.

Maricha tries to grab me but Legion snaps his teeth at her and she turns to face him instead. I force myself to keep going.

The hall into the cavern is lined with vampires in various states. I don't stop or look at them. Instead, I keep my gaze on the end of the hall where the dungeon door hangs open. Behind me, I can hear Maricha screeching orders as her vampires attempt to stop or slow Legion's dragon.

They won't.

They'll be destroyed trying.

But I don't intend to let him do it alone.

At the end of the hall, I clang the door shut, shoving the lock down and sealing me and everyone else inside. From the other side, more vampires slam into the iron bars, reaching through in their attempt to grab me.

"Open this door."

Uziah pushes his way to the front, glaring at me from the other side.

"You wanted me locked in," I said. "And now I am."

He curses at me, but I ignore him and turn back to where Legion's dragon is wedged into the hall that's nearly too small to hold his large form. Vampires claw against his scales, some of them attempting to stab weapons into wherever they can reach. Others climb the spikes on his back, looking for a vulnerable spot.

I glance around at the stone walls, sure that what I'm about to do will likely kill us all. If I hadn't accidentally done it up on that mountaintop, I wouldn't even know to try it now.

All I can do is hope that it's enough.

On a deep breath, I call out to the earth pulsing with plant life beyond these stone walls. The symbol carved into my skin is nearly healed, leaving my magic finally within reach again. It takes a few strained moments, but then my power slams into me, leaving me breathless.

The surge is overwhelming after being cut off for so many hours, but I don't hold back. Beside me, the wall cracks. Stone falls to the floor in large boulders, raining down along with smaller pebbles and sand.

At my feet, the floor opens, and the ground rumbles as a fissure appears and begins to expand. From the depths of the opening, thick, black vines creep up and out of the earth.

Poison.

I can feel it pulsing inside them.

Even without cursed skin, I still wield poisoned vines as easily as if they're a part of me. Their life force thrums inside me, offering their service willingly, and I urge them onward.

They climb swiftly down the hall, wrapping themselves around the vampires they find along the way. The vamps' legs are yanked out from under them as the vines coil around ankles and wrists.

The mate bond thrums alongside my magic, and I can practically hear Legion yelling in my head, telling me to get the hell out of here.

Not a fucking chance, death dragon.

At my direction, the vines pull taut around the necks of the Crimson Roses in their path. They struggle against the pressure, but I only squeeze harder—not stopping until the vines begin to cut through flesh.

From somewhere in the center of her pack of soldiers, Maricha screams for someone to get me. Most are too caught up in avoiding the dragon clawing through their ranks, but a few of them break away and run straight for me.

I don't move.

A step backward would put me within reach of Uziah and his men reaching through the bars of the door behind me.

Instead, I hold my ground, concentrating on the fissure I've opened. More vines pour out of it, creating a wall of vegetation that snags the vamps as they come up against it. Their blood coats my vines, dripping from the black leaves and filling the air with the scent of death.

Legion's dragon snarls, the sound sending a ripple of unease through me. I part the vines enough to see him writing against the bars of the cell we spent the night in. A small, carved blade protrudes from his scales.

I stare in disbelief and horror as the bond between us fills with pain.

"Legion," I scream.

Maricha whirls, the hatred in her gaze unhinged. "I will kill you slowly," she declares. "But he won't be so lucky."

Legion's dragon roars. Hellfire drips from his throat, evidence of his suffering.

"If you won't serve me, then you've outlived your use," Maricha tells him.

Legion snarls at her, and the mate bond snaps closed. For a horrifying second, I think he's gone, but then I realize he's only shut himself off from me. So I can't feel his death.

Idiot.

Hurrying toward them, I direct my vines toward Maricha, watching as they wind their way up her legs and around her wrists and throat. She utters another incantation, and the vines break, crumbling and dying at her feet. I send more in their place, but it won't be enough. I know it immediately. And I won't be there in time to save him.

Behind me, there's a loud clang.

I look back in time to see the door break open, and Uziah's crimson eyes blazing with fury as he steps into the cavern. Around him, Crimson Roses pour through, racing toward me.

Desperation and fear wrap around my throat as tightly as the vines.

This is it.

From behind the soldiers, the tunnel echoes with cries of pain and the clang of weapons.

A voice shouts my name. "Tori!"

I go still, unsure if I'm hearing things.

It comes again. "Tor, we're coming! Hold on!"

"Kendall?"

The first wave of vampires rushing through the door reaches me, distracting me from the sound of my sister's voice. My vines are fast, but these damn vamps are faster. I'm nearly bitten twice before they're dragged away from me by the ankles and dragged into the opening on the cavern floor.

I look up and find Uziah standing several paces away from me. His back is to me as he stares at the new threat.

My sister stands in the doorway from above.

Her cheeks are stained with dirt and blood. She wields a short blade in each hand, and the look on her face suggests she's been using them effectively thus far, though I have no idea how she learned. Beside her stands a wolf larger than I've ever seen. He glares at Uziah then lets loose with a howl that echoes off the cavern walls.

"Surrender, and we'll consider letting you live," Kendall tells Uziah.

Uziah snorts. "Put down that blade, stupid girl. You have no idea what you're doing."

"Why? Because I'm a girl?"

"Because you are a Seer, not a warrior,"

"You know, for a guy older than dirt, you're surprisingly limited in your world view." She grins, a flash of teeth that is more dangerous than amused. "That kind of small thinking is going to get you killed someday. I mean, why can't I be multi-talented?"

"You're no match for me."

"Maybe not," Kendall tells him. Her eyes gleam with a certainty that makes me pause. "But you've never met him. And death comes for us all."

The wolf rushes forward, teeth bared at the ancient vampire. Uziah blurs with speed as he rushes to meet his attacker. The two of them colliding is a gnarled, bone-breaking sound in my ears.

With Uziah and the wolf battling, the rest of the vampires throw themselves into the fight. I don't think beyond the power I'm wielding and nearly send a vine to attack my next incoming target when I realize it's Kendall cutting my way to fight at my side. Her blades sing where they clash against the vampires' weapons.

Our eyes meet.

I recognize the question in her gaze, so I hold up my gloveless hands. "The curse is broken."

She starts to speak, but something over her shoulder has my eyes widening in warning.

Kendall spins just as Uziah stumbles within her reach. She shoves her blade out to meet him, and he gasps as it pierces his heart. His weight sags against her, and I help her shove him back.

He falls to the stone floor, his eyes wide as if he can't quite believe Kendall managed to stop him. Blood leaks from his chest. It's thick and dark, pooling around the knife buried an inch to the left of his heart.

"You..." Uziah tries to speak, but his breath catches. He winces.

Kendall bends over him, her expression grim. "Me," she says. "Sucks to be finished off by a stupid girl, doesn't it?"

Uziah grunts.

The wolf prowls closer.

It looks intent on finishing off the vampire, but before it gets close enough, Uziah jumps up, snatching the blade free from his own chest and pointing it at Kendall's throat.

I shove her aside at the same moment the wolf plows into the vampire from behind. The blade he held clatters to the ground. I pick it up, closing the distance to where Uziah is attempting to scramble to his feet again. With both hands gripping the hilt, I shove it through his heart and twist.

Uziah falls again, and the wolf is there with claws and fangs, ripping out the vampire's heart.

I watch in silence, rage and relief coursing through me.

Kendall comes up beside me and gently takes the blade from my hands. The calm look she wears feels reassuring, as if she's the one comforting me. "Nice work, sis."

"What are you doing here?"

"Great question, and I'd love to tell that story, but it's not over yet. You have any of that vine magic left in you?"

"Plenty," I assure her.

"Show me."

I turn with her to meet the last of Maricha's soldiers. Kendall cuts through them with her knife, and I drag them off with my vines until the wolf rips them apart.

Between us, every last vampire falls.

When we're done, I look over to see the wolf already prowling toward Legion's cell where Maricha stands over him. He's back in his human form but he's no longer fighting her.

My heart lurches and I study the demon bitch, already planning how I'll kill her.

Kendall stops me. "Is that—"

"His mother," I tell her.

"Wow."

"And the wolf?" I ask.

"Klyn."

I nod, glad to have an ally like him in this moment. But I'm not sure it'll matter.

"You're all dead." Maricha's words are twisted with hate.

"Let him go and you can have me," I tell her.

"Take him. My work here is done." Her smug smile is pure evil.

I take a step toward her but Kendall blocks my way.

Legion groans but doesn't move. Maricha stands over him, murder in her eyes and in the whispered words she continues to utter, as if her grip on him depends on her continuous effort.

"She laces her knives with dark curses," I explain.

"I know," Kendall says, her eyes locked on Maricha.

Klyn merely stalks to meet her, his fur standing on end as he bares his teeth at the demon. Kendall grabs my hand and tugs me to follow Klyn.

"Come on," she says.

"Kendall, she's dangerous," I begin.

My sister looks back at me and winks. Like, actually *winks*. "She doesn't win," she tosses over her shoulder and waltzes forward to meet Maricha like it's already done.

I stare at Kendall, confused—and impressed. What-ever happened to my sister while I was away, I think I like it.

Klyn stops at the open cell door.

He bares his teeth, growling, and Maricha answers his challenge by stepping forward to meet him. Black wings unfurl from her shoulders. They are razor-sharp—weapons all on their own. She uses them as such, stab-bing one of them toward the wolf, but he darts out of reach, snapping his teeth at her. Maricha's movements are light, her feet barely touching the ground as she meets every one of Klyn's blows with a block of her own. She's not winded. She's barely even watching him as she moves left and right to counter him.

Despite Kendall's assurances, my insides twist.

Legion groans, and I look over to find him studying me. The bond is still quiet, but in his eyes, I see all I need to know. Maricha's magic is draining him. Even if Maricha doesn't win, I'm not sure how to stop what she's done to my mate.

Forgetting the danger, I rush forward, slipping past the fight and into the cell. Dropping down beside Legion, I grip his face in my hands until we're eye to eye. "Don't stop fighting," I tell him. "That's an order."

He snarls, but it's weak.

My eyes land on the hilt of the knife protruding from his shoulder. A whisper of voices sound in my ear. I can't understand the words, but I reach for the knife anyway.

"Stop!" Maricha's scream is unhinged. Desperate.

I look up in time to see her swipe the wolf with a sharpened wing. The wolf howls, and a bloody wound opens along his flank.

"Shit," Kendall says and steps in front of him. But Maricha is no longer focused on the wolf.

She rushes toward me. I have no idea why she's suddenly so unhinged about me touching her knife—so that's exactly what I do.

The moment my hand closes around the hilt, the dark magic slams into me. Whispers fill my ears. Shadows slither through my vision. The earth trembles around me, and I grip Legion with my free hand to keep from falling over. With all the strength I can muster, I yank the knife free from Legion's body.

Maricha falls to her knees, wailing.

The second knife she held clatters to the ground.

Legion shifts beside me, black scales sliding over his skin, replacing his flesh. I watch as the knife wound begins to pulse, the dark poison spilling out of him onto the ground. The symbol carved into his chest starts to heal and close.

Relieved, I look down at the weapon I hold. The knife is warm in my hands, coaxing me to never let it go.

My mind is a whirring of dark thoughts.

Death. Destruction. Domination.

I look up and see the second knife lying still on the stone floor. Without thought, I lift my hand, and the blade responds, sailing through the air and landing in my palm.

My fingers curl around the hilt possessively.

Power whooshes through me.

I look at Maricha, noting the way she's fallen to her knees. It was never her power that I needed to fear. It was the power of these blades. Rising to my feet, I step over my mate to where the dark demon cowers on the stone.

"Those don't belong to you," she accuses.

Her eyes aren't on me, though. They're locked on the blades.

"You will never hurt me or my mate again." The knives seem to echo my words, urging me to use them. I raise them both overhead, tips pointed straight at the monster who caused all this pain.

Before I can act, a dragon darts out of the cell, its teeth closing over Maricha's thigh. She screams, and the teeth bear down, crunching through bone. Maricha's wings stab at the dragon, but they bounce harmlessly off Legions' scales. Another crunch and Maricha's screams fall silent.

Her eyes remain open, her breathing shallow, as she stares up at her son.

Legion retreats into the cell, shifting back to his

human form. I can feel him standing beside me, watching me, just like Kendall and Klyn. But I can't shake the feeling that the task isn't complete. Nor can I seem to make myself let go of the blades.

Their whispers guide me, and I repeat their words. Words I still don't understand, but they flow from my tongue as if being coaxed or pulled by the magic itself. "Lissnim Roraouth Azrepkeer."

I watch as poison coats the wounds Legion left behind; a darkness seeping into Maricha's body just as it had done to me up on that mountain. It creeps into her blood. Her heart. Into the soul already damned to the realm of hell.

I watch her die, a grim satisfaction setting my expression.

The breath leaves her lungs, and the whispers finally, finally go silent.

The cavern is quiet.

It's over.

I start to turn away, but the whispers come to life again, calling me, coaxing me, asking me to rule them or be ruled by them.

"Wait," my sister calls.

I look up at her.

"Let me," she says gently.

"You don't understand. I can hear them."

"I know." She slides her own blade into a strap on her belt then takes the blades from my hands.

Instantly, the whispers intensify. She looks down at the blades, a strange look pinching her expression. I watch as she walks over to where Uziah's body lies. She holds up one of the blades and mutters a string of words I don't understand. Words that sound like the language Maricha used. The language I used just now. The language of the blades themselves.

At her words, the whispers instantly quiet.

Then she plunges one of the blades into Uziah's chest right through the space where his heart has been ripped free. He gasps, his eyes flying open despite his lack of the life-giving organ. I leap into motion, disbelief and fear sending me racing toward my sister.

"You could have been a great weapon for our side," he rasps.

"I am my own weapon," Kendall tells him.

She whispers something to the blade again, and poison leaks from its surface into Uziah's body. The vampire-god groans and then falls back again, motionless.

"It's done," Kendall says quietly. "He's gone. For good this time."

I stare at my sister, not sure whether to be horrified or relieved.

"What did you do?" I ask.

Kendall eyes me warily. "I sealed their deaths. And I claimed these blades for myself."

"How? And where did you learn to fight like that?" The questions I've been battling since she arrived spill out one after another.

She smirks. "You always underestimate me, you know that?"

Before I can answer, Legion is beside me, pulling me toward him and wrapping his arms around me. I cling to him, squeezing my eyes shut until the whispers filling my ears finally go quiet.

When I open my eyes, Kendall is watching me with relief in her eyes. "We have a lot to catch up on," she says, nodding at the way my bared skin touches Legion's.

"That goes for you too," I tell her.

We share a smile as I lean into the strength of Legion's arms around me. When he pulls away and meets my gaze, I see an uncertainty in his dark, depthless eyes.

"She won't hurt you again," I tell him.

"I killed my own—" He stops, and I grab his face in my hands, forcing him to meet my eyes. "You may have taken life, but you are not a killer. There's a difference."

His mouth quirks up at that, and I know he's going to be okay.

"Whoever told you that sounds very wise," he says.

I grin. "They seem to think so."

His smile is radiant—and free. "I told you I'd follow your orders." He kisses me and whispers, "Master."

"Ew, you just made it weird."

He laughs, hugging me tight. "I kind of like it. Unless you want to call me that instead."

I don't answer, too busy soaking up the feeling of no longer being threatened with death in order to be with the male I love. I cling tighter to him, closing my eyes and breathing deeply. His hand strokes my hair, his fingers brushing my cheek.

"It's over," he murmurs.

"It's over," I agree but then pull away to examine him. "Are you okay though? The poison—"

"Is gone." He looks at Kendall then the blades she holds. "You understand them."

"I do," she says quietly.

"They corrupted her."

Kendall doesn't look particularly thrilled with her own words as she says, "They were meant for me. I've seen it." Her gaze darts to me.

"Kendall," I say, utterly at a loss.

"I saw this too," she reminds me. "Back before this all started. I saw you and him, remember?"

"You said I had to choose," I tell her. "And my choice would determine whether I lived or died."

She nods. "You don't die alone anymore in case you're wondering. You live. Together. For a very long time."

Her gaze is sober, though. No hint of relief or victory.

My stomach tightens as I try to understand what it means. Her coming here. Understanding those blades.

She shoots a look at Klyn, who is still in wolf form. He's managed to get to his feet, but he's limping and bleeding from where Maricha's wing cut him.

"You okay?" she asks him.

He huffs and comes forward, nudging Legion with his nose.

"I'm okay," Legion assures his friend.

Klyn snarls and nods pointedly at the exit.

"Yeah, I second that idea," Legion tells him.

But I can't move. Not with so many questions swirling inside me. Kendall watches me as if she's read my thoughts. I look at her, pride radiating from me at the skill of her gifts. And more than a little guilt for the way I doubted her.

"You can really handle those blades?" I ask her.

She swallows hard but says firmly, "They obey me now. You're not in any danger."

"I don't get it. You sound like you knew about them before you saw them."

"I've seen them in visions," she says, which only gives me more questions. At my look, she sighs. "Death calls to death. These blades have been calling me for weeks now. I didn't know how to explain it to you."

The truth of her words hits me—along with guilt. "I wouldn't have listened."

She doesn't answer, but her expression softens.

Klyn whines.

Kendall glances to him then back to me, brows raised. "Look, can we get the hell out of here? I promise to answer all your questions once we're home. And when he's not naked," she adds, nodding at Legion.

"Fair point," he says.

I shake my head. "Let's go."

Legion holds me close as we make our way through the cavern. I notice Maricha's evil rune still healing over his chest. Before I can ask if he's really okay, awareness pours into me.

I look up at him and find him watching me.

The mate bond.

He's opened himself up again.

Now, instead of torture, all I feel is love. Relief and so much love.

It really is over.

I press myself closer to him, relishing our skin-to-skin contact, and climb the stairs beside my mate.

When we emerge from the cavern, I shake my head. "I can't believe we were beneath this stupid club this whole time. Carving that prison down there must have taken him years."

Kendall's expression hardens. "That's why he wanted me to work for him. To help him attain power—and prevent his defeat." She looks like she'd kill him all over again if possible. With her new blades, it just might be.

I shudder, thinking of all the things those knives can probably do.

"We should seal the doors," I say.

Legion nods knowingly. "Smart. Dead or not, what lies below deserves to be forgotten."

"Way ahead of you," Kendall says, "Come on. We don't want to be inside when this place goes down."

We follow her outside into what looks like a hurricane. I press myself against the wall of the club at my back, blinking into the sheets of rain that fall sideways thanks to the wind. Overhead, thunder rolls, and lightning cracks the gray skies.

"How does this help seal the cavern?" I call out.

Kendall nods at something. I follow the direction of her gaze and see a lone figure standing in the middle of the empty parking lot. Her clothes are plastered to her slight frame, the rain drenching every inch of her, but she doesn't seem to notice as she remains attentive to the skies she commands.

"Chaya?" I say.

"We needed something to help keep any reinforcements from being called in," Kendall explains. She grins. "Power's out, by the way. Cell towers too. Hell of a storm blew in this morning. Too bad the rest of the Crimson Roses never got a call to come when the boss needed them."

I grin right back at her.

Klyn trots out to where Chaya stands, nudging her hip with his snout. She looks down at him then over to where we're all huddled in the doorway.

"Now!" Kendall shouts to her.

Chaya makes a motion with her arms. Thunder and lightning crack. A loud pop resonates as lightning strikes the club. The ground rumbles, and over the whistling wind, I hear a rumble that vibrates the ground beneath me.

Legion, Kendall, and I step away from the building. I turn back in time to see the roof caving inward as the entire structure implodes on itself.

"Lightning did all that?" I ask.

"Klyn may have planted some explosives in strategic places," Kendall says.

Legion mutters his approval.

Out in the parking lot, Chaya lowers her hands to her sides. All at once, the thunder and lightning cease.

The rain slows then stops.

Overhead, the clouds begin to break apart, revealing blue skies on the other side.

Chaya and Klyn walk over to where we stand. "Are you okay?" she asks Legion worriedly.

"We're both fine," he tells her, and she visibly relaxes.

Then she throws herself against him in a tight hug. He catches her with one hand, the other still firmly holding mine. He smiles at me over her shoulder.

"I'm okay," he repeats. "I swear."

Chaya lets him go and then hugs me. I squeeze her right back, grateful for the ability to do so. When she steps back, Kendall's eyes are watering, and she finally looks properly happy.

I grab her hand and pull her in for a hug too.

She laughs and hugs me back tighter than ever before. By the time we're done squeezing each other, we're both standing in a puddle of water up to our ankles. But it's still the happiest I've felt in months. Maybe years. Maybe ever.

When I finally let go of my sister, Legion is there, planting a kiss on my mouth. "I didn't want to miss my chance to celebrate with you."

"Hells, there will be plenty of time for this shit later."

At Klyn's voice, we all look over.

He's standing in the empty lot, naked and bloody and looking more like a wild man than I've ever seen with blood and dust streaked through his beard. "Can we fucking go already?"

"Hey, we have a lot of time to make up for," Legion says, grinning.

Klyn looks at Kendall. "You and Chaya can stay with me for the next month if you want. Those castle walls are thinner than they look."

My sister snorts. "We might take you up on that."

I open my mouth to protest but then see the way Legion is looking at me and decide they're probably right to put some distance between us and them for a while.

Anticipation and pure happiness sing through the mate bond. I look up at Legion, smiling. "Take me home?"

He kisses me thoroughly enough to draw more groans from the others. "I thought you'd never ask."

EPILOGUE

TORI

Every day since returning to Tartarus feels like a vacation. Kendall keeps calling it retirement, at which point, I promptly remind her I'm way too young to be called retired. Besides, my new career is still young, but it's promising. Selling herbs and potions at the farmers market has been more fulfilling than I expected. Mostly because Chaya does the selling while I spend my time experimenting with the best recipe for face cream or brewing salve for burns. But also because none of it involves killing people. It's a nice change of pace, helping people rather than offing them.

The greenhouse Legion built for me is already packed with more plants than it can hold. The walls are covered in dark vines and black roses—inside and out—but so far, none of them have proven harmful. Legion thinks they're my magic's response to Tartarus' particular brand of shadow magic. As long as it doesn't interfere with me getting my hands on him every night, I'm all for it.

He's promised to build me something bigger soon—and it's not lost on me that we're not just planning a future together.

We're living it.

The Keep is feeling more like home every single day.

And the death dragon that rules it feels more like mine every single night.

Thanks to the mate bond, Legion's presence is like a gravitational pull. It's not only his location, either—it's his mood. His intentions. His lust. I feel it all, and I can't get enough. I'm not sure how I ever doubted our connection as mates, except that I know now how much my curse muted everything else in the beginning.

Now, the only things muted are my screams as I come for him at night—

but only after the rest of the house insisted we keep it down.

Standing in my bedroom, I assess my appearance in the mirror, wondering if I should change again. The black dress is tight around my hips and breasts, the straps thin, with a scandalously high slit up the side of the skirt. But trading my scarf and gloves for a slinky dress isn't the only change. My green hair is brighter than ever—permanently so—and my emerald eyes gleam with a life force that grows stronger daily. Tartarus is changing me. Making me in its image. Powerful, magical—and immortal.

Before I can move, strong hands land on my hips, and I watch through the reflection as Legion steps up behind me.

"Beautiful," he murmurs.

He dips his head and drops a lingering kiss to my bared neck. His tongue darts out, licking the scar where he bit and claimed me. I shudder, my skin tingling and my body already thrumming for more.

His hand slides lazily down the front of my dress, grabbing handfuls of fabric and pulling it up to gain access. I turn my head, and his mouth captures mine, his kiss possessive. Claiming. Promising a hell of a lot more where this came from.

I pull back, sighing against his lips.

"We can't be late," I tell him.

"Sure we can," he says. "They're going to be too drunk to notice anyway."

I give him a withering look and, with a scowl, he releases my dress. He grabs my hips and spins me around to face him. "Fine, but I'm getting double the orgasms out of you later as compensation for my loss."

I laugh. "Deal."

He takes my hands and leads me from our bedroom.

Downstairs, Kendall, Chaya, and Klyn are standing around chatting while they wait for us. Bron's voice drifts out from down the hall, asking if he can add sprinkles to the pastries. Brigita answers him in a gentler voice than I've ever heard her use on anyone else.

"Finally," Kendall says when she sees us. "I thought we were going to have to send up a search party."

"Ugh, that kind of dirty work is far outside my scope as a soldier," Klyn says, shaking his head disgustedly.

"Oh, gross, now that you mention it, I take it back. No search parties."

"Maybe just a lightning storm and a mysterious roof leak right over the mattress," Chaya says, eyes gleaming.

"You wouldn't," I say.

She laughs, and I realize she absolutely would.

"Come on, we don't want to be late," Legion says, grabbing my hand and pushing past everyone on our way to the door.

"Oh, now you want to be in a hurry," Klyn teases, falling into step behind us.

Our walk to town brings more laughter, and by the time we arrive at Osiris, my sides ache from listening to Legion and Klyn boast about whose team will win the next round of war games, which apparently involves laser tag with lasers that leave burns behind.

Inside the bar, four others are already waiting. Legion explained the bar would be closed to everyone else for the night, which makes sense, given the guest list. My stomach flips a little with sudden nerves at meeting someone so important and legendary, but I focus first on the faces I do know.

"Here they are," Styx says.

She and Reagan come forward, each of them grabbing me in a fierce hug.

"Really glad to see you," Reagan says to me, giving my hand a quick squeeze. "Without all the layers, I mean."

"Me too," I agree.

After that, it's a chaos of voices for a moment as everyone is introduced to one another.

"You must be Corvin," I say, offering my hand to the

male standing beside Styx. "I'm Tori. Nice to see you again."

"Ah, yes, the poisoner," he says, but he shakes my hand with a knowing grin.

"That's me. Retired, thankfully. Nice paintball skills, by the way."

He grins as Legion claps him on the back. "Speaking of which, I owe you a victory drink. And then Klyn owes us all a round for losing."

The bartender slides full drinks down the bar toward us.

"First round's on me," the male beside Reagan announces.

He meets my eyes, and my stomach flutters with nerves again.

"You must be Tori," he says, shaking my hand.

"And you're King Caius. It's an honor to meet you, Your Highness."

"Whoa," Legion says, stepping up beside us. "It's just Caius. We don't want him getting a bigger ego than he already has."

Caius grins and punches Legion in the shoulder.

"Too late," Styx chimes in.

Reagan laughs, and I feel my nerves lessen at the casual friendship between them all.

"He's right," Caius tells me. "You can call me Caius. All my friends do."

"Thanks," I tell him, feeling a wave of gratitude and happiness.

"Chaya, nice to see you," Caius says. "And you must be Tori's sister, the Seer."

"Kendall." My sister grips Caius' hand with confidence that impresses me. "It's nice to meet you, sir."

"Call me Caius," he tells her. "Legion speaks highly of your talents. I'd be interested in hearing more."

"Sure, what do you want to know?"

Kendall and Caius step away from the rest of us, locked in conversation.

Legion catches my eye, winking at me as Styx hands out drinks to everyone.

"Here," she says, giving Legion a glass with liquid slightly darker than the rest of ours. She holds her matching drink up to his, and they clink glasses.

"Is this...?" He sniffs it carefully.

"No point in drinking anything less at this point," she tells him.

Legion glances at me questioningly. "Is hers—?"

"Are you insane?" she fires back at him. "It took us five thousand years to build up a tolerance to this insanity." She clinks her glass with mine in a toast, telling me, "But hey, you can always catch up."

She grins at me and downs her glass, turning back to the bar and calling for another. I look over in time to see Legion gulp half of his own drink then wince.

"What is it?" I ask him.

"Magic infusion. Hell of a kick to it." He empties the rest of the glass.

"And mine?"

"Just Whiskey. For now." He offers a crooked smirk. "She's right. You have the next five thousand years to catch up."

Curious, I lean over his glass and sniff. "Hmm."

"What is it?" he asks warily.

"Smells a bit like opium. Mixed with..." I sniff again. "Ogre's blood maybe?"

I straighten and he stares back at me, horrified. "I've been drinking Meech's blood?"

"Who's Meech?"

He jerks a thumb at the bartender, and I bite my lip to keep from laughing.

His eyes narrow. "You think this is funny?"

"I think I can do better," I say, nodding at the drink.

His glare turns to an intrigued gleam. "How?"

I shrug. "Not sure if you've heard, but I'm pretty good with poisons."

He grins. "Oh, I know all about you, little assassin. Tell you what, next time we drink with Styx, we'll have a little taste test. You versus Meech."

"Challenge accepted," I say and then tip my glass up with all the others.

The next hour passes with toasts, jokes, and stories. The lifetime of memories shared between Legion and his friends only makes me feel closer to them all. It's a beautiful reminder of what I've become a part of. And it makes me think of Juniper and my parents with just enough sadness that I decide to get some air.

Slipping out the door into the darkness, I'm surprised to find Kendall outside.

"Hey," I say, "What are you doing out here?"

"Needed some air," she says.

I nod, noting the blades she wears in the leather holsters strapped to her middle. She never goes anywhere without them. We haven't talked about them since that day in the cavern below the club. Something tells me Kendall will talk when she's ready. And I still have some making up to do on that front.

"I'm glad you're out here," I tell her. "I've been wanting to talk to you."

"What's wrong?" she asks. "Is everything okay?"

"Everything's fine." I smile sadly as I realize it's going to take some more time before she accepts we don't live a life of constant danger anymore. It's going to take time for me too. "But I owe you an apology."

"For what?"

"Everything, really. For refusing to see how capable you were these last several years. For dismissing your visions. For going off without you to face Uziah and Maricha. I'm so sorry, Kendall. I hope you can forgive me."

"Of course I forgive you, Tor. You were being protective. You had to fill the role of a parent as well as a big sister. You raised me, and I'm so grateful for it, but it couldn't have been easy."

"Thank you, but it hasn't been easy on you either and that's on me. I should have made you feel like you could talk to me." I glance at the blades she wears. "You said you felt called to those things for a while. You should have been able to come to me."

"Don't blame yourself for that. I mean it. I wasn't ready to talk about it because I needed time to understand it for myself."

"Your gift is clearly more powerful than I realized. And the fighting?" I can't help but lift my brows at that.

She grins ruefully. "Yeah, my training with Natalia was a bit broader than I mentioned."

"She knew, didn't she? Natalia. That's why she wouldn't let you stay with her when this all began."

"She knew I'd been having visions about the knives," she says quietly. "It's why she helped me train."

I shake my head, nothing but proud. "I'm sorry I wasn't there for you like I should have been. I see now how much you've grown up, and I'm so proud of you."

"Thanks." Her eyes fill with tears. "That means a lot coming from you."

"Juniper would be proud too. And Mom and Dad," I add, tearing up at the thought of them looking down on everything Kendall has become. On what we've both become. The life we've built.

"They'd be proud of you too, punk," she says.

I laugh. "Thanks, punk."

She sniffles.

I reach for her, hugging her tight, grateful for the fact that we can do this again. When I release her, tears have tracked down her cheeks. She wipes them away hastily.

I smile softly. "What will you do now?"

"What do you mean?"

"You're capable of deciding your future for yourself. Just because I'm staying in Tartarus doesn't mean you have to."

Her eyes widen. "You mean that?"

"I do." I squeeze her hand reassuringly. "And I'm sorry about Chase. He was nice to you, and he didn't deserve what Uziah did to him."

"No," she agrees, her expression hardening at the memory. "He didn't."

I watch as she works to put aside her grief. So much stronger than I ever noticed. "So, where do you want to live?" I prompt.

"Well... Caius asked me if I want to come work for him."

"Seriously?"

"He said he can always use advisors with gifts like mine. Apparently, the glaistig annoys the hell out of him."

I snort. "Understandable. You'd be great at it," I add. "Are you going to say yes?"

"Not sure yet. It's nice hanging out with people who aren't going to die anytime soon." Her gaze flicks to something over my shoulder, and her expression changes. "But speaking of saying yes..."

She motions for me to turn.

When I do, Legion is standing in the open doorway, holding a small black box in his hand. Inside the bar, the others are all hushed and crowded around behind him, watching us expectantly.

My heart leaps. "What are you...?"

"Torissa Emerald Sage, I am willingly and joyfully bound to you, in blood, in spirit, in heart and soul. I will belong to you forever." He drops to one knee, uncapping the box to reveal a gorgeous emerald ring set against clusters of diamonds. "What I feel for you is something I want the world to witness. Will you pledge yourself to me before our friends and families in a Commitment Ceremony?"

Joy rushes through me. His. Mine. Everyone's.

I glance over at Kendall, who smiles and nods encouragingly. Behind Legion, Chaya clasps her hands together, looking hopeful. Beside her, Klyn grins. Reagan and Caius stand with their arms around one another. And Styx presses herself against Corvin, who stands behind her protectively.

Friends *and* family.

It's all I've ever wanted.

I look at Legion with all the love in my heart and the pure devotion that now runs through my veins. "As long as we get to start with the hunt."

"With you," Legion says, eyes gleaming with happiness and commitment, "the hunt never ends."

I hope you enjoyed Tori and Legion's love story. To read a special extended epilogue of Tori and Legion, join my newsletter at bit.ly/huntmebonus.

The following is a list of characters we saw in Hunt Me and the name of their book.

Caius & Reagan is MATE ME.

Styx and Corvin is SHADOW ME.

Stella is FORBID ME.

Spencer is CAGE ME.

And look for Kendall's story coming later in 2024!

PROTECT ME

Want a sneak peek of PROTECT ME, also set in the Immortal Vices & Virtues world? This standalone Why Choose Romance features 3 lion shifter bodyguards and the sexy silks performer they're sworn to protect. You'll also meet the other dragon that Legion senses during his conversation with Maricha and Uziah in Hunt Me.

"Ten out of ten! What a read! How I wish I could be Sway so that I can have three sexy yummy lion shifters." - Amazon reviewer

Turn the page for Chapter 1....

CHAPTER 1
SWAY

Breath wheezes in and out of my lungs as I hobble down the empty street. This particular section of No Man's Land is a stark void compared to the crowded party I've left behind. Trees surround me, the soft dirt muting my footsteps, slow as they may be.

Every step sends pain shooting up my limbs and ricocheting through my skull, but then sitting still isn't much better.

I'm a wreck.

Robert was drunker than usual, and shit, maybe I should have known better than to refuse him when he was so far gone, but I couldn't do it.

Not anymore. Never again.

I'll die first. As evidenced by the sheer number of bruises on my body and the fact that I'm only barely clinging to consciousness. Every pump of blood from my pounding heart is an anvil dropped on my brain.

When I ran, I had no destination. Hell, I've spent the

last four months telling myself running was only going to make things worse.

But then I realized it couldn't get much worse. Not while I still breathed. So, I ran. And somewhere along the way, the circus became my end goal.

I have no idea why I chose it.

No Man's Circus isn't exactly the haven I need right now. Hell, the Ringmaster is known for being cutthroat and merciless. But he's also reputed to be a fair business-man. If I can appeal to his logic or at least to his love of money, then maybe, just maybe, I have a shot at escaping this nightmare of a life.

It's the only chance I have left. I can't go back. I won't.

Up ahead, the trees part enough that I can see a large tarnished archway beckoning me. The Big Top is in the distance, the top of it barely visible behind the crumbling apartments and trees still standing between me and my salvation. I pick up my pace—which isn't saying much, considering my left leg is probably broken, forcing me to drag that foot a bit. The closer I get, the harder my heart pounds. Fear is a lump in my throat and a brick in my stomach.

I'm so damn close to what I can only hope and pray is asylum.

And if not? Well, then at least, I won't be suffering anymore. One way or another I'm escaping Robert once and for all.

Somewhere behind me, a male voice roars my name, "Swayyyy!"

The fear snakes through my insides, sending my

bones quaking. I stumble and fall. The ground scrapes into the palms of my hands, but it's nothing more than a whisper of an ache compared to the rest of the agony.

Tears spring to my eyes, burning on their way down my bloodied cheeks.

More pain. So much pain that I nearly give up right here. But the sound of voices murmuring urgently somewhere among the trees sends me surging to my feet.

I push on, pleading with whatever gods or goddesses are out there to let me live through this night. I may not deserve it, but I can find a way to make up for what I've done. There has to be a way.

The voices of my pursuers grow louder. Closer.

My pulse hammers.

Finally, I lurch forward, landing in the soft dirt beneath the large iron archway. It's covered in vines, but I can make out what used to say *Garden View Apartments*. Just ahead, the Big Top looms, a tall tent that stands in what was once the courtyard enjoyed by the humans who likely inhabited those buildings prior to Portland's fall fifty years ago.

Portland, Oregon is nothing like the city the humans once built. Now, decades of supernaturals vying for power and warring for their own corrupt causes have left it a shell of what it once was.

New boundary lines were drawn, and thanks to the portal that opened up here, Portland became yet another No Man's Land. It's ruled by no House, which is why I ran straight here rather than back to my own people—or his. None of them would have allowed me my freedom. At least here, I have a fighting chance.

I may not have the protection of a House, but there will be no one to turn me over either.

For most, the circus signifies entertainment. A way to pass the evening. But for me? The crumbling walls of these apartments combined with the red and white stripes of the Big Top signify hope.

Magic prickles along my skin as I pass through thin wards that most others likely don't even notice. My magic gives me an advantage there because I can sense things others cannot. I hold my head up just a bit higher, knowing that the Ringmaster has likely been alerted to my presence. The last thing I need is for him to see just how weak I am.

I know it won't be long before he shows up to investigate the after-hours breach, but I don't stop to wait. As long as I am out in the open, I'm still in danger.

The corrupt men hunting me will catch me unless I get out of sight. Remaining where I am is signing my own death warrant. Then again, a swift death would not be unwelcome at this point. But neither Robert nor his men will deliver that to me.

No, they want me to suffer. They want me to commit evil along with them. When I refuse, they'll only go to greater lengths to convince me. They'll break me. And that's what scares me most. Because I know they can.

If I'm lucky, the Ringmaster will take pity. But I chase that thought away. The Ringmaster's reputation paints him as shrewd in his dealings. There will be no pity. Only opportunity. If I can convince him I'm valuable, he'll keep me. If not, he won't. It's as simple as that.

At least, with him, I have a chance to offer value

beyond the magical gifts that will *never* be available. Not to him and not to anyone. Not even for the price of my life.

As Robert is so furiously figuring out right about now.

Asshole.

I sniffle, shoving down the guilt I shoulder for the part I played in Robert's downfall. If it weren't for me, he'd likely still be the charming man I'd met all those years ago. The one with a quick smile and bright eyes.

The image of his twisted expression as he slammed his fist into my jaw assaults me, and I clench my hands into fists.

My own fury fuels me, and I manage to make it nearly to the entrance before my body finally gives out. My knees buckle, and I go down hard, crying out sharply at the sudden pain it brings. I bite it off quickly, terrified I've alerted the asshole to my location.

But before I can twist around to see if I've brought him running, a heavy iron door opens in the center of the crumbling apartment complex. A figure steps out. Male, from the silhouette of him. And bathed in the light emanating behind him, though shadows make it impossible for me to make out features, the first stranger is followed by another. And a third. Security. The Ringmaster wouldn't come out here himself. These must be his guards.

I don't say a word. If I open my mouth now, all that'll come out is a scream, and I refuse to give in to the pain just yet.

The figures approach as a single unit, and I'm able to

make out their shapes. Definitely males. I manage to look up at them through blurred, puffy eyes before the adrenaline driving me finally wears off and I sprawl onto my side in the dirt.

"Whoa," one of them says. The front man. He steps forward, and the other two spread out on either side of him in a sort of "V" formation like they've done this a thousand times before. Like they're trying to assess what level of threat I am.

Desperation has me whispering, "Asylum."

"What's that?" The front man steps closer, crouching down.

I see stark blue eyes set against a hard jaw. Handsome. Too handsome. My stomach tenses because, in my experience, men who look like him behave like Robert. And I damn sure don't want to find out if that's a stereotype or fact. But it's this or let myself be discovered here by the demon himself.

"Ringmaster..." My ribs squeeze with every syllable, and I shut my eyes against the pain. Wheezing, I wait to see if they'll grant my request.

"What do you think, Duncan?" one of the others asks.

"She's asking for the Ringmaster," the front man says. Duncan, apparently.

"Is she drunk?" the third asks, mild humor coloring his tone. My fists clench at that, but I can't afford a reply.

"She's not fucking drunk, you dumbass," the second one shoots back. He steps closer, peering over Duncan's shoulder at me. Up close, I catch sight of multiple facial piercings glinting in the light against an angled jaw and green eyes that prickle my skin where they scan my body. I watch as he gets a closer look at my face, and his own expression registers shock.

"What is it, Kill?" the third one prompts, inching closer now too.

But Kill—whatever kind of name that is—doesn't answer. He blinks, his green gaze resettling on mine, and a dark sort of fury flashes in their green depths.

"She's covered in fucking bruises, dude." Duncan's tone has turned deadly. "Someone did a real number on her."

"I can fucking see that," the third snaps. "Drunken fight?"

"Do you smell liquor on her?" Kill retorts.

"No," the third replies.

Out among the trees, voices sound—male voices— all of them working for the asshole who did this to me. I tense, my wheezing cut short as I hold my breath and wait to see what my fate will be.

"Someone's out there," the third one says. "They might have done this to her. We should get her inside until we know."

"I've got her." Duncan reaches down and scoops me into his arms like I weigh nothing at all.

But the jostling makes me whimper, and I hear a, "Take it fucking easy," from the one called Kill; like he's actually angry at his friend for furthering my pain.

"He's just trying to fucking help," the third puts in.

They banter in a grouchy yet easy sort of way, and I wonder if these men are more than co-workers. Family, maybe. Their familiarity, even in the way they fuss at one another, suggests they're bonded somehow. The thought sends a pang through my already aching body. This one's more of a hollow echo in my chest. A deep sort of longing mixed with the grief of loss—for a bond I'll never have. That I can never afford to let myself look for.

I don't complain again, mostly to keep them from changing their minds about harboring me. Instead, I focus on deep breathing that doesn't sound like one of my lungs is drowning in its own fluids. Every inch of my skin hurts, but I also can't help but notice how safe I feel as I'm carried by the front man of this security trio, no matter how grouchy he is about having to help me.

The three men continue grunting at one another while we walk, and I lose all sense of direction as we make a few turns down a series of halls.

Finally, we stop, and one of the men knocks sharply on a door.

From the other side, I hear, "Come in."

I'm carried into a warm space that practically glows orange from a fire crackling in the large hearth. From this angle, I can't see much else beyond the ceiling, but I can sense there are others present here.

"What the hell happened?" a female asks. She doesn't wait for an answer before rushing over and looking down at me.

Through my swollen lids, I meet her eyes and find a surprisingly friendly face peering at me. Her near-white hair is pulled up in a messy bun, and her cheeks are slightly flushed, but she doesn't flinch away from the sight of my battered body. Instead, her kind eyes flash with a fury that seems out of place on her otherwise soft face.

"What is this?" asks a gruff male voice from somewhere behind the woman.

"Found her outside," one of my three rescuers says.

"Who did this?" the female demands.

"Liv, calm down," the gruff male warns.

"D's right," says the man holding me. *Duncan.* "You can't let yourself get worked up."

"Do not start with me, Duncan," she warns. Before he can answer, she leans in close to me and smiles. "I'm Liv. Can you tell me your name?"

"Helen," I lie through a busted lip. It's my mother's name. I cannot let them know who I really am because the one hunting me has friends all over, even in No Man's Land.

"Helen, can you tell me who did this to you?" she presses.

I don't answer that. Instead, I say, "I'm looking for the Ringmaster."

Liv smiles wryly. "Well, you've found him." She nods toward the figure behind her. The gruff-voiced male straightens, and alarm spears through me.

Shit. The Ringmaster is here? Watching me get carried around like a rag doll?

I scramble, trying to free myself from the strong arms holding me, but they only tighten their grip.

"Put me down," I insist.

"Not happening," Duncan says.

"I am ordering you to put me down." The words—

and the bitchy tone I use to say them—completely exhaust me. But Duncan gives in and sets me on my feet.

I'm vaguely aware of Liv nodding to give him the order to do it, but I ignore that. Instead, I pretend it was all me and that Duncan gave in because of how scary I sounded. That feels better than this helplessness.

The minute Duncan lets me go, I wobble, knees buckling.

"Dammit." Duncan is there immediately. But he doesn't swoop in and grab me again. He only yanks a chair underneath me so that I sink into it rather than the floor.

He remains directly behind me, close enough for me to reach back and touch him if I wanted to. Which I don't. The other two stand on my left, too far back for me to see their faces. Liv, the woman, takes the chair opposite mine. As she sits, I note the large, round belly she cradles with her hand.

My mind tries to put all the pieces together, including who all these people are to each other, but the pain is making it hard to think. Exhaustion doesn't help.

No one else speaks.

I exhale, shaky but determined. Then, I lift my gaze to the man standing beside the hearth. He glares at me, his piercing copper eyes narrowed on my face. His dark hair is cut short on the sides and left a bit longer on top, and scruff darkens the lower half of his face. Even so, I note the strong, stubborn set of his jaw and the raw power emanating from him.

Of fucking course this is the Ringmaster. Everything about the man demands respect even when he's silent.

My head starts to throb, but I force myself to hold his stare. There's a hardness about it that I've never encountered in anyone else before, but it's not cruelty. I hope that means he'll have mercy. Or at least just give me a chance to prove my use.

"I have come offering my services," I say when it's clear he's not going to speak first.

"Your services?" he asks, arching a brow in challenge. "And what exactly can you offer?"

He's fishing to find out what type of supernatural I am, which means he's not able to sense me. No one else can, but still, after everything I'd heard about this guy, I'd wondered. *My first stroke of luck. Perfect.* I lift my chin. "I'm a performer. This seems like a place where my talents could be useful."

"And what exactly are you?" the man asks. "You don't look like you have much to offer me. So, unless you are—"

"I am a performer," I interrupt. "A talented one at that." Years of learning to cope with my anxiety led me to the silks. While I've never performed for a large audience, I'm damned good. Good enough to make my way here until I can figure out my next move.

"Talented?"

He doesn't believe me—that much is clear from his voice. I can't blame him. I look like a hot mess, and it's not like I'm up for proving my skills right now. Fear licks at my mind. If this doesn't work—

"Arial. Mainly silks, but I am experienced on the lyra, too."

Liv's eyes light up. "D, the lyra. We need—"

"Quiet," he says, but it's not nearly as forceful as he is with me.

She scowls but continues to watch me.

I look back at the Ringmaster. "I'll do whatever you need. I just..."

"Need a place to hide?" he finishes.

I don't argue because, hello, hot mess. I can't exactly deny I'm in a bind here.

"I'm not going to pretend there isn't something in it for me," I say, refusing to cower.

He grunts.

I have no idea what that means. Hopefully, I get points for honesty.

"I don't give freebies," he says at last.

"I'm not asking for a handout," I snap.

"Well, you're also not in a position to prove your worth, are you?"

"D," Liv hisses, but he ignores her, clearly waiting for me to say something.

Behind me, Duncan, the one who carried me here, is utterly silent. Not that he owes me any favors, but damn. The man found me collapsed outside; the least he could do would be to try to buy me some time, right? Even as I think it, I dismiss it, though. Since when can I count on a man to have my best interests in mind?

Easy answer. Never.

My entire fucking body feels like I was just run over repeatedly, but I straighten as best I can. "If that's what you need, I'll show you. Take me to the Big Top."

"No. Absolutely not," Liv snaps as she turns to D. "She is in no state to perform."

The Ringmaster eyes her with amusement glistening in his gaze. "She says she can."

"D," Liv warns, and I get the sense he's playing with her somehow and she knows it. Either way, watching her refuse to back down to a creature like him is impressive as hell.

"Fine," he says, turning back to me. "Answer me this. What are you doing here?"

"I told you; I'm offering my services."

"And whoever did this to you? Will they come looking for your *services* as well?"

I flinch but otherwise don't dignify that with an answer.

Liv gives him another exasperated look.

He clears his throat. "You have three days to recover. You'll have one audition, two minutes. If you prove unskilled, you'll be asked to leave, no arguments. Do you understand?"

I keep my breath even, mostly to hide my excitement but also to keep from hurting my bruised ribs more. "I understand."

"If you can perform as you say you can, I will give you three months. That's all I can offer you. Nightly performances, five days a week—once you're fully healed, of course."

"Thank you." Hope soars, inflating my chest and straightening my shoulders.

He nods. "At the end of the three months, you're no longer my concern. We have no room for two aerial acts at this time, and I don't do charity." He glances at Liv, and she gives him an approving smile.

"I'll take it." The weight on my chest that's been threatening to crush me eases slightly. I inhale, still wheezing but lighter.

Duncan speaks up from behind me. "She needs a healer, boss."

The Ringmaster frowns but nods. "Put her in a room. I'll send Adaya over to take a look at her." He turns back to the fire, making it clear this meeting is over.

But Duncan doesn't move. "Sir, there were people in the woods outside the grounds." The Ringmaster turns back. "I think they might have been looking for her."

My breath catches. Shit. Had I really believed they'd keep that to themselves?

"Check it out," the Ringmaster says. "Settle her first, though."

"What about the wards?" Duncan asks.

"Take her to Uma on your way," the Ringmaster says as he looks me up and down. "Shouldn't be too hard to get blood from her right now."

"You got it, boss," one of the other guards says.

"Blood?" I ask, fear burning a hole inside of me. But they don't answer me, and I don't press. Whatever they need the blood for seems small in comparison to what's waiting for me if they throw me out.

Duncan comes around and scoops me back into his arms. I don't bother protesting about being carried. Now that I've secured my safety, I can afford to admit how badly I'm broken.

Besides, the Ringmaster only gave me three months. And I have a feeling all my complaining will do is make me look weak in the eyes of such a powerful man. The last thing I need is for him to throw me out before I can prove myself. I didn't come this far only to let my asshole fiancé win. I have three months to heal and figure out my next move.

Three months to figure out how to escape my fate. I will not be used to burn down the world. He'll have to kill me first.

PROTECT ME is available now!

About the Author

Heather Hildenbrand lives in coastal Virginia where she writes paranormal and fantasy romance. Her most frequent hobbies are cuddling with her goldendoodle, riding country roads on the back of her husband's motorcycle, and avoiding killer slugs.

You can find out more about Heather and her books including signed copies delivered to your door at www.heatherhildenbrand.com.

ALSO BY HEATHER HILDENBRAND

One Dark Spark

Two Blazing Hearts

Three Scorched Kingdoms

Dark Wolf Soul

Deadly Wolf Bite

Broken Wolf Heart

Protect Me (Immortal Vices & Virtues)

Hunt Me (Immortal Vices & Virtues)

To Hunt A Wolf

To Kiss A Wolf

To Keep A Wolf

Midnight Cursed

Midnight Hunted

Midnight Bound

Wolf Cursed

Wolf Captive

Wolf Chosen

Wolf Revealed

A Witch's Call

A Witch's Destiny

A Witch's Fate

A Witch's Soul

A Witch's Prophecy

A Witch's Hope

Twisted Tides

The Girl Who Cried Werewolf

The Girl Who Cried Captive

The Girl Who Cried War

The Winter Witch

The Spring Witch

A Witch's Heart

Midnight Mate

Goddess Ascending

Goddess Claiming

Goddess Forging

Kiss of Death

Knock Em Dead

Death's Door

Dead to Rights

Dead End

The Girl Who Called The Stars

The Girl Who Ruled The Stars

Alpha Games

Alpha Trials

Alpha Chosen

Dirty Blood

Cold Blood

Blood Bond

Blood Rule

Broken Blood

One Hour: bonus novella

Imitation

Deviation

Generation

Guarded by the Alpha

Alpha Undercover

Mated to the Wilde Bear

The Bear's Fated Mate

Protected By the Bear

The Badge and the Bear

Tragic Ink: A Havenwood Falls story